The Way Home

Galloway, Volume 2

Tom E. Hicklin

Published by Ol' Pard Publishing, 2019.

THE WAY HOME

First edition. September 20, 2019.

Copyright © 2019 Tom E. Hicklin.

ISBN: 978-0-578-56936-9

Written by Tom E. Hicklin.

Also by Tom E. Hicklin

Galloway
Road to Antietam
The Way Home

Watch for more at https://tomehicklin.com.

Chapter One

Private Christopher Galloway of the 8th Ohio Volunteer Infantry left the house he and his messmates had slept in the night before and stepped out into bright sunshine. The sun's heat covered him like a warm blanket and made him want to shed his greatcoat. Stretching, he took a deep breath and immediately bent over coughing, overcome by the smoke from the many still-burning buildings around the city—testimony to two days' hard fighting between the Army of the Potomac and the Army of Northern Virginia. The 8th Ohio, his regiment and home for nearly two years, had crossed over the Rappahannock River into the town of Fredericksburg the evening before. Today would be their turn.

It was December 13, 1862. Almost three months since the Battle of Antietam and the death of his brother, Daniel. The 8th had spent most of that time stationed on the heights above Harpers Ferry, reconnoitering the countryside or, as Christopher liked to call it, chasing shadows.

Since that terrible day on the banks of Antietam Creek, Christopher had slept little and ate less. He was thin and worn despite the relatively easy assignments the regiment had enjoyed for the last three months. Only the anticipation of another big battle and the chance to avenge his brother's death drew Christopher out of his apathy.

He rubbed the wispy beard he'd let sprout on his chin and looked over at his friend, Ezra, already sweating under his greatcoat. He flicked his eyes to the heavily laden knapsack Ezra wore on his back and thought of that day at Camp Dennison, so long ago, when he and Daniel had been forced to march for two hours wearing knapsacks full of rocks as a punishment for fighting. "You're going to be sorry, Ez."

Ezra tried to shrug and winced. "It's worth a try. You got the tobacco?"

Christopher nodded in response. He thought of the bundle of weed they'd pilfered from a warehouse the day before, tucked into his own knapsack underneath a change of clothes and other personal items—and a stack of intricately embroidered handkerchiefs he planned to send back to his mother as soon as they got back to their current winter camp on the other side of the river.

He'd felt a pang of guilt as he took the handkerchiefs from a beautifully carved chest of drawers in the master bedroom of the house they were bunked in, but everyone else was stripping the home bare, and, if he didn't take something, he'd miss out. Besides, the people who lived there were just secesh. That's what they got for rebelling.

Ezra had stuffed his knapsack with every piece of silverware he could find in the home, and Christopher could see the pain on his friend's face as he adjusted the shoulder straps for the hundredth time. If they had to run at the double quick, Ezra would probably pass out.

The bugle call for assembly rudely interrupted Christopher's musings on their spoils from plundering secesh homes. They all lined up, and, as the lieutenants and sergeants conducted roll call and inspection, the company captains conferred with Colonel Sawyer on the front porch of a large, stately home. Christopher watched the officers sipping coffee and eating soft bread as they huddled around a table covered with what he assumed were maps and whatever else officers stared at when getting ready for battle. Occasionally someone would point to the tabletop and ask a question. Otherwise, Sawyer did all the talking.

"I wonder how many of us will die today because of their planning?" Christopher mused. He spoke to no one in particular and no one responded.

Sergeant Parker Bonnett, two files down from Christopher, leaned forward to see past the man between them. "It might be better to think we could go home soon because of their plans."

"You been in the same army as me these last two years, Parker?" Christopher spat.

"That I have, bub. And I know same as the next man, this can't go on forever. Sooner or later, one side is gonna give, and the only way that will happen is if we keep pressing forward."

Christopher nodded. "Don't worry. I'm more than willing to kill my share of rebs."

Parker straightened back up. "That's what I'm afraid of."

At that, the shelling began. The air filled with the sound of whistling projectiles, followed by explosions that added to the destruction of the city. Soon, great clouds of smoke hung over the city and threatened to block out the rising sun. Christopher thanked God the rebels were shooting blind. So far, none of the shelling had come anywhere near the 8th.

Christopher looked down the street to where the houses ended. Beyond was an open field with only a few buildings scattered about, and beyond that, a stone wall hid the waiting rebels. That's where they were heading. Once they stepped out into the open, the rebels would no longer be shooting blind.

The officer's meeting ended, and they all started down the porch steps toward their respective commands. First Sergeant Howe barked out, "Company! Attention!"

The sound of hundreds of heels clicking together was added to the cacophony of explosions going on around them.

Colonel Sawyer mounted his horse and addressed the 8th from atop the skittishly prancing animal. Because of losses from battle and disease, and the many still out recovering from wounds received at Antietam, the regiment numbered just over three hundred men. If not for the constant shelling, they all could have easily heard him. But, as it was, Christopher only caught about half what Sawyer said and conjectured the rest.

"Gentlemen! Our task this morning is to make a way for the rest of the Second Corps to reach the enemy." He pointed down the street to the open area. "The field down there that separates us from the enemy position is bisected by a canal. The few bridges across that canal have been stripped down to the pilings by the retreating enemy. Stacked before you are planks and railroad ties which we will carry to the canal and use to repair the bridges. That way the rest of our corps can attack the enemy without getting their feet wet."

The men laughed. Despite having missed the last few words, Christopher join in. He'd heard enough to get the gist of the joke.

Christopher looked at the pile of wood, then down the line at the other men in his company, most of whom had knapsacks full of loot or cases of tobacco strapped to their backs.

"We will leave our packs here," Sawyer continued. "That includes the tobacco you pilfered from that warehouse yesterday...and anything else you may have on your person that will slow you down."

Sawyer seemed reluctant to address the looting issue head on. *He has more important things to worry about*, Christopher surmised.

"Don't think it will be that easy, though," Sawyer said. "Before we can lay the planks, we will have to drive back the skirmish line guarding the canal." Several men groaned. Sawyer's voice rose. "The 1st Delaware and 4th Ohio will come up the streets parallel to ours on either side. Once we have driven off the defenders, laid the new bridge planks, and crossed over, we will march by the left flank and join up with the 1st. The 4th will do the same behind us and join us at the other end. That will put us in the center. Then we will advance on the enemy position behind that stone wall. The rest of General French's division will be right behind us. Are you ready?"

"HUZZAH!"

Christopher thought of all the obstacles they faced: the guarded canal, the open field sloping uphill to a stone wall, behind which a thousand rifles waited, all within the sites of several rebel batteries. His huzzah felt like a lie.

THE MEN LEFT THEIR packs and greatcoats in front of a house with the Quarter-Master Sergeant and his staff. The company commanders assigned the larger men to carry the materials, the rest were to carry the rifles and provide protection. Ezra was assigned to be a wood bearer, and Christopher was to carry his rifle. The men ate a breakfast of hardtack and coffee, lined up on the street, and waited.

The sun rose to its zenith, and the day grew warmer. The men sweated and drank from their canteens, grousing and fretting about leaving their new plunder behind. The shelling continued, and the sound of gunfire was so constant it became a natural part of their surroundings. The men ignored it and tried to forget that soon that gunfire would be directed toward them. Finally,

General Kimball arrived with his adjutant and spoke with Colonel Sawyer. It was time.

The regiment marched down the street in a column of four at the double quick, many of the officers and regimental staff out front with the color bearers. Leaning over to see around the man in front of him, Christopher saw the head of the column pass the last two houses and go down a slope toward the canal. The bugler was just beginning the command to shift left flank into line when the rebels guarding the canal rose up and fired a volley into the head of the column. Officers and men dropped like tenpins.

The colors went down, and Christopher felt a jolt of panic sweep the regiment as men stopped, stumbled, or ran into one another. The officers still standing screamed for order, joined by company first sergeants. Most of the men quickly regained their composure and reformed the column. Those who hesitated were physically shoved into place by sergeants and corporals.

The men in the first company in line carried the dead and wounded to the side of the street. Someone grabbed the regimental flag and raised it up. The column resumed its march at the quick-step. As Christopher passed, he saw Master-Sergeant Henthorne lying on the side of the street with a jagged hole in his forehead. Next to him a captain whose name Christopher couldn't remember lay squirting blood out of a leg wound. There were also several other men lying on the ground writhing in pain and calling for help.

The wood bearers discarded their planks and retrieved their rifles as the regiment spilled out into the open field and onto the sloping bank, shifting into line and descending on the rebels who had fired the volley. Christopher took comfort from the pressure of shoulders pressing his on either side. It was reassuring to know he was not alone, and that he was where he belonged.

Time seemed to slow, and tunnel vision robbed him of his peripheral vision at the realization they were within the sight of the enemy batteries. Before them, the rebels guarding the canal were close enough it would be almost impossible for them to miss.

The rebel line rose up for another volley. At the site of the rifles aiming at him, the now familiar cold, aching terror gripped Christopher's stomach, and he clenched his butt cheeks in response. He wanted to get through a battle without soiling himself for once.

The force guarding the canal was at most fifty men. Facing a whole regiment must have made them nervous because, despite their close proximity, their second volley did little damage. Trapped with the canal behind them and outnumbered, the rebels then surrendered. As the prisoners were led away, Ezra passed his rifle to Christopher and went to retrieve the wood he'd been carrying.

Christopher watched the prisoners march away and felt a fleeting sense of resentment. By their surrender, he'd been denied his first chance for revenge against the enemy.

While he waited, Christopher noticed the constant buzz of passing Minié balls coming from the rebel riflemen behind the rock wall on the hill before them. Thankfully, they were still too far away to be much of a threat. Not so for the rebel batteries, though. They had begun a steady fire at the newcomers to the field, adjusting their fuses and sights with each volley until shells were exploding all around the regiment.

Christopher's skin tingled with the expectation of a jagged chunk of hot iron tearing his flesh. He was still partially deaf from the explosion that almost killed him at Antietam, and he thought of putting cotton in his ears but feared if he did he wouldn't hear the commands. His nerves got worse with each explosion until his hands were shaking and his right leg twitched involuntarily.

The plank bearers returned, passed through the ranks with their burdens, and headed down the slope to the canal. As Ezra passed, he said, "Looks like I'm gonna get wet."

"Better wet than dead," Christopher responded and hitched up his and Ezra's rifles.

Christopher stood in his place in the line, watching the men construct the makeshift bridges over the canal. The ditch was at least fifteen feet across and almost as deep as a man was tall. None of the materials they brought would reach that far, so they had to use the existing pilings from the bridges the rebels had destroyed. That meant there would only be a few bridges available when the rest of the corps arrived. If they tried to cross using only the bridges, it would create a bottleneck that would bring their advance to a halt. Given the choice between standing in line while being shot at, or wading the canal, many would climb down into the canal and wade through the water at the bottom.

A shell exploded nearby, and Christopher heard the buzzing growl of flying shrapnel and the thud of hot iron hitting the ground. The shaking and twitching grew worse until he feared if they didn't move soon, he would turn and run. How would he ever be able to face his pards after something like that?

Finally, Ezra and the others returned and took their place in line. The bugle call for forward march sounded, and the regiment stepped out. They immediately shifted the battle line into columns of four to cross the bridge. The planks they'd laid were hastily secured and clattered and bounced with each step. Christopher was willing to bet they would fall apart before the first division had crossed, and the rest of the corps would have to wade the canal anyway. Christopher could only imagine how that would go: each man scurrying down the embankment, wading the ice cold water, and then clamoring back up the other side—all while under fire from rebel sharpshooters and artillery.

Once on the other side, the regiment shifted back into battle line and moved out at the double quick at a left oblique. Looking to his left, Christopher could see the 1st Delaware moving up to join them. The two regiments came together, forming a single battle line, and then shifted their line of march directly toward the stone wall.

Being the first on the field, they had to break down fences so the men coming up behind them would have an easier time charging the rebel position. Every delay seemed to cost them a man or two.

As they got closer, the enemy rifle fire increased and became more accurate. They were now close enough that Christopher could see rebel reinforcements coming down the hill and approaching the wall from the other direction. Soon, this field would be a kill zone that nothing could cross without being hit. Yet this was where the big bugs chose to attack.

The sound of passing Minié balls was now a constant buzz, and Christopher could feel their passing by a puff of air on his cheek or a ripping tug at his clothes. Up and down the line, men were falling with frightening regularity. As they stopped at one of the many fences they had to deal with, Christopher raised his rifle to strike one of the planks and the man to his right stumbled into him. Christopher shoved back to keep from being pushed over. The man fell and Christopher spotted fresh blood on his sleeve. He didn't look—there was no time, and he thought it best not to for fear of losing his nerve. Christopher hit the fence with the butt of his rifle as hard as he could and kept hitting long after the plank had broken loose. The line moved forward, and he followed, the hell they now found themselves in intensifying with each step.

Christopher's hat flew off his head, and he felt a burning sensation on the top of his skull. Ezra cried out behind him, and Christopher tried to look over his shoulder to see if his friend had been hit. He tripped and stumbled and had to look forward again to keep from falling. He continued advancing toward the enemy, not knowing if Ezra was still behind him.

They reached a point where the street they'd originally lined up on curved to the left and intersected the street next to it. There was a cluster of buildings at the intersection, and the enemy fire was now so overwhelming that what was left of the battle line came apart and men scattered, seeking shelter wherever they could.

Christopher joined the rest of Company D behind a house on the right side of the street, just before the intersection. He frantically looked around until he saw Ezra leaning on his rifle and panting.

"Are you all right? I thought you'd been hit!" Christopher yelled over the constant noise of gun and cannon fire.

Ezra nodded. "Your hat hit me in the face. I thought they'd shot my eyes out."

Christopher almost laughed. "I think if they'd shot your eyes out, you'd have felt it."

Ezra grinned. "How do you know? You ever had your eyes shot out?"

Christopher was thinking how to respond to that when a bullet passed between them.

Christopher felt a moment of panic. *That came from the left.* "Captain Reid! We're being flanked!"

Captain Reid, who was conferring with the company lieutenants and sergeants, ignored the panicking private.

"Damn officers," Christopher grumbled as he tried to see where the shot had come from.

Across the street was a line of houses. As Christopher watched, a puff of smoke appeared in one of the upstairs windows, followed by the report of a rifle and the buzz of a passing bullet.

Christopher and Ezra dropped down behind a fence.

"The captain's gotta know we're under fire," Christopher said.

"Maybe a bullet up his ass will get his attention," Ezra responded.

Christopher was tensing to rise and run over to Captain Reid when the group broke up, and Parker Bonett headed their way.

Christopher waived his arms and pointed toward the line of houses. "Parker, look out! There're snipers in those houses over there!"

Parker waived Christopher's warning away and kept walking. Suddenly the sergeant was jogging, and Christopher assumed a passing bullet had gotten his attention.

As Parker jogged, he motioned for Nathan Jump and John Finn to join him. The five convened at Christopher's and Ezra's spot behind the fence.

Ezra gave Nathan and John a hearty hello and slapped Nathan on the shoulder. Christopher gave the two a curt nod but refused to make eye contact.

Being around Nathan Jump made him uncomfortable. They had both lost older brothers at Antietam—Christopher by death and Nathan by desertion. Shortly after the battle, Nathan's older brother, Joe, disappeared one night, and no one had seen him since. He hadn't even told his younger brother he was leaving—or so Nathan insisted. Christopher thought that was worse. At least Daniel hadn't left him voluntarily.

John Finn was a year older than Christopher. Born in Ireland, he lived with his parents and eight siblings and had worked as a day laborer before the war. The family went to the same church as the Galloways, and Christopher and John had gone to school together. When they were younger, they had shared a bond in their hatred for Ezra, but since Christopher and Ezra had become pards, John had become stand-offish.

"Boys," Parker began. "We have orders to clear the snipers out of those houses over there." Four heads slowly rose over the fence and peered at the houses in the distance then scanned the open ground between them and their current position.

"We gotta go back out in the open?" Ezra whined.

"That's right," Parker replied. "And besides the snipers before us, we still have the line of rebs behind that stone wall shooting at anything that moves. So we have to go fast. We will not line up and march over there—there won't be any of us left to clear the houses. Instead, we're going to break up into squads—you four are with me—and run like hell until we get to the other side. Our squad is to take the house on the far left."

Christopher looked again, this time taking a particular interest in the house they were to "take." Most of the houses were brick, but this one was a two story clapboard home with a small porch in front of the door. The siding was a bright and festive yellow, with dark blue shudders. A large, jagged hole marred the siding next to one of the upstairs windows—presumably from a cannon ball. Christopher imagined as they got closer they would see a lot more holes in the siding from bullets and shrapnel.

"How we going to take the house when we get there?" Ezra asked.

"We'll be pretty exposed so we'll just kick the front door in and rush inside. Hopefully, whoever is in there will be too busy looking for targets outside to shoot us down in the doorway."

Ezra glanced at Christopher with a sour look on his face.

Parker continued, "Once we've taken care of the snipers we'll take any prisoners we've got and all meet Captain Reid in the middle house. Any more questions?"

Everyone shared a nervous glance. Christopher shook his head.

"Good. Follow me."

Parker stood up and strode to the end of the fence. His squad followed him bent over single file. *Like a mother duck and her ducklings*, Christopher thought.

The company came together on the other side of the fence. Both lieutenants and every sergeant had a squad with four or five men. First Sergeant Howe and a small squad were to accompany Captain Reid to the house designated as the rendezvous point.

Captain Reid straightened up to his full height and raised his sword straight over his head. Christopher kept his eyes on the sword as his whole body tensed.

"For Ohio!" Captain Reid called out, and the sword came down.

"Ohio!" the men screamed as they took off running across the street.

There was a smattering of fire from the stone wall, but fortunately Company D had caught the enemy on that part of the wall unaware. But, a couple puffs of smoke ahead told Christopher that the snipers were expecting them.

As they crossed over the open ground, the enemy fire intensified. Several men dropped, unable or unwilling to continue.

Christopher heard the bullets buzzing by, and sometimes even felt the breeze of their passing. They seemed to come from everywhere, and he knew every breath he continued to take was a blessing from God.

As they reached their destination, the five men barely slowed down, slamming into the side of the house and pressing up against the wall while they caught their breath. Christopher noted with a strange sense of satisfaction that he'd been correct, and the siding was completely pockmarked with bullet and shrapnel holes.

Parker grabbed the door handle and slowly twisted. It was unlocked. He gave the door a shove inward and stepped back, raising his rifle.

As the door swung open, Christopher could see the parlor was in complete disarray. All the furniture was turned over or broke into pieces. Shards of glass littered the floor, and he could smell spilt whale oil from the broken lamps. The windows were broken out and their curtains torn down. He assumed anything small enough to be carried away had been taken by pilfering soldiers.

The front door opened onto a foyer with a hallway leading to the back of the house and a staircase going up to the second story. Parker swung his rifle back and forth, then stepped inside. "Rouse and Galloway, search the rooms to the left, Finn and Jump take the room on the right. Once we've made sure no one is down here, we'll go upstairs."

As they split up, Parker moved down the hallway, his rifle leading the way.

Christopher raised his own rifle and slowly stepped into the room on the left. He tried to move as quietly as possible, but the iron-shod heels on his brogans seemed to boom with every step on the hardwood flooring.

The room he and Ezra entered appeared to be a dining area. Like the parlor on the other side, it, too, had been ransacked. The table and chairs had been smashed and everything but the large table top taken for firewood. Nothing remained on the walls. Any pictures or mirrors not taken by the owners when they fled were now piles of broken wood and glass on the floor below.

Another door at the back of the dining room led to the kitchen area, where the boys found Parker. He shook his head.

"Nothing down here." He looked up and pointed to the ceiling. "They have to be up there."

"Unless they ran when they saw us coming," Ezra said. "Snipers ain't known for their courage."

"No such luck, Rouse," Parker replied. "They're up there."

Christopher's feelings were mixed. He would like nothing more than to take down a couple of dastardly snipers, but running into a room with armed opponents ready for them seemed downright suicidal.

John and Nathan entered the kitchen. John shook his head.

Parker started back down the hallway. "I'll go first. Make sure your rifles are on full cock and the primer hasn't fallen off. And whatever you do, don't shoot me in the back."

The stairs creaked and groaned with every step. To Christopher's mind, every step on the wooden planks was as loud as a gunshot. Half way up the stairs was a landing and a 180-degree turn. Parker eased around the corner, his rifle raised upwards.

The farther up the stairs they went, the harder it became for Christopher to breathe. It seemed no matter how much air he sucked in, it wasn't enough. A black ring formed around his vision, much like what happened when he marched into battle. His arms burned and trembled. The barrel of his rifle dropped a little with each step.

After what seemed like a lifetime, they came to the top of the stairs—and another 180-degree turn. After another achingly slow maneuver around the blind turn, they found themselves at the end of a long hallway with four closed doors, two on either side. Christopher groaned internally, and Parker blew out a breath of frustration.

"We're going to have to take them one at a time," Parker whispered.

"What are you whispering for?" Ezra asked. "It's not like they don't know we're here by now."

Parker gave Ezra a look that made Christopher cringe, and he wasn't the recipient. Crammed in the tight space at the top of the stairs with four others, all Ezra could do was lower his eyes.

"Most likely," Parker continued, "they're going to be in one, or both of the first two rooms, since those are at the front of the house. But, as Ezra pointed out, they know we're here and have had time to prepare for our arrival, so they could be anywhere." He looked down the hall and thought a moment. "We'll take the first door on the left first. Ezra and I will go in, you other three hang back unless we need you."

Ezra's eyes almost bugged out of his head. "Me?"

"You," Parker said without looking back.

Ezra gave Christopher a pleading look—to which Christopher could only shrug—before following the sergeant.

When he reached the door, Parker realized their rifles were too long to hold in a horizontal position across the hall, so they removed their bayonets. Christopher watched the two men slide their bayonets into their scabbards and wished he could as well. His arms were so tired already it was all he could do to keep the rifle barrel up high enough to keep from gouging the floor.

Parker was going to open the door while Ezra held his rifle up ready to shoot at whatever may be inside, then Christopher had an idea. "Here, let me," he said and moved next to the door frame. "Two rifles ready are better than one."

Parker nodded and stepped back next to Ezra. When they both had their rifles up and ready, Christopher placed his hand on the knob and turned. Before pushing the door open he put his ear up against the wall and listened.

"Just get on with it!" Ezra moaned.

Christopher gave the door a shove, and it flew open. Ezra and Parker tensed so much they almost stumbled forward. Then, Parker stepped into the room and Ezra followed, rifles still up and ready.

After a moment, they came back out, pale and sweaty. Parker shook his head.

"Next," Christopher said.

Parker gave him a single, curt nod. "Remember, that's the more likely side, so be ready."

"If I was any more ready, it'd kill me," Ezra whined as he shook out his left arm. "They need to start making lighter rifles."

"They do," Christopher replied. "They're called carbines, and the cavalry carry them."

"Well, bully for the cavalry."

"Quiet you two! Let's get this done."

Parker stepped in front of the door across the hall. Ezra stepped up next to him. Christopher moved to the other side of the door and put his hand on the knob. He turned until he heard the click of the latch, then, just before he pushed the door open, he thought he heard another click.

Christopher pushed, and the door flew open. At the same time, two simultaneous gunshots, the blast as loud as a cannon, came from inside. Smoke and flame billowed out the door. A hole appeared in the opposite wall next to Ezra's head. Parker fell back, a surprised expression on his face. Ezra screamed and fired blindly into the room.

The hallway was now full of gun smoke, but Christopher could still see the spreading pool of blood on Parker's jacket as he slid down the wall, leaving a red stain in his wake. He could hear John and Nathan running down the hall. Ezra was screaming at him to get up and shoot. But that red stain overpowered all thought or reason. The image of Daniel's shocked face as the bullet pierced his heart filled Christopher's mind.

Nathan reached Parker, pulled him away from the doorway, and the spell was broken. Without any thought to the danger or consequences, Christopher rose up and ran into the room, his rifle at the ready before him.

As he cleared the smoke, he saw two thin and dirty rebel soldiers, rushing to reload their rifles. Seeing Christopher, they stopped what they were doing, threw down their rifles, and raised their hands.

"Don't shoot! Don't shoot!"

Their actions failed to register, and Christopher kept going until the tip of his bayonet caught the first rebel just below the breastbone. The man reached down and grabbed Christopher's rifle in a desperate attempt to keep from being stabbed, but Christopher's fury and momentum was enough to carry him back against the wall. He stopped, but Christopher kept going. His bayonet sliding into the rebel's body until the tip came out his back and into the wall another inch.

The man started screaming and crying, his hands fluttering over the barrel of Christopher's rifle. The other rebel was screaming in fury and anguish, "We was tryin' to surrender! We was surrenderin' you bastard!"

Christopher heard the other rebel move toward him. Then there was a thud, and the rebel dropped to the floor. Now he was crying.

But Christopher never took his eyes of the rebel he'd run through. He was young—maybe even younger than Christopher. Beneath the dirt was a freckled face with a pug nose. His whiskers were no more than a wisp of hair on the tip of his chin. He looked Christopher in the eye and said, "You killed me, yank."

Christopher suddenly wanted out of that room more than anything in the world. The anger that had consumed him was replaced with overwhelming guilt and sorrow. He pulled on his rifle, but it was stuck. He tugged again, but it didn't budge. With each pull the young rebel jerked and cried out.

With a growing sense of desperation, Christopher leaned forward, and then threw himself back as hard as he could. As he did, his right hand slipped and brushed the trigger, still at full cock over a fresh primer. The rifle discharged into the young rebel, who responded with an ear-splitting scream that hit Christopher's whole body like a wave.

That final effort, aided by the recoil of the rifle, dislodged the bayonet and the young man sank to the floor, his ragged shirt and jacket smoldering on the edge of a now free flowing pool of blood.

Another scream filled the room, then the still-living rebel cried out, "You killed my brother, you dirty yank bastard! Ya killed him!"

The man crawled to his brother and took his head in his lap.

Christopher fixated on the young rebel's eyes, so full of pleading and fear. So like Daniel's. Then, nothing.

"Why?" It was almost a whisper. A quiet plea directed at no one. "We was tryin' to surrender."

Chapter Two

Christopher rushed out of the room and into the hallway. He fell back against the wall, squeezed his eyes shut, and tried to block out the sound of crying coming from the room. That had been him three months ago. Then a low moan caught his attention.

Opening his eyes and looking down, Christopher saw Parker sitting on the floor with his eyes closed, propped up against the wall. Nathan was pressing a dirty rag against his wound while John stood with rifle ready, staring at the still-unopened doors.

Christopher knelt next to Parker.

"Parker? You still with us?" he asked. *At least the blood's not pumping out,* he thought. *If we can get him help, he may stand a chance.*

Parker opened his eyes and looked at Christopher. He tried to smile. "I guess standing in front of the door wasn't such a good idea," he rasped.

Nathan shook his head. "Quiet now. We gotta get you back to a hospital."

John jutted his chin down the hall. "What about the rest of the rooms?"

"To hell with 'em," Christopher said. "Let's get out of here."

Ezra stepped out into the hall. "What about our prisoner?"

Christopher looked into the room at the man weeping over the body of his brother. He started to shake. He thought he might throw up. After a moment, he managed to speak. "Break their rifles and leave him. He can't do no harm if he's not armed."

John shook his head. "I don't know, we got orders—"

"To the devil with the orders!" Christopher snapped, louder than he'd intended. "Like Nathan said, we have to get Parker to a doctor. Our orders were to stop the flanking fire. We done that. Now we have to go."

"Our orders were—"

"I don't care." Christopher wanted to slap John and his damn orders. "That was the intent, and it's done."

"I'm with Christopher," Nathan chimed in. "We have to get Parker out of here."

Ezra nodded. "Me too."

John let out a big breath and seemed to deflate. "OK. Let's go."

After removing the breech nipples and smashing the stocks of the two rebels' rifles, they picked up Parker and left. Ezra and Nathan carried Parker down the stairs with Christopher and John following, carrying all the rifles.

Christopher took one last look into the room before leaving. The living soldier sat against the wall with his brother's head in his lap. He was stroking the dead boy's hair while quietly singing a children's song Christopher didn't recognize.

Christopher rushed to keep up with the others. All the while the events that took place in the room played over and over in his head. His chest hurt. He wanted to take it all back. Images of Daniel's dead body flashed through his mind, intermingling with the image of the young boy he'd just killed. Flowing tears created streaks on his powder-blackened cheeks.

Once out of the house, the four each took a limb and jogged back toward the town. Parker's head bounced with each step, causing him to scream and moan until he passed out.

Christopher thought by now the rest of their division should be crossing the field, but it was still empty except for the 8th pinned down around the houses behind them.

They reached the canal and had to transfer Parker back to Nathan and Ezra so they could cross one of the rebuilt bridges. The planks shifted with each step, and again Christopher wondered how long they would last once a few thousand more soldiers tried to cross them.

Once they were back in the town proper, the sounds of battle seemed to lessen somewhat, and they could hear the stamp of thousands of feet approaching.

"Here they come," Ezra grunted.

"'Bout time," Christopher gasped to himself.

Just ahead was an ambulance tied to the hitching post of a large building. The four carried Parker up the steps and into what appeared to have once been a meeting hall.

Somehow, the sight of the main hall drove home to Christopher the impact of the war on this small town in a way that the random fires and damaged buildings outside did not. The walls, once a bright white, were blackened from the smoke of multiple oil lanterns and in places streaked with blood from the arterial spray of dying men. Whatever furniture occupied the room before had been removed, broken up for firewood, or used to prop up makeshift operating tables made from doors and rough-hewn planks. The floor was covered with straw, upon which the many wounded from yesterday's street fighting lay—some writhing in agony, some staring at nothing, indifferent to their own suffering and the suffering of those around them. Some were comatose and near death, others already there.

An orderly directed them to lay Parker on a table. Once they did that and stepped back, he removed the bandage and cut away Parker's clothing from around the wound. As he worked, Christopher looked again at the wounded men lying around him. It couldn't be more than fifty degrees in the room and he was sure much colder at night. Yet most of the men were in various states of undress, their clothing cut off them like Parker's, with nothing but a single blanket to keep back the night's chill and the thin layer of straw separating them from the cold, hard wooden floor.

The orderly shook his head at the sight of Parker's wound. "You boys done good bringing him in; he's lost a lot of blood." As he continued, he propped up Parker's head and shoulders. "The bullet probably nicked a lung. I'm surprised he didn't drown in his own blood the way you were carrying him, though."

"We did the best we could," Christopher said, more forcefully than he intended.

The orderly only nodded and motioned a surgeon over. As the doctor examined Parker, he gave orders that set in motion a flurry of activity around the unconscious soldier. More orderlies converged on the group, one carrying a brass cone and bottle of ether, another with a leather satchel full of medical tools. The first orderly continued to clean and prepare the wound for surgery.

As they worked, they ignored the cluster of men who had brought their patient in. Christopher and the rest of his squad stood and watched them administer to their sergeant and friend. After a while, a provost sergeant approached the group.

"You boys better get back before someone notices you're gone. You ask me, you done the right thing bringing your pard in like you did—specially now before the fighting really gets going and the doc has time to give him good care—but your officers may see different."

Christopher nodded. The sergeant was right. Who knows what Captain Reid was thinking happened to their squad. With one last glance at Parker, he turned and walked back outside, the others following.

The four men stood on the porch and watched a river of men in blue march up the street toward the open plain and rock wall beyond. Christopher imagined them like ants, their lines spilling out of the town from every street, crossing the canal and spreading out across the field. And like ants before a bored child's foot, they would be crushed and swept away by the entrenched enemy waiting to meet them.

"I don't know about you, but I ain't in no hurry to go back," Ezra said.

"But, Captain Reid will be wondering where we got to," Nathan replied.

Christopher sighed. "We got our duty, same as these boys," he said, waving his hand toward the column marching before them.

Ezra waved his own hand toward the column and countered, "Look at all of 'em! those bridges we rebuilt can't hold all that. We'd just be in the way."

"You're right. I imagine a lot of those boys will get their feet wet," Christopher said. "I guess we will, too." Inwardly he cringed at the thought of those steep banks, as high as they were tall, and the cold water at the bottom. "Come on, let's go back."

"Wait a minute. I don't see any more stripes on your arm than the rest of us." Ezra straightened up and turned his arm toward Christopher to drive home his point.

"I'm with Notch," John said.

Christopher looked at John and almost smiled in appreciation. Nathan looked back and forth at the two, then nodded. "I'm game," he said.

Ezra shook his head and frowned. "I don't wanna cross that killing field again. Those rebs gotta have a good bead on anyone crossing by now."

"They'll be aiming for the battle lines. We'll stay to the side and go between," Christopher said.

Ezra leaned over the edge of the porch and spat a stream of tobacco juice. "I don't like it."

"None of us like it, Ez. It's just what we gotta do."

The four left the porch and jogged up the street, making sure not to get mixed in with the column. At one point an officer called out to them, but they pretended not to hear and picked up their pace. Soon, they passed the last of the houses and were back into the field, where the canal was proving to be a major bottleneck to the advancing troops.

As Christopher predicted, instead of waiting their turn, many men were sliding down the embankment and wading the frigid water. Getting up the other side, though, was proving to be a challenge. Christopher watched a corporal, standing on the opposite bank, pulling men up the embankment one by one, until an exploding shell sent him flying to the bottom of the canal. Looking down into the trench, he saw several bodies, and the water was taking on a reddish hue.

But the squad made it across the canal without incident. Being the tallest, Ezra climbed out first and helped the others up the opposite embankment. With no worries about keeping a straight line, the four of them ran down toward the houses where they'd left the 8th as fast as they could.

The newcomers to the battle were forming battle lines and moving forward as quickly as they could. At first they were protected from direct enemy fire by a large swale, but eventually they had to come up out of the swale and face the line of rifles behind the rock wall. As Christopher and his squad ran up the street on their right, the first battle line did just that.

As the men crested the rise, the explosion of hundreds of rifles firing at once overwhelmed the cacophonous battle noise. The sudden burst of sound and passing bullets drove Christopher and his companions to their knees, and the battle line disintegrated as dozens, maybe hundreds, of men fell under the onslaught.

Christopher watched in horror as the next line stepped up and over the bodies that were once the line before them, only to meet the same fate. He looked at the lines filling the field, being fed by the unending columns marching out of the town, and realized they would all meet the same fate. There was just too many enemy soldiers, too well entrenched. As long as the rebels' ammunition held out, they would never take that hill.

He looked ahead to where they'd left the rest of the 8th. Every space behind a fence or building that offered any kind of protection seemed to call out to him, *come rest a spell*. But, they had to make it to those houses.

Ezra got his attention with a shove. "Forward or back, pard! We can't stay here."

Christopher nodded once. "Our place is up there—with the 8th."

Ezra sighed. "I was afraid you'd say that."

The four rose back up and ran, ducking and cringing as the fire intensified.

When they reached the buildings at the fork in the road, they dropped behind a fence already occupied with men, many of them wounded, trying to hide from the constant barrage.

"Company D!" Christopher called. "Anyone know where Company D is?" Those who bothered to acknowledge him shook their heads. "Captain Reid! Where are you, dammit!"

Ezra spat again. "We risk our necks to join our regiment and now we can't even find our own company."

"We'll find them," Christopher spat.

The four of them duck-walked along the fence line, calling the names of their company officers. Whenever they came to a gap in the cover, they ran as fast as they could, then resumed their search on the other side.

They found the 8th command in a house, the floors crowded with wounded men, and the windows occupied with soldiers exchanging fire with the enemy behind the stone wall a couple hundred yards away. As they approached, Colonel Sawyer looked up and recognized the four from his old company. His eyebrows shot up in surprise. "How did you four get here?" he asked.

Christopher exchanged glances with the other three of his group, sure they were in trouble. He steeled himself for the consequences and told the colonel everything.

When he finished, Sawyer slowly shook his head and gave the boys a half grin. "And you came back... Truth be told, I don't know if I would have had the courage myself."

Ezra let out a quiet harrumph.

"We need to get you to your company," Sawyer continued. "Unfortunately, they are pinned down on the other side of the street and about to be overrun. I was just getting ready to send them some reinforcements. You four can join them."

Ezra choked and coughed as he swallowed his plug of tobacco.

"Yes, sir," Christopher, Nathan, and John replied together. Ezra followed suit after he managed to stop choking on his tobacco.

"Good, report to Lieutenant O'Reilly out in the yard." Colonel Sawyer resumed writing out orders. Christopher and his squad took that as their dismissal, saluted, and left the building in search of Lieutenant O'Reilly and the reinforcements for Company D.

Christopher felt a thrill of fear and trepidation as the squad of twenty men lined up in preparation for the mad dash across the street to the same houses they'd cleared earlier. In an upstairs room in one of those houses lay the consequences of his blind rage—the sin he could not take back.

Lieutenant O'Reilly raised his sword. He didn't bother trying to make himself heard over the now constant battle noise, he just looked around to make sure everyone was watching, dropped the sword to point across the street, and ran. This time the enemy was more prepared, and as soon as they were in the open, a withering fire from the stone wall commenced, dropping one man almost immediately and forcing several more back with wounds that prevented them from continuing.

Christopher aimed for the same house they had cleared earlier, and the other three followed. Once they were up against the pockmarked wall, Christopher thought about going back inside to see if the two brothers were still there, but Lieutenant O'Reilly motioned them over to the middle house, where the rest of the squad had gathered along with several members of Company D.

Still, he hesitated. Ezra must have sensed some of what he was thinking because he placed a hand on Christopher's shoulder and, once he had his attention, shook his head. He leaned his head toward Christopher and loudly said, "There's no redemption for you in there pard. Let's go on and join the others."

Christopher nodded, and the four ran across the yard to the other house. When they got there, Lieutenant O'Reilly had gone inside to talk to Captain Reid. The rest of the reinforcements had hunkered down as close to the brick wall of the home as they could get. But there were also many of their pards from Company D leaning against the wall with bloody bandages covering wounds or huddled around the corners of the house taking turns leaning out and shooting at the enemy.

Charlie Locker was there, and he smiled in relief when he saw Christopher and Ezra. Then he did a double take. "Where's Parker?" he asked.

Christopher leaned in to be heard. "Shot in the chest. We took him back to a hospital."

Charlie's face briefly contorted with anger and concern and then wonder as he looked out over the open field between them and the town, now littered with countless dead and wounded. He looked Christopher in the eye. "And you came back? Through that?"

Christopher shrugged. "It wasn't so bad when we started."

Ezra leaned forward. "I swear, if I didn't know better, I'd say someone was bucking for some stripes."

With a flash of irritation, Christopher started to respond, then Charlie interrupted.

"Listen! I need you four to get ready; there's some rebs moved forward who've occupied a house near the stone wall. We think they're getting ready to assault this position."

Christopher shook his head. "Why? All they have to do is hunker down behind that wall and shoot us as we come up. Look around you—they're wiping out the whole army without even trying."

"Doesn't matter. Some have come out from behind their hidy-hole, and Captain Reid wants to make sure they don't get very far. We didn't risk our lives taking these houses for nothing."

Christopher shrugged. He'd learned long ago not to bother trying to second guess officers—and you definitely didn't argue with them. Since the corners of the house were already crowded, he and Ezra went inside to see if they could get a window position. Even though when they rejoined the company

their mission was complete and the squad ceased to exist, Nathan Jump and
John Finn followed.

Inside the house, they saw the same destruction they'd witnessed in the
other house—furniture destroyed, wall hangings and knick-knacks shattered
in heaps on the mud covered floor, and blood stains showing where someone
had been hit. A thick pall of gun smoke hung in the air, causing Christopher
to wrinkle his nose in disgust at the urine-like smell.

Ezra took one whiff and said, "Smells like my grandma's house."

"Your grandma do a lot of shooting, does she?" John Finn asked.

"No, she has a bunch of cats."

The four laughed. *At least now,* Christopher thought, *we can hear ourselves think.*

He went to a window facing the enemy and looked out while trying not
to expose himself too much. The house and its occupants were drawing a
steady fire from the enemy. It was his first good look at the enemy position
other than from a distance.

The wall looked to be about three or four feet high, thick and made of
stone. Nothing short of a direct hit with a cannonball would penetrate it.
The well-entrenched position of the enemy made him think of the Bloody
Lane at Antietam, only much longer. There was no way they could flank this
entrenchment, he thought. And the rebels had good artillery support.

An almost solid line of rifles lay over the top of the wall, behind which
was a mass of heads, firing at the constant flow of Union soldiers crossing the
open field. Few of those Union soldiers were making it to the houses the 8th
now occupied. And no one had made it any farther.

Not for the first time Christopher wondered if the big bugs were mad, or
just stupid.

He saw the house Charlie was talking about and could see that the enemy
indeed occupied it. But he could see no reason for them to attack. They were
winning just fine where they were.

They stayed there the rest of the afternoon, taking turns shooting out
windows and holes in the walls created by exploding shot and shells. The
middle of the downstairs rooms and the side yard of the house filled up with
wounded.

Toward dusk, several Union batteries were brought forward and lined up just the other side of the canal. When they opened fire, the noise surpassed even the constant barrage they'd been experiencing all day. The whole house shook.

For a few moments, there was a respite from the constant enemy fire, and some of the assaulting troops made it past the houses occupied by the 8th only to be shot down in waves when the enemy resumed shooting. Those who were not killed outright dropped to the ground and lay there, not moving except to crawl behind a dead body for cover.

In the increasing darkness, a runner got through to Captain Reid, informing him the 8th was falling back. As the company formed up in the yard, Christopher said a silent prayer thanking the Lord that he'd lived through the day and to keep him safe until they were back in the town. The moving lips on many of the surrounding men said he wasn't the only one.

As they marched back toward the town, a final assault was being attempted. Christopher knew that French's division had been the first—they were supposed to have to joined them in the assault—but they hadn't even made it to the houses. He wondered how many other divisions had been shattered against that wall of hiding rebs and said a prayer for those now marching forth, futilely trying not to step on bodies as they advanced.

There was another deafening roar, and what was left of that final assault came running back before the 8th even made it to the other side of the canal.

The canal itself was now clogged with the dead and dying. Christopher imagined the bodies in the water swelling and was thankful the waning light blanketed the crevasse in shadow.

It was a demoralized army that went into camp that night in Fredericksburg. While officially, they were to camp along the Rappahannock, most reoccupied the abandoned homes. Where the night before the soldiers plundered the homes, justifying it to themselves that was the price for rebellion, the angry and demoralized soldiers that night needed no justification for their actions. They took their anger out on the homes of the hated secessionists, leaving the houses gutted ruins the next morning when the army began its exodus back across the river.

THE FOLLOWING MORNING, Christopher and Ezra stood in line waiting to cross the Rappahannock River along with several thousand others. Though the bridges were wide enough to accommodate a four-man column, the line was moving at a crawl.

Ezra, weighted down with his knapsack full of stolen silverware, was particularly frustrated by the delay and not afraid to show it. Beads of sweat covered his face, and he hunched over, constantly shrugging and shifting the knapsack in a futile effort to get comfortable.

"What in tarnation is taking so long? If we don't get moving soon my back is gonna break."

"You reap what you sow, pard. All that ill-gotten gain is weighing you down, body and soul," Christopher replied.

"My soul is just fine, thank you. It's my body that's ready to give out—preacher." Ezra raised an eyebrow. "Besides, I know for a fact you got a little booty of your own weighing you down."

Christopher blushed. "Just a little something for my mother."

"Uh-huh. A little frilly something taken from one of those secesh homes without a by-your-leave is all."

"Let's drop it," Christopher snapped.

Ezra looked out over the river and tried unsuccessfully to shrug his shoulders. "Just saying...you know the old saw about casting stones..."

As they inched forward, they saw the reason for the slow movement. A group of provost guards were at the base of the bridge, relieving soldiers of any obvious contraband. Ezra cursed under his breath.

Turning his back on Christopher, he asked, "Is anything showing?"

"Just your guilt. You're sweating like a pig, and those straps are fit to bust any minute now. I don't see how you're going to fool anyone into thinking all you got in there is some spare socks and underwear."

"I could say it was my great coat."

"You're great coat don't poke out like that."

"Well...what am I gonna do?"

Christopher shrugged. "Give it back I guess."

"Right," Ezra responded. "You think any of that stuff they're taking off the foot soldiers is gonna make it back to the secesh? More likely it's all going to some officer's quarters to be sent back home."

Christopher frowned. There didn't seem to be any effort to identify the owners. They were just taking the stolen goods and piling them up by the road.

Christopher looked at the pile, and his eyes got wide. Besides the obvious small stuff—dishes, silverware, picture frames, and various personal items—there were chairs and tables and even a piano. He wasn't proud of what he'd taken. In a way, the stack of folded handkerchiefs and bag of tobacco in his knapsack seemed as heavy as the silver in Ezra's. But what they'd taken paled compared to some of the goods in that pile.

As expected, when they reached the roadblock, the guards honed in on Ezra's knapsack.

"What you got in there, Private?" the sergeant asked.

Ezra smiled and tried to appear relaxed. "Just my personables."

"That so?"

Ezra nodded. A little too enthusiastically, Christopher thought.

"Open up. Let's see," the sergeant said in a bored voice.

Ezra worked his mouth open and closed a couple times like a fish out of water. "Why, why, I'm offended by the affront on my personal liberty."

"You're in the army, bub. You have no personal liberty."

"Still, there are limits a patriotic American fighting for his country should have to put up with."

"Not when there's thieving involved," the sergeant's voice went up a notch. It was clear he was near the end of his patience.

"Give it up, Ezra. You can console yourself with a smoke when we get back to camp," Christopher said to remind him they still had the tobacco.

Ezra looked at Christopher's knapsack for a second. Then he nodded.

As the guards relieved Ezra of his plunder, the sergeant looked to Christopher. "How about you? You got anything?"

Christopher thought of the silk handkerchiefs and tobacco in his knapsack. He thought of the possibility of either ever getting back to their rightful owners. He thought of how insufferable Ezra would be for the rest of the day if they lost the tobacco, too. Then he looked the sergeant in the eye and said, "I have nothing to declare, Sergeant."

The sergeant looked at Christopher, looked at his pack, looked over at the pile of silverware retrieved from Ezra's pack, then looked at the unending line winding out of the town and down to the bridge. He sighed and waved them through.

Anger and a lightened load gave Ezra the energy to stomp across the bridge at a brisk pace, winding his way through other soldiers and cursing under his breath. Christopher followed a few paces behind.

At the top of the opposite bank, Christopher stopped and looked back. Except for an occasional rifle shot, the guns were silent. A few columns of black smoke rose from burned-out buildings. But other than that, the horizon of homes and shops, punctuated by a few steeples, appeared unaffected by the battle. If Christopher could somehow rid his memory of all the dead that still lay in that field on the other side of town, he could imagine a lazy summer morning, bobbing in a boat on the river, fishing and thinking all the inconsequential things people thought when they didn't have death hanging over their heads almost every day. It almost made him smile.

Almost.

Chapter Three

It took Christopher half the morning to find Parker Bonett in the maze of tents that made up the Second Corps hospital. Despite his familiarity with post-battle suffering, the sights and sounds that assailed him that morning made him nauseous and weak-kneed. He stumbled through rows of men in blood-soaked bandages, many missing limbs, most feverish and moaning. Those who were conscious and still had the energy constantly thrashed about in a futile effort to ease their pain.

As he was moving toward the exit of the first tent, a skeletal hand reached out and grabbed his pant leg. He looked down at an older man, maybe thirty, his skin and clothing drenched in sweat, with a bloody bandage wrapped around his midsection.

"Water," the dying man croaked.

Christopher knelt down and looked at the man with what he hoped was a look of compassion and not the fear and disgust he felt. "You been gut-shot, pard. I can't give you no water."

The wounded man's head fell back, and he squeezed his eyes shut. "Please."

It was no more than a whisper, but it cut through Christopher's resolve like the bark of a drill sergeant. The *man's dying*, he told himself. *What difference is it going to make?*

"What do you think you are doing, Private?" yelled a surgeon as he stormed up to the other side of the wounded man. "I will thank you to not interfere with the patients."

Christopher scrambled to his feet. The man wasn't wearing a coat, but he knew all surgeons were officers. "Sorry, sir. It's just he was so thirsty. I thought... I mean..." Christopher lowered his voice to a whisper. "He ain't gonna make it. I figured what harm could it do?"

"He *ain't* ain't he?" the surgeon mocked. "Is that your expert medical opinion, *Private?* Tell me, where did you get your medical training?"

Christopher squared his shoulders back as a surge of defiance coursed through him in response to the surgeon's tone. "He's gut-shot... sir. Everyone knows there's no coming back from that."

The surgeon put his fists on his hips. "Do they, now? I tell you what, young man, I've seen worse than this survive and make it home to their loving families. When it comes to medicine and the human body, what everyone knows *ain't* worth a picayune penny. Now, run along and don't let me catch you interfering with these patients again."

Christopher made a hasty retreat, making sure not to look at the wounded man again on his way out.

After that, Christopher kept moving, looking at each face only long enough to see if it was Parker or someone else he may know. The only ones who seemed to be resting were those still unconscious from the ether administered during surgery, or dead. Christopher prayed he wouldn't find Parker that way.

He found him laying on a pile of straw covered with a bloodstained sheet. Parker's shirt and shoes were missing, and a single blanket was all that protected him from the cold December air. A bloody piece of cloth was tied over his chest wound, and he was sweating and shaking from the fever and the cold at the same time.

Christopher knelt beside him and whispered, "Parker, you awake."

There was no response.

"Parker?" Christopher thought of shaking him, but didn't want to cause his friend any more pain than he was already in.

He sat like that a few moments, fretting that Parker would not awake before he had to leave. Finally, the wounded man mumbled something.

Christopher leaned down. "What? What was that?"

Parker shook his head.

Christopher lay his hand on Parker's forearm. "Parker, can you hear me?"

Without opening his eyes, Parker whispered, "Chris. What are you doing here?"

"I came to see you. The battle's over, and we're back in camp. They wupped us good, Parker. I never seen anything like it. Not even at Antietam."

Christopher's eyes got a faraway look as he continued. "We kept coming, wave after wave, and they kept knocking us down, and they kept sending more and more, like grist to the mill. By the end of the day bodies covered the field.

"And worst of it was, a lot of them were still alive. Those that made it close to the wall couldn't move without getting shot, so they just laid like that all night long. I bet it was a cold one for them."

Christopher came back to the present and looked down at his friend. Parker had been there since the beginning, looking out for the Galloway brothers and acting as the voice of reason when they argued. After Daniel's death, Parker stepped up, keeping him sober and out of trouble. Whatever happened now, this war was over for Parker, and Christopher didn't know what he'd do without him.

"How you feeling, Park?"

"I been better. Hear tell they're sending me back to Washington City in a couple days. I hope by boat. I wouldn't want to go that far in an ambulance on those rutty roads."

A wave of fear crawled down Christopher's spine. The returning wounded he'd talked to said the ambulance ride was almost the worst part. The things had no suspension, and the slightest bump sent you flying. Christopher wondered how many men might have lived if they had a more humane mode of transportation.

"Washington City should be good," he said, shaking off his fear. "I hear tell they have female nurses now. Maybe you'll get a pretty one."

Still not opening his eyes, Parker gave a half smile. "More like a sour-puss old biddy."

Christopher laughed despite himself.

With a groan of pain and effort, Parker reached out and grabbed Christopher's arm. He opened his eyes and looked into Christopher's. "You have to be strong, Chris. Whatever happened in that Confederate prison, Danny's death, all the killing and the hate...you have to stay above it. Or this war will kill you sure as it's killed me."

Christopher shook his head. "Don't talk like that, Parker. A couple months in the hospital you'll be back in the line-up with the rest of us. You'll see."

Parker shook his head, sweat spattering the bedspread. Then he let his hand and head drop, and he let out a sigh. "I don't think so."

"I know so, Park!" Christopher voice rose and his words grew forceful. "You pull through, dammit! We need you...I need you."

"I'm sorry, bub," Parker said before dropping back into a deep sleep.

Tears filled Christopher's eyes, and his chin trembled. "You get better, Park, you hear me," he said. He stood and made his way out of the tent and into the weak winter's sunlight.

CHRISTOPHER DIDN'T like the shack he, Ezra, and Charlie shared at the winter camp just north of Falmouth, Virginia. Ever since his forced confinement while sick at Camp Dennison, he found the windowless huts the soldiers built wherever they stayed a while small and restricting. Also, they seemed to bottle up odors so they lingered for hours.

But he had to admit, this shack wasn't too bad. Ezra had "found" a small cook stove from somewhere, and they lined the floor it set on and the wall behind it with a thick layer of mud. As the stove burned, the mud not only kept the shack from burning down, it also hardened and reflected the heat, which Christopher appreciated as the temperature continued to drop.

The only drawback to such a nice abode was the worry. All it would take was for the three of them to be away on picket duty for a day or two, and they would more than likely come back to an empty hut. That's probably what happened to the previous owner of the stove.

Christopher didn't ask where Ezra got the stove. All he knew was that he'd woken one morning, and there it was. He and Ezra spent the day hauling mud and shaping the hearth. Getting the mud to stay on the wall long enough to dry proved challenging, so when Charlie came into the shack they still weren't done. The sergeant stopped at the sight of his mud-covered messmates. Then he saw the stove, and his eyes got big as saucers.

"Where did you get that?" he asked.

"Do you really want to know?" Ezra responded.

Charlie shook his head. "All I know, and all I want to know, is that there is an officer with the 67th who's been haranguing anyone who'll listen about how he ordered a new stove from back home and only had it a few days before it up and disappeared. I suggest you two not go bragging about your new acquisition."

"We weren't planning to," Christopher said with a pout. "It's not like we're the type to put on airs."

"I'm not saying you are," Charlie said. "Just be careful is all. That officer said if he finds who took his stove, he'll see the man is flogged until there's no skin left on his back."

Ezra paled a little at that but quickly recovered. "No need to worry, Charlie. We'll keep it on the quiet."

Charlie nodded, then smiled. "I say, that is a nice addition to our humble abode. Just don't burn the place down."

"Yes, sir, Sergeant, sir!" Ezra said with a mock salute.

"Pshaw!" Charlie exclaimed, waiving his hand at Ezra.

CHRISTMAS CAME ONLY a couple weeks after the battle at Fredericksburg, and a collective funk hung over the camp like a death shroud. There were few festivities, and the baggage trains and sutlers still hadn't arrived, so there was nothing to be festive with. The closeness of the enemy required a heavy picket presence, and the men spent half their time at a forward picket camp, sleeping on the cold, wet ground with no tents to protect them from the snow.

Charlie made sure at least one of them was off duty at any given time, so when they got back from picket duty, there was always to a warm place to sleep.

Christmas morning, Ezra and Christopher both had the day free, though with no packages from home and their personal items still somewhere between camp and Washington City, there was little to celebrate. They had a breakfast of fried beef and soft bread, with plenty of fresh-ground coffee, then they spent the morning lying on their cots complaining about army life.

"You know," Ezra ruminated, "it strikes me as odd that this army can move us down here on foot in a matter of days, but our baggage, which is traveling by wagon and rail, takes weeks to go the same distance."

Christopher sipped his coffee and leaned back, taking on the same thoughtful air as Ezra. "It is a particularity unique to the army, that's the truth. I guess they're just more careful with the baggage.

"Tell you what." Christopher winked at Ezra. "Next time you're having tea with ol' Backside, why don't you ask him to do something about it."

Ezra laughed a short, bitter laugh. "Another disaster like Fredericksburg, ol' backside-Burnside will be manning a picket line with us."

"Hmm." Christopher rubbed his chin. "I wonder who'll replace him—Sumner, Hooker, or Franklin? Maybe they'll bring someone else up, like Couch."

"Pshaw," Ezra spat. "He's the one caused us to lose all our goods at Fredericksburg."

"Not all," Christopher reminded him.

"Not all," Ezra mimicked back. "Goody-two shoes Galloway slipped some doilies and tobaccy past the guards. La-de-da."

"You enjoying your nightly smoke, or not?" Christopher shot back.

"Hmmm." Ezra returned to the original subject. "Maybe they'll promote Kimball!"

Christopher burst out laughing. "I heard tell he made a real ass of himself with his little speech to the rest of the brigade before the battle."

"To be fair," Ezra got out through fits of laughter, "what can you say to a few thousand men about to march to the slaughter? 'Hip-hip, boys. You go on now, and I'll be right here if—I mean—when you get back...doing whatever it is generals do while the rest of you are off dying.'"

"Coordinatin'," Christopher said.

"That's right! Coordinatin'!"

"It worked, though!" Christopher continued. "The boys were reluctant to go, but by the time Kimball was done, they were clamoring to be the first on the field, bare their chests to the enemy, and yell, 'Here I am, Johnny, shoot me now!'"

The boys were still doubled over with laughter when Charlie walked in, went straight to his cot, and dropped down as if he'd just finished a twenty mile march.

Christopher stopped laughing. Even in the meager light of the hut, he could see Charlie's blue eyes glistening with tears. A cold fear clutched his gut. "What is it?"

Charlie looked at them both for several moments before he could speak. Finally, he managed a whisper. "Parker...Parker's dead."

To Christopher it was as if someone turned the shack over and sucked all the air out. The room spun, and he had trouble catching his breath. Ezra's face crumpled like that of a toddler about to cry.

"How? When?"

Charlie hung his head. "Two days ago. Fever got him."

A deathly quiet fell over the room. Christopher stared at the light of the candle lantern and remembered the first time he really got to know Sergeant Parker S. Bonnett. It was the train ride from Camp Dennison to West Virginia. Parker lived in Ridgefield, Ohio, about five miles west of Norwalk, and was older than Christopher and Daniel, so they didn't know him before the war. On the train the men had been cooped up drinking and working themselves up into a fighting frenzy. When the train stopped for water and fuel, they made a mad rush toward the doors. Non-commissioned officers in the cattle cars with the men had to restore order before the officers would allow the doors to be opened. Parker, then a corporal, moved through the crowd with a leather blackjack he kept in his pocket, pushing men into line and cracking those that resisted on the head.

That was Parker. Sometimes sarcastic, he took no guff from anyone. But, if he was your pard, there was none better. He did his best to fill Daniel's shoes after Antietam and kept Christopher out of trouble. He was the undisputed leader of the mess and respected by men and officers alike.

Inside, Christopher's heart hurt so badly he could hardly breath. He felt as if he'd lost two big brothers now, and there would not be another. But he didn't cry. He had no tears left. He never cried for Parker Bonnett, and that was a regret he carried with him the rest of his life.

Chapter Four

The snows of December turned into the rains of January. Soon, the entire camp was a sea of mud that clung to feet, hooves, and wheels in big heavy clumps that made any kind of movement exhausting.

Fortunately, before the roads got too bad, the 8th's supply wagons arrived from the Washington depot. Unfortunately, while in storage a lot of the men's personal items had been "lost." Not even Colonel Sawyer was immune. Christopher saw him dressing down a poor private in the quartermaster corps, demanding to know where his camp chest was.

There was little drill during this time because of the mud and the heavy picket schedule. When they had drill practice, the men stumbled and cursed the entire time. Within minutes, Christopher's shoes would be covered with a layer of mud almost an inch thick, and his leg muscles would start to quiver from the exertion.

After one such aborted attempt at drill, Christopher and Ezra returned to their hut to find a flyer tacked to their door. There were several such flyers going around camp, and Christopher knew what it was, but he pulled it down and looked it over anyway. At the top was a drawing of a monkey in a black coat and top hat with a beard along his chin and jawline. Above that was a thought balloon that said, "Another ten-thousand dead soldiers, I get a banana!" It described how the president and congress had mismanaged the war and Lee and Jackson were running circles around the northern armies. All was lost and, if the average soldier wanted to live another year, he should just pack it up and go home. It did not mention the possibility of being executed for trying to do just that.

Christopher sat down on the large rock they'd put in front of the door as a porch and used the pamphlet to wipe the mud off his shoes.

"All is lost, Ezra. The government is corrupt and stupid, and we're committing atrocities against the innocent civilians of the South."

"Is that what it said?" Ezra asked as he worked the mud on his own shoes with a stick.

"Well, not this one. That was the last one. This one just talks about how Abe Lincoln is an ape and throwing away our lives for bananas."

Ezra barked a laugh. "That's a new one."

"Never let it be said the copperheads lacked imagination, that's for sure." Christopher threw the now mud-covered pamphlet into a puddle and rubbed his aching thighs. A twitch had started on the left one, and he hoped some deep massage would make it stop.

"At least we've had a couple days of no rain or snow. Maybe now it'll dry out," he said as he massaged his leg.

Ezra spat. "Don't count your chickens, pard."

Christopher glanced toward the hazy, weak sun. "I'm not. Just wishing, I guess."

Christopher took off his brogans and stood to go inside. As he reached for the door, it burst open, and two men came running out of the hut, their arms full of blankets and tin cookware. Christopher was almost knocked over, but caught himself just in time.

The men jumped over Ezra and slogged through the mud as fast as they could.

Christopher yelled, "Stop, you damn thieves!" as he fumbled into his brogans.

Ezra stood and started after them. "I see you Si Hineman! I know where your camp is! You bring that stuff back, or we'll be paying you a visit tonight with twenty of our pards!"

The shorter, stocky thief glanced over his shoulder. "You ain't got twenty pards, Rouse. You ain't even got that many left in your company," he cackled and kept running.

By that time, Christopher had his brogans on and had joined the pursuit, though he hadn't had time to tie them. The four men slogged down the company street in slow motion, the mud gripping their feet with each step.

Christopher passed Ezra and was gaining on the two thieves when his right shoe caught in the mud and stayed there. With his next step, Christopher put his stockinged foot into a puddle and stopped, shocked by the icy water that enveloped his already-cold foot. "Dammit all to tarnation!"

He looked up at the receding backs. "Stop, you damn thieves!"

By that time, the four had gotten the attention of other members of Company D, and they moved to converge on the two in front. Then, a rock sailed passed Christopher's ear and hit Hineman between the shoulder blades. The thief cried out and dropped his load of blankets. His partner, sensing imminent capture, dropped his own load and tried to pick up speed.

Ezra came up beside Christopher and handed him his shoe. "That'll teach 'em."

Christopher took the muddy brogan, now full of brown water, with a grunt of disgust. "At least they didn't get our equipments. It'd be damn cold tonight without any blankets."

The thieves were cut off by Nathan Jump and Lucius Hoyt and, with the help of other Company D men, quickly surrounded. Christopher poured the water out of his brogan and slipped in his wet, muddy foot. He took a moment to tie both shoes before stepping forward.

The sounds of an argument between the two thieves and members of Company D grew louder with each step. By the time he and Ezra reached the group, the yelling was coming non-stop so fast from so many people it was unintelligible.

"Quiet!" Christopher yelled. Already angry from the near loss of their possessions and the thought of his brogan now muddy inside and out, he was ready to lash out at anyone, friend or foe.

Christopher looked the two would-be thieves up and down. The one Ezra had called Si was short and oddly fleshy for someone in the infantry. His partner was tall—over six feet—and rail thin.

Christopher addressed the short one first. "Ezra called you Si, that your name?"

"Might be."

"You're in no position to be acting smart, Si."

"You can't be holding us here against—" Christopher boxed Si's ear.

Si's partner took a step forward, and Ezra stepped up to meet him. The two stood chest to chest and stared into each other's eyes with open hostility. Christopher noted that the stranger was taller even than Ezra.

"Who might you be, beanpole?"

The tall one took his eyes off Ezra long enough to answer Christopher. "They call me Shorty."

Several men laughed, and Christopher squinted at Shorty for a moment, sure he was the butt of some joke. When he saw the man was serious, he smiled. "Shorty, huh? That's right funny. Who gave you that moniker?"

Shorty shrugged. "I've always been Shorty."

Christopher nodded. "Maybe so, but I doubt you've ever been short."

Sensing the shorter of the two was the leader, Christopher turned his attention back to Si. "What do you mean by taking our plunder? In broad daylight, no less."

Si shrugged. "We thought you was out drillin'."

"We was out drillin', you chubby little mudsill," Ezra responded. "Then we came back."

Si straightened and puffed up at the insult. "Well then, I guess we shoulda been quicker."

"What're we gonna do with them, Notch?" someone asked.

Christopher had no idea. What were they going to do with them? Give them a thumping? Strip them and send them back to their regiment buck naked? Several options ran through Christopher's mind. Everything but taking them to an officer. But nothing seemed appropriate. And, other than getting everything muddy, no harm had come from the little escapade. In fact, it had broken the monotony for a while.

Christopher shrugged. "Who are you with?" he asked.

Si and Shorty exchanged a glance. Si squinted at Christopher, his eyes slits. "Why you want to know? You going to report us?"

Christopher sputtered at the insult. "What do you take me for?" He shook his head. "We just need to know where to go if next time you're more successful in your endeavors."

Si shook his head. "That's for me to know and—"

"And me to beat out of you if I have to." The look Christopher gave Si made him blanch.

"I know where they're from," Ezra said. "They're with the 14th Indiana. Their camp's not too far from here."

Christopher put his hands on his hips. "Well, Si, Shorty. We'll let you off this time. But next time you can expect some payback."

The two gave Christopher an uncertain look. "You saying we can go?"

A chorus of objections came from the crowd. Christopher raised his hands for quiet. Once everyone settled down, he nodded. "This time."

Si' hesitantly turned to go. As he did, Christopher glanced down.

"Wait!"

Si jumped. "I knew it! As soon as we turn our backs, you're gonna thump us!"

"If I wanted to thump you, I wouldn't wait 'till your back was turned." Christopher pointed to Si's trousers. "Turn out your pockets."

"What?" Si feigned confusion, but his cheeks reddened.

"Both of you, turn out your pockets."

Shorty reached in and turned out his pants pockets. They both were empty. Si continued to hesitate.

Christopher took a step forward, and the crowd closed in around the two men. "Turn out your pockets, Si. Or we'll hang you upside down and shake out whatever's in there."

Si seemed to deflate. He reached into his pockets, which were clearly bulging, and pulled out the silk handkerchiefs Christopher had brought back from Fredericksburg. He still hadn't mailed them to his mother out of shame for how he'd gotten them.

Christopher angrily reached out and ripped the handkerchiefs out of Si's hand, dropping several in the mud. The two men froze. Christopher felt the anger building up, threatening to consume him. Si's eyes were so wide, he could see white all around the irises.

Christopher clenched the silk cloth until the veins stood out on the back of his hand. He took several deep breaths. He whispered, "Get out of here."

Si and Shorty didn't wait for him to change his mind. The two turned and resumed their slow, slogging run back to their regiment.

Christopher watched the two's semi-hasty retreat for almost a minute, thinking of the immoral impact war seemed to have on men—himself included. Then he went to help Ezra pick up their possessions. As he turned he saw First Sergeant Howe watching him. The man had a peculiar expression on his face, and for a moment Christopher thought he was in trouble. Then the sergeant turned and walked away without saying a word.

TWO DAYS LATER CHRISTOPHER received a summons to report to Captain Reid's quarters. This was it. Whatever obscure regulation he'd broken in their encounter with the Indiana boys was now coming back to bite him. *Well,* he thought as he entered the captain's hut, *let's get this done and over with.* He couldn't help feeling a little pride thinking at least this time, if they want him to parade around in a knapsack full of rocks, it would be like a Sunday stroll compared to what he and Daniel endured back in Camp Dennison so long ago.

As Christopher's eyes adjusted to the dim light he looked around, taking in the cot, the frock coat hanging on a hook on the wall next to a shelf with a shaving kit and toothbrush, and a small shelf of books on the wall opposite. A closed chest sat at the foot of the bed, and Christopher inwardly smirked at the idea that, while Sawyer's camp chest had gotten lost in storage in Washington City, Reid's had made it back to the 8th. That could only have made the loss more infuriating for the colonel.

The captain was sitting in a chair next to a portable writing desk. Sergeant Howe stood next to him, further enforcing the idea in Christopher's mind that he was in store for a dressing down. He removed his hat and came to attention with a snap of his heels. "Private Galloway reporting as ordered, sir," he said to the room.

"At ease, Private," Reid responded. He took one look at Christopher's face and said, "You're not in trouble."

Some of the tension left Christopher's shoulders. He looked at the captain with his head slightly cocked to one side.

"First Sergeant Howe and I have been talking about you, Galloway. You've even come up in conversation with Colonel Sawyer." Christopher felt a stab of panic. He didn't see how being the topic of conversation between the big bugs could be a good thing.

Reid smiled slightly at the now-obvious nervous confusion on Christopher's expression. Howe gave no sign he was even listening. He just stood there, back straight, eyes focused somewhere in the distance, his hands clasped behind his back.

"It's nothing to worry about, Galloway. The colonel was impressed that you and the rest of your squad came back out onto the field at Fredericksburg after taking Sergeant Bonett to the hospital. Most men would have taken that opportunity to sit out the battle. Especially one going as badly as that one."

Christopher opened his mouth to protest, but Reid raised a hand, cutting him off. "The colonel was also under the impression that it was you who led those men after Bonett's wounding. Furthermore, Sergeant Howe observed you in an encounter with a couple of soldiers who'd tried to rob your hut. He said you were clearly in command of the situation."

"I don't know about that, sir," Christopher said. "I was just trying to impress on those two bummers not to come around the 8th's camp tryin' to make off with anyone's plunder."

Reid nodded. "Precisely. Despite your best efforts, Galloway, you've shown some leadership skills, and Lord knows, after these last two battles, we're getting short on leaders."

With that, Captain Reid picked up a set of corporal's stripes sitting on his desk and handed them to Christopher. "Here, sew these on your jacket sleeves. There will be a formal announcement at tomorrow's dress parade."

Christopher didn't take the stripes. Instead, he shook his head and sputtered, "But... I don't... Captain, sir... Whatever for..."

"This is not a request," Reid responded. "You will take these stripes and sew them on your uniform. And tomorrow, *Corporal* Galloway, Sergeant Howe will assign you a squad. At which point, you will assume your duties as a non-commissioned officer. First Sergeant Howe will provide you with a manual and answer any questions you may have. That is all."

Christopher tried one more time to protest, but First Sergeant Howe cut him off. "Corporal Galloway, you are dismissed!"

Christopher felt himself deflate in acceptance. "Yes, sir. Thank you, sir." He turned to go.

"Corporal..."

Christopher kept moving.

"GALLOWAY!" Christopher jumped and spun around, staring at Howe wide-eyed. *What now?*

"Aren't you forgetting something?" Howe's eyes dropped down to Reid's outstretched hand.

Christopher reached out and took the stripes as if the captain was handing him a dead rodent. He nodded once and left the hut.

CHRISTOPHER'S FIRST assignment as corporal was to lead a four-man work detail in building a corduroy road. Work details had cut out a road through the trees behind the camp and the trees they had cut down in the process were being used to create the corduroy. Everywhere, the local forests were being cut down to supply more logs for the road, as well as to keep the camp supplied in firewood. Mostly, it was men from Wisconsin, Michigan, Minnesota, and Maine, with previous logging experience doing all the cutting. They would then drag the logs to the work site using mule teams, where hundreds of infantrymen—anyone without logging experience—would line the logs up in a row along the path and drive long wooden spikes through pre-cut holes in cross-bars to hold them in place.

The road ran parallel to the river, and once the woods were stripped bare, the rebels on the other side came out to watch.

Ezra had just dropped his end of a log in the mud and was wiping his brow as he looked out at the line of Confederate soldiers in the distance.

"Looks like the cat's out of the bag," he said.

"What cat's that, ya think?" Nathan Jump, standing at the other end of the log, asked.

"You know, our secret plan to flank the enemy," Ezra said.

"That what we doing? Flankin' the enemy?" Nathan asked.

Ezra shrugged. "What else? They wanted to keep us busy they could have found easier ways to do it than this. There's always trash to police, sinks to dig, buttons to polish... Hell, I'd almost rather be drilling than doing this."

Christopher had heard enough. "All right. The road's not going to build itself. Get that log lined up with the one next to it, and go get another."

Ezra wiggled into an approximation of an attention stance and saluted Christopher while wagging his fingers. "Ay, Ay, Corporal Galloway," he said snickering.

Christopher sighed. When he'd returned to their hut after his meeting with Captain Reid and First Sergeant Howe, Ezra had burst out laughing at the sight of the stripes in Christopher's hand—and had not let up since. "Well," Ezra had said when he stopped laughing. "It always pays to have friends in high places." Then he'd burst into laughter again. To him, Christopher's promotion was a testament to the vagaries of army life and an opportunity for personal gain.

To Christopher, though, it was a bitter injustice. *What were they thinking promoting me?* he thought as he sewed the stripes onto his sleeves. *I never wanted these stripes and never should have gotten them. These are Danny's, not mine.*

But he was stuck with them now. The only thing worse than being a corporal would be getting busted back down to private. He would just have to make the best of it and keep Ezra from taking too much advantage. This first assignment was putting that to the ultimate test.

Christopher looked out at the river and enemy beyond. He knew as well as Ezra that this was the prelude to another attempt to take Fredericksburg. The thought sapped his strength and left him feeling depressed. *Burnside won't stop until that town's taken or we're all dead.*

He looked up at the sky. He'd thought about saying a brief prayer asking the Lord to see him through, but the slate gray sky, laced with wisps of white, distracted him, and he thought of snow. Not the slushy stuff down here that covered the ground for a couple days and then turned to mud. The snow back home. Soft and light, glistening under a bright winter sun. Huge drifts and piles, some as high as a man. The temperature so cold it made your nose and chest hurt.

He thought then of his family and wondered how they were doing. They'd not written in a while, or at least he'd not gotten anything. He remembered that prayer and said it for them instead of himself.

A thud, and the sounds of men cursing, drew Christopher back to the present. Looking over he saw that Nathan and Ezra had dropped the log they were carrying. Nathan was rubbing his leg, and Ezra was cussing. Taking a big breath, he moved in to sort things out.

BEFORE THEY HAD FINISHED the corduroy road, the rain returned. The final logs were laid in standing water, the ground too wet and soft to secure them with the vertical piles. To make matters worse, the rain brought warmer weather that melted what snow remained on the ground. The camp was a quagmire of brown soup. Anyone not on picket or fatigue duty was indoors, cleaning their equipment and brushing the mud off their clothes. Everyone knew another attack was imminent, but the mud made trying to move an army impossible.

The rains eventually stopped, but the mud remained. When the sun came out, the standing water that lay everywhere almost glistened. Everything else was a uniform brown that seemed to suck the light into itself and drain man and beast of energy. So they continued to wait for the attack everyone knew was coming, but no one seemed to know when.

Then, someone decided they could wait no more. As bugles blew the call to assembly, men lined up in the mud and water for inspection and distribution of rations and ammunition. Artillery brigades lumbered by, their horses and mules straining to pull the heavy pieces and caissons though the muck. It took two days to get the army moving, and when it did, the corduroy road they'd constructed just for the task sunk into the ground as if the earth was reclaiming the logs taken from its forests.

The 8th was on picket duty on the lawn of a mansion that looked out over the Rappahannock River and Fredericksburg beyond. The officers were billeted in the house, while the enlisted men, when not on picket, slept in dog tents spread out across the lawn.

Christopher had been assigned a post near the river, so he couldn't see the army's progress, but he could hear the rumble of wagons and cannon on the corduroy road accompanied by the tramping of thousands of feet. The sounds of neighing horses, braying mules, and cursing men accompanied the sounds of marching. Never a fan of picket duty, Christopher for once was glad to be where he was. Given the condition of the road and countryside, he didn't think the army would make it ten miles much less to whatever ford they'd decided to use for the crossing.

The day passed. Usually, enemy soldiers would pass the time by coming down to the river to harass the pickets, but today they were nowhere in sight.

With all the trees cut down, there was nothing to stop the cold wind that blew off the river, and the wet, muddy ground soon made Christopher's feet numb with cold. With his rifle in the right-shoulder shift position, he marched back and forth, expecting nothing from the other side, and for several hours they did not disappoint. Then, there was a flurry of gunfire. Crouching low, Christopher brought his rifle down to the ready position and strained to see what was happening on the other side of the river. Even if the army were to make it across the river and attack the rebel flank, it was much too soon. Christopher expected nothing until tomorrow afternoon at the earliest.

It was late afternoon, and the shadows cast by the town's buildings were beginning to lengthen when Christopher spotted a line of soldiers marching out onto the street that ran parallel to the river. Only, they weren't marching so much as prancing. Occasionally, someone would shoot a pistol into the air, and someone else would whoop out a rebel yell, but they showed little interest in the pickets on the other side of the river.

Christopher looked to the next picket over, who had also stopped and was watching the display. The two just shrugged at one another. Then, the unmistakable blast of cannon fire came from the town. Christopher tensed as he waited for a shrieking shell to come flying his way. But it never did.

By now, officers had come out of the mansion and stood on the porch watching the spectacle with field glasses. After a couple minutes, Christopher could tell they were cursing, deepening his confusion. What was going on? What had gotten into the rebels, and why did it have the officers so angry?

As the enemy soldiers marched and pranced their way down to the docks, they held up signs, and, as they drew closer, Christopher could finally make out what they said: BURNSIDE IS STUCK IN THE MUD!

As Christopher had guessed, the army never made it anywhere near the ford before bogging down in the mud. To make matters worse, the lack of trees exposed the spectacle to the enemy who was now rejoicing at the Army of the Potomac's latest failure. *Damned ol' Backside*, Christopher thought. *He's made a fool of us all.*

Chapter Five

General Burnside was relieved of command shortly after the infamous Mud March. In his place, General Joseph Hooker, former commander of First Corps and one of Burnside's Grand Divisions during the battle of Fredericksburg, was made commanding general.

Hooker assumed command of an ill-fed, ill-equipped, and demoralized army and took immediate steps to improve conditions. As soon as the roads were clear enough, a steady supply of food, clothing, tents, and other military equipment started arriving. Other, personal items, having no military purpose whatsoever, appeared in sutlers' row in sufficient quantities to keep prices low. Hooker also came up with a different badge for each corps, intended to foster unity and *esprit de corp* among the troops. But the thing that had the men talking the most was a system of furloughs available to every unit for men with clean records who had seen action. The possibility of going home—even if only for a short time—had the men more excited than all the badges, clean clothes, and fresh food combined.

Christopher and Ezra sat up late almost every night talking about what they would do if they had the chance to visit home. Christopher thought their chances of getting passes were good—since the incident at the drinking shack a year and a half ago, he and Ezra had stayed out of trouble, and there was no doubt they'd done their part at both Antietam and Fredericksburg. They just had to stay out of trouble.

GUN SMOKE, THICK AS a deep fog, swirled around Christopher, hiding the horrors that lived in the shadows. Christopher thought it odd that that much gun smoke wasn't burning his nose and lungs. In fact, it had no smell at all. Despite its clean nature, though, it hid monsters that immobilized Christopher with fear.

In the swirling fog lay mangled corpses, fields of green splotched with puddles of bright red blood, faceless men, somehow still alive, grunting for mercy in pig-like squeals. In the shadows, Spaulding—his tormentor while a prisoner of war and the first man he killed—lurked, ready and able to rob Christopher of everything he owned, including his pride. He shivered as a trill ran down his back and the remaining strength drained away from his limbs.

Soon now.

But it wasn't Spaulding that lurched out of the fog; it was Daniel, blood-soaked and stiff, his face still frozen in the look of fear and horror he'd worn as he died. His eyes looked at Christopher in pleading sorrow. Then, as Christopher watched, frozen in fear and anguish, Daniel's face slowly changed, his cheeks grew rounder as his nose receded, leaving a little button-like bulge at the end. It was the boy in the house at Fredericksburg, and the pleading sorrow in his eyes hardened to hatred and accusation. *You killed me*! A hand, stinking of death, reached for Christopher's face.

"Aaagh!" Christopher sat bolt upright, fist clenched, his body soaked in sweat despite the cold. The fire had gone out several hours ago, and as he relaxed, Christopher began to shiver. He sank back down, burying himself as far into his blanket as he could. Listening to the sounds of the night, he realized there was no deep breathing or snoring coming from Ezra.

"Ez, you awake?"

"Um-mmm."

"Why ain't you asleep?"

"I don't know. Maybe it was the screaming."

"Sorry."

"Don't fret it. You ain't the only one with night demons."

"You have dreams, too?"

"Sometimes. Sometimes my pa comes and tells me I don't deserve to still be living when so many good boys are under the sod."

Christopher was silent for a moment, unsure what to say. Then, "What a bastard."

Ezra barked out a short, humorless laugh. "You got that right."

The two were silent for a while, lost in their own guilt and terror.

Finally, Ezra broke the silence. "What do you see, Chris?"

"What? When?"

"In your dreams. I ain't never seen someone so vexed with bad dreams before. What's getting your goat so bad you wake up hittin' and screamin'?"

Christopher was quiet for a time. He wanted to tell Ezra everything, but the words seemed to stick in his throat. Then he was talking, and he talked about starving, about the courthouse basement in Winchester, about Spaulding and how he robbed them of everything—their food, their blankets, even their dignity—and about how they eventually killed him, and that it was Christopher who had dealt the fatal blow.

"Sounds like a right bastard who got what he deserved."

"Maybe, but that's for God to decide, not me."

"It's no different from shooting men on the battlefield. It was him or you. God forgives us for doing what we have to do to survive."

"I hope so."

"So you should, too."

"Only, it's not just Spaulding anymore. Since Antietam, Danny's been there, too. He used to help me, like from the grave or something. But, since Fredericksburg and that kid in the house, he's not been so helpful anymore. I fear I've gone too far for God's forgiveness, or Danny's."

"That's balderdash. That was no different than if you'd shot him from across the field. How many of our boys do you suppose he laid low that morning? It's just cause it was up close that makes it hard. Them's the worst."

"I guess. But, I don't like the way it makes me feel afterward."

"That's why you're a better man than Spaulding ever could be."

There was another long pause.

"But only after," Christopher whispered.

"What?"

"Only after. While it's happening, I don't feel guilty at all. In fact, I think I'm starting to like it."

After a pause that had Christopher thinking he'd said too much, Ezra laughed.

"What the hell? What's so funny?"

Ezra stopped laughing long enough to say. "I feared it was just me. It can't be right to like fighting, but it...it's a thrill, like horse racing or a high stakes game of poker. While it's happening, you're alive and excited at the prospect of beating the other guy and hoping like hell you don't lose, but for that moment, you're alive more than any other time in your life—until the next race or game or battle."

Christopher didn't know what to say. It was true. He'd felt it, he just didn't want to admit it. He was starting to like war—at least the fighting part. Except for the feelings of sorrow and guilt that followed, it was the best time of his life—the best, and the worst.

Christopher still wasn't comfortable with the man the war was shaping him into, but he was more relaxed and at ease with himself than he had been in a long time. It seemed to help just to talk about it with someone going through the same things. It didn't change anything, or make it better, it just made it easier. With that realization, sleep took hold once more. His eyelids grew heavy, and he let out a languorous yawn. As he drifted off, he said, "You know, Ez, for not having any book learning, you're one of the smartest men I know."

Christopher slept a deep, dreamless sleep for the rest of the night, unburdened by his demons of guilt and sorrow.

BUT THE DREAMS CONTINUED, just not as regularly, and the conflicting emotions that plagued Christopher left him sullen, withdrawn, and quick to temper.

The dreams were not a problem when Christopher was sleeping in the hut he shared with Ezra and Charlie Locker. They knew well enough to let him be when he started moaning and thrashing. If he had to wake Christopher, Ezra kept a long stick by his bed that he would use to poke his troubled friend until sat up, punching air.

But, with the enemy so close, the army kept a heavy picket line along the banks of the Rappahannock, and Ezra and Christopher spent half their time bivouacked in the picket camp. Ezra kept watch when Christopher slept, but he couldn't always be there. It was just a matter of time before someone tried to wake Christopher and got a punch in the nose for their troubles. They just hoped that it wasn't an officer.

One morning, Christopher marched in with his picket detail well before sunrise, where the corporal of the guard, a man from Company B named James Kelly, assigned everyone post numbers and relief schedules. As the detail fell out, Kelly pointed to the newly sewn stripes on Christopher's sleeves and said, "Next time, maybe you'll be in my spot."

Ezra snorted and glanced away. Christopher smiled and nodded, but inwardly groaned. He welcomed the couple extra dollars a month the stripes provided, but he didn't like the added responsibility.

Ezra's schedule required him to be on post at sunrise, but Christopher's relief wasn't until later in the day. They both ate a breakfast of sliced beef and soft bread, washed down with coffee, then laid down in a two-man tent to get some sleep.

Ezra was asleep almost as soon as his head hit the pillow, Christopher lay for what seemed like ages listening to his friend snore and staring at the top of the tent, only a few feet above his face.

As Christopher would start to nod off, the face of the boy at Fredericksburg would appear, then slowly change to that of Daniel's—his cheeks flecked with frothy blood coughed up from his ruined lungs. Christopher would jerk awake, jostling Ezra, who would rustle in response without waking.

Finally, exhaustion won out over guilt and sorrow, and Christopher drifted off to a troubled sleep. Despite his tired state, the dreams seemed to start almost immediately. First was the hunger, the panicky feeling that he was slowly dying from lack of nourishment. The panic would rise as the hunger pangs increased until Christopher started licking crumbs off the floor. Then, Spaulding came.

That morning on at the picket camp, Ezra was already at his post when the sergeant on duty, Thomas Galway of Company B, came to wake him. "Up! Up, Corporal! Your relief is coming up."

Christopher stirred. In his dream, Spaulding's lips were moving, so he knew the man was saying something, but he couldn't make out the words. Dream Christopher clutched the bowl of gruel in his lap and snarled.

"Come on, you want time for something to eat and your constitution before you have to fall in don't you?" Galway nudged Christopher's foot with his.

Again, Christopher stirred. Spaulding had moved closer until his face was only inches from Christopher's. The man's breath stank from rotting teeth, and Christopher gagged. He felt the nudge as a kick to his leg. He was ready to strike when Spaulding's face transformed into the face of the rebel boy. The big face melted down to gaunt cheekbones over a downy beard, his eyes changed from black to bright blue, and the stench of rot disappeared. But, when the boy opened his mouth, it was full of blood. Blood poured down over his chin and his teeth and gums were coated with the thick, red fluid.

All the fight left Christopher and was replaced by a deep, almost painful regret. He could hear the boy's brother crying, "You killed my brother! You killed my brother!" But, when Christopher listened closer, he realized it was his own voice crying out.

Christopher felt another kick, a deathly cold swept over his body, and he was sure the dead boy had come for his revenge. Christopher struck out, crab walking back on his hands and feet as he screamed for mercy. Then he came to.

Sergeant Galway sat on the ground spread legged before him, his eyes as wide as saucers. The cold, Christopher realized, came from the ground he'd been laying on. It had seeped through the gum and wool blankets he'd been laying on and chilled the sweat that covered him despite the near-frigid temperatures.

Seeing the sergeant on the ground before him produced a wave of fear in Christopher. What if he'd struck a superior? Even if he had been asleep, it could still cost him his stripes or the chance for a furlough. Not to mention the whatever other diabolical punishment the army may come up with. There was a large wagon-yard in the camp, with plenty of spare parts. Christopher had a brief glimpse of himself stripped to the waist and tied to a wagon wheel, his back bloody from the lash, and he shuddered.

"Are you all right, Sergeant?" he asked.

Galway grinned. "No thanks to you I am," he said. "If I hadn't jumped back, you would have thumped me good." The sergeant looked down at his shoes and continued, "Unfortunately, my feet didn't jump back as fast as the rest of me."

Both men struggled to their feet. Although both were still in their teens, they moved like a couple of old men, stiff with cold and fatigue. Once they were standing their eyes met, and Christopher saw the chagrin he felt echoed in Galway's eyes.

Then the sergeant cocked his head to one side. "Say, don't I know you from somewhere?"

Christopher shrugged. "We're in the same regiment. I'm sure you've seen me many times."

"No. That's not it. Somewhere specific..." Galway continued to stare at Christopher for what seemed like hours, then his eyes lit up. "That's it!" He snapped his fingers. "The wayward drinker!"

Christopher groaned inside. Galway had been the provost sergeant the night he and Ezra had gone to the drinking shack up by Romney.

"It's really your brother I remember. He was beside himself the day you disappeared. But once you were back I'd seen you two together so much, I put two and two together quick enough." Galway's expression darkened, and he suddenly found his brogans extremely interesting. "I was sorry to hear we lost him at Antietam. He seemed like a good man."

"He was," Christopher whispered through the sudden tightness in his throat.

Galway grinned and slapped Christopher's sleeve over the stripes. "You're doing right by yourself now. I saw you at Fredericksburg with your squad. They say you boys were all over the field, shooting rebs and saving men. Good job."

Christopher shook his head. "I only shot the one reb, and that was half by accident." He looked down at his own brogans. "The man we tried to save didn't make it."

Galway frowned. "That was a meat grinder that day it was...Whelp," he said, suddenly back in the present, "get something to eat and take care of whatever you need to take care of, I'll be calling line up for your relief soon."

With that, the sergeant turned and left. Christopher watched him walk away. *That was close*, he thought. *Good thing Galway is an all right sort. It could have been much worse.*

A WEEK LATER, CHRISTOPHER received a summons back to the captain's hut. *What now?* he thought after the orderly left. *Did Galway file a complaint after all?*

When Christopher entered Captain Reid's quarters, he almost fell over in shock and fear. Sitting at the captain's desk was Colonel Sawyer, Captain Reid sat at the end of his cot, and First Sergeant Howe stood back behind the two men, trying to maintain a rigid stance, but clearly in some discomfort as he kept shifting his weight from foot to foot and grimacing.

This is it, Christopher thought. *I've lost my stripes, I'm going to be whipped, maybe even thrown in the stockade. Lord, why did it have to come to this? I can't be held responsible for what happens in my sleep. I can do better, I know I can. I just need more time. The dreams are coming less often now. I just need...*

"Good afternoon, Corporal," Sawyer said with a slight grin, clearly aware of Christopher's discomfort.

Christopher snapped to attention and stared at the other end of the hut. "Good afternoon, Colonel!"

"I imagine you're wondering why we asked you here."

"That would be an understatement, sir."

The officers chuckled, and Christopher relaxed a little. They would not be so jovial if they were preparing to court martial him. And, come to think if it, there were no provost guards lurking about.

"I'm sure you've heard of the problems we've had with recruiting after Antietam—and now Fredericksburg." Colonel Sawyer stood up and lifted two pieces of paper off the desk. "We're going to give it another try. We're going to send some of our brave fighting men back home to reassure the folks that not everyone is dying down here."

Sawyer handed Christopher the first piece of paper. "Here are your orders. When you leave here report to Lieutenant Daniels. You two will be our representatives from Company D. You leave for Cleveland in two days with several representatives from other companies of the 8th. Your assignment will be to spend two weeks in Cleveland and environs giving speeches and encouragement to the populace. I expect an enthusiastic countenance from the members of this detail. You have to be cheerful and patriotic and encouraging to the hopeful soldiers in the crowds. Understood?"

Christopher nodded although he was having trouble grasping what the colonel was saying. He was leaving the front? He'd be sleeping in a real bed, eating real food? His clothes would be louse free? It was almost too hard to imagine.

"For you, there is an added bonus. Consider it a reward for your efforts on the field at Fredericksburg." Sawyer handed him the second piece of paper. "Here is a weeklong furlough for you to spend in Norwalk—since you'll be in the vicinity anyway." The colonel's eyes sparkled with pleasure as he handed Christopher his furlough. "I envy you, young man. What I wouldn't give for the opportunity to see Norwalk and my dear wife..."

Christopher took the piece of paper with a hand that seemed to weigh a thousand pounds. He couldn't move; he couldn't think what do to next. Home. Family. Suddenly fear punched him in the gut, and he sucked in a deep breath. How would he face them without Daniel? His lips moved but nothing came out. He should say something, but the words wouldn't come. Home.

Chuckling, Colonel Sawyer stood and guided him to the door. "Go back to your quarters, Corporal, and get your wits about you. Then go see Lieutenant Daniels." He squeezed Christopher's shoulder. "You're going home, son." those last words were like hammer blows to Christopher's conscience. Home.

Christopher stood outside Captain Reid's quarters for several moments. Unable to think or move. He was going home. He should be ecstatic. Instead, an overwhelming fear engulfed him. It was like going into battle, it was so overpowering.

Home.

Chapter Six

Elizabeth Galloway stood at the kitchen counter cutting an onion for the evening meal, but, as was more and more the case these days, she was finding it impossible to focus on what she was doing. It seemed the family had fallen apart since Daniel's death. Her sisters constantly clung to Elizabeth's skirt, their tear-filled eyes wide with fear; her father, silent and distant, spent more waking hours at work than home; her mother... Elizabeth choked back a sob. Her mother lay upstairs at death's door. The doctor said it was typhus, but Elizabeth knew it was sorrow, her mother's weeping whenever she thought no one could hear told her that.

Elizabeth looked up and out the window at the budding trees in the yard, their visage distorted by the swirls in the glass. Spring was here, but there was no joy in the Galloway household.

Finished with the onion, Elizabeth sat down the knife and picked up a jar of home-canned peaches. Put up in one of the new Mason jars last summer using the boiling method that created a vacuum, the seal was extra tight. The ring came off easily enough, but the lid refused to budge. She picked the knife back up and tried to work the tip between the lid and lip of the jar. But the blade slipped and sliced open her finger.

"Ahhh!" She slammed the knife and jar down on the counter and reached for a towel. As she grasped the towel, the sleeve of her dress brushed the bloody roast that sat waiting for the oven to get hot.

The hated black dress. It was the only black one she had, and now she would have to wash it tonight. She had promised her mother she would wear it for a year following Daniel's death. Her mother too wore mourning black, but where Elizabeth looked forward to the day she could once again wear colors, she thought her mother would wear black for the rest of her life.

She hated it. She hated the black bunting that hung on the front of the house over the door like some kind of dark, evil spider web, but she especially hated the black dress. She was just sixteen, yet it made her feel like an old maid.

It wasn't so much of an exaggeration, she thought. All the men and boys who had gone to soldier were coming back weakened by disease or mangled by battle or in boxes—if at all. By the time this cruel war was over there would be no one left for her to marry, and she really would end up an old maid.

Quit feeling sorry for yourself, Lizzy, she thought. *Grow up and be strong.* Her eyes filled with tears. She wasn't ready to grow up.

She was dabbing her eyes with the clean end of the bloody towel when she heard the door open. Fear sliced her heart. Da was out of town, Rachel and Rebecca were at school, and mother was upstairs in her bed being tended to by Auntie Mae. There was no one who should be coming through that door uninvited at this hour.

Elizabeth grabbed the knife and spun around toward the door. She held the knife out before her and channeled her fear into anger. She was angry at the invasion and the fear it invoked and angry at the interruption to her feeling sorry for herself.

"Who's there!" she yelled. "You best turn around and go back the way you came. My da will be home any minute and he doesn't take kindly to uninvited strangers in our home!"

Heavy, deliberate steps sounded on the wooden floor of the front room. The steps of a man. The sound grew louder as the steps got closer. Elizabeth thought of running, but her anger kept her rooted to the spot, unable to go forward, unwilling to retreat.

Then he was in the doorway. A soldier. He wore a long dark-blue frock coat and one of those ridiculous-looking Hardee hats, one side of the brim pinned up by a brass eagle and sporting a black ostrich feather tucked into a light blue cord with tassels. The front of the hat was adorned with a brass horn and the letter D. A blue three-leaf clover was sewn onto the left breast of the soldier's coat.

The hat brim shaded a pair of the most cold, wicked eyes Elizabeth had ever seen. If the eyes were the window to the soul, this man's soul was black.

She shuddered to think what those eyes had seen, and what this man might be capable of.

Then he smiled, and the eyes lit up with a familiar twinkle. His lips formed a smirk that Elizabeth knew all too well.

"Hello, darlin'. Did you miss me?"

Suddenly the room was spinning, and the floor was dropping out from under Elizabeth. She felt as if she were falling through space though she never moved.

"Christopher?" she whispered before she started choking on huge sobs that racked her shoulders. She dropped the knife and sprinted across the room, throwing her arms around her brother's neck and burying her face in his coat collar. The cloth was course and smelled of coal smoke and sweat, but she didn't care. Her brother was home.

She stood like that for what seemed like several minutes, crying into Christopher's collar as they clung to each other. When she regained control, she stepped back and took a good look at him. He'd seemed so foreign to her when she first saw him, she was curious what had changed.

Looking into his face, she saw his eyes were glassy and his cheeks were wet. He quickly wiped the tears away, and even through the deep tan she could see his cheeks redden.

A short burst of laughter escaped her lips, and snot bubbled out her nose. It was her turn to redden with embarrassment, and she quickly covered her face with her hands. She turned around and wiped away the mess with the towel. She blew her nose and threw the dirty towel toward the counter. It fell short, but she didn't care. She turned around and faced her brother once more.

Christopher was looking around like he was seeing their home for the first time. His eyes were alive with curiosity, and his lip curled up in that infuriating little smirk of his.

"It all looks the same as I remember," he said, almost in awe.

"Well, what did you expect? You've only been away for a couple years." Her voice trailed off as the realization of what she was saying sunk in. *Only* a couple years. They were the longest, most miserable two years of her short life. *His too*, she thought.

His eyes met hers. Thankfully, they were their regular blue and full of life—not the black empty orbs she'd seen before. "It's just... I can't believe I'm here, you know? I...I..." He shook his head. "You wouldn't understand."

The frustration was clear in the tension in his jaw and the sharp line his lips had formed. Elizabeth wanted to reassure him, to tell him he was home now and everything was all right. But was it?

She was grasping for something to say when he asked the question that she feared most.

"I guess Rachel and Rebecca are at school, and Da's at work, but why are you here? And where's Ma?"

Elizabeth's eyes flashed toward the ceiling. Christopher's face hardened once more. She gasped at the cold emptiness that filled his eyes.

"Christopher..." she began, then hesitated.

Christopher grasped the door jamb and squeezed. His knees buckled.

"No! No, it's not that. She's, she is upstairs. Sick. It's typhoid fever, Chris."

Christopher's whole body seem to deflate. His head dropped until his chin touched his chest. The Hardee hat fell from his head to the floor. Neither stooped to retrieve it.

"Aunty Mae's upstairs tending to her. She's been a Godsend."

The words were no sooner out of her mouth before Christopher was bolting out of the room and running for the stairs. He took the steps two at a time and was gone down the upstairs hallway before Elizabeth was even at the foot of the stairway.

Rushing up the stairs, down the hallway, and into their parent's bedroom—now Mary Galloway's sick room—Elizabeth found Christopher locked in a bear hug with Mae, unable or unwilling to break free. Mae pushed Christopher out to her arm's length and looked him up and down.

"My, my, my," she exclaimed. "Look at you. Little Chrissy all growed up and gone for a soldier." Her eyes flashed with pride and her smile lit up the darkened room.

Mary was asleep, her face shiny with sweat, her breathing labored. Christopher looked at her and asked, "How is she, Mae?"

"Don' you worry, child. Your ma's a fighter. She'll be up and about 'for you know it."

Elizabeth stood in the doorway, her eyes going from Christopher's shocked expression to her mother's face, grimacing in pain even in sleep. It was as if she was seeing her mother for the first time as well and it was frightening. She seemed to have aged ten years in the last few weeks. Her hair was almost all gray, her complexion white and waxy where it wasn't inflamed with angry red splotches. Her cheeks, and even her eyes, were sunken into her face, and her lips formed an inward pucker for lack of teeth.

Elizabeth stifled a sob and stepped into the room. Her eyes met Mae's, and she managed a small smile. Mae held out her arms and Elizabeth rushed to the comfort of her embrace.

Mae was a free black woman who used to work as a seamstress with their mother. Both the black woman and Irish immigrant experienced the prejudice of the native born American, each in their own way, and it drew the two women to each other. While Jack Galloway was eventually able to open his own cobbler's shop, Mae's husband, Rufus, struggled to get anything more that temporary laborer jobs. Jack brought Rufus on as an apprentice, despite the lost business it cost him, and the two worked together until Rufus was killed in a wagon accident.

That was when Elizabeth was just a baby, Christopher and Daniel were toddlers, and Rachel and Rebecca hadn't been born yet. The customers who left Jack because he was working with a free black came back, and the Galloways could afford to hire Mae as a nanny for the children. Jack used to say how those people who wouldn't pay a black man to make them a pair of shoes would have a conniption if they knew their money was now helping to support that man's window.

Christopher sat on the edge of the bed and took his mother's hand, her skeletal fingers a sharp contrast to his rough, calloused ones. He stroked the back of her hand and whispered, "Ma?"

It surprised Elizabeth to see her mother stir, her sleep had been frighteningly sound since she got sick, and it sometimes took a great effort to wake her. As she watched, Mary Galloway's eyes fluttered open. She looked around in confusion. "Daniel?"

"No, Ma. It's me, Chris."

Mary's eyes continued to flutter for a few seconds before they finally settled on Christopher. Then they flew open and her mouth made a little "O." Her red, bloodshot eyes filled with tears.

"My baby boy." It was more than a statement, it was a plea.

"It's me, Ma. I got leave and came home." Christopher was struggling to get the words out, and Elizabeth knew he was crying. She and Mae both wept and clung to each other.

Mary's hand came up and stroked Christopher's cheek. "So skinny. The army doesn't feed you enough."

"No, ma. Not like you."

Like a weakened tree struggling but failing to stay upright against the elements, Christopher slowly pitched forward, picking up speed as his face rushed to bury itself in his mother's neck. He began to weep.

Unable to take any more, Elizabeth ran out of the room and down the hall. She ran into her room, slammed the door, and threw herself on her bed.

So much pain. Everywhere, so much pain. Why couldn't it stop?

After a time, she heard Christopher and Mae talking in the hall. Then footsteps going down the stairs. Christopher's heavy steps resonating on the hard wood floor, getting quieter as he continued down to the first floor.

A man. Christopher. Her brother, the eternal brat, was a man. Not just any man, but a man of purpose and conviction. Those eyes. That black stare. She found it thrilling and frightening at the same time. She wondered if all the boys who'd gone to war would come back like that. Then she pushed the thought away. There was no time to be thinking such things.

She lay there, her mind seesawing back and forth from death and misery to hope and redemption. *This too shall pass.* Then, as she thought of all there was to do, and all the things she wanted to ask Christopher, she fell asleep.

Chapter Seven

Christopher descended the stairs and stepped into the living room where he'd spent so many nights as a child, playing with his siblings, listening to his mother sing, or asking his father endless questions. Though it was still April, and a chill hung in the air, he could almost feel the warm glow of the fireplace and smell the aroma of fresh-baked cookies. He remembered how bored and frustrated he was at the sameness of it all, night after night, the close-knit family bonded together in simple repetition. God, how he wished he could go back there.

But, it was all now as foreign to him as an Arabian maharaja or an Indian elephant. And as distant. It was like a dream. One you woke up from and basked in the glow of for a few minutes before it faded away, and time forced you from your warm bed to the harsh coldness of the here-and-now.

Christopher slowly unbuttoned his frock coat, fresh from the quartermaster's stores and so clean and shiny. He brushed the eagle embossed on one of the brass buttons with the tips of his fingers. The symbol of the eagle was everywhere—on banners and posters, in books and newspapers, even on the clothing he wore and the equipment he carried into battle. The eagle had called him to war, tempted him with promises of fame and glory. Damned that eagle.

He draped the coat over the back of a chair and went into the kitchen to retrieve his hat. He figured he would leave them both and go back to the sack coat and forage cap stowed away in his knapsack when he went back to the regiment. The frock coat and Hardee hat were all right for meeting halls and bandstands but too uncomfortable for daily wear. Though he knew of some Wisconsin boys who dressed that way—even into battle.

Picking up the hat, Christopher looked around at the half-prepared meal. Cut up onion and potato littered the counter next to a slab of beef.

He smiled at the thought of a steaming bowl of homemade Irish stew, but there was no one to make it. His mother, God bless her, was...was...Mae was with her, and Elizabeth had disappeared into her room. *Flighty as ever*, he thought.

Well, old boy I guess that leaves you. He grinned at the thought of everyone's astonishment at being served a meal prepared by Christopher, the master of getting out of chores. Then he got to work. The stove was hot, so he found a pan to brown the beef. After cutting up the beef and putting it in the hot pan with some grease and flour, he finished chopping the vegetables and placed them in a pot with a scoop of salt and some other seasonings he found in the cupboard. He filled the pot with water from the spout his father had installed just before he and Daniel left for the war and set it on the stove. He added some kindling and small pieces of wood to the firebox and blew on the embers until he until he had a fire big enough to get the water boiling.

While the water was heating, he took off the now-browned beef chunks and threw them in the pot with the vegetables. He stirred the stew and thought how it needed some crushed-up hardtack to thicken it up. Then he laughed outright. Nothing and no one ever *needed* hardtack—except to survive. And, even then it was a last resort. Instead, he used flour to thicken the broth.

Once the water was boiling, he moved the pot to a cooler spot on the stove so it could simmer. After it had simmered and thickened for a while, he tasted the broth. It wasn't anything like his mother or Mae made, and even Elizabeth could probably do better. It was simple army fare, but it would do with some fresh bread. Maybe there was even some butter down in the cellar. Now that would be a treat.

Lost in the routine of fixing a meal, Christopher paid no attention as the shadows lengthened and slid across the room—until the sounds of the front door opening and children chattering came from the front of the house. He looked around and estimated it was late afternoon. That must mean Rachel and Rebecca were home.

As Christopher left the kitchen, the chattering stopped. One of the girls, Rebecca he thought, said, "What's that?"

"I don't know," the other said. Then Christopher realized the first voice was that of Rachel, the youngest, though now void of the toddler lisp she had had when he left. "Looks like a couple of bags."

"That one stinks."

"Yeah. What do you think is in it?"

"Poop."

The girls were giggling when Christopher stepped into the room. "That, my darlins, is a Standard Issue, Regulation, Federal Army Knapsack, and the smaller one is a haversack. That's where I keep my lunch."

Christopher thought the resulting squeal would burst his eardrums.

The girls spun around, their eyes flew open, and their mouths made large 'O's, much like his mother's had earlier, only much more animated.

"Chrissy!" they screamed in unison.

As much as he still hated that nickname, Christopher couldn't help but laugh. The girls ran to him and threw themselves into his arms. He caught them both though he stumbled back several paces. *My Lord, they're getting so big,* he thought as he struggled to stay upright.

He sat Rebecca down, but Rachel held on. She wrapped her legs around his waist and grasped his cheeks with her small hands. "It's you," she whispered in awe.

His smile was so big it hurt. "It is me, and I've come home to see the two prettiest girls ever."

"What about Lizzy?" Rachel asked.

Christopher almost said "and her too," then thought better of it. That was something the old Christopher would say. Instead, he said, "You're right. The three prettiest girls ever." Rachel beamed in response.

As he sat his youngest sister down, Christopher saw Rebecca was crying. Then Rachel saw it, and she started crying.

"What's the matter?" he asked perplexed.

Rebecca shook her head and started crying harder.

"Becky, please...What is it?" Christopher felt himself panicking. This was the last thing he expected, and he didn't know what to do.

"It's...I...you...I wanted...you're here, and I wanted it so bad...you...you...Danny!" Rebecca wailed, and Christopher dropped to his knees. Now he was crying. He took both girls in his arms and pulled them to him. They stayed like that until Elizabeth's voice made them jump.

"Christopher Galloway, you haven't been home a day and already you have your sisters crying." She'd said the words in jest, but Christopher knew too well the truth behind them. He'd been selfish and hurtful. It had cost him so much for so long, but that was all going to change now. He loved his family and would never again disappoint them or let them down.

He looked over Rebecca's head at Elizabeth. Her hair was still mussed from her nap, and her eyes were puffy and red from crying and sleep. But, she was one of the prettiest girls he knew. That was not a lie.

Her face went from mock anger, to confusion, to understanding, in a blink of an eye. Then she rushed to the group. Christopher held out an arm and dropping to her knees, Elizabeth folded herself into their embrace. The four of them stayed like that until the smell of stew pulled Christopher back to the present.

He quickly extracted himself from the group hug and stood. "I need to take care of supper before it burns," he said as he headed for the kitchen.

"What?" Elizabeth asked as she stood and rushed past him.

Christopher entered the kitchen and almost burst out laughing at the look of wonder on Elizabeth's face. Her head swiveled back and forth from the counters, empty of all vegetable cuttings, and the warm stove with the steaming pot atop it. "You cooked a meal," she said, slack jawed. She looked him up and down as if a stranger had taken his place.

"I've cooked quite a few meals in the last two years, I'll have you know." He straightened with pride as Rebecca and Rachel entered to room oohing and ahhing.

"Is it army food?" Rachel asked.

Christopher nodded. "Only better," he replied. "'Cause it's made with the Galloway touch." Rachel laughed as his voice took on an Irish brogue, and he gave her an exaggerated wink.

Elizabeth retrieved a loaf of soda bread and cut it into pieces while Rebecca retrieved a tub of butter. Elizabeth took two bowls and some bread up to Mae and their mother while the rest set places at the kitchen table and served up the meal. Once they were all seated, Elizabeth had Rachel say grace.

"Bless us, oh Lord," she began in her child's voice, "for these, my gifts..."

"Thy gifts," Elizabeth corrected.

"...thy gifts we are 'bout to receive, from my...from *thy* bounty, through Christ our Lord. Amen."

"Amen," they all echoed.

The stew was bland compared to their mother's, and the bread was getting old, but Christopher thought it the best meal he'd ever eaten.

After dinner, the girls insisted on carrying Christopher's bags up to his room, which was fine with him. The last thing he wanted to do was face the room he'd shared with Daniel for the first seventeen years of his life. But then they balked at touching his haversack.

"It stinks," complained Rachel.

Elizabeth approached the offending bag then stopped several feet away and covered her nose.

"What is in that thing?" she asked.

Christopher shrugged. "Not much right now. That's where we carry our campaign rations."

She took another step, now pinching her nose closed. "Why is it here?" she whined. "Are you expecting a campaign in Northern Ohio?"

"No," Christopher huffed. "I just brought some things with me to eat on the train. I had to put them somewhere."

"When was the last time you washed it?"

Christopher looked at her askance. "Washed?"

"Good God, Christopher. You mean to say you've been putting food in that bag and you've never washed it? No wonder it smells like the dead." Elizabeth took two big strides forward, grabbed the haversack, and headed for the back door. "Rachel, Rebecca—take that funny looking bag upstair—"

"It's a knapsack," Christopher interrupted. "You wear it on your back."

"—that *knapsack* upstairs. This thing is going out back until it has had a rendezvous with a tub of hot water and a bar of soap."

"Don't let King get it," Rebecca cautioned.

"Don't worry," Elizabeth replied. "I wouldn't want the dog to get sick."

Offended by the clear reprimand regarding his sanitary habits, or lack thereof, Christopher grabbed his frock coat and stepped out onto the front porch for a smoke. Once outside, he sat down on a wicker chair by the front door and retrieved his clay pipe and bag of tobacco from the inside pocket of his coat. As he smoked, he thought of all the campfires he'd sat around with Daniel, Ezra, Charlie Locker, and Parker Bonett. Now Parker and Daniel were gone, and Charlie's duties as sergeant were taking him away from the mess more and more. Sometimes Nathan Jump would hang around with them, but Christopher still wasn't comfortable with their shared experience of losing older brothers. It was a club to which he didn't want to belong.

As the sun set and Christopher smoked, his lids grew heavy, and his reminiscing took on a dream-like quality. He felt as if he were lighter than air. He clutched the arms of the chair even as his head fell forward. His chin met his chest and woke him up. He jerked his head back and looked around.

The large maple trees were bare but already budding. Soon it would be summer, and the fighting would begin again. More boys would die, and more would kill and maim. That was the "glory" he'd signed up for.

He heard the front door open, but he didn't look. He assumed it was Elizabeth, and he was right. She took the chair across from him and folded her hands in her lap. Looking down at her hands, she said, "In the morning we'll go to the telegraph office and wire Da that you are home. He's not expected back until next week, but I'm sure he'll want to see you before you go."

"Hmmm," Christopher replied. He was appraising the slope of the yard across the street and wondering how effective a couple of cannon would be at its crest.

He had a thought that shattered his tactical analysis of the small town neighborhood. He shifted in his seat and clenched his jaw. "Next week, you say?" He gave Elizabeth a steely glare. "How can he go off and leave Ma like this for that long?"

Elizabeth blanched, and Christopher was embarrassed for having scared his sister so. He realized on this trip that there was a hardness to soldiers coming back from the front that made civilians uncomfortable. Though he didn't feel it, he assumed he was no exception.

His sister clasped and unclasped her hands, then fidgeted with the thread on a seam of her dress. "You have to understand, the pressures are immense," she began, then the words flowed out quickly. "The competition for government contracts is intense. And some of the products being sent to the boys are horrible, just horrible—so poorly made they just fall apart." She stopped and her cheeks reddened. "But, I need not tell you that, you've probably seen them firsthand."

Christopher nodded. "But still. She could go at any moment."

Elizabeth swallowed before answering. She spoke so quietly Christopher had to lean forward to hear. "She could. But it would make little difference to her if he's here or not—she's rarely awake or aware of what's going on around her. Today is the first time I've seen her so animated in days. Your presence is like an elixir." She smiled.

"This contract Da is negotiating is one he's been after for a long time. If he doesn't get it, they'll give it to some Cincinnati interest. Though Da doesn't do much of the work himself anymore, you know what he produces will be good quality and serve our dear boys in blue well. Besides, he is in constant contact via telegraph and could be here in a day if need be."

Christopher nodded. He looked at his sister out of the corner of his eye and gave her his best smirk. "How do you know so much about business all of a sudden?"

Elizabeth smiled, and her face lit up. "Da's been talking to me about business a lot since...lately. I read his trade magazines and the papers to make sure my conversations are titillating for him. It's quite fascinating, really."

"It sounds like you like it. Won't you be disappointed once all the men return and you have to give it up?"

Elizabeth's face fell, and her voice became guarded. "I suppose Da will want to bring you on once you're home."

It was Christopher's turn to be uncomfortable. He looked away as he answered. "We tried that before, remember? It didn't go over so well."

Elizabeth leaned forward to catch Christopher's eye. "But so much has changed since then. You've changed. I saw it the moment you walked in the door. You're not the brat that left here two years ago—not by a long shot."

Christopher shifted in his seat, fighting an urge to bolt. "That was always Danny's place, not mine. Business and book learnin' were never my strong suit."

"Not because you weren't capable. You're plenty capable. You just weren't willing. Now, Da needs a male heir to keep the business he's created going."

Christopher shook his head. "You can have it."

Elizabeth laughed, but there was no humor in it. "A woman running a business, that'll be the day."

"Stranger things have happened," Christopher countered.

Elizabeth stood and smooth down her skirt. "Maybe when pigs fly and men walk on the moon. But not today." She went inside and left Christopher alone with his now cold pipe and thoughts of life after the war.

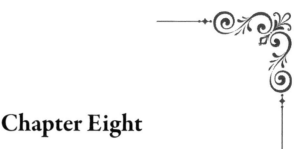

Chapter Eight

That night Christopher slept in the backyard with the dog. He was still unwilling to face the room he'd shared with his brother and still found sleeping in a soft bed somewhat suffocating. All the girls gave him curious looks when he came inside the following morning, his hair disheveled and his clothes covered in dog hair, dragging an old wool blanket. But no one said anything.

Christopher grabbed a mug and poured himself a cup of coffee. He wrapped his hands around the warm porcelain and relished its smooth delicate nature—so much more inviting than an old, battered tin cup. He took a cautious sip of the still-too-hot coffee and sighed.

Then, like an artillery volley, Rachel and Rebecca started talking all at once, so fast and breathless, Christopher could only make out a word here and there. "Wait until all the other girls hear you're here, Chrissy—" "Can you help me with my primer later?" "They'll so want to see you—" "Can you come to class with us one day?" "Yeah! And wear that funny hat with the feather." "When do you have to leave?" "What do those stripes on your sleeve mean?"

"Girls!" Elizabeth cried over them. "Quiet!"

Silence.

"That's better. Now, one at a time, and quietly, like proper ladies."

By the time Christopher finished his first cup of coffee he'd explained to them what a Hardee hat was, what his stripes meant, what a corporal did and had agreed to make an appearance later that week at their school if the headmistress approved.

Elizabeth fed him a breakfast of eggs with the remaining soda bread. Then he went upstairs to see his mother.

Mae had not yet arrived, and she was alone, sleeping. Christopher sat on the chair by her bed, and one whiff told him the sheets needed changing. She was so old and frail—not at all like he remembered. Tears clouded his vision, and he angrily wiped them away.

Damn this war. Damn it to hell.

After a few moments, he went down to talk to Elizabeth about changing the sheets. He had no idea how they did it without his mother getting off the bed. About that time Mae arrived, and Elizabeth told Christopher they would take care of it. They would have to clean her, she explained, and it wouldn't be proper for Christopher to be there when they removed her nightdress.

Christopher blushed and hurried out the door with his pipe and tobacco.

Afterward, Christopher and Elizabeth walked down to the telegraph office on Main Street to send a message to their father. Elizabeth hooked her arm in Christopher's and, as they passed the shops and offices, would call out a cheerful greeting to everyone they met. "Yes, yes," she'd proclaim, "it's my brother home from the war."

Christopher was uncomfortable with the attention and thankful that most people responded with polite reserve, refusing to make eye contact. He was struck by the number of black dresses on the women and black armbands or crepe on the hats of the men. Had the town lost that many men? He knew that the 8th wasn't the only regiment to which Norwalk had contributed. Just the first. After all, that was why he was here, to recruit more young men for the war to consume.

One woman stopped.

"Mrs. Prentiss," Elizabeth said. "You remember my brother, Christopher, don't you? He's home from the war."

Mrs. Prentiss looked Christopher up and down and nodded. "How could I forget? You were quite free with my apples, young man. Barely left me enough for canning."

Christopher tipped his hat. "My apologies, madam. That was a long time ago."

The old dowager pursed her lips and nodded. She looked Christopher up and down again. "You look hale enough, young man. Tell me, what brings you home before the task is complete?"

Christopher looked her up and down in turn and noted that she was not dressed in mourning attire. "I've been in Cleveland recruiting more young men for the *task*," he replied.

"Christopher's here on vacation," Elizabeth said in a strident tone.

"Furlough," he corrected, squeezing his sister's arm. "In the army they call it furlough."

"Well, what's the difference?" Mrs. Prentiss asked.

Christopher shrugged. "I don't rightly know, ma'am. This is my first time for either."

Mrs. Prentiss nodded. "Never took to this new-fangled concept of vacations myself—too much idleness and temptation if you ask me. Well, thank you for your service young man. We'll beat these ungrateful secessionists yet."

"Yes, ma'am. Thank you, ma'am." Christopher tipped his hat and pulled his sister down the street.

"Sour old bitty," Elizabeth muttered.

Christopher chuckled. Then it occurred to him it technically wasn't his first furlough. He assumed that the passes Ezra had finagled back in Romney counted as a furlough. Given that one had cost him six months in a Confederate prison, Christopher hoped this furlough turned out much better.

After sending the telegraph notifying their father of Christopher's arrival, they walked to Pennewell's Grocery to get some things for dinner. When asked, Christopher said he'd eat anything as long as it wasn't salted pork or hard cracker.

On the way to Pennewell's they passed Peak Bros. Clothing and almost ran into a young woman exiting the store carrying a hatbox. Christopher took a quick step back and started to apologize, but Elizabeth lit up when she recognized who it was.

"Susan! What a fortuitous event. Look who's here." Elizabeth pointed to Christopher with a huge grin.

Susan Johnston looked at Christopher curiously for a moment. Then, as recognition took hold, she smiled and reached out a hand. "Christopher. It's so good to see you."

Christopher didn't smile, didn't take her hand, and didn't make eye contact. Instead, he looked down the street as he tipped his hat. "Miss Johnston."

"Christopher is home on furlough. Isn't that right, Christopher?"

Christopher nodded.

The smile on Susan Johnston's face faded as she looked from brother to sister and back. Elizabeth gave Christopher a curious look, and her own smile shifted to a bewildered frown.

"We were just on our way to get some groceries." She looked at Susan. "It was so good running—quite literally—into you." She managed a short giggle. "Come by when you have a chance, and we'll catch up."

Susan nodded shyly. "That would be nice." She nodded to Christopher. "I'm glad to see you well, Christopher."

Christopher harrumphed, tipped his hat again, and moved past her toward the grocer. Elizabeth had to jog to catch up. When she did, she grabbed his arm and spun him around.

"What was the meaning of that? You were so rude. To your late brother's fiancé, no less."

"She wasn't his fiancé," Christopher shot back.

"Well, maybe not officially. But once they gained her father's approval—"

Christopher shook his head. Reaching into his pant pocket, he pulled out a crumpled envelope, stained black and brown. "Here, read this."

Elizabeth looked at the envelope for a moment, then, curling her nose, she reached out and took it with her thumb and index finger. She opened the envelope while trying to touch it as little as possible. "What is it? And what's this mess all over it? Something disgusting from your haversack?"

"It's Danny's blood."

She thrust the envelope back at him, hitting Christopher in the chest with it and holding it there until he took it. "Oh, my... Why would you hand me something like that?"

Christopher put the envelope back in his pocket. "It's Susan's last letter to him—breaking off their relationship. Only a few months before he was killed. She doesn't have the right to wear mourning clothes for him."

Elizabeth looked down the street in the direction Susan was heading. "I don't understand. She was so upset...she came to the service and wept. I don't think there was anyone there who showed more grief and sorrow except for Ma." She looked Christopher in the eye. "I don't believe it. She loved him."

"Probably just felt guilty," Christopher said. "All I know is what I read here in this letter. She told him it would never work—that their backgrounds were too far apart. She cast him aside, I tell you. Cast him aside while he was off in the service of our country. Who would do such a thing?"

Elizabeth watched Susan receding in the distance. "I can't believe it. I know what I saw—and I saw a person grieving for a loved one. And for weeks after, when we would stop to talk in the street, she was always on the verge of tears." She shook her head. "I just can't believe it. Why? Why, if she loved him, would she do such a thing?"

"Only one way to find out," Christopher said and started after Susan.

"Wait!" Christopher heard Elizabeth's footsteps on the boardwalk, trying, but unable, to catch up to him.

Christopher had developed a long stride and a quick pace that he could maintain for hours on end from hundreds of miles of hard marching. Elizabeth quickly fell behind. Within moments he was within hailing distance of Susan Johnston.

"Miss Johnston!"

She stopped and looked around.

"Back here, Miss Johnston. Could you wait a moment?"

She turned around. Even from a distance, Christopher could see the color drain from her face. But she waited for him, and Christopher noticed her back get a little straighter as she lifted her chin and stood her ground.

Soon he was standing before her and, what seemed so clear just a moment before, was now cloudy and murky. He looked into her piercing green eyes and was suddenly speechless.

"Mr. Galloway," she said.

Christopher removed his hat. "Miss Johnston. Uh...thank you for waiting."

"My pleasure. I think."

Christopher looked to the ground as his hand slid into his pocket and clasped the envelope. The feel of the brittle paper gave him courage, and he pulled it out and held it before her. "Do you recognize this?"

She looked at the envelope for a moment, then, as recognition took hold, her shoulders slumped and her eyes filled with tears. "You must hate me," she whispered.

"I've hated you since the moment I read this letter. Read it as Danny was being buried in an apple orchid near the spot where he was killed. He carried this letter for months but never said a word. Now, I want to know why. Why did you break my brother's heart? And what now gives you the right to wear mourning attire for him?" As Christopher spoke, his voice got louder, and Susan started to cry.

"Christopher!"

Startled, Christopher and Susan whipped their heads around at the same time, their anger and grief interrupted by surprise. Elizabeth stood before them with her hands on her hips, frowning at Christopher in disapproval. It reminded him so much of his mother he almost gasped.

"Christopher," Elizabeth said in a softer tone. "You're making a scene."

"I just—"

"Not now."

"But—"

"No!"

Elizabeth stepped forward and took Susan's arm. "Forgive my brother. Danny's death has been particularly hard on him."

Susan dabbed her eyes with a handkerchief and sniffed. "I understand. And...and he deserves an answer." She looked up and down the street. "But, I'd rather not get into it out here in the middle of town. Maybe we could meet later?"

"Yes, of course," Elizabeth said. "How about the diner—"

Susan shook her head. "Too near the courthouse..."

Elizabeth nodded, her eyes suddenly full of compassion and understanding. Susan's father worked at the courthouse, and he didn't approve of her continued involvement with the Galloways. Christopher felt his righteous indignation undermined as events developed beyond his control.

"Why don't you come to call later. We could have tea and discuss this like civilized people." Elizabeth gave Christopher a pointed look, and he huffed at her in response.

Susan nodded. "That would be fine. Would three o'clock be all right?"

"That would be perfect. Come along, Christopher, we still have groceries to purchase. Oh.." She looked at Susan. "Could you stay for dinner?"

Susan shook her head. "I don't know, I—"

"Please do. Rachel and Rebecca would love to see you."

Susan looked as helplessly adrift as Christopher felt.

"You may not want me to stay after we talk."

"Nonsense. I get the feeling once we talk, all this will seem 'much ado about nothing,' as the bard would say." Elizabeth gave Susan a disarming smile.

"I suppose it would be all right. I'll leave a note for Father letting him know I won't be home for dinner."

"Wonderful. We'll see you then." Elizabeth grabbed Christopher's hand and pulled him down the street. He looked over his shoulder and saw Susan still standing where they'd left her with a look of perplexed unease on her face.

CHRISTOPHER DECIDED to face the bedroom he'd shared with Daniel, partly because he needed a change of clothes, and that was where Rebecca had put his knapsack and partly because he knew he couldn't put it off forever. But mostly because it he didn't want to be downstairs when Susan arrived.

As he opened the door, he was struck by how musty the room smelled. The furniture had been dusted and the beds made, but it still smelled like a room that was not lived in. Christopher walked to his side of the room, noting that the toys and childhood bric-à-brac he'd left scattered across the top of his dresser had all been put away. His knapsack and haversack (now clean and empty) sat on the bed. His old hunting rifle (a .32 caliber smoothbore with a short stock) still leaned against the wall in the corner. With a sharp pang of sorrow, he thought that after the last couple of years he'd never enjoy a night in the woods again.

Slowly, Christopher turned to Daniel's bed. It, too, was made and the furniture next to it dusted. A framed image of Daniel hung over the head of the bed. It had been taken a couple years before the war, and in it Daniel sat stiff and straight, giving the photographer his most serious and thoughtful stare, wearing his Sunday finest.

Christopher felt a lump swell in his throat and turned to the bookshelf on the opposite wall holding Daniel's novels. Impulsively, he went to the shelf and pulled down a book. It was *Moby Dick* by Herman Melville. He opened it and read the first sentence: "Call me Ishmael." Immediately, an image came to mind of Alex Melville, the half-grin on his face belying the anger in his tone: "*Don't* call me Ishmael!" Christopher burst into a near hysterical laughter that quickly turned to tears. He dropped the book and stumbled to his bed. He sat down heavily, making the bed squeak and shake, gripped his knees, and rocked back and forth. He squeezed his eyes shut and tears ran down his crumpled cheeks. He bit his lip to stifle the moans and cries that threatened to burst forth. *Damn it all!* he thought. *What's wrong with me?*

He stood up and started pacing. Alex died on the field at Antietam with Daniel and so many others, and it wasn't fair that their memories should be so painful. Not the good ones, anyway.

The heavy clomp of the iron-shod heels of his brogans on the wooden floor almost drowned out the sound of the front door knocker. Christopher stopped. There it was again.

He looked around. There was no clock in the room. Even if there was, no one would have bothered to wind it. Then he heard Elizabeth's greeting and Susan's response. He couldn't make out the words, but he was sure it was them.

He pulled a handkerchief out of his pocket and wiped his face. He went to the mirror that hung on the door of the armoire and inspected his appearance. His eyes were red and puffy. There was no way he could go downstairs just yet.

He went into the hallway and headed for his parents' room. He hadn't looked in on his ma since that morning, and there was a basin of water there he could use to splash his face.

As he entered the room, Elizabeth called up from the bottom of the stairs. "Christopher, Susan's here. Could you come downstairs, please?"

His mother was sound asleep, and, maybe it was just wishful thinking, but he thought her breathing seemed less labored than before.

Aunty Mae was sitting in a chair by the bed reading the bible. She looked up, took one look at Christopher, and burst out laughing. "Boy, you got that same look on your face you used to get when I'd catch you with your hand in the cookie jar. What have you done now?"

"Nothing. Honest. I just came to check on Ma."

Mae squinted to see him better, but the shades were drawn and the room was dark beyond the pool of light cast by the oil lamp next to her. "Hmm, mmm. Wasn't that Lizzy calling you just now?"

Christopher nodded and moved to the other side of the bed. "In a minute." He sat down and took his mother's hand. "How is she?"

"She's doing pretty well, it seems to me. Sleeping sounder anyway."

"I thought her breath seemed less labored."

Mae nodded. Elizabeth called again. Christopher rubbed the back of his mother's hand like it was a talisman.

"You should probably go see what your sister wants," Mae said. "Lest you're afraid of somethin'."

"I ain't got nothing to be afraid of," Christopher shot back. "Can't a fellow check on his poor sick mother?"

Mae nodded. "They can 'cept when they have more pressing matters to attend to. I don't think Lizzy's going to go away, so you might as well go face the piper."

Christopher stood. "There ain't no piper to face. I wanted to see Ma is all."

"Hmmm, mmm," Mae responded and went back to her bible.

Christopher slipped out the door and headed for the stairs. With each step his legs got heavier. *I feel like I'm marching onto the battlefield,* he thought incredulously. For months he'd carried that letter and the anger it fostered. Now that the time had come to do something about it, he found himself reluctant. The last thing he wanted was to face another bout of Susan's tears.

As Christopher entered the drawing room, he saw Susan sitting on the divan next to Elizabeth. She was wearing a black skirt, but her blouse and shawl were gray. *Half-mourning attire,* he thought. He supposed he could begrudge her that much, though he still thought it inappropriate that she had dressed in mourning for Daniel when they were no longer a couple.

He sat in his father's wing-back chair, feeling like an imposter usurping a role he did not deserve.

"Miss Johnston," he said.

Susan's eyes flitted to his and then back to the handkerchief she was holding. "Mr. Galloway. I want to thank you for seeing me and giving me the chance to explain."

Elizabeth put a hand on Susan's, stopping them from twisting her handkerchief. "Think nothing of it," she said. "We all loved Danny, and I for one am sure there is a perfectly reasonable explanation for this situation."

Susan nodded. Christopher sat in silence, waiting. He noticed Elizabeth had not looked him in the eye since he'd entered the room. *Who's side was she on?*

Susan took a deep breath and let it out slowly. Then she spoke. She told them of how Daniel had come to see her father before they'd left for training, how the two had reached a tentative agreement that, if Daniel wanted her hand, he would have to prove himself in battle.

Christopher felt a stab of fear and was instantly thankful for the lack of autonomy given the enlisted man in battle. Given the opportunity, he was sure Daniel would have tried some grand romantic and stupid gesture on the field. Not that it had made any difference.

She went on to explain how her father had seemed mollified and accepting of their continued correspondence for a while. But, as time went on and Daniel still lived and their relationship showed no signs of cooling, Benjamin Johnston started pressuring his daughter to forget about Daniel Galloway and return to her studies back east.

As she spoke of the ongoing campaign of seemingly innocent remarks designed to make her feel guilty, and fights with raised voices and things said better left unsaid, Christopher understood the pressure she was under. He, too, had experienced similar campaigns with his father, meant to instill a sense of responsibility and maturity into him—to make him "grow the hell up."

Finally, the constant pressure, and worry that Daniel would yet do something rash, became too much for her, and Susan Galloway wrote the infamous letter, now crumpled and stained with Daniel's blood, that Christopher had carried every day for the last six months. When she finished speaking, the three sat in uncomfortable silence, punctuated by the steady tick-tock of the grandfather clock by the door.

Christopher shifted in his seat, and the sound of the creaking leather was like that of a passing shell—offending and dangerous in its intent. He saw Susan flinch and was suddenly ashamed. He understood now why she did what she did, and he couldn't blame her. His only regret, and he suspected hers, too, was that Daniel would never know.

When Christopher finally broke the silence, his voice was low, almost raspy. "Miss Johnston—"

"Susan. Please call me Susan." She looked at him with pleading eyes as if what he now called her meant everything to her.

Christopher nodded and cast a glance at Elizabeth, who still refused to match his gaze. "Susan. I had no idea what you and Daniel were going through. I...I always thought it was a done deal. If I'd have known—"

She leaned forward expectantly. "Would you have hated me less?"

Christopher didn't know how to respond. Everything was all mixed up now. He had hated her for all this time. Hated her with a passion that sometimes kept him up at night. But now... He suspected that, even if he didn't know what he did now, he would find it hard to maintain that hatred. But, he didn't want to lie. "I don't know. Maybe."

Her eyes dropped back to her lap. There was that stab of guilt again. He fought a sudden urge to reach out and take her hand. "Please understand what I was going through as well. My brother, my older brother..." His eyes teared up, and the words caught in his throat. It was a moment before he could continue. "...Died in my arms," he whispered.

Elizabeth gasped, and Susan took her hand. The two held onto each other and looked at Christopher expectantly, yet fearful.

"I was devastated," he continued. "I felt an anguish and loss like nothing I'd ever felt before. I...I was...I was adrift without him. After the pain subsided, hatred took its place. I hated the rebs most of all, but I found that letter, and I came to hate you as well."

Christopher took a deep breath and remembered that dark time after the battle when the army sat inactive—standing guard over the killing fields and woods while work details buried the dead. He'd drunk himself into a stupor more than once, and it was only the steadfast support of his messmates that kept him from falling into the abyss. Eventually, he sat aside the bottle, vowing to be done with it once and for all, and focused his energy on hating anyone who he thought contributed, no matter how indirectly, to Daniel's death. He would be a good soldier and kill as many of the enemy as he could; and he would then come home and make sure everyone knew of the duplicity and disloyalty of Susan Johnston.

Now that hatred was crumbling at every turn. First, in that house in Fredericksburg, when he'd killed that unarmed boy, and now with Susan Johnston. Nothing was as easy as it had seemed, and his revenge seemed hollow and misplaced.

The sound of Elizabeth's tears drew him back to the present. He looked at his sister and felt an overwhelming love for the young girl so brokenhearted over the loss of her older brother. It was one thing to read about it in a letter, or to see his name on a casualty list. It was another to imagine him bleeding out on the ground, hurting and afraid.

Christopher got up and went to her. He knelt down before the divan and put his hands on Elizabeth's. Susan's hands were still there and the three of them held onto each other, connected by their sorrow and their shared love for someone taken from them too soon.

"Lizzy, I'm sorry you had to hear it like this. I had no intention of ever telling you how Danny died. Not any of you. I wanted to shield you from that particular horror."

Elizabeth sat up straight, extracting one hand to wipe her eyes and cheeks. "Christopher Galloway, it's not up to you to protect me from the truth. I deserve to know what happened just as much as anyone."

That she'd left one hand in his lessened the sting of her words, but they still left Christopher shamed and confused. He didn't think he would ever understand women, and especially not this headstrong, outspoken, mature woman his little sister had turned into. He briefly wondered if she'd ever find a man strong enough to tame her.

"Still, I never wanted to hurt you." He looked at Susan. "Either of you, truth be told."

Susan gave him a wane smile and nodded.

"I was just full of so much pain and sorrow, anger seemed the only thing strong enough to drive it out. But I wasn't fair to you," he said to Susan.

"And to me," he continued, now looking at Elizabeth, "you were still this gawky little thing, all limbs and freckles, dreaming of boys and whatever else young girls dream of. I had no idea you would have grown up so much so fast."

"Yes, well," Elizabeth replied. "While you boys were off playing soldier, someone had to stay back here and hold things together when you started coming home in caskets."

"Amen," Susan whispered.

Christopher stood. "You think it was easy for us?"

"Not at all," Elizabeth answered evenly. "I just think you underestimated the impact your actions would have on those you left behind. I would love to still be able to dream of boys and 'whatever,' but that option was taken from me. We have all lost more in this war than loved ones. Even the survivors have lost a piece of themselves."

Christopher frowned. Surviving was everything.

"Do you know why I didn't recognize you when you first came in, Christopher?"

He had thought it was because he was so grown-up and manly in his uniform, but now he suspected it was more than that—and she would tell him.

"It was your eyes."

"My eyes?"

"Yes. Your eyes. They were empty, soulless. I thought you were a brigand come to do me harm. There was no life in those eyes, Christopher. Oh, sometimes it comes back. You get that twinkle, and I see the boy you once were, but something of you died with Danny. And I pray...oh I pray you get it back," she finished with a gasp.

Christopher went back to his seat and sat down, stunned to silence. Was that why she wouldn't look at him? Was his own sister afraid of him? The image of a freckled face with a button nose and wispy beard filled his thoughts. What kind of monster had he become?

He shook his head. This would not do. He couldn't doubt himself. Not now. Not yet. He needed to hold on to that hate until this was over. He suspected it was the only thing keeping him alive and sane.

He stood up. "I'm sorry you feel that way, Elizabeth. I am what I am now because it keeps me going when any sane man would run shrieking in terror. And I will have to hang onto it for a while longer now."

He looked to Susan, "Miss Johnston. Please accept my apologies for doubting your dedication to my brother. I hold you no ill will and wish you well."

Christopher walked across the room, took his hat off the hook and opened the front door.

"Christopher," Elizabeth called. "What about supper?"

"Please proceed without me," he said without turning around. He stepped out into the late afternoon sun, shut the door behind him, and headed out to the street. The tavern on Main Street called to him, but he ignored it. He turned the other way and headed toward the edge of town. He would sleep in the woods tonight, where he would find comfort in the familiar feel of the cold, hard ground.

Chapter Nine

The train sat at the station in Columbus, creating a cacophony of noise as water was added to the boiler and wood to the wood bin. Christopher sat staring out the window thinking how different this train trip to Virginia was from his last one. Before, he'd traveled by cattle car with close to a thousand other men, all drinking and singing and dreaming of glory, the drunken boasts getting more outrageous with each passing mile and bottle consumed. Now, he sat in a passenger car, and, though the seat was upholstered, he found the upright back unforgiving and wished for the cattle car where he could lay back in a bed of straw and get some sleep.

Before, the tracks had been lined with well-wishers, waving flags and kerchiefs, the children jumping up and down in their excitement, the adults yelling blessings and encouragement to the passing cars. The stations had been filled with brass bands, local politicians, hot meals, and stolen kisses from pretty girls. Now, most people barely acknowledged the uniform he wore. It seemed to make them uncomfortable, as if it were a reminder of their loss, or the dangers their loved ones faced.

He sighed and leaned his forehead against the window, watching with idle fascination as the imperfections in the glass caused the passersby to stretch and contract in odd shapes. He'd expected change when he'd gone off to war, just not like this.

JACK GALLOWAY HAD RETURNED home the day after Christopher and Elizabeth met with Susan Johnston. Despite his intentions to sleep out of doors the night before, a cold rain moved in after midnight and drove Christopher home. The rain showed no signs of letting up the following morning, so Christopher spent the day indoors, sitting with his mother, and passing the time by the fire. At one point, he'd gotten out his "housewife" to mend some of his clothing, but Elizabeth insisted on doing it for him. So he'd tried reading another of Daniel's books, this time a Walter Scott novel all about knights and damsels in distress. But he'd found the flowery language boring and almost incomprehensible, and he spent more time dozing than reading.

He and Elizabeth had been sitting in the parlor. Christopher was dozing with the book half fallen out of his lap, and Elizabeth was repairing a loose hem on one of her skirts. They had spoken little since the night before, and the things said and unsaid hung between them like the haze from a smoky fire. Elizabeth had tried to apologize, and Christopher had tried to accept that apology and offer one of his own, but the thought that his own sister found him frightening left him feeling even more depressed and adrift that he had been before. He could tell Elizabeth was sorry by how she went out of her way to be nice to him and do things for him, such as replacing lost buttons on his shirts and darning his socks.

The sound of the front door opening, followed by his father's cursing of the weather, woke Christopher with a start. As Jack Galloway strode into the room, still shaking water off his hat and coat and cursing the weather, Christopher and Elizabeth stood and stared at him expectantly.

"Well, I'm home just as you asked," Jack growled.

Elizabeth ran to him and took his hat and coat. "Oh, Da. I'm so glad you made it back in time to see Chrissy—Christopher before he has to go back."

Jack eyed his son up and down. "Well, where's your uniform?" Christopher was wearing an old pair of dungarees and a shirt his mother had made for him a couple years before. Elizabeth had insisted he send his uniform out to be cleaned, though he couldn't imagine why, he'd only been wearing it a couple weeks.

"At the cleaners, Da. And it's good to see you, too."

"Ba!" Jack responded. "If I'd known you were coming, I'd have been here to greet ya."

"Well," Christopher said. "It all happened sudden like. Burnside was out; Hooker was in. He was passing out furloughs and such trying to make the boys happy, and the 8th needed more men. They sent me up north with a recruitment detail and tacked a weeklong furlough on the end. So..." Christopher took a big breath. "Here I am. Also, I thought it would be fun to surprise you all."

Elizabeth laughed nervously. "That you did. Though I wouldn't exactly call it fun."

"Men have commitments, Christopher. You should know that by now. What, did you think I was just sittin' here waiting for you to show up and surprise me?"

Christopher felt nauseous, and his legs weakened. Of all the homecoming scenarios he'd played in his head since getting his furlough, none of them included his father being angry and put out. "No, Da. I just...Like I said, it happened fast. When the army says go somewhere, you go. You don't check first to see if it's convenient for all parties." As Christopher spoke he got louder and more assured until the last sentence came out almost as a rebuke.

Jack held up a hand. "Don't think I'm not glad to see ya, safe and sound and all. Especially with your ma took sick like she is. Seeing you must have been a comfort to her."

"Oh, that it was, Da," Elizabeth said. "You should have seen her face light up." Elizabeth had hung the hat and coat and was running her wet hands down her skirt as she talked, then stopped. "You know, I think it may have had some kind of healing properties for her. She seems less raspy and maybe even a little more energetic since Chris came home."

"What? After two days?" Jack gave her an incredulous look, and she shrugged.

"It just seems that way to me is all I'm saying."

Christopher walked to his father with his hand outstretched. Jack took the offered hand, and the two squeezed each other's hands, their backs straight, and their eyes locked. *Like two pugilists, preparing to spar,* Christopher thought.

"You're looking well, Son," Jack said.

"As are you, Da," Christopher lied. His father looked old and angry, his hair almost all white, and the perpetual scowl he wore emphasized the deep wrinkles on his pale face. "I hear business is good."

"That it is. At least something good has come from this cursed war. I just hope my good fortune continues after the meetings I had to cancel to get here."

Christopher pulled his hand back and returned to his chair. "I'm sorry for the trouble, Da."

Jack headed for the stairs. "No trouble, Son," he mumbled. "I'm just going to go up and check on my sweet Mary." As his attention turned from Christopher to Mary, much of the anger seemed to leave Jack's tone and countenance.

After he was gone, Christopher let loose a growl of frustration. Elizabeth came and knelt down beside him, reached out, and took one of his hands in hers.

"Oh, Chris. I don't know what's gotten into him. You two always butted heads as long as I can remember, but this..." She shook her head. "I think as long as I live, I'll never understand you men."

Christopher leaned back and smacked his head on the back of the chair, the way he used to do as a child when he was preparing to throw a fit. Why was his father acting this way? He thought things had gone well last time he'd seen his father back at Camp Dennison, at least after they had gotten past the whole fighting in camp thing. He'd hoped that things between them would be different now—more like it had been with him and Danny. Didn't his father realize he could die at any time? Maybe that was it. Maybe he was just afraid of losing another son to the war. Maybe he thought that by keeping his distance, the loss would be easier to take.

Christopher thought of all his pards back in the 8th who he used to be so close with, sharing a snort when someone had a bottle, gambling away their paychecks before they even arrived, ruminating about what combat would be like and who would be brave and who would run...wherever there was fun to be had, Christopher was there. Now, he just kept to himself. He hardly had anything to do with anybody but Ezra, and there was no getting rid of Ezra. Maybe he was afraid. He didn't know how much more pain and loss he could endure after Antietam. And maybe his da felt the same way.

And there was the guilt after a fight when thinking of those that didn't make it. Why them and not him? Why did he deserve to live and they didn't?

He'd done nothing special. He'd not shirked, nor had he taken foolish risks. It was just the way it was. The bullets flew at random, and if it was your time, it was your time. Still, sometimes you couldn't help feeling guilty.

He looked over at the stairs. Was that it? Was he afraid? Was his father feeling guilty because his oldest son had died and he'd let him go off to war?

Did he hate Christopher because he had lived and not Daniel?

That last thought made the nausea worse. Would his own da prefer he'd died so his brother could live?

Christopher snatched his hand from Elizabeth's, stood up, and started pacing. It was like all the air had been sucked from the room. He couldn't breathe. His thoughts were whirling around his head so fast he couldn't keep up. His father's hate—his father's fear. He felt the scream coming on and there was nothing he could do about it. It let loose as he was running out of the house, toward the setting sun.

Christopher wandered the streets of Norwalk long after the sun had gone down. He passed the tavern on Main Street more than once and marveled at the growth the town was experiencing. Soon, he found himself wandering among the large estates along West Main Street—where town founders and prominent civilian big bugs lived. A nervousness overtook him, replacing the brooding funk he'd been in since leaving the house. He was soaked from the rain and shivering from the cold. He felt like he was in enemy territory, and he was being watched. Watched, judged, and found wanting. He turned around and headed home.

He returned to find his father sitting in his chair by the fire, smoking his pipe, and reading the paper. Rachel and Rebecca were home and playing with their dolls on the living room floor. Elizabeth was in the kitchen—he could hear the pots and pans banging out her frustration. When Christopher entered the room, Jack Galloway folded his paper and sat it on his lap.

"Girls, take your dolls up to your room why don't you," he said to Rachel and Rebecca—while looking at Christopher. "Your brother and I need to talk."

"Ah, Da...Do we have to?" Rebecca whined. "We want to stay down here with you and Chrissy. He can tell us some more stories about the war."

"Yeah, I wanna stay, too," Rachel added.

"Not now, girls," Christopher said, staring at his father. "I'm all storied out. Maybe after supper."

The girls looked at each other as if their father's words were merely a suggestion, and they were contemplating its merit. Finally, Rebecca shrugged. "Okay. Come on, Rach," she said, taking her sister's hand. "Let's go get the doll house out and make tea."

Rachel responded with her own shrug. "Okay."

Christopher watched them ascending the stairs, hand in hand. There were six years between Elizabeth and Rebecca, and the two youngest girls lived for each other. There was no doubt they loved their older siblings, but more like they would aunts and uncles than brothers and sisters.

Once they were gone, Jack cleared his throat. "Chris. I apologize for the way I acted before. I was out of line. You're home safe, and I'm glad for it. I just wish you didn't have to go back is all."

Christopher looked his father in the eye. "Do you wish it was me that died at Antietam instead of Daniel?"

All the color drained from Jack Galloway's face. He sputtered. "How dare you suggest such a thing!"

But Christopher saw the moment's hesitation in his eyes.

"It's no secret Danny was your favorite."

"That's not true, Son. Sure, Danny was easier—he took to book learnin' and helping out in the shop, whereas you...well you always went your own way." Jack's gaze dropped to the floor. "That doesn't mean I loved you any less. It was just different."

"Then why the cold shoulder now? I feel unwanted in my own home...My studies or prospects in the shop don't matter now. I'm here for only a few days, then I go back—to the war where I could just as easily get killed as Danny did."

Jack flinched.

Maybe that was it, Christopher thought. *Maybe it was the fear—not the hate.*

Christopher went to his father and knelt down beside the chair just has Elizabeth had earlier—though he didn't take his hand.

"Da. I don't know what tomorrow will bring. I don't even know if there will be a tomorrow for me. So I want to make the most of every moment I can while it lasts. And right now, that means being with my family because I may not get another chance."

Jack's eyes glistened, and Christopher could sense the struggle going on inside of him. It was the same mastery of self-control that made it possible to put one foot in front of the other when they stepped out into the field of battle. Only now it just created a wall between them.

Jack took a deep breath and said, "If that's so, maybe you shouldn't be rushing out the door at the drop of the hat."

The air rushed out of Christopher's lungs, and his shoulder's slumped. Then he realized the tone of the statement wasn't of reproach but of humor.

Jack placed his hand on Christopher's shoulder. "I'm sorry, Son. The death of Danny took everything out of me until there was nothing left for anyone else. It's been hard on us all."

They were so intent on each other, neither Jack or Christopher heard the soft, slippered steps on the stairs, or the labored breaths. They were both startled by a soft, raspy voice. "There are my men, together."

Christopher stood and spun around. Jack lurched out of his seat.

"Mary, what'cha doing out of bed?" Jack cried.

"Ma!" Christopher ran to take his mother's arm as she slumped against the wall. "What are you doing, Ma?"

Jack was right behind Christopher, and the two of them helped Mary Galloway to the divan. Jack sat beside her, giving her something to lean on, and Christopher knelt at her feet.

Elizabeth rushed into the room. "Ma! What'cha doing out of bed?"

Christopher let loose a small giggle, and Mary offered her daughter a wane smile. Even the ends of Jack's mouth turned up a little hearing his daughter's words echoing his own.

"I had to see me boys is all," Mary said.

"We coulda seen you in your room, Ma," Christopher answered.

"I couldn't wait."

Christopher stared at his mother's face. It seemed some color was back and the red splotches a little less inflamed. Her eyes were clear, and she was looking at him, not through him. At that moment he felt an overwhelming hope and a determination to survive the war. His family needed him to live.

Then the tears were back, washing over him like a wave. He gulped for breath and buried his face in his mother's night dress. It smelled of sickness, but he didn't care.

As he felt himself losing control more and more, Christopher grabbed the ornate wood frame of the divan and squeezed. This was not how it should be. War was supposed to bolster his manhood, not rob him of it.

Mary ran her hand through his hair and cooed to him. Elizabeth placed a hand on his back, and he could hear her own tears matching his.

After what felt like an eternity, but was only a couple minutes, Christopher regained control and leaned back. His father was staring at the opposite wall, his eyes glassy, and he seemed embarrassed and unsure what to do or say. His mother was smiling at him, and he was sure he saw strength in that smile. She was going to be all right.

Christopher stood and held his hand out to Elizabeth. "Come on, Sis. Let's go finish supper." Elizabeth smiled and let him help her up.

Christopher looked toward the stairs and saw Mae standing at the base, her cheeks shining with tears. As their eyes met, Mae came forward. "I'm so sorry, everyone. I stepped away for just a moment, and when I came back, she was gone."

Jack looked at their old friend and nanny to his children and smiled. "It's all right, Mae. We were just having a moment."

Mae's gaze flitted down to the floor and back. "I saw."

"Come," Jack continued. "Join us. Sitting up seems to be doing Mary good, and I'm sure you'd appreciate some time out of that dark, smelly room."

Mae shook her head. "I don't know, it looks like family time to me."

"Nonsense," Mary said. "You *are* family."

"Besides, the kids were about to go make us some supper. That'll give us old folk the opportunity to sit and chat. I've been in a daze so long we could stand with some catching-up."

"Well, all right," Mae said. "Just let me get you a blanket, Mary. Then we'll sit down here for a little while. Then it's back to bed for you, old girl. We don't want to overdo it."

THE SCREECH OF THE train whistle accompanied by the increasing huffing and chuffing of the engine pulled Christopher back into the present. He leaned back and looked out the window, watching people scurrying about as the moment of departure approached.

A man in a business suit sat down next to him, nodded once and buried his head in a newspaper. Christopher wondered if he had been in the crowds lining the tracks two years ago as their train passed through Columbus on its way to Virginia.

He took off his frock coat, rolled it up, and put it between his head and the window. He leaned up against the wall with his head on the coat, steeling himself for the long, uncomfortable ride to Wheeling in the new state of West Virginia. So much had changed...

FOR THE LAST LEG OF the trip back to the camp along the Rappahannock River, Christopher caught a ride with a supply train. He regretted it the whole way as the wagons struggled up and down the hard dry ruts left over from the winter rains. But the ride made him think of the time he rode in a wagon train from Romney down to the suspension bridge where he and Ezra drank and gambled with Company B and a bunch of Indiana boys. That little adventure ended with him in a Confederate prison and almost cost him his life.

He then thought of the tavern on Main Street in Norwalk and the many times he'd passed it without going in. He'd hardly thought of drinking and was glad to have that devil off his back. Though a strong snort now would surely ease the dull ache that had developed in his lower back from the constant swaying of the wagon.

Christopher arrived at a camp in chaos. Everywhere men were running around, animated with a sense of purpose and excitement. A company-sized contingent of men descended on the wagons and, armed with ledgers and pencils, attacked the contents.

He jumped off the seat of the ammunition wagon he'd been riding in, barely missing a private carrying a box of Enfield rounds. He stretched and groaned like an old man, grabbed his knapsack and haversack (much cleaner than before, but still smelling like rancid bacon), and set out in search of the Second Corps and the 8th.

Christopher wandered the camp streets, following flags and asking directions, for almost an hour before he saw the 8th's colors flying next to an Ohio state flag in the distance. He hurried toward them, an excitement building in him that was as strong as that he'd felt when the train pulled into Norwalk. It surprised him, but this felt as much like home than his actual home did.

Chapter Ten

Christopher's first stop was the quartermaster's tent, so he could draw a new rifle and traps and hopefully trade the Hardee hat for a new forage cap—the brim having come off his old one. Quartermaster Sergeant Daniels was not at his desk, and a corporal Christopher did not know was in his place. Christopher approached the desk and waited to be acknowledged.

"Afternoon, Corporal," he said after waiting several minutes for the man to look up from his paperwork.

"Whatever you need, we ain't got time," the man responded without looking up. "We got goods coming in and goods going out so fast we can't keep up." He finally looked up at Christopher. "There's a war on, in case you hadn't heard."

"That must explain all the bullets keep buzzing by my head," Christopher shot back, taking off his hat so the man could get a good look at his ear with the chunk missing off the top. "I guess if I spent all my time behind a desk with my nose buried in a ledger I'd be more on top of these things." He knew he was close to being dismissed empty-handed, but he had his hackles up at the man's disrespect. Part of him knew it wasn't fair, but Christopher had a deep dislike for logistics personnel. They never had to put themselves in danger, and it always seemed the men on the line were left wanting while they lived in the lap of luxury.

The corporal leaned back in his chair and, to his credit, acknowledged Christopher's point. "Forgive me, Corporal. It's been extremely hectic around here the last few days, what with the upcoming campaign."

Christopher's respect for the man shot up, and he softened his tone. "I just got back from a recruitment drive. Hooker going to have a go at Lee?"

The man nodded.

"Hopefully not another assault on Fredericksburg."

The corporal sneered. "Definitely not. I don't think anyone wants to try that at this point. No, the way I understand it, Hooker's going to try going around Lee and flank him. We're..." He cleared his throat. "Er, you all, will cross the Rappahannock somewhere to the east and head south so you can come in behind Lee's army. Maybe even cut him off from Richmond."

Christopher nodded. "Bully. I'm ready to give them a taste of what we got at Fredericksburg."

The corporal leaned forward again. "Looks like you'll get your chance. So, what do you need?"

The tone of the last question, though no longer dismissive, told Christopher it was time to get down to business and be on his way. "I turned in my rifle and traps when I went north, so I need to check out new equipments. Also, if you have one, I'd like to trade this Hardee in for a forage cap."

"I can definitely set you up with a new kit. The hat will have to wait, though. We're short of clothing at the moment. The supply train that just arrived has some clothing in it. Try again in a couple days."

Christopher got a rifle, bayonet, and scabbard; fuse and cartridge boxes; a belt; and—since they were preparing for a campaign—forty rounds of ammunition. The corporal also threw in a new haversack. When Christopher pointed out his old one with still in good shape, the man just waved his hand in front of his nose and said his pards will appreciate it.

As he turned down the street for Company D, Christopher's pulse quickened, and he picked up his pace. He was now seeing many faces he knew and was smiling and nodding continuously. There was Nick Apgar, who joined up with his father and brother in '61 (both of whom had been discharged for disability, so it was just Nick now); Joe Dewalt, wounded at Fredericksburg, now out of the hospital and cleaning his rifle; Bill Gridley, who'd helped Christopher at Red House when he'd got the top of his ear shot off, now with a third stripe on his sleeve; and Virgil Ennis, recently promoted to Company D's first sergeant.

Christopher reported to Sergeant Ennis, who recorded him as present in the company ledger and sent him to his hut to prepare to move out under full marching orders. He entered the hut he'd been sharing with Ezra since Parker Bonett was killed, and Charlie Locker had moved to the non-commissioned officer's quarters. As expected, Ezra was there packing his knapsack.

Unexpected, though, both Jump brothers were there packing their knapsacks as well.

"What? You didn't think I was coming back?" Christopher said as a way of greeting.

Ezra strode across the room with a big grin on his face. "Welcome back, pard!" He drew Christopher into a bear hug, lifting him up off the ground and knocking off his hat in the process. "How was Ohio?"

Christopher extricated himself from his friend's hug and retrieved his hat. "It's still there."

Nathan Jump came forward, almost jumping up and down with excitement. "Chris! Look who's back!"

Joe Jump nodded his head. Christopher nodded back.

Christopher didn't know what to say or how to react. Joe Jump had been wounded at Antietam and had deserted from the hospital as soon as he was able, leaving his little brother alone. Christopher had gotten along well enough with both Jump brothers prior to that, but now he didn't know how he felt about Joe—not so much because he'd deserted the army, that Christopher could understand—but that in doing so, he'd also deserted his younger brother. Christopher thought he should get some credit for coming back, but not much.

"I tell you, Chris," Nathan was chattering. "I was on my way back from the sinks, and who should be standing by the fire chatting away with First Sergeant Ennis but my big brother, Joe." The statement ended on such a note of admiration that Christopher looked at Nathan and cocked his head in confusion. *How could he not be mad?*

Christopher remembered days where he'd been angry, feeling like Daniel had deserted him, but Daniel hadn't had a choice in the matter. He supposed if Daniel suddenly appeared, Christopher would be just as over the moon as Nathan was. "So, what brings you two here?" He looked sidelong at Ezra as he spoke.

"Well," Nathan responded. "There weren't no room in the cabin I was in, so when Joe showed back up Ezra was good enough to let us move in here. You don't mind, do you, Chris?"

Christopher shook his head. "More the merrier."

"Sorry I didn't consult with you beforehand, pard, but I didn't figure you'd mind."

Christopher shrugged and threw his knapsack on his bunk. "I guess we gotta prepare for moving out.

"Who was gonna carry the other half of your dog tent if I hadn't shown up?" he asked Ezra.

"I was gonna do without."

"Well, no need to now. Let me unload some of this stuff from my knapsack, and I'll carry my half." Christopher opened the knapsack and started removing clothing—some he'd taken with him but also several new shirts and socks his sister had sewn for him. He retrieved his old fatigue jacket and replaced the frock coat he'd been wearing. Then he pulled out his old forage cap will the bill hanging half off.

"I guess I'm stuck with this Hardee for now," he said. He sat down and worked on removing the hunting horn from the front of the hat. "Better take all this brass off."

"Why's that, Chris?" Nathan asked. "I think it looks sharp."

"Yeah, well. I figure Johnnies are like chickens—their eyes are naturally drawn to shiny objects. I don't want a ball in the head because of a shiny horn on my hat."

Nathan nodded. "Good point. But what about the D?

"That I'll keep. I have an eight around here I can add, too. They're not too big, and that's who were are. Sure, we got the fancy clovers now to tell everyone we're with the Second Corps, but there's a lot of boys in the Second Corps. Few left though that can say they're in Company D of the 8th Ohio."

"Here, here," Ezra said. He jutted his chin toward Christopher's belongings. "I see you got a new bread bag."

Christopher nodded. "Yeah, apparently the old one was getting rank."

Ezra chuckled. "You can say that again."

"So, I guess I was the only person who didn't think it stunk," Christopher huffed.

"Yep," Nathan and Ezra said in unison.

"It was getting pretty ripe even before Antietam," Joe added.

At the sound of the bugle call to assemble, they dropped what they were doing and exited the hut. Christopher felt a little self-conscious being the only one wearing a Hardee hat, but at least it was unadorned now. Just a plain black hat. And he was back in his old fatigue jacket, so he fit right in.

They were issued a week's worth of rations, with instructions to cook them up and store them in their haversacks. *So much for the new clean haversack*, Christopher thought. They were also issued forty rounds of ammunition. Christopher already had his forty rounds, but he knew from experience that wouldn't last long in a real fight, so he took the forty more and loaded up his haversack and pants pockets until his suspenders dug into his shoulders from the weight.

The next day, three corps moved out, but the Second Corps was not one of them. Christopher and his messmates—new and old—sat and watched the bustle of an army on the march while they drank coffee and consumed much of the rations they had been given the day before.

It was a bloated and uncomfortable Christopher that woke the next day and donned his traps, hoisted his rifle, and moved out with the rest of the Second Corps. The lightness of his haversack countered the fullness of his stomach, and he worried about running out of food if the campaign should go on for long. The winter rains that had plagued the army back in January and February had turned to spring rains, and the road was still a muddy mess, just barely passable after the thousands of men and wagons that had marched out the day before.

Soon, Christopher's thighs were burning, and he was regretting the long months of inactivity. There had been little drill over the winter months, and he'd not done much that could be called exercise while he was back home. He remembered the first march they'd undertaken after arriving in West Virginia almost two years before and vowed he would not fall behind like he did then. But it was going to be a long couple of days before he had his marching legs back.

He was distracted for a time by watching Joe and Nathan Jump, marching side by side, occasionally leaning toward each other to share an intimate thought, or just walking together in amiable silence. The intensity of the jealousy he felt toward the two brothers surprised Christopher and left him feeling ashamed. It made no sense. There were many family members serving together in the 8th and plenty of other regiments. He was not the first person to lose a brother in this war, nor would he be the last. But, he'd thought after Antietam that he and Nathan shared a unique bond. But, that feeling made Christopher uncomfortable, and he never befriended Nathan. He'd just been around. It was just the way it was, and only death or the end of the war would change that. Now, Nathan had Joe and he had...Ezra.

Christopher looked over at the man who'd become his best pard in the whole damn army. Big-boned, broad shouldered, not at all handsome or book smart, Ezra was the most loyal friend anyone could ask for. "Hey, Ez. You have any rations left?"

"Yeah, ya want some?"

"Naw. Just checking. We're going to have to watch 'em from here on out. No telling how long this campaign will last."

Ezra nodded, then gave Christopher a wink. "Don't worry, I'll find us something."

Ezra was not known as the best "forager" in the company for nothing.

The Second Corps stopped along the northern bank of the Rappahannock, and the 8th was assigned picket duty. They spread out along the bank of the river where Christopher could watch as the engineers constructed a pontoon bridge. God, he hated pontoon bridges. They swayed and bobbed and made a soldier feel like he was in a turkey shoot, and he was the turkey. But, he had to hand it to the engineers, he only had to be on the bridge for the time it took to cross it, they had be there for as long as it took to build. Rebel sharpshooters had killed a lot of those boys outside Fredericksburg.

They crossed the river the next morning, marched down a turnpike, and met up with the other three corps where the turnpike intersected with another major road. A large house stood on one corner of the intersection. That, someone said, was Chancellorsville.

"Well, I'll be damned," Ezra exclaimed. "I thought Chancellorsville would be at least as big as Fredericksburg. Hell, the names bigger than it is."

"Look on the bright side," Christopher said, chuckling. "We don't have to worry as much about reb sharpshooters, and we'll know exactly where to find the big bugs when we need them."

"Got that right. They'll be in the parlor, sipping tea with the lady of the house."

Sergeant Ennis was passing by and stopped long enough to add to the conversation. "The important thing is, we're now behind Lee's fortifications. He's going to either come out and meet us or slink back home like the dog he is. And we crush Lee here; there's nothing between us and Richmond."

The war could be over this summer, Christopher thought but kept his mouth shut. *If there's a way to mess this all up, the high command will find it.*

They continued on a little ways south of the house and went into a defensive position spread out on either side of the turnpike. They spent the afternoon digging trenches that ended up never being used. Toward the end of the day, they were drawn back to Chancellorsville and made camp. All day they heard fighting off in the distance, toward Fredericksburg, but thought nothing of it. That was just the distraction to keep Lee occupied while they got situated.

The next morning, they formed battle lines, and the men threw up some minor fortifications—little more than slight mounds with no abatis before them to slow down an attack. They then settled in to await the frontal assault everyone knew was coming.

Sometime after the noon hour, Colonel Sawyer assembled the 8th to read a letter to the men from General Hooker. The letter highlighted the success of the army's maneuvers and how victory was within their grasp. As Christopher listened he realized he wasn't afraid this time, just excited. The upcoming battle was a chance for a much-needed victory, one that may even end the war. And, though he'd never admit it, he was looking forward to the excitement, the charge that came with fighting a dangerous enemy just as hell-bent on winning as you were, and facing death head on. There was no feeling like it in the whole world.

As Sawyer continued on, talking about the glorious victory to come, he wondered if going home would be like his furlough—long periods of feeling isolated and melancholy, arguments with his da, crying jags that would come out of nowhere. If so, maybe he didn't want to go home. Maybe he could join the regular army and go west to fight Indians. He remembered reading a book once for school where the author described the plains as a sea, the rolling hills like waves, the grass constantly moving in the breeze. *Danny would have liked that.*

He was just thinking he'd have to get better at horseback riding when the sounds of a major battle erupted off to the right. Colonel Sawyer stopped reading. Everyone looked around confused. That was the wrong direction. The enemy was the other way—toward Fredericksburg.

Then, the sound of drums echoed throughout the camp as musicians beat out the long roll. Hooker's letter forgotten, everyone scrambled for their rifles. Officers and sergeants called out for order. Men frantically asked what was going on though they knew full well no one could answer them.

Each company reassembled in front of their rifle stacks. Captains yelled, "Take!—" Every man leaned forward, grabbed his rifle in the stack before him with one hand, and waited for the rest of the command. "—arms!" The men stood and pulled their rifles to them, the stacks coming apart like Chinese puzzle boxes.

The men marched to their places in the line and waited. By now, artillery fire was exploding with uncomfortable regularity behind the line. As Christopher dropped into his place behind the minor fortifications, he thought he could hear something coming in the trees. It was a faint rustling, almost undetectable over sounds of officers shouting commands and the explosions of incoming shells and outgoing artillery fire.

Then he saw movement and was sure something was coming. He squeezed his rifle as adrenaline coursed through his body. Without waiting for the command, he brought the butt up to his shoulder. Whoever it was, they would be here any moment and, at the rate they were moving, there would barely be time to get off one round before they were upon them.

Suddenly, men in blue streamed out of the woods to their right, hatless and without rifles, their eyes wide with fright; they ran across the 8th's front and kept going, not even slowing down to acknowledge their fellow soldiers.

The right flank was moving to face this new threat, whatever it was. In a matter of seconds the right half of the battle line was at a seventy-degree angle to the rest. And they waited.

The sounds of battle off to the right grew in intensity. Christopher was sure the generals were responding, and something would happen soon. But the Second Corps received no orders, so they continued to wait, still harassed by incoming artillery but under no immediate threat before them.

A shell exploded behind Christopher's right shoulder so close that he felt the heat of the blast and the concussion almost knocked him over. His Hardee hat flew to the ground before him. He couldn't breathe. He squeezed his eyes shut, tensed his whole body, and willed himself to relax. His ears rang, and the smell of gunpowder was so strong he could taste it.

Once he'd overcome the shock, he reached down and grabbed his hat. *God, I hate artillery.*

After a moment, the panic subsided, and he went back to waiting. Somewhere on their right front men were facing much more than just a few stray artillery rounds. By the sound, a couple of corps were engaged, fighting over hotly contested ground. If their side lost, the whole army could fold. Christopher imaged the army in flight, every man for himself, running through the brambles and thick underbrush of the wilderness that separated them from the Rappahannock.

Their own men continued to pour out of the woods, and the 8th was ordered out of their entrenchments and into line with fixed bayonets to stop the steady stream of deserters. Christopher stood at port arms, with his rifle in front of his body at a forty-five degree angle, and waited. Soon, another wave poured out of woods, and everyone raised their rifles yelling at the oncoming men. No one wanted to point their rifles at their fellow soldiers, and they certainly didn't want to use their bayonets, but the retreat had to be stopped.

Nicholas Apgar was on Christopher's right, and a man came running up to the line and tried to push his way between them. Nicholas and Christopher closed ranks and pushed back. The man stopped, but tried to claw his way between them, talking fast in German.

"What's he sayin', Nick?" Christopher asked.

"Got me, I ain't Dutch."

"Hey! Pard! Stop your runnin'! Do you speak English?"

The man stopped and looked at Christopher quizzically. He tried again, but slower.

"Do! You! Speak! English!?"

"Ja," the man nodded.

"Where you going in such an all-fired hurry? The enemy's that way." Christopher pointed his rifle toward the woods.

The man cast a nervous glance over his shoulder and shook. "They have kilt us all," he moaned.

"Who? the rebs attack you?"

He nodded again.

"Well, why the hell didn't you fight back."

The man shook his head. "We was reserve. In the back...the, the rear. There wasn't supposed to be any fighting."

Nicholas barked a humorless laugh. "We've all been sayin' that since '61. But they just keep coming.

"Who you with?" Christopher noted with disgust that there were no gunpowder stains on the man's face. He'd not fired a rifle at all that day.

The man sighed and his shoulders slumped. All the fear and tension seemed to leave his body. "The 45th New York," he said to the ground before him.

"Well, New York, you have a chance to redeem yourself. They're issuing men who want back into the fray rifles and gear over there." The man looked to where Christopher was pointing.

To drive his point home, Christopher pointed to the woods. "Here that fighting? Those are your pards in there, fighting to hold on. They go, this whole army goes. Then we'd be in a real fix. Now, go get yourself a rifle and get back in there. We'll be along shortly." Christopher gave the man a kick to the rear and sent him on his way.

The same scene was playing out up and down the line, and soon there were groups of men marching back toward the battle, being led by their officers if someone found them or by staff officers if they couldn't.

As the steady stream of men became a trickle, the 8th moved back to the defensive line. From there, they listened to the battle raging before them somewhere beyond the woods. As the sun set, the trees were lit by a kaleidoscope of flashes, some large, some small, but so constant it was like pulsing daylight.

Ezra took a swig from his canteen and spat half of it back out. A habit they'd all picked up trying to wash out the gunpowder that constantly filled their mouths from biting off the ends of cartridges. "If those boys need help up there. I'd be willing," he said to no one in particular.

"I know, Ez. Our turn will come."

"Let's just get on with it then. Why are they holding us back?"

"We're in reserve, I suppose."

"Reserve." Ezra spat again. "I hate reserve. There's our boys up there dyin', and all we're doing is watching. Let's get in there and get it over with already."

Christopher could see Ezra's knee bouncing up and down, and from the light of the flashes he could tell his friend's knuckles were white from gripping his rifle. "Careful what you wish for."

"All I wish for is that this be done with. I can't stand the waiting. Always waiting. I want to fight!"

Christopher didn't respond. Ezra's blood was up, and nothing he could say would change that. While he struggled to maintain an outside air of calm confidence, inside he felt much the same way.

The shelling continued for most of the night. Not that anyone could sleep anyway. The thought that they'd been outflanked and outmaneuvered by the rebel army once again had everyone on edge. When the shells exploded overhead, they lit up a sea of anxious faces staring in the same direction, expecting disaster at any moment.

Sometime before dawn, Christopher drifted off into a shallow, half-sleep, where he dreamt of Daniel and Susan Johnston. He and Daniel were wearing dress uniforms, cleaned and pressed. Their skin was so clean it shone, and the sores and pimples that had plagued them since joining the army were absent. Susan entered wearing a white dress, and her radiance outshone them both. Christopher looked at Daniel, who was looking back at him smiling.

A nearby explosion, close enough to rain dirt and debris down on Christopher's head, woke him. He opened his eyes to the feeble light of dawn. The battle had recommenced with the rising sun.

The smell of wood smoke and coffee pierced the acrid stench of gunpowder. Christopher's stomach rumbled, and he sat up, trying to determine which need was greatest—the need to pee, or the need for coffee. He decided to pee.

He asked for and received permission to leave the line. No one seemed concerned about an imminent attack on their position. The fighting was still somewhere beyond the woods. As he wandered through camp, Christopher noted that little had changed since the night before. The same men occupied the same positions. The only thing different from that time the previous morning was their attitude. Instead of bursting with confidence and the desire to engage the enemy and "finish the job," the men were edgy and nervous.

Christopher returned to his position and retrieved his tin cup and a piece of hardtack from his haversack. After pouring a cup he sat down on the line between Ezra and Nicholas. There was no banter or joking, not even any griping or speculating what the big bugs would do next. Christopher dunked his hardtack in the hot coffee and joined the others in staring at the woods. Though they could not see what was beyond the trees, they could all easily imagine. Occasionally, a man would stumble out of the trees, sometimes wounded, sometimes not.

As Christopher was taking his first bite of hardtack, the call for assembly sounded. He responded with a string of curse words he didn't even know existed before joining up. He bit off as big a chunk of hardtack as he could fit in his mouth and surrounded it with coffee still hot enough to make his eyes water.

The part of the army not engaged retreated a couple miles south of the Chancellorsville house—farther from the Rappahannock and safety. They built up new defensive positions, and then the 8th was pulled away to guard a nearby farmhouse, or, more specifically, the battery that had taken up position in its front yard.

Not having shovels, they used their bayonets to loosen the soil and their tin plates to scoop it up and pile it before them. Soon, they had a line of dirt that could almost be called a parapet. As they dug, Ezra finally found his voice. "It ain't seemly, us digging in the dirt like niggers."

"Ezra," Christopher replied. "You know I don't like that word."

"Yeah, well, you're about the only man in this army that don't use it. You're also about the only one who joined up to free the ni—darkies."

Darkie wasn't any better, but Christopher let it slide. If he complained too much, people would shun him.

"Well, you want to go back to standing in a line, trading shots with the enemy? I don't like digging any more than you do, but I like a couple feet of dirt between me and the rebels' bullets."

Ezra chuckled. "And we get to lie down while we're fighting, too."

They settled in and built another fire. Soon a fresh pot of coffee was adding its aroma to the smells of wood smoke, unwashed men and clothing, gunpowder, and rotting food. The life of a soldier was a smorgasbord of smells to which the men had grown immune.

Though they were never called up to join in the fighting, they were not idle. They received tools, including shovels and axes, and built up proper parapets complete with abatis made of fresh-cut logs, sharpened on the end. They even dug rifle pits beyond the main defensive line and set up a skirmish line. The officers feared the thick woods before them would prevent them from seeing an attack in time, so the skirmishers were to be their early warning system or, as Ezra put it, "The canary in their coal mine."

For most of the day, they watched a steady stream of men shuffling down the pike, mixing with ambulances, caissons, and staff officers, riding to and from the fighting. The chaotic bustle that went on behind the front lines was fascinating to the men who were more used to being out front. At one point, a column of black smoke rose up in the distance, standing out in sharp contrast to the silvery-gray and white pall of gun smoke that bleached the color from the sky.

That night, the fighting did not continue after sundown. After the constant noise, the quiet was disconcerting, but fatigue and apathy had replaced the nervous tension that had possessed them before. Soon, most of the men not on the skirmish line or assigned a picket post were fast asleep.

Sometime in the night, Christopher was awoken by a burst of gunfire on their right. He sat up and gripped his rifle, expecting an attack. Looking around, he could see by the feeble light of the moon the tension on the faces around him. Soon, the shooting tapered off, replaced by angry shouting. Everyone surmised that a nervous picket had shot at a shadow and set off a chain reaction. The now quiet night was filled with the exhalation of hundreds of held breaths.

The following morning dawned sunny and quiet. But soon they could hear a battle taking place somewhere in the distance.

"That sounds pretty far away to me," Ezra said.

"It's definitely not right in front of us," Christopher responded. "I wonder what happened."

"Maybe we out-flanked those flanking flankers and got behind Lee for a change."

Christopher shrugged. "At this point, I'd believe anything, except maybe a Federal general could outsmart Lee."

"Anything is possible—except that."

"Amen, brother."

As the day progressed, it remained quiet. Ezra and Christopher took their turn in the rifle pits on the skirmish line, feeling vulnerable and exposed the entire time.

"If a horde of Johnnies comes running out of those trees, how long do you suppose we'd last?" Ezra asked.

"Long enough to fire once and run like hell," Christopher said. "Which is about all they want from us, I think."

"Yeah, maybe," Ezra said. "I wouldn't want to get shot in the back though."

"I've long ago given up such notions of dying a hero's death or being branded a coward if I'm shot in the back. And from the way the 11th folded yesterday, so has the rest of the army."

"Still, what would my pappy say?"

"You're pappy would never know how you bought it. Besides, it's not the how that matters to family. Believe me, front or back, or in-between, doesn't mean a thing to them. Only thing that matters is that it happened at all." As Christopher talked, his voice got quieter.

Toward evening, they were replaced on the skirmish line and returned to their spot behind the parapet. They were idle the rest of the day. They watched the woods before them and listened to the fighting, like distant thunder on an otherwise cloudless day.

Mid-morning the next day, though, everything changed. Christopher was just pouring himself his third cup of coffee of the morning, hoping to fill his belly with liquid since the food in his haversack had run out the day before, when he heard the distinctive boom of an artillery battery, followed by several explosions in and around their defensive works. He poured out the coffee, grabbed his rifle, and ran for the pits.

He reached his place in the line at about the same time the skirmishers and pickets came scrambling over the abatis and pushed their way behind the battle line.

"They coming," one of them yelled, his voice betraying just a hint of the panic he must have felt.

Christopher looked up, and, sure enough, a line of Confederates, at least a brigade in strength, was pouring out of the woods and approaching their position at the double-quick, yipping and howling their distinctive rebel yell.

"We hold here, men. Reinforcements are on the way," Sawyer yelled from somewhere behind Christopher.

Suddenly conscious of his stripes, Christopher felt he should say something to bolster the surrounding men. "Steady, boys. Wait for the command."

"Fix! Bayonets!"

A thrill of panic coursed down Christopher's spine as he pulled his bayonet out of its scabbard and attached it to the end of his rifle. He did not want to have to stab anyone with a bayonet again.

"Prime!"

He pulled a primer out of its box on his belt and placed it on the breach-nipple of his rifle. His hands were steady though his heart was running like a race horse.

"Firing by number! Ones—Ready!"

Since they were not in a normal battle line, the regular fire commands didn't work. Instead Sawyer thought of having them fire by number. In that morning's line-up, Christopher had been a one, as had Ezra behind him. Now, in the pits, Ezra was at his side, and they both raised their rifle butts to their shoulders.

"Aim!"

Christopher took a bead on a single ragged soldier in the middle of the line. He thought he could see the hate in the man's eyes even from that distance.

"Fire!"

The rebel line disappeared in a cloud of smoke and flame as Christopher's rifle bucked against his shoulder. Something splattered over his face and neck. He assumed it was partially burned powder, but it seemed wet.

"Ones! Load!"

He reached for another cartridge.

"Twos! Ready!"

Christopher could sense the activity around him, but he was focused on loading his rifle. About the time he finished ramming the bullet home and reseating his ram-rod, he heard the command, "Ones! Ready!"

He barely had time to replace the primer and get the rifle to his shoulder before he heard the command, "Fire!"

"Load!" Sawyers voice was already hoarse and scratchy. Christopher thought he should have the company captains giving the commands.

Christopher sensed rather than saw the reinforcements arrive. Men crowded into the firing line, and the command changed to "Fire at will!" It was every man for himself.

He had no idea how long the fight lasted. Probably only a few minutes. At one point, he realized the enemy charge must have faltered, or they would have been upon them by now. But he continued to load and fire into the thickening bank of gun smoke before them. Then, a breeze blew an opening in the cloud, and he saw the rebels falling back. The firing slackened, and the smoke cleared until it became clear that the rebels were in full retreat, running for the distant trees. Christopher continued to load and take pot shots at the retreating enemy until someone called out, "Cease fire!"

Christopher took a deep breath and wiped his face with his sleeve. It was hot work, and he was sweating. Then he looked at his sleeve and he could tell by its darkened appearance that it was not all sweat. He ran his finger over his cheek and looked at it. The pad was smeared with blood.

Frantically patting himself down, Christopher jerked his head back and forth as he searched for a wound. Not finding one, his breath caught at a troubling thought. "Ezra?" His voice was small, and there was a pleading tone to it.

"Here, pard."

Christopher looked down. Ezra was kneeling next to the body of Nicholas Apgar. Poor Nick had caught a bullet in the face and had gone down without a sound. That was probably the spatter Christopher felt.

Ezra looked up at him, his eyes glassy. "That's all the Apgars gone now," he said.

Christopher leaned back against the parapet. All he could do was nod.

Chapter Eleven

Once again, it was a dejected and demoralized Army of the Potomac that crossed back over the Rappahannock River. As they approached the pontoon bridges, the 8th fell out with their brigade, letting the rest of the Second Corps go on ahead. Their orders were to take a brief rest before falling back to join the rear guard. The men stacked their rifles and dispersed, many gathering firewood for cook fires, hoping to get a cup of coffee before having to march again. Others just sat by the side of the road, chewing on the leavings from their haversacks, if there were any, or having a smoke from the last of the tobacco from Fredericksburg.

Christopher and Ezra joined a group of men from another company in building a fire. Though the wood was damp, Christopher had a few dry linen scraps in his haversack he added to the kindling, and they soon had a fire large enough to create a bed of coals big enough to heat all their tin cups.

As they sat back to wait, one man muttered to no one in particular, "You know, boys, I'm starting to have my doubts about this army. I don't think these generals could out-think a pack of savage injuns let alone one of the finest military minds of our time."

There were nods all around, then another responded, "I for one am about ready to pack it in. We can't win for nothin', and what are we fighting for anyway? I thought it was for the Union, then Lincoln went and made it all about the nigger with his proc'amation."

"Here, here," replied the first man. "I ain't willing to die to set some darkie free. They'll just come north and take our jobs."

Christopher sat squirming until he couldn't take it anymore. Ignoring an intense warning look from Ezra, he chimed in. "You don't think there's enough work for everybody? Look at all we're producing for the war. Way

I hear it, they're so hard up for workers they're hiring women to do men's work."

"How long you think that'll last once this ball is over? They won't need all this equipment no more, and we'll all be back home looking for work. Throw a few thousand niggers in the mix willing to work for half of what a white man will, and we won't be able to make enough to feed our families."

"What makes you so sure they'll all come north. The work they're doing now will still need to be done, just now they'll get paid for it."

"You think their former masters gonna look kindly on having to pay for what they were getting for free?"

"Doesn't matter what they think. That's the way it's gonna be."

"Hell, boy! You seen them contraband. Ain't a one of them fit to do much more than pick crops and propagate."

"Yet they're gonna come to your home town and take your job."

"All I'm saying is those that run things will pay as little as they can get away with, and if they can get a bunch of ignorant niggers to do the job for less than they pay a white man, that's what they'll do."

"Not if they want a good product, they won't."

The man flapped the sole of his brogan, the toe of which had come undone from the top of the shoe. "You think they give a damn about quality?"

"The government buying big lots, sight unseen; ain't the same as a customer coming into a shop and buying something for himself."

"Boy, you're as ignorant as you are dumb. If you love the black man so much, why don't the rest of us just go home and let you finish the war by yourself. I'm sure you can find enough rabid abolitionists to fill a regiment or two."

Christopher was seeing red. He was tired of sitting quietly by and listening to this talk night after night. Men like Rufus deserved a chance to earn a living just as much as anyone. Why couldn't these ignorant jackanapes see that? He and the other man were rising, ready to take their argument to the next level, when the bugle call for assembly sounded.

"I guess you're off the hook, *bub.*" The man stepped forward until he was standing over Christopher. "I'll have to thrash you some other time."

"Any time—*bub.*"

The men parted, knowing no one would follow through on their threats. As angry as they were now, the argument wasn't worth being whipped or bucked and gagged for.

THE WEATHER WARMED up, and soon the closed-in huts they'd built for winter became too hot to occupy. The army moved camp fifteen miles north to a hilly area with a nice breeze where trees still existed and water was plentiful. Once again, the army tried to bolster the men's spirits with a steady flow of supplies. The men were well-fed, well-clothed, and paid up, so they had plenty of scratch for gambling or buying liquor and other goods from the sutlers.

As the Union army moved north, so too did the Confederates. The two armies, or some part thereof, always seemed in proximity, making picket duty dangerous and nerve wracking. At least at first.

The picket line was so close to the Confederates that, when the wind was right, Christopher could hear the comings and goings of their camp. Sometimes, he thought he could even smell them.

One afternoon, as he stood in nervous readiness, fearful of an enemy charge, or a sniper's bullet, a voice called out from the brush. "Hey, Billy!"

Christopher dropped into a crouch and brought his rifle closer to his shoulder. "Who comes—"

"Oh, we don't need none of that foo-for-all now. It's just us chickens."

"What? Who is that? If this is a trick, it ain't funny!" At the thought someone was pranking him, Christopher's nervousness flamed to anger.

"Ain't no trick, pard. Name's Jim Taylor, from Alabamy. I thought you and I could work out a trade of some kind."

A trill of terror crawled up Christopher's spine. He crouched lower, and every muscle tensed. After a moment, he realized he was holding his breath and let it out in a sharp exhalation.

"What do you want?" he asked.

"Got any coffee?

"What?"

"You shore ask what a lot. You hard of hearing?"

"Wha—No! I...I...Well, what are you after?"

"I told ya! Coffee ya fool."

"But, why me?"

"Why not you? We ain't had no coffee in a month of Sundays and, I'm guessin' you boys are flush with the stuff. Am I right?"

"Well...Yeah. When we ain't campaigning."

"Well, iffen you were campaignin' now, we wouldn't be talkin.'"

Christopher nodded to himself. He figured—he hoped—that the reb couldn't see him that well.

"Well! Iffen we're in agreement, let's palaver."

So much for not being seen. "Where are you?"

"Over here. Iffen I stand, you promise not to shoot?"

Christopher thought for a moment. This was so strange. But try as he might, he couldn't see the harm in it. Like the man said, they weren't campaigning, and he was tired of fighting.

"Okay. Let's see ya."

A gray, dirty scarecrow came up out of the brush not more than fifty yards in front of Christopher. His breath caught in his throat, and he took a step back. It seemed unnatural not to try to shoot the man. His legs did not respond at first, but eventually he took a step forward.

"Howdy," said the scarecrow name Jim Taylor.

"H-h-hello."

"I take it you ain't done this before."

Christopher shook his head.

"You'd be surprised how many boys make little truces up and down the picket line, lookin' for a little peace where otherwise there ain't none.

"How about you set your rifle down, too, and we meet half-way, all right?"

Christopher nodded, and, without taking his eyes off the man before him, he slowly crouched and sat his rifle on the ground, making sure by feel that the breach side was up.

Jim slowly walked forward, as if he were approaching a skittish doe, murmuring. Christopher found himself mesmerized by the man's easy demeanor and quiet words, and he, too, started slowly walking forward.

"I been watchin' you couple days now. You seem all right. Maybe a bit of a prig, marchin' back and forth with your rifle on your shoulder, or starin' out all serious like. But mostly you just look homesick, like the rest of us. Pining for a pretty girl, or missin' loved ones. Am I right?"

Christopher nodded again. He was slowly relaxing, but the thought a rebel soldier had been watching him for the last two days was disconcerting.

Soon, the two men, one in a blue, one in gray, were within arm's reach. Jim held out his hand.

"Glad to meet'cha, pard."

Christopher looked at the hand. It was so dirty, the nails were almost black, and the pores looked like brown freckles. But that wasn't why he hesitated. This seemed like a betrayal—of his oath, of his country, of his fellow soldiers...maybe even of Daniel. But still, he was damn tired of living in fear and hate. He took a step forward and took the outstretched hand in his.

"Name's Chris Galloway."

Jim's face burst into a wide smile, exposing a mouthful of brown teeth, some well on their way to rotting out. "Well, I'll be. An Irishman."

"Second generation."

"Funny. We got a lot of you boys on our side, too."

"Funny how?"

"Well, we get to know each other, we ain't all that different. I often wonder why it had to come to this."

Christopher nodded. "Me too. The more I think about it, the less sense it all makes."

"Well, nothin' to do now but get the job done and go home, I guess."

"I guess."

There was a moment of silence as both thought about what "getting the job done" meant, and if it would involve shooting each other. Then Jim broke the silence.

"I sure could go for a cup of coffee. And I'm guessin' you boys got plenty. You have any on you?"

"I got some beans in my bread sack. What you got?"

"How about some tobacky? I'm guessin' you don't get much good, southern tobacco these days.

Christopher thought of the cases his regiment had stolen from the warehouse in Fredericksburg but didn't mention it. He'd heard that the looting the Federals had done during that battle was a sore subject for most of the South. Besides, it was all gone now.

"I smoke a pipe now and then but can take it or leave it myself. I suppose there's some would appreciate something fresher than what's coming in from overseas though.

Jim pulled a healthy size plug out of his haversack as Christopher retrieved a sack of coffee beans from his. Jim looked at the bag, which wasn't that large, and bit off the end of the plug. "There, that seems fair."

The two exchanged product.

"I have three more days of picket duty," Christopher said. "You going to be here tomorrow?"

Jim nodded. "I got a couple more days."

Once the deal was done, Christopher's mind kicked into gear as he thought of the possibilities. He was sure Ezra could scrounge up more coffee, and if they could get enough tobacco, it'd be as good as money back in camp.

"If you can get a case of tobacco, I can bring a pound of coffee tomorrow."

Jim's eyes lit up with greed, but then he frowned. "That's all tall order. I don't know iffen I can get a whole case."

"Bring what you can, I'll have a pound, and we can do a fair trade for anything up to that amount. Deal?"

Jim smiled and held out his hand. The two shook once more, all the while Christopher wishing his new friend would keep his mouth shut when he smiled. Those rotting teeth put off a powerful odor.

CHRISTOPHER'S PICKET trades proved to be lucrative. The tobacco was as good as money, and he could barter for most everything he needed that the army didn't provide, even after splitting the take with Ezra. Once the paymaster arrived, and they drew their back pay, Christopher found himself with a pocket full of cash and nothing to spend it on. He thought of sending some home. His parents didn't need the help, but he thought his da could put it away for him so he'd have something to get started with once the war was over.

Then he discovered chuck-a-luck.

Chuck-a-luck was a simple game of luck. Anyone with a gum blanket, a charcoal pencil, and three dice could be a chuck-a-luck dealer. Some men made their own dice carved out of wood or bone, but most of the players preferred the sutler-bought dice because they could be sure those were properly balanced. The game was so random though, there was no incentive for the dealer to weight the dice.

The would-be dealer would draw the numbers 1-2-3-4-5-6 on the white side of his gum blanket. Then, the players would place a bet by putting money on a number. They would then roll the dice, and, if their number came up, they won. The payout was one-to-one, so each time the player matched a number, he would double his money. If their number did not come up, the dealer won the whole thing.

With the whole army just getting paid, games cropped up everywhere. Any open space would do, be it the parade ground, the field used for sermons, or even along the company streets. In their new location, the men had made lattices from saplings and long, thin branches and, when not on duty, would sit in the shade for hours and play chuck-a-luck or other gambling games.

There was always at least one canteen filled with whiskey being passed around at any game. To avoid the temptation of the alcohol, Christopher would focus on the game with an intensity normally reserved for the battlefield. He won and lost what to him was great sums of money. At the height of his gambling, he walked away from a game with over a hundred dollars. The next day, he was broke and had to borrow two dollars to get back in the game.

When Christopher gambled, his desire to win was all-consuming. He couldn't say why, he didn't need or want the money. It wasn't about that. It was about winning at all costs. Something they did every time they went into battle. It was as if he was trying to capture that thrill, that rush of adrenaline.

Christopher slapped a dollar down on the six painted on the underside of a gum blanket and rolled the three dice. Two came up six. The dealer put two dollars down on his one and Christopher let it ride. The next roll there were no sixes. The dealer took all three dollar bills with a satisfied smirk.

Christopher reached for another dollar, and Ezra grabbed his hand. Christopher tried to tug his hand away but Ezra held on. "What in tarnation, Ez?"

"Don't you think you've had enough, pard?"

"If I thought that, I wouldn't still be playing, now would I?"

"Ya think?"

Christopher opened his mouth to respond, but could not think of a retort. *Could I?* the words niggled at the back of his mind.

The two friends stared at each other until Christopher let out a breath and slumped in resignation. "Fine." He handed the dice on to the next person and stood, surprised to discover his feet were asleep from kneeling so long.

Christopher looked around. The field looked like an outdoor revival meeting, with hundreds—maybe thousands—of men, all on their knees. Christopher's smile was short-lived as the thought popped into his head that the comparison seemed sacrilegious.

Looking up, the waning sun startled him. It was late afternoon already, and he had guard duty that night. Not only that, he was the corporal of the guard for his section.

"Come on, Ez. Let's go get a fire going and fix up some grub."

Wiping his mouth and passing a canteen back to the man on the other side of him, Ezra smiled at Christopher, his eyes glassy and out of focus. "Now you're talking."

As they headed back to their company street, Christopher marveled, not for the first time, at his friend's ability to go from responsible soldier to irreverent beat on a dime. That was the thing about Ezra, you never knew which one you would get. By the time they reached their fire pit, he realized that, since the incident at the drinking shack outside Romney, they were both like that, passing the roll of the responsible one back and forth, helping each other keep their baser instincts in check. Except for the gambling, it worked.

Ezra went to draw their rations, and while he was gone Christopher moved the coffee pot around the fire so it wouldn't boil over. He was still thinking of his and Ezra's relationship and how it had evolved over the last two-and-a-half years—from uneasy alliance, to tentative friends, to drinking buddies and hell raisers, to best pards looking out for each other. Suddenly, he decided to quit gambling. Maybe even attend the Sunday services put on by the 8th's chaplain. He'd gone before but always felt self-conscious and unsure how to act in a non-Catholic service. But, closeness to God was the same no matter the ceremony, and it would do him good. Help him get away from all the many vices that army life threw before him.

But, like the Lord, the army giveth, and the army taketh away. Where one day Christopher would find himself surrounded by temptation, be it liquor-filled canteens, games of chance, or the prostitutes that set up tents on the outskirts of camp and enticed the boys by stepping outside in their skimpy nightclothes, the next day they would be on the march with no time to even think of all those sins. So Christopher never had the chance to test his resolve. The next day, the Army of the Potomac began the slow, laborious process of putting over one hundred thousand men, complete with artillery and supply support, in motion. The rebel army was on the move, and this time they would not catch them flat-footed.

It seemed no one knew where Lee was going, or what he was doing, but most were sure he was gearing up for another invasion into the north—probably Maryland again.

For the next couple of weeks, the 8th was on the move. Sometimes they would march at night, sometimes during the day. Some days they only marched a couple hours, other days they marched from sunup until the middle of the night.

THE BLARE OF BUGLES, the roll of drums, the call of officers and sergeants all convened on Christopher's senses and drove him from a sound sleep. Cracking an eye, he could see that the sun was not yet up. They had packed up the night before and bivouacked under the stars so they would be ready to move at the crack of dawn. But, even a pre-packed army took time to get moving, so they were being woken well before their planned departure time.

Groaning, Christopher rolled off his blanket to his hands and knees, hawked up some dusty phlegm from the road the day before, and climbed to his feet. He stumbled to a nearby clump of trees, peed, and stumbled back. Someone had a cook fire going, so he got out his tin cup, threw in some coffee grounds and water, and sat it on some hot coals. While the coffee was coming to a boil, he chewed on some salt pork he'd cooked the night before, staring bleary eyed at the shadows moving around him as the army prepared to move.

Once the coffee in his cup had boiled for a couple minutes, he took it off the fire and dunked a hard cracker in it while it cooled. After breakfast, Christopher packed up his blanket and personal items in his knapsack and cinched everything down. He was ready to go.

The sun came up. The sky was clear and the air already warm. After a few minutes, Christopher checked on the privates in his squad to make sure they were ready. Since everyone was all together, packed and waiting, that took about ten minutes.

The sun continued to rise. As it neared its zenith, Christopher did another check on the men in his squad to make sure no one had unpacked anything while waiting. No one had. After listening to Ezra call him a "mother hen," Christopher returned to his own pack and rifle and sat down.

About an hour later, the head of the column moved out. The men stood as the generals rode by, accompanied by their staffs. When first division started out, Christopher settled back down. The 8th was part of the rear guard, so they were in for a long wait.

Several hours later, the bulk of the army had passed, and the supply wagons were just starting to roll. Christopher checked his equipment and then checked on his men. Someone had started up another cooking fire and several of the boys had gotten out their tin cups and coffee. Christopher had them douse the fire and put everything away. They could move out any minute now.

Two more hours went by, the last of the wagons passed, and the rear guard fell in. By now, the sun was well past its zenith and on the wane. Christopher made a wry smile and shook his head as he realized that it would be dark in a couple hours.

THE SUN WAS LONG SET, and the men were marching in darkness. Having been up since well before dawn, most of the men were already dragging. Then, a ripple of commotion started somewhere ahead in the column and worked its way back. The army was turning around. They'd gone the wrong way.

The call to halt sounded down the line, and the men fell out along the side of the road. The bone-weary men watched in disgust as the head of the column came marching back the other way. This time, the officers had to prod, cajole, and threaten their men to get them to stand as the generals passed.

After another long delay, the 8th was again on the march—going the opposite direction. Christopher knew when they'd reached their previous campsite by the trampled vegetation, the smell of human waste, and the piles of trash glistening in the moonlight. They kept going and took a different road.

Finally they stopped for the night. They'd been waiting or marching for almost twelve hours. Christopher figured they were probably about five miles from the old camp site. But, he didn't care. He dropped at the first decent spot he could find and, using his knapsack as a pillow, was soon fast asleep. They were woken four hours later to do it all again.

SOMEWHERE IN ALL THE long days and nights of marches to nowhere, Hooker was replaced by Meade, but it didn't matter. Christopher didn't think there was a general in the whole damn army worth his salt.

Marching had always been Christopher's bane, and in the early days of his enlistment, when they had trekked all over the mountains of northwestern Virginia, he was always straggling, stumbling into camp long after the rest of his mess had a fire going and coffee brewing. But, in the two years since, he'd become a strong marcher and rarely fell behind his regiment's place in the line. But, some of the marches during June of 1863 proved too much for him even in his hardened condition.

The first several days the heat was unbearable. Several of the men still had whiskey in their canteens instead of water and they were the first to fall out.

Christopher would pass them laying along the side of the road delirious from alcohol and dehydration. It felt like the sun was baking through his hat, and several times he imagined the top of his head as a loaf of bread, rising in the oven. When they stopped for breaks, if he sat his hat upside down and left it for a while, when he tried to put it on the leather sweatband would be hot to the touch. Many men were unbuttoning their fatigue jackets, pulling the bottoms out of their belts, or even taking them off and throwing them away.

By the afternoon, sweat and heat would build under Christopher's knapsack, and the constant rubbing of the straps created sores that became more painful with every step. Many men were abandoning their knapsacks along the side of the road, and Christopher had thought about it. But, there were personal items in the knapsack—a picture of his family, the infamous letter to Daniel from Susan, a stack of letters from various family members, and a new letter he'd just received, from Susan Johnston. Those were things he didn't want to lose.

Particularly the letter from Susan. That was something new, and he still hadn't decided how he felt about it. Not that there was anything wrong with the letter. It started out reiterating what she'd said to him and Elizabeth that day in Norwalk, then asking if it was all right for her to be writing and describing various goings-on around town. It finished with the perfunctory "hope you are well," "be safe," and other such things you wrote to soldiers at war and a request for him to write her and let her know how he was and if it was all right for her to continue writing him until the war was over.

Christopher read the letter probably a dozen times. He'd started writing a response almost as many times, but could never get past the salutation and opening paragraph. What should he say? He didn't know because he didn't know how he felt. On one hand, it thrilled him to have gotten the letter, and he imagined her face as he read every word in her neat, feminine handwriting; on the other hand, it felt like a betrayal to his dead brother. Worse, there was no one to talk to about it.

He looked over at Ezra, picking his nose as he walked and examining its dusty, sticky contents before wiping it on his jacket. Nope. No one.

Officers and sergeants weaved their way through the ranks trying to stop the men from throwing their belongings away, but they couldn't be everywhere at once. By noon the route of the army could be identified by the line of discarded equipment alongside the road. *Like breadcrumbs in the forest,* Christopher thought.

Though they filled their canteens from streams or water barrels every morning it was usually the only water they saw all day. By afternoon the men's canteens would start to run dry. Then it wasn't equipment dropping—but men. Christopher had heard that more than a few had even died, their corpses discovered when the provost guard would try to roust them back into the march.

Late one afternoon, Christopher watched as Ezra took the cork out of his canteen, gave it a shake, and turned it over, giving it another shake for emphasis. Nothing came out.

Christopher took his own canteen and handed it to his pard, who shook his head. Christopher shook the canteen back at him. The pantomime argument continued for several minutes, both too tired to speak. Eventually, Ezra took the canteen, removed the cork, put the canteen to his lips, and tilted his head back. He even flexed his neck like he'd taken a drink. Then he smacked his lips and handed the canteen back.

Christopher was sure Ezra had kept his lips pressed together and had drunk nothing, but he was too tired to continue the argument. He put the canteen to his lips and drank the last little bit. The warm trickle was only a thin line of wet in his dry, swollen throat.

They dropped back until the 8th and the Second Corps were too far ahead to hope of catching up, even if they'd had the energy, so they spent the night in a barn with about fifty other men, all representing a cross-section of just about every regiment, brigade, division, and corps in the army.

The next morning, wagons full of water barrels made their way up the road, refilling canteens and giving the men hope that there was an end in sight. But the damage was already done. The Army of the Potomac was spread out along the Virginia roads for miles, a good portion of them too sick with heat exhaustion to be fit for duty.

Then the rains came.

The dry, dusty roads that had made it difficult to breathe; left eyes and throats scratchy; and turned hair, skin, and clothing the same dull, washed-out color soon turned to rivers of mud.

The rain cooled the temperature, but the mud caking the men's shoes and pant legs made every step like walking with a ball and chain attached to each leg. Christopher knew this to be true; he had worn a ball and chain more than once when he was a prisoner of war. To make matters worse, wagons and caissons became bogged down in the brown muck, and infantry men, so exhausted they could barely put one foot in front of the other, would have to stop and push them out. The rains eventually cleared, but the mud hung on for days, adding to a sense of misery that permeated the entire army.

As they worked their way north, the 8th marched through the area where the Second Battle of Bull Run had been fought. That introduced the men to a new horror. As they marched across the fields, they saw the skeletal remains of hundreds of casualties of that fight. Casualties buried in shallow graves that were now expelling their contents thanks to the heavy rains.

As they made their way across the battlefield, everywhere Christopher looked were skeletons, still dressed in scraps of uniform crisscrossed with belts and cartridge box straps turned brown from exposure to the elements. Everyone responded with horror and anger at the way their fellow soldier's remains were being ignored, but for Christopher the response was visceral. Panic and guilt at the thought of Daniel's remains working their way up out of the ground where they'd buried him made Christopher sick to his stomach.

He passed a hand sticking up out of the ground, the index finger pointing up to the sky, and he thought of Daniel, pointing up at him. "You can't even bury me right," it seemed to say. He saw a skull sitting on the ground, still wearing a ragged forage cap, and experienced a moment of panic when he imagined the brass letter on the hat, now tarnished a dark green, was a D. His breath caught in his throat, and he stumbled. Only after a second glance did he realize it was a B. And, he told himself, they were still a long way from Antietam.

As they continued northward, they were soon in the Shenandoah Valley. Christopher had missed much of the 8th's tour in the Shenandoah, having been a POW at the time, and wasn't there for the taking of Winchester or the battle two weeks later when Jackson tried to take it back. He spent several months in Winchester, but it was while the town was still in rebel hands, so he'd been locked in the courthouse basement the entire time.

But the area brought back memories of the short time he did spend there after his return. Mostly memories of joy at being free and reunited with his brother and pards of the 8th but also of chasing, but never catching, old Stonewall Jackson. It seemed any happiness he felt was always tainted by an underlying frustration that they were not doing enough to hasten the war's end.

Now Jackson was dead, killed by his own men at Chancellorsville. *Maybe now the Army of the Potomac has a fighting chance*, Christopher thought.

They continued north and soon passed into Maryland. The rumor going around was that Lee was moving north, into Pennsylvania, and that they would just be passing through Maryland. Still, they came much too close to Sharpsburg and Antietam Creek for Christopher's peace of mind. Part of him wanted to slip away and go visit Daniel in his grave. They were so close he knew he could do it in a day. But, after seeing the horrors of Bull Run, he feared what he would find.

Two days later, they heard heavy fighting ahead and knew that the two armies had found each other.

"What's at the end of this road?" Christopher asked a passing officer.

As the man continued on without stopping, his answer was short and succinct. "Some little town called Gettysburg."

Chapter Twelve

One of the oddities of battle is that ear-splitting, death-yielding sounds and sights that surround you when you're in the thick of things become so overwhelming that the body shuts down to the point where you become numb. The fear doesn't go away, it just recedes until you can function, and is often replaced with an exhilaration like no other.

But, the distant sounds of battle are like a nightmare that wraps itself around your heart and lungs until you can barely breathe, and the slightest noise can make you jump and cry out. All that day, Christopher and the 8th marched toward a thunderous conflagration that told them death and destruction lay ahead. As the day progressed, the sounds grew in volume and intensity until by the end of the day the battle sounded like it was just over the next ridge. But, by that point they had crossed several such ridges, with the battle always just ahead.

When they stopped for the night, Christopher collapsed in an exhaustive state well beyond the rigors of marching. Every muscle twitched with fatigue, his nerves tingled as if exposed to the elements, his neck and shoulders were flexed to near immobility, and a headache raged just behind his eyeballs.

It was well after nightfall. The sounds of battle had slackened to the occasional gunshot or artillery blast, and they were well behind the front lines. But the smell of gunpowder hung in the air, and the roads were busy with the comings and goings of staff officers and ambulances. This was shaping up to be a major battle, maybe even the one that would decide the fate of the nation, and it wasn't over yet.

There was no line up, no roll call. The men dropped where they were. Some didn't even bother to remove their knapsacks and traps before falling asleep. Christopher took off his knapsack and took out his gum blanket, spreading it out on the ground. He lay his knapsack at one end and sat his traps along the side. Then, he laid his rifle down, loaded but not primed, breech side up on the edge of the blanket. When he lay down, using the knapsack as a pillow, he was asleep within five minutes. His last thought was, though he was only nineteen, he was as slow and stiff as an old man.

It was still dark when the sound of reveille being blown on several bugles pierced the night air, resulting in a cacophony of coughs and curses. Christopher struggled to his hands and knees, his aching muscles protesting his every move. He looked around. A few fires were already lit, and the smell of boiling coffee pierced the lingering stench of gunpowder. His stomach rumbled, and he fumbled for his haversack and canteen.

A few feet away, Ezra sat up and stretched. He rubbed his eyes and scratched his belly and looked around like he was welcoming the new day.

"You ready for this?" Christopher asked.

"What?" Ezra asked, his mouth hanging open and his eyes half closed.

"The battle, ya dang fool. What do you mean, 'What?'"

Ezra shrugged. "It don't matter whether I'm ready or not. It's coming, and we'll be there." For emphasis he followed up with a yawn and loud fart.

"Good God, man!" Christopher exclaimed as his friend's stench drifted his way. "Don't you have to have food in your system to stink like that?"

Ezra shrugged again. He stood and, pulling his haversack and canteen over his shoulder, looked around as if he was trying to decide what was the most immediate need—sinks or firewood. He settled on the former and headed for a copse of trees that had already attracted a line of men intent on the same purpose.

Before going, Ezra stopped by Christopher's blanket and looked at him with a half-smile. "All I know is, since you got back from Norwalk, you ain't had a single dream you woke up swingin' from. Now, if we can just do something about your disposition, you'll be almost back to normal."

Christopher froze and watched Ezra walk away. It was true, he hadn't had a dream like that in weeks. *Hallelujah!* He crossed himself and smiled as he stood to follow Ezra to the trees receiving a massive infusion of fertilizer.

The two opposing armies greeted the dawn with overwhelming artillery bombardments. Meanwhile, the 8th found a nearby stream, filled their canteens, and made coffee. No one had time for more than a couple swigs of lukewarm brew and a couple bites of whatever was in their haversacks before they called assembly. Once the regiment was formed into line, roll call was taken, rifles were inspected, and ammunition was distributed.

Christopher heard a staff officer talking to the master-sergeant as they walked past. The master-sergeant was telling the officer that the regiment had just over 250 men. He remembered back to the days at Camp Dennison when they numbered almost a thousand. How many would there be come nightfall?

They marched through the woods and picked up a road heading northwest. As they marched, the sun rose in a cloudless sky and, with it, so did the temperature. The sounds of battle, somewhere ahead and to the west, grew as they marched. What started out as distant rumblings were now close and distinct enough for Christopher to discern the different ordinance being used. There was the higher-pitched pops of rifles, so frequent and close together that it sounded like a rattle. And the deeper, throaty booms of artillery, followed by the freight-train-like shriek of a cannonball, or the high-pitched whistle-boom of timed shells. Christopher thought he could even tell the difference between the newer three-inch rifled cannon and the old Parrot guns.

Soon, Christopher could see the white pall of battle ahead. Clouds of gun smoke ebbed and flowed across the field throughout a battle, sometimes hiding everything, sometimes blowing away in violent swirls that exposed the enemy in the distance and the devastation between, but a grayish-white pall always hung in the air over the battlefield. *Was it a veil to cover man's atrocities so God wouldn't have to look at them?*

As they marched, the landscape became hilly, and they were always marching either up or down hill. They left the road, crested a hill, and marched down behind the Federal line. For a moment Christopher had a panoramic view of the battlefield. The two armies were lined up along ridgelines on either side of a picturesque valley of fields and orchards, dotted with farmhouses and barns. A road bisected the valley, leading northward to a small town in the distance. To the west of the town were some imposing buildings, one of which sported a tall steeple.

That, Christopher surmised, must be Gettysburg. And the buildings must be some kind of seminary. The Federals were in a good defensive position in a line that extended south as far as he could see and farther and north to a grouping of hills just south-east of the town, where the line bulged out into a U-shape and curved out around the hills. But the Confederate's position wasn't bad either. They commanded the entire western side of the valley and, from the puffs of smoke that appeared from time to time in the upper-floor windows of various buildings, the town as well. Both armies were in good defensive positions, but someone would have to attack eventually. It was just a matter of who went first.

If Burnside had still been in command, Christopher figured he'd throw them to the slaughter the way he did at Fredericksburg. But the army had a new commander, General Meade. Christopher hoped would be a smidgen smarter that the last couple. Also, the way he saw it, the rebs wouldn't be able to stay this far north for long, cut off from their supplies and support, so he was sure that, given time, they would be the first to blink. Then all they'd have to do is lie behind that little stone wall he saw up ahead and mow the rebs down the way they had done at Fredericksburg. As they marched downhill, Christopher was feeling good about their prospects.

They marched behind the Federal line until they reached a spot where it bulged out around a hill. There they stopped, right in the middle of the bulge. Before them lay the valley, with a road in the middle heading north into town. The line continued to curve around to their right until it was hidden from view by the hill. Given the proximity of the town, Christopher surmised that they were near the end of the right flank. Somewhere on the other side of that hill was the end of the line.

Knowing the enemy was not only before them but also to their right was disconcerting, but the rock wall provided good cover toward their front, and there were a couple corps at their back. As they fell out, being put in reserve, someone said it was the 11th Corps on the other side of the hill. Christopher remembered them being the boys who'd skedaddled out of the woods at Chancellorsville. He hoped they'd show more fortitude today.

The men did not stack their rifles but kept them so they would be ready to go at a moment's notice. As soon as their company commanders dismissed them, they descended on the multitude of small cooking fires scattered throughout the area. The men already there were laughing and joking, their spirits and optimism higher than Christopher had seen since the ear-ly days of the war. Sure, that was the hated and feared Army of Northern Virginia before them, who'd whipped them time and again. But this time it would be different. This time, all they had to do was sit and wait for the ene-my to come to them, breaking themselves like waves on a rocky shore in futile attacks that would not budge the mighty Army of the Potomac. They beat them at Antietam, and they'd beat them here. And this time, they wouldn't idle the days away afterward while the enemy slinked back across the Po-tomac. This time they'd pursue them all the way to Richmond, where they'd hang Jefferson Davis and Robert E. Lee and anyone else they felt like and put an end to this madness once and for all.

Ezra had retrieved a raw slab of salt-pork from his haversack and slapped it down on a flat rock by the fire while he dug around for his skillet. Christo-pher was using his finger to scoop out a couple big globs of tar-like essence of coffee into two cups of water when they heard the regimental musician blow assembly. "Damnation!" Christopher grumbled. *We just got here.*

Ezra threw the raw meat back into his haversack with a sigh, and the two shuffled off to find their spots in line, their stomachs grumbling almost as much as their mouths.

Once the regiment was formed up, Colonel Sawyer rode up on the back of his horse, attracting the buzz of Minié balls like nectar attracts bees. His skittish horse neighed, flicked his head, and chewed on his bit as the colonel addressed his troops.

"Gentlemen! There is a heavy force of enemy skirmishers taken up posi-tion in the ditch that runs alongside the road to our front. They are wreaking havoc on the artillery corps and high command trying to coordinate the bat-tle, so we have been ordered to drive them back to their side of the valley!"

Ezra groaned. "I knew it was too good to be true."

"I assured Colonel Carroll that the 8th would not let him down, and, him being well acquainted with the caliber of soldier in the Gibraltar Brigade, and the 8th in particular, he fully agreed."

"You'd think with the unwanted attention he's getting, he'd move things along a bit more spritely, wouldn't you," Ezra whispered in Christopher's ear.

At that moment, a passing bullet ruffled the mane of Sawyer's horse and the animal bucked and almost threw its rider.

Christopher smiled and nodded. "That ought to get things moving, I'd think."

The colonel tugged violently on the reins until his horse was once again in his control, then called out, "Eighth Ohio! Attention! At the right oblique, forward, march!"

The regiment marched out in line, angling to the right and heading toward the road. At the rock wall, the formation fell apart as the men scrambled over; all the while the men crouching down in relative safety behind the barrier gave them guff and laughed at their expense.

One man looked at Christopher as he spoke. "Hey, Ohio! When you're finished winning the war, come on back; we'll be here sippin' a warm cup of brew and awaiting your return."

Christopher gave the man a quick glance. "Sorry, we'll be up there, sipping coffee with real men." He heard the man's compatriots laughing at his expense and couldn't help smiling as the regiment reformed before the wall.

Colonel Sawyer jumped the wall on horseback, withdrew his sword, and addressed the regiment. "Regiment! Fix! Bayonets!"

The metallic rasp of hundreds of bayonets being affixed to the ends of rifles filled the air.

"Prime!"

Christopher pulled the hammer on his rifle back to half-cock and quickly affixed a primer to the breach nipple. He then tucked the rifle into his right shoulder at the order arms position.

"Charge! Bayonets!"

As one, the men of the 8th Ohio took a half step back with their right foot, brought their rifles down to a forty-five degree angle facing the enemy, and gave a loud "Huzzah!" By now, they were attracting unwanted attention from the entire force of rebel skirmishers, and bullets were finding targets. Christopher marveled at the calm he felt, despite the circumstances. A year before he would have been screaming inside in terror and frustration.

Colonel Sawyer raised his sword. "At the double-quick step! Forward! March!"

Almost immediately, a bullet struck the colonel. Christopher saw him hesitate and tremble, but he didn't go down. Instead he kicked the sides of his horse and led his men into the valley at a run.

After that, Christopher forgot about Colonel Sawyer and everything else except for what was right before him. He was yelling as he ran, as was the rest of the regiment. Bullets flew by at an alarming rate, nicking clothes and equipment, piercing canteens, and felling men. As they neared the road, the rebel skirmishers rose into a battle line of their own. The 8th came to a stop and, at the command from Colonel Sawyer, fired a volley into the enemy. Then, as one they surged forward, their rifle-mounted bayonets before them, right into the ditch the enemy was using as a rifle pit.

The fighting was brutal and quick. Men thrust their bayonets and swung their rifles like clubs. Those too close to use their weapons resorted to fists and feet, kicking and punching in a frenzy of pent up hatred and fear. Within minutes the rebels turned and ran. Those that couldn't were taken prisoner.

Christopher shook his rifle and jeered at the retreating enemy along with most of the regiment—those still standing anyway. As his peripheral vision returned, and he could take in his surroundings, Christopher saw Colonel Sawyer had dismounted and was leaning against his horse. Both were bloody from multiple wounds, but still standing.

After taking a moment to catch his breath, Colonel Sawyer began barking orders. He was still in the fight. Christopher watched as a man took the reins of Sawyer's horse and led the poor animal back to the Federal position. Christopher hoped the beast would live. While they were out here of their own volition, the poor horses did not understand what was happening or why. And the large animals made for easy targets.

Christopher and Ezra sat down on the edge of the ditch and drank from their canteens. But their rest was short lived. The forward position was too small for the whole regiment, so Colonel Sawyer left Companies A and I as skirmishers and took the rest of the regiment back to the main line.

They jogged back across the field. Christopher tried to maintain an air of calm indifference, but going back, all he could think of was the randomness of death on a battlefield.

An itch began on a spot between Christopher's shoulder blades and grew until his whole back and neck seemed to be crawling with insects. Soon, he was wiggling as he ran, and, when they reached the rock wall, he leapt over it without breaking stride. He dropped to his knees, gasping for breath, and, as quickly as it came, the itch was gone.

There was no call for assembly—the 8th just dispersed and went back to whatever they were doing before being called up to take the forward skirmish line. Christopher returned to the cook fire and rooted around in his haversack. *Maybe now I'll get something to eat*, he thought.

As the sun rose, the July heat became oppressive. Christopher was reluctant to remove his traps, fearing a sudden attack would leave him empty-handed, but all around him, men not on the line were doing just that. He took off his belt and cartridge box, setting them on the ground next to him along with his rifle. Unbuttoning his jacket, Christopher considered removing it, but he knew what a stickler Sawyer was for decorum, so he just lifted the bottom of the jacket and shook it so the sweat under his arms could dry. He then took off his hat and fanned his face. He'd learned to appreciate the Hardee hat now that it was broken in. It did a much better job of protecting his head from the sun. The only drawback was the black wool felt seemed to hold in heat until it felt like his brains were cooking. He fanned until his eyes watered from the bright sun and he felt his forehead burning. Then, he put the hat back on and waited for the heat to build back up. Then he repeated the process all over again.

As the morning progressed, the fighting to the south intensified. Christopher could see the smoke billowing up where the armies clashed, but he couldn't see any of the actual fighting.

"Sounds like they're earning their pay down there," Ezra said.

Christopher nodded. "I wonder who?"

Ezra shrugged. "It ain't us. That's all I care about."

As the sun continued to rise, Christopher wished they would get called up to man the wall. He imagined the coolness of the rock pressed against his skin and smirked. Those who knew no better would call him noble and brave—ready to step forward and do his duty. But in reality it was just a selfish desire to be more comfortable.

As the day progressed, the cacophony created by the fighting to the south continued unabated. They could follow the ebb and flow of the fight by the volume of fire and the direction from which the sound was coming. But it never let up. Silently, he agreed with Ezra: *I'm glad it ain't us.*

The ongoing sound masked the sudden attack to their front. Christopher was first aware of a sudden tensing of those on the battle line—backs tightened and rifles coming up to the ready position. A low murmur began, and heads bobbed back and forth looking for a better view without going up any higher than they had to.

Being further back, Christopher felt comfortable enough to stretch his neck out a little so he could see over the wall and its defenders. And he didn't like what he saw—not at all.

An enemy force about the size of the entire 8th regiment had come up and were attempting to take back the skirmish position along the road. The companies left to defend the position—outnumbered four to one—were fighting for their lives. Christopher quickly surmised the only reason they hadn't broken and ran already was the fortifications of torn-down fencing and dirt thrown up on the road before the ditch they occupied provided the only safe place to be. If they broke and ran, many of them would get a bullet in their back for their troubles.

Beside him, Ezra cackled. "I guess our boys giving back some of what they'd been dishing out this morning, and they didn't like it none."

Christopher shook his head. "It's a good position for sniping officers either way."

Ezra nudged him. "You say that like it's a bad thing."

"Company D, line up!"

Christopher looked around. Ezra cussed.

First Sergeant Ennis, the latest in a long line of first sergeants, was, at twenty-two, the youngest first sergeant the company had so far, and, since they'd been in reserve for most of the battle of Chancellorsville, this was his first real test under fire. The way he was standing up straight and strutting around, Christopher got the impression the young first sergeant felt he had something to prove. He hoped it didn't get anyone killed.

Christopher donned his traps, grabbed his rifle, and ran to the spot where the company was forming up. He took his position between Nathan Jump and Thomas Mathews. Mathews was a good ten-plus years older than most of the rest of the company and had gained the respect of the younger soldiers. Most privates over thirty had long since gone home on disability.

Behind him, Ezra chattered as he usually did when he was nervous. "Looks like it's just us. Sawyer's over there nursing his wounds from before, so Reid's taking D in by hisself."

Christopher looked over his shoulder and spotted the colonel up the ridge aways, his jacket unbuttoned and his torso swathed in bloody bandages. He was staring through a pair of binoculars at the fight his men were in.

"Load!"

Whipping his head around, Christopher quickly retrieved a cartridge and loaded his rifle. By now, he could load and fire in a matter of seconds, and the knowledge that there were fellow regiment members needing help drove him through the motions even faster.

"Fix! Bayonets!"

A few men had removed their bayonets to skewer chunks of salt-pork for cooking, but the rest still had theirs affixed to their rifles. Once everyone was ready, Captain Reid addressed the company.

"Men, we haven't time for formalities. Those are our comrades out there, and we're going to go help them. Try to stay together, shoot if you have a target, and do your duty to God, your country, your state, and the mighty 8th!

"Huzzah!" came the resounding response.

Reid swung his sword forward and yelled, "At the double-quick! Go get 'em!"

The company leapt over the rock wall and ran across the field, laughing and cheering at their captain's informality.

But the laughter didn't last long. The enemy was close, and the wet thuds of lead on flesh, and the occasional cry of pain, told Christopher many of the bullets flying past them were finding their marks.

Christopher jumped into the ditch and crouched behind the makeshift parapet. He reloaded his rifle and took in the situation. All around him were dead or wounded men. Lying on his back was the captain of Company I, the left side of his uniform drenched in blood. Even his long, black beard dripped red. Christopher pegged the man for a goner and went back to loading his gun.

The man next to Christopher was still alive but out of the fight. He sat propped up against the side of the ditch clutching at a wound on the side of his neck. In-between loading and firing, Christopher would look over and watch the blood pumping out between the man's fingers, torn between wanting to help and fighting to keep from being overrun. Once he looked up into the man's eyes and saw a world of pain and sorrow and a look that said he knew he was going to die. As the rebels continued to press the attack, and Christopher continued to fire as fast as he could , he would glance down at that pulsing wound, and every time he looked, the interval between pulses lengthened, and the flow weakened, until it stopped all together, and the sorrow in the man's eyes was gone.

Christopher jumped up and fired his rifle, screaming. As quickly as he came up, he dropped back down and reached for another cartridge. He should have done something. But the pressure of the rebel attack was too great: Focus on the fight, take care of the wounded later. That's what they said. Besides, there's nothing you can do for a hit like that. He was a goner even before Christopher sat down beside him.

But he should have helped.

Ezra waddled over to him, keeping his head tucked down between his shoulders as far as it would go. He took one look at the now-dead man next to Christopher and grunted. "Excuse me, pard," he said and pulled the dead man out of the ditch. He laid the body out in the grass alongside the road, crossing the man's hands over his chest. "I need that cover more than you do."

As Ezra settled in next to Christopher, he peeked up over the fence rails piled up before them. "So much for hanging back in reserve."

"You got a break at Chancellorsville. You think you deserve another?"

"It'd be nice. I wouldn't complain if we spent the rest of the war in reserve."

Christopher cast a glance at his friend. He opened his mouth to respond, but a volley from the other side drowned out anything he had to say, so he returned to loading and shooting.

There was no telling how long the fight for that ditch continued. Christopher had learned that in battle, time seemed to have little meaning. Hours seem like minutes and minutes like hours. All he knew was, by the time the rebs were finished, his cartridge box was empty. During that time, the Confederates charged their position several times and were driven back each time, leaving the ground carpeted with dead and wounded. But, it was not until Company B came forward to offer additional support that the enemy decided a forward skirmish line wasn't worth the cost.

Afterward, Christopher and Ezra sat with their backs against the side of the ditch, their faces and hands black from gunpowder, and drank from their canteens. The first swig they spat out in an effort to wash off the grains of gunpowder stuck to their dry lips.

"I guess we're stuck up here now," Ezra stated in a tired, monotone voice.

"Yep," Christopher said, looking back at the stone wall protecting the rest of the Federal forces on that part of the line.

"Look on the bright side," Ezra continued in a voice that made clear he didn't believe there was a bright side, "maybe while we're sniping at them Johnnies we'll hit a general." Christopher didn't respond and, after a moment, Ezra's eyes widened just a little. "Maybe even General Lee hisself."

Christopher managed a short chuckle. "I can see the headline now: *The War Between the States Ended by Ezra Rouse from Norwalk, Ohio.* My how the girls would swoon over you then."

Ezra smiled back. "Anything is possible."

"Yep." Christopher was almost laughing now. "And then Sam Hill will need a new pair of galoshes."

ONCE IT WAS APPARENT the enemy was not going to try another attempt to retake the skirmish position, Companies A and I were sent back behind the line, leaving Companies D and B in their place. They took their wounded with them. The dead they left. The field between the skirmish line and the main battle line was still a killing field, and anyone who crossed it attracted the attention of sharpshooters and artillery. It was one thing to risk life and limb to save a wounded comrade, quite another to risk anything for a dead body.

Christopher thought of the indifference the men had developed toward the dead. Most everyone had seen a dead body before, but usually laid out in a wooden coffin in the parlor, not mangled and bloody. After two years of fighting, though, violent death was the norm. Now when Christopher saw a dead body, his first thought was to wonder if the man had any extra rounds or food on him. Some had taken to calling the bodies that littered the ground after a battle dead-meat, or just meat. A life full of hopes and dreams, laughter and sorrow, reduced to a bag of flesh and bones.

Before they left, the boys of A and I gave their extra cartridges to those replacing them. Christopher and the others pilfered the cartridge boxes of the dead. Self-conscious of his indifference, Christopher avoided looking at the dead faces of the men whose cartridge boxes he went through.

That still left them short on ammunition if the Confederates should try to retake the ditch again. As they were leaving, Christopher heard Captain Reid ask Captain Smith of Company A to have ammunition and rations sent up as soon as possible.

Captain Smith nodded, self-consciously touching the patch over his left eye as he did so—his own constant reminder of Antietam. "I'll personally see to it, John. You have my word."

Christopher watched the captain as he jogged back to the main line. He thought of Captain Nickerson, of Company I, who had long since been taken back to some field hospital—probably to die. He didn't have much use for staff officers, except for maybe Colonel Sawyer, but he had to admit, the company officers put themselves out there just as much, if not more, than their men. Christopher could freeze up in battle, the way he did at Antietam, or hide behind a pile of fence posts the way he was now, and no one would notice. But, if a company officer froze up in battle, it put the whole company in jeopardy.

Fingering his cartridge box, Christopher looked at Ezra and smiled wryly. "I don't know how they expect us to harass the enemy if we ain't got nothing to harass them with."

Ezra nodded. "Got that right, pard. I ain't gonna spend no rounds shootin' at nothin' I can't even see and then have nothin' left if things get hot.

I'll wait until we have enough ammo to fill our boxes and then some." He looked around at the ground alongside the ditch. "Hell, these Dutch farmers are so efficient there ain't even any rocks to throw if we run out of bullets."

The day passed with no sign of relief or replenishment. The sounds of battle to the south continued to ebb and flow. Christopher figured whatever was going on down there would make what they'd just been through seem like a Sunday stroll. As the afternoon passed, the searing July heat continued to intensify. Soon they were out of water. Now overriding the constant fear was an overpowering thirst.

Everyone seemed to share Ezra's sentiment about maintaining harassing fire, and the line was quiet. Once Christopher tried to look over the fence posts to see what was going on with the enemy, and a bullet hit the barricade by his face. He dropped back into the ditch with nothing more to show for his curiosity than a few splinters in his cheek.

At one point, the need to shit became too much, and Christopher had to squat in the ditch. As he worked his way out of his jacket and suspenders, his head came up high enough that the Hardee hat he wore stuck out above the parapet. Afterward, as he squirmed his pants back up, his head came up again. Apparently, an enemy sharpshooter was waiting for just that and Christopher's Hardee hat went flying across the field with a ragged hole near the crown.

Christopher thought about leaving it out there, but it was the only shade he had for his head and face. He scurried out on his hands and knees, grabbed the hat, and scurried back.

As the sun crawled across the sky, it created some shade in the ditch. Christopher lay on the bottom of the ditch, fixated on the piece of hardtack and half-cooked salt-pork in his haversack. It was right there for the taking, but he knew one bite with no water to wash it down, and he'd instantly regret it.

Eventually, Companies C and E came up to relieve them. They brought no extra water with them. Everyone going back was so thirsty they tried to bum a drink before they left, but the newcomers refused.

"To the devil with ye, lad," said the man Christopher asked for a drink. "There's plenty of water where you're goin', and what I got has got to last me."

BEHIND THE LINE, WATER and ammunition were available, but still no food. As the sun set, Christopher and Ezra got together with the Jump brothers and Charlie Locker, and the five of them pooled together their remaining rations. From the pitifully small pile of salt-pork, hardtack, and some desiccated vegetables they made a thick stew. There wasn't enough to fill anyone up, and no one could say with a straight face that it was tasty, but it was something.

The battle to the south continued, and Christopher was wondering if they'd keep fighting into the night when the rattle of rifle fire and boom of artillery exploded behind him. He grabbed his rifle and jumped to his feet.

Charlie laughed and patted the air with his hand, indicating Christopher should sit back down. "Don't worry, that's the northern end of the line just the other side of that hill there. It's probably just an enemy probe trying to determine how far our line goes. There's a couple corps over there, so I doubt they'll break through."

Christopher shook his head. "Yeah, but one of those corps is the 11th, and remember how that turned out at Chancellorsville."

Charlie's face darkened as he frowned, and Christopher feared he'd offended his friend. He said nothing about the Germans' courage or reliability, but since Chancellorsville many had. Constantly listening to your countrymen's honor being besmirched must be frustrating.

"All the more reason not to worry—they have something to prove," Charlie responded.

The sounds of fighting intensified, and it quickly became apparent that it was more than just a probe of their defenses. The enemy was attempting to turn the right flank. The fighting raged on to the south as well, and the sounds of battle on either side of them made it impossible to relax. Christopher sat still, but he was breathing hard and getting a headache from the strain of constantly tensed muscles. He tried to relax, telling himself there was no need to worry until called upon, or something happened on their part of the line, but it did little good. Though he'd cleaned his rifle after coming off the skirmish line, he wiped it down until it shone. He ran patches down the barrel until they came out as clean as they went in. Several times he reached into his haversack though he knew that it was empty.

Soon it was dark—except for the blasts of artillery and rifles lighting up the landscape in a strobe-like effect that, under other circumstances, would have been beautiful. Sometime in the night, Company D moved back up to the forward skirmish line. As expected, the men they relieved were just as parched as they had been several hours earlier.

Christopher and Ezra worked out a schedule where they would take turns trying to sleep while the other kept watch. But, though the fighting on either side of them eventually stopped, the artillery kept up a constant fire in intervals just long enough apart to ensure no one on the battlefield got any sleep.

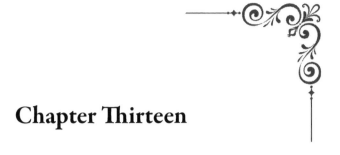

Chapter Thirteen

As dawn approached, all grew quiet. Leaning back against the side of the ditch, Christopher watched the eastern sky brighten to a steel gray. Golden beams of sunshine pierced the clouds—a testament to the beauty of God's creation. He could almost forget he was in the middle of a battlefield. Only the creaking and rattling of artillery being moved into place and the omnipresent cries of the wounded told him he lay in a valley of death. *Yea, though I walk through...What about sleeping in?* He closed his eyes and said a quick prayer, asking the Lord's mercy and protection for him and his pards—for he knew the peaceful feeling was a lie.

Christopher heard Ezra shuffling and grunting beside him, then came the sound of a stream of urine hitting the dirt. Now that the sun was up, exposing any part of the body above the fortifications they'd built up before them was sure to attract enemy fire. The men learned yesterday it was best to relieve themselves while laying down. It was messy and hated by everyone, and after only a day, the ditch was taking on the smell of the sinks—as were the men that occupied it.

Ezra finished and shoveled dirt over the wet spot he'd just created. He then rolled over onto his back, scratched his neck, and let out a loud fart. Before he'd met Ezra, Christopher didn't think a human body could hold that much gas.

"Think we're gonna get some breakfast?" Ezra asked.

Christopher shook his head in resignation. "I doubt it."

"Maybe some coffee at least..."

"Don't get your hopes up."

"Dammit, they're gonna starve us at this rate."

Christopher looked sideways at his pard. "It's only been a day. You'll survive."

Ezra threw some dirt over his shoulder. "Mebbe."

As the morning dragged on, nothing more than a skirmish here or there disturbed the uneasy peace that had descended on the battle line. As noon approached, Christopher was sure either Meade or Lee was gearing up for a major attack. Christopher's money was on Lee.

"Look at it this way," he told Ezra, "he's attacked both our flanks. The only thing left for him to do now is attack the center."

"Where we're at," Ezra said.

"Well, close anyway," Christopher responded. He peeked over the parapet but saw no sign of an imminent attack. Then, a thunderous explosion of artillery fire drove him down to the bottom of the ditch, where he put his palms over his ears.

It was as if the entire force of enemy artillery fired a single, well-timed volley. The blast created a sharp pain in his ears, followed by a loud ringing. Shot and shell flew over the valley in a screeching symphony of death, leaving contrails of white smoke that created an unnatural cloud pattern of straight lines. Then there was another series of explosions as the shells detonated somewhere behind their line.

There was a slight pause, then more artillery fire rent the air. This time not a single thunderous explosion but a series of well-timed volleys from different batteries, creating a rolling blast that melded together into one unending explosion that overwhelmed the senses. After less than a minute of this Christopher found himself curled up in a fetal position on the bottom of the ditch, his hands cupped over his ears and his mouth open in a silent scream.

Despite the ongoing sensory assault, after a time Christopher regained his senses enough to take in what was happening. First, he noticed clumps of dirt bouncing on the ditch bottom before his eyes. He'd heard of earthquakes—the bible was full of stories of God making the earth shake—but this was the first time he could say he actually saw it happening. Looking up at the sky, he saw that the white strands of smoke left by the flying shells were now a solid white pall that hung over the entire valley. This was something he was familiar with.

Then, he lifted his head to look back at the Federal line. By now their own batteries had joined in, matching the rebs their deadly, thunderous roar. A wall of smoke, which was lit up in a strobe-like light show from the blasts of cannon and exploding shells, completely masked the ridgeline. Sitting up, Christopher stuck his head over the parapet and saw a similar scene on the other side of the valley. Though he kept his hands over his ears, and the constant rumble of cannon-fire drowned out anything else, he could imagine the screams of horses and men from within those clouds as solid shot and shrapnel found unlucky targets.

Ezra sat up beside him. They exchanged glances but didn't speak. Even if they could have heard each other, there wasn't anything to say. They knew when the artillery stopped the enemy would attack. And they were part of a couple undersized companies stuck out in the middle between the two lines. They sat and watched the light show among the smoke-filled trees along both ridgelines and waited.

Christopher didn't think either side would have been able to keep up that rate of fire for more than an hour, but by the time they stopped, and a death-like silence descended on the valley, it felt like the constant explosions had been going on all day. Christopher expected that, if he could have seen the sun, it would have been hanging low in the west, ready to set.

Except for a loud ringing in his ears, Christopher couldn't hear anything. Ezra said something, but it sounded as if it was from far away instead of right beside him. He watched men scurrying about as the big bugs moved them around like pieces on a chessboard—bringing up a regiment here, sending back another there. Today they were all coming up, reinforcing the line to prepare for whatever Lee was fixing to do.

Christopher turned around and pulled himself up so he could see over the barricade. Rising up made his head spin, and he grabbed a fence post to keep from staggering. Slowly, he raised his head until his eyes were just above the top. Then he pulled himself up further for a better view, the sight before him making him forget about shooting or being shot at.

Men in butternut and gray were coming out of the still-smoke-shrouded trees to form up into a battle line that seemed to stretch from one end of the valley to the next. Multiple flags blew in the wind to designate all the different regiments and brigades that made up the force preparing to attack. Their mounted bayonets caught the weak sunlight—peeking through the thinning smog that hung above the valley—and winked at him with beams of reflected light that bespoke the care their owners put into them. Though they were too far away for Christopher to see individual faces, in his mind's eye he saw the grim determination, mixed with fear, on the face of almost every man before him.

"Here comes the colonel," Ezra said.

Not stopping to realize he could now hear better, Christopher turned around to see what Ezra was talking about. There, marching across the field toward their skirmish line, came Colonel Sawyer and the one hundred and fifty some men that made up the balance of the 8th Ohio.

"What in tarnation..." Christopher muttered to himself.

"I think our colonel may have a screw or two loose," Ezra said.

Christopher shook his head. While he had done just as much complaining about officers as any enlisted man, he'd never said a bad word about Colonel Sawyer. Even when the colonel had punished Daniel and him so severely back in Camp Dennison, he'd not held it against him. Christopher knew he was just doing his duty—and that it was things like that that had made Christopher the soldier he was today. But this was too much. Maybe there was something to the rumors of Sawyer's drinking.

The force Sawyer brought up split into two lines; the first line squeezing into the ditch with its current occupants and the second kneeling just behind. Christopher watched as Sawyer slapped Captain Reid on the back and said, "We couldn't stay back and leave you boys up here by yourself, now could we?"

"You coulda called us back," Christopher muttered to himself.

Ezra made a hand gesture as if tipping a bottle up to his lips and gave Christopher a wink.

Christopher said, "You know, if we're part of the 'Gibraltar Brigade,' then the 8th is that one rock under the water that sticks out so all the boats run into it."

"What's wrong with that?" Ezra asked. "Don't all the boats sink?"

Christopher nodded. "Yeah, but every hit chips off a piece of rock until eventually there's nothing left."

MOST OF THE ENEMY FORCE was lining up to the south, so for a time Christopher hoped that the attack would pass them by. Then, another large body of Confederates lined up along the ridge before them. By the number of flags, he guessed it to be a division—though it seemed small to be a whole division. Maybe the rebels could no longer replace their casualties. If that was the case, it was only a matter of time. *Just keep up the pressure*, he thought, *and maybe we'll be home for Christmas. Those still living, anyway.*

Christopher's anger at their colonel was somewhat mollified by the fact that the 8th was going to stay behind the makeshift barricade. At least Sawyer wasn't crazy enough to have them line up out on the field. Still, once the rebels started to move, nowhere between the lines would be safe—they'd be in just as much danger of being hit by fire from their own lines as from the enemy.

"What'er they waiting for?" Ezra grumbled.

"Maybe Lee's waiting for Meade to send him an invitation."

Christopher smiled wanly at his joke. Then he pictured a tall man in white gloves, tails, and top hat strolling across the corpse-strewn field, carrying a silver try with a white card on top. As the imaginary butler strolled up to the silver-bearded general on his big gray horse and raised the tray up, Christopher started to chuckle. Then, the butler spoke: "General Lee, sir, you and your army are invited to a small cotillion, hosted by the Army of the Potomac, just on the other side of this road." At that, Christopher burst out laughing. He laughed until his sides hurt and tears streamed down his dirty cheeks.

Ezra cast him a sidelong glance. "What? You ain't that funny."

Shaking his head and stamping his foot, Christopher tried to stop laughing. But, every time he thought he had control, a big guffaw would burst out as if of its own volition. With a sigh, the humor passed, leaving Christopher with a sense of melancholy that seemed to deflate and weaken him. He wiped his eyes and nose with the sleeve of his jacket and sighed again. *Let's just get this over with.*

As if in answer, the sound of bugles and drums drifted across the field, punctuated by loudly barked commands and the stamp of thousands of feet as the massive line of rebels stepped off.

The enemy before them was just a half-beat behind the main force, as if hesitant to proceed. But onward they came, their lines straight, their step in unison. The flags caught the wind and rippled out as if with pride at who they represented. Even from a distance, Christopher could see how ragged and dirty they looked, but their heads were high as they advanced with their rifles at the charge position.

As they moved across the uneven landscape, littered with their dead and dying comrades, the enemy lines began to undulate, their steps not so even and precise, hampered by obstacles not seen from a distance. But, still they came.

Then the Union artillery started firing. The boom echoed off the rocky ridgeline, and suddenly the air over the field was full of exploding shells. Christopher heard the shriek of cannonballs as they flew overhead, then watched the line part here or there as a ball passed between the files, sometimes taking an arm or leg, or disemboweling someone too slow getting out of the way.

"Eighth Ohio!" came the unmistakable voice of Colonel Sawyer. "Ready!"

Christopher brought the butt of his already-loaded and capped rifle to his shoulder, anticipating the familiar kick of the recoil and the acrid stench of gun smoke that would soon engulf their position.

The enemy lines came back together and continued on, seeming to grow larger with each step.

"Aim!"

Christopher looked down the barrel of his rifle. He tried not to aim at any one particular man, focusing instead on the forward site as he brought it up before the approaching wall of gray.

"Firing by company! Company A, fire!"

The first rifle volley of the engagement went out and staggered the enemy line. By the time the firing sequence got to Company D, they seemed to be faltering. Maybe they were surprised to be under rifle fire already, or maybe they expected their massive artillery barrage would have silenced the enemy guns. Whatever the reason, their heads were no longer high, their backs no longer straight. Instead, they were bent over like old men fighting a massive headwind. But still they came.

Then they stopped.

To the man, the 8th crouched down as the enemy line brought their rifles up and, firing by rank, returned fire. Bullets filled the air; some slammed into the fence posts stacked before them and a goodly portion passed them by, but a few found their mark with a wet thud or crack of bone.

Then, the Federal line behind them started firing, and there were bullets flying in both directions. At that point, Christopher decided the best place to reload was crouched down in the bottom of the ditch they'd been using as a rifle pit. Every couple minutes he would pop up, fire and drop back down. Soon, most of the 8th was doing the same. Even Colonel Sawyer was down on his knees, trying to keep his head below the top of the barricade.

By now, the advance before the 8th had completely stalled, and soon the artillery had them in their sites. Still, the rebels held out a little longer, dropping down into swales or anywhere the landscape offered them some cover. They even lay down behind corpses when there was nothing else available. But there was no hiding from the artillery.

A couple times, they tried to resume their advance, only to be halted again by a few well-timed volleys from the 8th and the soldiers behind them.

The attack didn't fall apart all at once. Peeking over the top of the barricade, Christopher watched as enemy soldiers began abandoning their positions, retreating at a run in ones and twos. Soon, there was not enough left to sustain an adequate defense, let alone attack, so the whole line folded up and ran.

Christopher and the rest of the men jumped up and began cheering and yelling taunts at the retreating rebels. Christopher and Ezra hugged and slapped each other on the back, smiling like fools.

But, the sounds of battle continued. If anything, it was getting louder. Christopher looked over and saw that the main attack to their left had not been stopped. Though badly mauled by artillery, the enemy forces had continued on. The front line—or at least what was left of it—had now reached a fence, the same fence the 8th was now using as a barricade, but there it was still intact. They had to stop and either go over the fence, or break it down. Christopher tried to maintain a martial-like indifference, but his heart went out to those poor men, so brave, so doomed. But, he realized, once the enemy got past that fence, they would soon be beyond the 8th's position and able to cut them off from the Federal line.

By now the enemy was within rifle range, and, in addition to the constant artillery fire they had been subjected to since stepping off into the field, they were now being hit with a steady fire from thousands of rifles. As Christopher watched, the men trying to scale the fence were being mowed down in droves. In some parts, they had managed to dismantle the fence, but the pause to do so had made them sitting ducks, as evidenced by the line of bodies marking where the fence had been.

Now there was no attempt to maintain straight lines—it was every man for himself as the rebels continued to die by the score for a few more feet of ground.

"Eighth Ohio! Line up on the road!"

Startled by the command, Christopher looked around. The rebels before them had quit the field, but some were still out there, offering token resistance should the Federals choose to attack—which Christopher feared Sawyer was about to do. He looked over at his commanding officer and saw that Colonel Sawyer had already scaled the barricade and was in the road, indicating with his sword where he wanted the line to be. Sergeants and company officers were joining him, and slowly the regimental battle line was taking shape.

Christopher wasn't the only one watching. As the men lined up, the enemy took note, and was soon subjecting the 8th to a steady stream of lead. The surrounding air seemed alive with the constant buzz of passing Minié balls. As he climbed up onto the road, Christopher wanted to fold up into himself. Every muscle in his body was so tight it hurt. And he was not alone—every man in the regiment was bent over and moving in stiff, jerking motions. They looked like a line of methuselahs instead of the young men that they were.

As he paced before his men, Colonel Sawyer's eyes were bright, and only a slight wince with each step gave testimony to the wounds he'd received the day before. Christopher didn't know if it was excitement or alcohol that gave Sawyer his indomitable spirit. He didn't see how a sober man would be ordering them to line up between enemy lines in the middle of such a massive battle.

"Regiment! Attention!" The men stiffened, and some clicked their heels together for emphasis, but no one straightened up completely.

Colonel Sawyer raised his sword. As he did, a bullet nicked the blade and twisted it out of his hand. Sawyer stood there, eyes wide with confusion and what Christopher hoped was doubt. Lieutenant DePuy, the colonel's adjutant, picked up the sword and handed it to his commander. Sawyer nodded and, after a slight hesitation, raised the sword again.

"Forward! March!" The sword came down toward the enemy line and the men stepped off.

Almost immediately they were off the road and back in the field on the enemy side.

"Regiment! Left wheel!" All eyes turned to the pivot man on the left end of the line. "March!"

The men in Company I on the left all slowed down and shortened their steps. The man on the end of the line ceased all forward motion and began stepping in place. The men of Company A, at the other end of the line, increased the length of their strides. Everyone in between adjusted according to how close to the pivot man they were.

The object of the wheel command was to turn the facing of a battle line by pivoting in a circular motion around a stationary point. The battle line became, in essence, the spoke of a wheel and the man on the end, the hub. For a full-size regiment, it was an extremely difficult maneuver, but the 8th hadn't been a full-sized regiment since Camp Dennison.

The difficultly for them came from the many bodies the men had to step over and the fact that they were coming under intense fire, with bullets now finding their targets with alarming frequency. As they continued wheeling to the left, several men grunted or cried out, falling or staggering back. Christopher felt the tearing of cloth and burning of flesh as a bullet creased his abdomen. He flinched and sucked in his gut, but kept going. He felt the passing breeze of several other near misses, and the sound of flying lead was a constant hum.

"Regiment! Halt!"

They stopped. Two hundred wild-eyed young men, their faces ashen beneath a layer of dirt and gunpowder, their chests heaving as if they'd just run across the field. Christopher sucked in air through his open mouth, but it never seemed enough. His head spun, and his knees had started to shake.

A tableau of a once-beautiful valley, littered with the dead and dying, lay before them. And the enemy, decimated by constant fire, yet still numbering in the thousands, had not yet noticed the minuscule regiment threatening their left flank.

"Regiment! Load!"

Those whose rifles were not already loaded did so. As soon as everyone was in the ready position, Colonel Sawyer continued.

"Firing by rank! Rear rank, ready!"

The barrel of Ezra's gun came over Christopher's shoulder, and he heard over the battle sounds the click of the hammer.

"Aim!"

Christopher considered covering his right ear but decided at this point it hardly mattered; he was already half deaf from the earlier artillery barrage.

"Fire!"

The explosion of Ezra's rifle created a ringing in Christopher's ear, and Sawyer's next command sounded as if he were far away and Christopher's head was under water.

After the front rank volley, they went to fire at will, with each man loading and firing as fast as he could with little attempt at aiming. Christopher hoped that as soon as their cartridge boxes were empty they could get out of there, and apparently that hope was shared by most of the regiment.

As the smoke of the initial volleys cleared, Christopher could see the confusion they had wrought in the enemy lines before them. The rebel soldiers, already near the breaking point from the long trek under constant fire, suddenly found themselves under fire from a new direction, and many had thrown down their rifles and run. Others were rallying under officers to change fronts and take on this new threat. Now the 8th was taking fire from two directions, and bodies began to drop with increasing regularity.

Christopher was reaching into his cartridge box when a bullet snapped its strap, taking out a chunk of his shoulder muscle in the process. He staggered back and grabbed the cartridge box before it fell to the ground. Step-ping back into line, he did an assessment of his condition. Blood was soaking his jacket and already starting to run down his left side, and there was noth-ing to hold up his almost empty cartridge box. He noticed several other tears in his clothing that had not been there that morning, and, to his great frus-tration, at some point he'd wet himself. Again. Just one battle, he thought, just one battle he'd like to make it through without losing control of his bod-ily functions.

Then a bullet tore his hat off his head, and he forgot all about bodily functions. He pulled the remaining cartridges out and stuffed all but one in his pocket. As he reached into his haversack to retrieve his bandana, he turned to Ezra to get his help stuffing it into the tear in his jacket over the bleeding wound on his shoulder.

But Ezra wasn't there.

He frantically looked around thinking his friend had been moved as they closed up ranks to fill the empty spaces in the line, but didn't see Ezra's famil-iar face anywhere. Then he looked down and saw Ezra laying on his back, a large circle of blood on his left upper chest.

Christopher froze as a horrifying sense of déjà vu overcame him. His knees buckled, and he collapsed to the ground. His head spinning and his stomach roiling, he dry heaved several times before he could get a hold of himself. As he crawled to his friend, his field of vision collapsed until he saw nothing but the man laying before him. *Not again, Lord, please not again*, he silently prayed over and over again.

Then, Christopher gasped with relief when Ezra's eyes locked onto his. He was still alive!

"Ezra! What happened?"

"What...think...happened..." Ezra gasped and dropped his head to the ground.

All thought of his own wounds gone, Christopher tore open Ezra's jack-et, frantically searching for the hole the blood was pouring out of. As he pulled back Ezra's shirt and wiped at the wound with his bandana, he stopped and looked at it in confusion. There, poking out of a jagged hole in Ezra's chest, was the misshapen base of a Minié ball.

As he thought it through, Christopher decided it must have been a spent bullet, lacking the energy to pierce Ezra's ribcage. Still, it had left a ragged hole in his flesh that was turning purple and swelling, and he was still losing a lot of blood. Christopher scooted in closer to Ezra so he wouldn't have to reach to hold the bandana over his wound. By now his left arm was getting numb, and it was all he could do to hold the now bloody bandana on Ezra's chest.

He looked around at all the other wounded and dead of the 8th scattered around him. There was Sergeant Gridley, on his knees holding a misshapen and bloody arm to his side. Christopher remembered the first time he'd been shot in the regiment's first skirmish, just outside the town of Red House, Virginia. It had been Gridley, then a corporal, who'd helped him, staunching the blood flow with his own bandana and reassuring the shocked young teenager that it would be alright. Now, Christopher sat helplessly and watched as Gridley sank to his knees, swayed back and forth, then pitched forward like a felled tree. He looked away and spotted Sawyer on his knees, obviously wounded again. *Serves you right, you bastard.*

Suddenly, those still standing were on the move, running into the crowds of retreating rebels, looking to take prisoners and capture battle flags. *Someone's going to get a medal out of this*, he thought. Meanwhile, he, Ezra, and many other good men lay bleeding out on the fertile Pennsylvania soil.

Christopher looked around for help, but there didn't appear to be anyone uninjured left. Those who hadn't run after the retreating rebels were in as bad a shape as Christopher and Ezra. A stab of fear churned his gut, and he looked down at his friend. Ezra's eyes were closed, but he was still breathing—though each breath seemed to require a mighty painful effort. He thought of trying to drag Ezra back to the Union lines, but Ezra outweighed him by at least thirty pounds. It would have taken all Christopher's effort to drag him at the best of times—light headed from blood loss and with his left arm now completely numb, it was impossible.

Christopher lay back on the ground next to Ezra and resigned them to their fate—whatever it may be. He closed his eyes and silently prayed: *Jesus, Mary, and Joseph, I ask that you have mercy on my soul, and that of my good friend, Ezra Rouse, and all the boys who've been stricken this day and the days previous... I ask that you embrace the fallen, and grant healing to the wounded. That you...you... grace and mercy...Lord...beseech...*

Chapter Fourteen

A burning pain shot down his left arm, and Christopher came awake screaming. The sky had been replaced by a veil of white canvas. Was it his burial shroud? If he was dead, where was Jesus? And why did it still hurt so much? Then, with an icy start, he noticed a chorus of moans from all around him, and despair wash over him until he wanted to cry. He didn't make it. He was on his way to hell.

He struggled to a sitting position and realized he was in an ambulance, full of wounded men. Then he heard the snap of a whip, and the wagon started with a jerk that turned many of the moans to screams. Christopher bit back a scream of his own and looked around for Ezra.

He saw his friend lying next to him, still out cold, but still breathing. The front of his jacket was black and shiny with blood. *How could someone still be alive after losing that much blood?* He pulled back Ezra's open shirt and jacket. The bandana was gone, probably having fallen when they lifted him into the ambulance. The remains of the bullet were still there, and the wound swollen and reddish purple, but the bleeding seemed to have slowed almost to a stop. Maybe there was hope yet.

The ambulance ride was a special kind of hell. Each bump (and there were many) caused a jolt of pain in Christopher's shoulder. It seemed to have the same effect on the other occupants because each bump elicited a cacophony of screams and moans that filled the wagon. At one point, the man on the other side of Christopher went still and quiet. His eyes were closed, and he appeared to be peacefully sleeping, but Christopher had seen enough death to know the difference. *Besides, there's no rest for the living on this ride.*

At the hospital, Christopher wondered why they'd even bothered putting him in an ambulance. An orderly took one look at him and had him go lay down under a shade tree with the other ambulatory wounded. Most of the men had flesh wounds, but one man had his eyes and half his face wrapped in thick bandages that were already red with new blood. Most of the wounds had no covering to keep the blood in and the dirt out.

They had taken Ezra into the hospital tent, but only after Christopher raised a fit. From the amount of blood he'd lost and the location of the wound, they had assumed Ezra had a serious chest wound and would not survive. So they were going to put him with the others waiting to die. Christopher grabbed the stretcher bearer by the arm and yanked, almost causing the man to spill his load.

"Watch it, ya damn fool!" the man cried angrily. "Ya don't want to be causin' this poor soul any more pain than he's already had—let him go in peace."

Just as angrily, Christopher spat back, jabbing a finger in Ezra's direction. "He ain't gonna die if he's looked after. Look at his wound."

The man shook his head. "I just take 'em where they tell me."

Christopher looked around. "Who do I have to talk to around here to see my friend gets a fair shake?"

The stretcher bearer jutted his chin toward a tired-looking man who appeared to be directing the incoming traffic. Christopher recognized the man as the hospital steward by the green half-chevron with the distinctive snake entwined staff on his sleeve and stomped over to the man, his determined movements causing a sudden dizziness that threatened to topple him over. He stopped and fought off a wave of nausea, then proceeded to make his way through the wounded lying on the ground almost shoulder to shoulder, filling the whole field.

"Say!" Christopher tugged on the steward's sleeve, earning a withering look, then continued before the man could object. "My pard over there's in the wrong place. He ain't gonna die."

A moment of compassion passed behind the man's eyes and then disappeared. "If they moved him to that corner, there's nothing we can do for him."

"Did you even look at where he got shot? It was a spent bullet. He bled pretty good, but the bullet didn't pierce his chest. He'll have a chance if you'll give it to him."

"How do you know it didn't pierce his chest? Have you had medical training?"

"The dang thing is poking out his body. You don't need training to see that."

The steward sighed and seemed to deflate some. He gave Christopher an appraising look that reminded him of the look Lieutenant Sutton had given him his first night of picket duty, when he'd shot at a cow, but he persisted. He wasn't the same wet-behind-the-ears kid he'd been back then.

"Well," the steward said with more than a trace of annoyance. "Lead the way."

Christopher made his way back to the spot where they'd put Ezra, looking back a couple times to make sure he was being followed. When they reached him, the steward took one look and just shook his head. Christopher understood; his friend was so pale he was almost white, and his jacket front was covered in blood.

Christopher knelt down and pulled back Ezra's jacket and shirt. The steward knelt down beside him and looked at the wound, which had by now completely clotted up around the mini-ball that protruded from it.

"Well, I'll be..." he said. "Not only did the bullet not penetrate, it formed an effective barrier against excessive bleeding." He looked at Christopher. "I won't lie to you; despite that your friend has lost a lot of blood. But, maybe there's hope for him after all." He slapped Christopher on the back, causing a bolt of agony across his left shoulder. "Good job, Corporal. You may have just saved this man's life."

The steward stood and flagged down an orderly. "Put this man in the queue to see a surgeon."

"Don't worry, pard," Christopher said, his voice catching. "We're gonna get you help. It'll be all right."

As Christopher returned to his spot with the lessor wounded, he couldn't help feeling a sense of satisfaction and relief. But, his last words to Ezra rattled around the back of his mind. Would it be all right? They'd gotten Parker help, but he had died anyway.

Christopher found a spot and sat down to wait. The volume of wounded coming into this hospital was overwhelming, and he knew it would be a long time before they could deal with anyone not already on death's door. Many of the surgeons and orderlies had been working almost non-stop for the last three days.

And this was not the only hospital set up for this battle.

As the hours passed, Christopher wondered how many of the walking wounded would still be that way by the time someone got around to seeing them. Many of the men were getting increasingly listless. The wound on Christopher's shoulder was aching and throbbing, and all the dried blood caused his shirt to stick to the wound, creating a tearing pain and renewed bleeding whenever he tried to move his arm.

An older man, maybe late twenties, came and sat next to Christopher. His head was swathed in a bloody bandage from which a thick shock of black hair poked out, and his eyes were a deep, vivid green. He introduced himself as Dylan Jones.

Welsh, Christopher thought. *That's okay. I won't hold it against him.*

"I tell you, I was kneeling down behind that little wall, thinking I was pretty safe. Then, when I poked me head up to take a shot—bang! A Minié ball hit me right upside the head. Damn near split my hat in two."

"Something similar happened to me once," Christopher said. "Took the top of my ear off." He pointed to the mangled ear and lifted his hair so the man could see the ragged scar that ran a couple inches along the side of his head.

"Well, I'll be. Good thing them rebs aren't better shots, isn't it?" Dylan laughed at his own joke, and Christopher smiled, thinking back to Red House and what it had been like to be that innocent.

After a while, Dylan started slurring his words and seemed to have trouble focusing. Then, he fell asleep.

Good, Christopher thought. The rest would do him good.

A young lad, no more than thirteen or fourteen, came by with a bucket of water, ladling out drinks. Christopher thought Dylan shouldn't miss the opportunity, no telling when someone would be by with water again. When he shook the man's shoulder, he wobbled and fell over.

Christopher stared at the body. He couldn't decipher what he saw. Dylan was all right. He just had a scratch, same as Christopher at Red House. He knelt down and shook the man's shoulder. Nothing. He tried to lift him back up to a sitting position, but it was like trying to set up a bag of flour. He put his ear to Dylan's chest. Nothing. At some point Dylan had stopped breathing.

Christopher sat back on his heels and bowed his head. They thought they were safe, but it was an illusion. Any of them could still die from this battle at any time—blood loss, an infection, or just falling asleep, never to wake again.

He looked around at the faces of the wounded men watching him. Curious, maybe a little afraid, their fragility hung over them like a poised fist. Christopher's arm throbbed, his shoulder burned, and his fingers felt thick and numb. He wondered if the cause of his death was already there, waiting to take him as soon as he closed his eyes.

No. He gritted his teeth and stood up, then stopped and waited until the dizziness past and he stopped swaying. Pointing at the water bucket, he asked the young lad, "Could you get us another one of those? And maybe a pot to boil it in? How about some clean bandages?"

The boy responded with a bobble of his head, somewhere between a nod and a shake, his eyes wide with fear and confusion. "I, I...others need water to..."

"It's all right," Christopher said in a more soothing tone. "We just need to clean our wounds while we're waiting. We don't want to get an infection."

The head bobble started to lean more toward a nod.

"You'd be helping the surgeons out. They would have less to do once they get around to seeing us if we're cleaned up. And hopefully we can prevent anyone from getting worse."

"I suppose I could get more water," the boy said. "But bandages are hard to come by. We've already had to take sheets from people's homes and tear them up, spare shirts, and undergarments, anything we can get. More's a comin', but no one knows when."

"That's okay. If you get us the water, we'll make due."

The boy's nod became a vigorous up and down motion that almost toppled his hat off his head. Then he ran off, the remaining water in the bucket he carried sloshing on the ground and his pant leg.

"Don't forget a pot for boiling!" Christopher yelled after him. He then turned his attention to the dozens of wounded men that lay or sat around him. "Well, pards, while he's off fetching the water, let's get a fire going."

"Fuck off, ya whippersnapper. We need to rest."

Christopher looked around to see if could tell who'd spoken. Since no one stood out in defiance, he spoke to the crowd.

"We need to get our wounds cleaned up the best we can to give us a fair shake. You can take your chances with the surgeon if you want, but I intend to walk out of this hospital."

"Ha!" came the immediate response. "What hospital. All I see is a few trees and a fence—and a whole passel of boys waitin' to get in that tent over there. We might as well just take it easy and nurse our wounds best we can. We're going to be here a while."

"That's what I'm saying." Christopher had identified the man responding and now addressed him directly. "While we're waiting, we should do something to improve our odds—clean up our wounds, bind them if we can. So we don't bleed out or our scratches get worse before someone can see them."

A blond man with a thick, short beard, speckled with dirt and blood, stood up next to Christopher. "I am wit you. What you say makes sense."

Christopher nodded and shook the man's hand, wincing as each up-down motion sent a bolt of pain shooting down his other arm. "Anyone else? If we all work together to help each other, it shouldn't take too much effort." He watched as the looks of doubt and confusion slowly gave way to nods of approval. There were still a few hold-outs, such as the first man who spoke out, but mostly, men came to accept the idea they could do something for themselves to make their plight less uncertain.

Those that were able went to work dismantling a nearby fence. One man used a bayonet to dig out a fire pit, and another gathered kindling and tinder to get the fire started. By the time the youth returned with a fresh bucket and pot, they had a good blaze going.

While the water was heating, everyone went to work tearing their shirts into strips to make bandages and wash cloths. They washed and dressed each other's wounds as best they could. Once cleaned, many of the wounds proved to be not that serious, and those men wandered off in search of their regiments. Some revealed more serious concerns, such as an exposed bone or bleeding that wouldn't stop, and Christopher was able to get the hospital steward to reassess those cases and get them re-prioritized.

As the sun set, torches and oil lamps were lit and placed around the entrance to the hospital tent. The steward came by and inspected what he called

Christopher's "walking wounded corps," most of whom were now resting as comfortably as was possible under the circumstances. He looked Christopher up and down where he lay, propped up on one elbow, and nodded approvingly. "You did good here, Corporal. I'll make sure the head surgeon is made aware of your efforts."

Christopher lay back. As he realized he could finally relax, a tiredness that made his eyes droop and his thoughts jumble overcame him. His wound still hurt like the dickens, and he could hardly move his left arm, but he felt that the cleaning and rebinding had helped. The throbbing had lessened considerably, and he thought his hand and fingers were a little less red and swollen.

"Thank you for the compliment, sir, but that's not necessary," he said sleepily. "I'm just glad we could do something for the boys." He closed his eyes and drifted off as the sun set on the third day of the Battle of Gettysburg.

SOMEONE SHAKING HIS good shoulder, causing spasms of pain in the wound on the other side, woke Christopher.

"Lay off ya dang fool," he slurred. "That hurts like Hades." He licked his lips and tried to swallow, but without success. He smacked his lips and grimaced. His tongue felt like an old leather shoe. "Ya got any water?"

It was still dark, and the man leaning over him was nothing but a shadow behind the oil lamp he carried. "There's water inside," the shadow said. "The surgeon will see you now."

The shadow helped pull Christopher up. Once standing, he saw it was the hospital steward, his uniform now a blood-spattered, rumpled mess. The bags under his eyes were so dark, they stood out even in the poor pre-dawn light. He followed the exhausted man into the tent.

Inside, the tent was illuminated by several oil lamps with steel reflectors to enhance the light. The space was big enough for several beds, occupied by the worse cases who still had a fighting chance (*in other words—officers*), and four operating tables, or at least doors and planks lain over saw horses that the surgeons used as such. Sleeping surgeons, snoring loudly in a state of unconsciousness deeper than mere sleep, their aprons and arms black with dried blood, occupied three of the tables. The air stank from the multitude of un-washed bodies that had come through there in the last couple days, leaving behind puddles of blood and bodily waste that no one had the time or energy to clean up.

Christopher's stomach churned, and he felt bile come up, burning his throat. For once he was thankful he had eaten nothing in the last twenty-four hours. He followed the steward to the only table still active, doing his best to step around the worst of the puddles.

The surgeon was an older man, with iron gray hair, a large gray mustache, and a pointed goatee. He hadn't shaved in several days, and his cheeks bristled with white whiskers. Christopher hadn't thought it possible, but the man looked even more tired than the steward. His eyes were blood-shot orbs at the center of blue-black skin so sunken he could see the outline of the sockets. The lines on his pale face so deep and dark, it looked like a porcelain vase that had been broken and badly glued back together.

"Remove your jacket, Corporal," he said in way of greeting. He didn't bother to ask where his wound was—the torn and blood-soaked shoulder of his jacket made that clear.

Christopher unbuttoned his jacket one-handed and shrugged it off. The surgeon took one look at the strip of shirt tightly bound around Christopher's chest and shoulder and turned to the steward. "Is this the one?" he asked. The steward nodded in response.

The surgeon turned back to Christopher. "I'm Dr. Kennawick. And you are?"

Christopher's pain and exhaustion had worn him down to the point it relaxed him before this officer, but he immediately stiffened at the sudden interest in his person. "Corporal Christopher Galloway of the 8th OVI, Company D, sir."

"Very good, Corporal Galloway. I understand you had something to do with these freshly bound wounds I've been seeing for the last couple of hours. Is that true?"

Christopher gave a slight nod. "Yes, sir. Me and the boys decided to help each other out while we was waiting."

"Yes, well, what everyone is telling me is one particular corporal—a slight fellow, but strong headed is how he was described...this one corporal organized the walking-wounded and had them building fires, boiling water, cutting up shirts and bandanas to make bandages, all manner of things they came here to have done for them. Now, they come in here, and there's not much for me to do but put on a fresh bandage, maybe apply a stitch or two, give them a dose of opium, and send them on their way. Are you trying to put me out of a job, Corporal?"

Shocked by a dose of adrenaline, Christopher snapped to attention. "No, sir! That was not my intention, sir!"

Kennawick laughed. "Relax, Corporal. I was kidding. You did me and my fellow doctors a great service. As you can see, a few of us are getting some much-needed sleep thanks to you."

"Sir?"

"I need not tell you, these last few days have seen some of the most brutal fighting of the war. The number of wounded has completely overwhelmed us. We haven't slept in days. The wounded just kept coming and coming." Kennawick's eyes lost their focus, as if he were looking at that unending stream of pain and suffering and not Christopher. "The men that come in here, no matter the wound, are scared and in need of assurance as much as they are physical care. We do the best we can, but it's rarely enough. These men put themselves in our hands, but we haven't time to do anything but lop off a limb, or administer a dose of opium, and move on to the next one. The men you inspired to help themselves weren't as afraid, they already had a pretty good idea of their state, having taken care of much of the work themselves. All we have had to do is put the finishing touches on the process. Thanks to you, several men will more than likely keep their limbs, and most will be back with their regiments in a fraction of the time if they'd been left to lie out in the dirt for hours on end letting bad humors take hold in their wounds.

"Tell me, how did you know to wash the wounds with hot water?"

Christopher shrugged with his good shoulder. "That's what my ma would always do when we got hurt. I noticed small cuts that I let go would sometimes hurt worse than the bigger ones she took care of. After two years of fighting, I seen it more times than I care to. Someone gets a flesh wound, doesn't seem like no big deal and then, next thing you know, they're dead. I just remembered those childhood scratches that my ma used to care for and applied the same idea here."

Kennawick was smiling. "In other words, your ma already knew what it's taken us two years of war to figure out. No one knows why—hell, we may never know. But, you're right, a clean wound is a healthy wound. You allow dirt or other foreign matter to get in it, the body can't handle it. I'm going to send a note to your commanding officer; you deserve a commendation for your efforts.

"Now, let me have a look at that shoulder."

Christopher took a dose of opium mixed with whiskey and Kennawick went to work on his shoulder. The man tugged and prodded and sometimes bolts of pain would find their way through the haze. Afterward, Christopher's shoulder was bound tight and felt even stiffer than before.

"That's the stitches I put in to hold the wound together. It limits your mobility, but allows the cut to heal faster. A couple weeks, you're be swinging a rifle again like it was nothing."

Christopher couldn't imagine ever feeling whole again, and he didn't want the surgeon writing Sawyer about him, but he was too tired to argue. An orderly led him to a spot under an oak tree where he lay down among hundreds of men in various states of consciousness. There he relaxed and let the effect of the drugs and exhaustion overcome him.

Chapter Fifteen

The following morning, Christopher's shoulder hurt with a throbbing pain that pulsed down his arm with each beat of his heart. They had given him a sling to wear and instructed him to keep his arm as immobile as possible for the next few days. But he wanted to know how bad it was. He wiggled his fingers and moved his arm around—first at the elbow, then the shoulder. Though they were still a little swollen, his fingers worked fine, and moving his elbow only seemed to increase the pain that was already there, but moving his arm at the shoulder created a sharp pain that made him cry out and left him light-headed. He took a pill from the small bottle of opium the grateful Dr. Kennawick had given him and thought of breakfast, finding Ezra, and finding the 8th—in that order.

Finding breakfast proved easy, there was a commissary wagon set up near the field hospital. He only had to stand in line for half an hour with several dozen other wounded and weary soldiers. After a breakfast of coffee, soft bread that was probably less than a week old, and a partially cooked piece of meat from a cow that had probably met his fate that morning, Christopher went back to the hospital tent to inquire about Ezra.

To his surprise, the yard he'd waited in yesterday was now filled with Confederate wounded. After getting over the shock of finding himself surrounded by gray and butternut uniforms, he learned Ezra had probably been taken to the nearest depot and transported to Taneytown, Maryland. He figured Colonel Sawyer would get a report on all the regiment's wounded faster than he could hitch a ride down to Maryland, so that just left finding the 8th.

He spent the morning wandering through the post-battle chaos of troops marching hither and yon; roads clogged with artillery batteries, supply wagons, and ambulances; and everywhere men separated from their units, some wounded, others wandering with blank expressions on faces blackened by dirt and gunpowder.

Many officers rode through the mess with an air like they knew what was going on and where they were going, but they didn't have time to stop and talk to a confused and overwhelmed lowly corporal.

Christopher decided to follow the empty ambulances because he assumed they would be heading back to the battlefield to pick up more wounded. He followed the traffic for almost an hour, but it was slow going, and it looked as if they were following the road the long way around. He suspected the battlefield was on the other side of the ridgeline to his left, and, knowing how spread out the fighting had been, he figured if he crossed over he'd come out somewhere on the Federal line—hopefully near where the 8th had fought.

The climb was not as bad as he feared but still left him light-headed and out of breath. When he reached the crest, he found himself with a commanding view of much of the battlefield. The ridge on the other side sloped down a couple hundred feet to the valley floor, covered with the mangled bodies of men and horses.

He'd seen his share of violent death and its aftermath in the last two years, but the sheer volume of what lay before him made Christopher stop and gasp. The corpses numbered in the thousands, spread out as far as he could see and, he suspected, even farther. A deep sadness overwhelmed him, and he almost sat down right there. The thought of finding the 8th or doing much of anything suddenly seemed like too much effort.

He watched an army of caregivers, both army and civilian, as they swarmed the field, doing what they could to slow the ever-rising death toll as the wounded that still lay exposed under the hot July sun bled out or died from exposure. They carried canteens and satchels full of first-aid supplies, or stretchers, and were going from body to body in search of those still living. It was a gruesome task, and many of those battlefield angels had wrapped cloths around their noses and mouths.

In the distance, he could just make out the remnants of the enemy battle line. It looked to be still manned. But they were letting the caregivers go about their business in peace. As they should—most of the wounded that lay out in the valley were theirs.

Most of those civilians had just had their lives violated by a massive battle that had brought destruction to their town and much of the countryside. But, there they were, now offering their services to the authors of that destruction. Christopher was moved by their Christian charity, but the sadness still lingered, and with it a sense of ennui that seemed to rob his limbs of all strength.

Despite the scene before him, Christopher felt there was still too much indifference to the continual suffering of the soldier. Otherwise, they'd be trying much harder to bring the war to an end. Everyone was too wrapped up in their sense of honor. Their side was right, and the other side was wrong, and they didn't care how many men had to die to prove it.

He sat down on a rock, feeling the July sun rising high in the sky behind him, bringing with it a summer heat that would cause the bodies to blacken and swell long before they could be buried. It was a final insult to the brave men who fell here over the last three days.

Then he thought of the suffering his own family was going through. No one was free of the consequences of this war. He would need to write them as soon as possible and let them know he was all right.

Christopher could see the rock wall off to his right, so he was farther south than where they'd fought the last two days. He struggled to his feet and began the hike downhill in that direction, hoping to find the bulge in the line that wrapped around the hills at the end of this ridge. If they were still on the field, that was where he'd find the 8th.

Soon he was in the valley walking along the rock wall, behind which lay a concentration of bodies and discarded equipment. For two days, they'd held that line and now commanded the entire field. The aftermath looked horrible, but it gave him a small sense of satisfaction to be on the winning side for a change.

He reached the bulge in the line, but the 8th had moved on. A sergeant, grimy and blood-spattered but with no visible wounds, sat on the rock wall trying to light a pipe. Christopher could see a tremor in his hands was preventing him from getting a good enough strike with the lucifer to ignite the sulphur tip. He took the match, struck it on a rock, and held it out, cupping it with his other hand to protect it from the wind. The man leaned forward and sucked until the tobacco in his pipe glowed and began to smoke. He nodded his appreciation as he furiously puffed away. So far, neither man had said a word.

Finally Christopher spoke. "You doin' all right, pard?"

The sergeant nodded, the stem of his pipe quivering in his still shaking hand. "I'm fine." He sighed as if disappointed in his own lie. "That was a tough one," he said.

Christopher's eyes lit on a bloated torso. He looked around and wondered where the man's legs were. "I don't know if we can take much more like it."

The sergeant's eyes got hard as he fixed them on Christopher. "We'll take whatever they throw at us, we will. And we won't quit 'til the job is done." He tried to spit out a speck of tobacco that'd stuck to his tongue, but lacked the saliva to do the job.

Christopher felt chastened, and his eyes dropped to the ground. "I reckon you're right."

The sergeant continued to suck on his pipe as if he needed to finish the bowl as quick as possible. It took several minutes for his eyes to return to the vacant stare he'd worn when Christopher came upon him.

"Say," Christopher said in a soothing tone. "You wouldn't happen to know where the 8th Ohio's got off to, would you?"

Christopher waited, but the man continued to suck on his pipe, looking out over the field. He'd almost given up when the man finally spoke. "Were them the damned fools that marched out on the field yesterday and did a left wheel in the middle of the rebel attack?"

Christopher wanted to point out that the rebels on their front had already retreated when the 8th moved forward but didn't want to agitate the man again, so he just nodded. "That was us."

The sergeant shrugged. "They collected their dead and headed out over that away," he said, pointing over his shoulder with the stem of his pipe.

Christopher felt a wave of optimism and thanked the sergeant. He headed in the direction the sergeant had pointed and eventually came upon a field next to a farm house that was now full of freshly dug graves. There he saw many familiar faces. He looked for Captain Reid but couldn't see him anywhere, so he looked for Charlie Locker but couldn't find him either. He looked for the Jump brothers without any luck. Finally, he spotted First Sergeant Virgil Ennis, who was also sporting a new sling, but over his right arm instead of his left.

Christopher walked up to the sergeant who was resting under a tree.

"Sergeant. It looks like between the two of us we can muster up a full set of hands."

Ennis peeked at Christopher's sling from beneath the brim of his forage cap. "Corporal Galloway. I was starting to think you were one of the dead too mangled to identify."

"Nah, someone picked me and Ezra up and took us back to a field hospital. I got patched up and sent back. Ezra was a little worse off, so he's going to be out of it a while."

Ennis nodded. "Uh-huh. There's a lot of that after yesterday."

"Say, you seen Captain Reid?"

"He's still getting patched up, I reckon. I don't think nary a one of us made it off the field yesterday without a new hole somewhere—some worse than others."

Christopher knelt. "How about Charlie Locker? You seen him?"

"That stubborn Dutchman. He's limping around here somewhere. Got a calf shot all to hell, but he won't go get it looked at. Afraid they'll want to take his leg."

"I'll talk to him. If the bone's not broken, they won't take his leg unless it gets infected—and there's less chance it'll get infected if he lets a surgeon take care of it."

Suddenly it occurred to Christopher that he had no equipment, no hat, not even a shirt under his torn and bloody jacket. "I'm going to need a new rifle and some traps."

"There's a pile over there. Help yourself. Check in with Lieutenant Manahan; I don't expect to see Captain Reid back today. I'll change your status to present and accounted for and transfer Ezra to Company Q."

"Thanks, Sergeant."

Christopher walked over to the pile of equipment. He found a rifle that was relatively clean, its owner probably having fallen early in the fight. Then, he dug up a belt that fit, and draped a cartridge box and canteen over his right shoulder. He'd already cut off the left strap of his suspenders, he would have to cut the strap off the cartridge box and attach it to his belt—he wouldn't be putting anything on his left shoulder for a while.

He found Lieutenant Manahan sleeping in the shade on the edge of a wood lot. He let the lieutenant sleep and went looking for Charlie Locker. The camp was quiet. No one was gambling or swapping stories around the fire; no games were being played in the open field. Some had erected dog-tents, and men lay in them resting. Those without tents found shade where they could and apparently intended to sleep the day away.

Charlie was sitting by a fence, gingerly removing a bloody rag that was tied around his lower leg. Christopher knelt down next to his old messmate and shook his head. "Charlie, Charlie, Charlie. You need to take better care of yourself. We can't afford to lose you, you old *fiesling*." Christopher hadn't forgotten the German word for bastard, having earned the moniker himself during training at Camp Dennison.

Charlie looked up and smiled. "Christopher Galloway. I'm glad to see you alive."

"Glad to be alive, Charlie. How's the leg?"

"It hurts is how it is. At least the bleeding has almost stopped."

"You need to get it looked at—make sure there're no pieces of cloth or metal still in there. Otherwise you'll lose that leg for sure."

'Ya, ya. I'll do that as soon as I can. It's just we're shorthanded here if you hadn't noticed. Gridley got hit pretty bad. They took him back to a field hospital. Same with the captain. Ennis has been directing burial details all morning. Bill Wells is around here somewhere, but he hasn't been sergeant for long. We're all shot up, Chris, and someone has to keep the company moving.

Christopher looked around at the resting men. "They ain't moving now."

"No. And that is why I'm going to take care of my leg now. I think we're all done for the day."

"Well, here. Let me take a look." Christopher knelt down, wiped Charlie's wound off with a cloth wetted from Charlie's canteen, and looked for any sign of foreign matter. There were two angry red holes on either side of his calf, the edges of which were swollen and puckered. But, as well as Christopher could tell, there was nothing in the wound that would cause it to become infected. They seeped blood, but there didn't appear to be any danger of blood loss.

He wrapped Charlie's leg with the tail of the sergeant's shirt and tied it off tight. "Next ambulance comes by that's not too full, you hop on and go have that looked at."

"Yes, sir...*Corporal*."

Christopher bristled. Rank ain't got nothing to do with it. I don't want you to lose that leg, ya here?"

Charlie smiled and nodded. "Yes *mein* friend, you order out of love, not authority."

"Uh, yeah...I guess. Speaking of which, here, I got a little spot of opium. Take a pill. It'll help with the pain."

"Ah, you are an angel of mercy, Christopher Galloway."

Christopher settled down next to Charlie. The haversack he'd taken out of the pile was empty, but Charlie had a piece of hardtack he broke in half with his bayonet and shared with his friend. They each took an opium pill and were soon asleep, their hardtack half eaten.

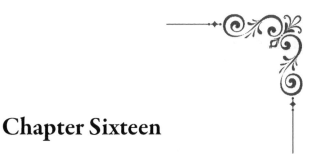

Chapter Sixteen

The crack of thunder woke Christopher. Shivering, he sat up and rubbed his arms. The sudden downpour had soaked his clothes, and he had no blanket. He remembered they had left their knapsacks behind the line when on the skirmish line. Hopefully, someone had thought to retrieve them when they gathered up the regiment's equipment. He went back to the equipment pile and rooted around until he found his knapsack. It took a while—there were still many unclaimed knapsacks.

Sometime while he'd slept, a wagon had come up and resupplied the regiment with food and ammunition. Now they would be ready to move when the order came.

Christopher had his half of the dog-tent he normally shared with Ezra in his knapsack. He found two sticks, and, using a rope and a couple stakes, he and Charlie created a lean-to, under which they spent the rest of the day and night.

The following morning, Christopher and Charlie walked out to the battlefield where all but the enemy dead and unidentified bodies had been removed. Those remaining were lined up in long rows and work details were digging trenches in which to bury them. Among this morbid scene wandered curious citizens with handkerchiefs over their mouths and noses, their eyes wide with horror.

Souvenir hunters carrying large burlap sacks over their shoulders also littered the field, picking up discarded clothing and gear, spent bullets and anything else they could find. Christopher came up behind one man bent over going through the pockets of a headless corpse and kicked the man in his ample rear. The man pitched head first onto the bloody corpse he was robbing, soiling his tan suit and straw boater hat. He recoiled from the corpse and scrambled to his feet, his face flushed beneath the streaks of gore than dripped down his cheeks and beard. His eyes flashed as he spun on Christopher.

"How dare you—"

Christopher took a step forward and grabbed the man by the lapel. "How dare I? How dare you, you worthless piece of—"

"Chris!" Charlie put a hand on Christopher's arm. "You made your point." He then looked at the other man. "You sir, are a grave robber—the lowest form of thief. I suggest you absquatulate before I let my companion go, and he has his way with you."

The man looked in Christopher's eyes and saw the truth of his predicament there. He saw a man to whom violent death was commonplace, who'd partaken in the battle that had produced all these mangled bodies. So far, the blood on his face was not his own, and he preferred to keep it that way.

"I meant nothing by it," he whined. "I just got carried away is all. I took nothing off these fine men. Honest."

"See, Chris. He didn't take anything."

Christopher let go of the man's lapel. "Then, like my pard said—absquatulate!" Christopher shoved his face in the other man's, who responded by stumbling back several steps, tripping over the feet of a corpse, and falling hard on his butt. Moaning, he crawled over to his hat, shoved it on his head, got up, and took off running.

Christopher laughed at the man, but there was no humor in it.

"Vultures feeding on the carrion of battle is what they are. I don't blame your anger, Chris. But sometimes restraint is the better part of valor."

"I heard that before, is that a German saying?"

"Shakespeare."

"Oh," Christopher sneered, wrinkling his nose.

Charlie gave him a half grin. "What, you don't like the bard."

"I had to read a couple of his sonnets in school. Didn't have a clue what the damn fool was saying most of the time."

Charlie laughed. "Few do is my guess."

———— ❦ ————

MISSING MEN OF THE 8th straggled in throughout the day. In the early afternoon Joe and Nathan Jump appeared. Nathan had a torn and bloody pant leg, beneath which was a fresh bandage. Joe seemed none the worse for wear, but was sticking with his little brother as if the two were glued together.

Charlie went to help First Sergeant Ennis, and Christopher swapped stories with the Jumps. He told them about his own and Ezra's wounds and their experience in the field hospital. After taking a grazing wound to the thigh, Nathan made his way back to the rear with Joe's help. Joe carried both their rifles while Nathan leaned on him the whole way.

"Glad to see you boys back in the fight," Christopher said. We get moving soon, we can finish up ol' Lee and his boys and be home by Christmas.

"Yeah, I heard that last year after Antietam," Joe said bitterly. "We don't get moving soon, he's going to get away again."

"You okay to march?" Christopher asked Nathan, who nodded in response.

"I'll make do."

"I have some opium if the pain gets too much."

Both the Jumps eyes got big. "How do you rate? They were just about out of any painkiller except some local stump-liquor when we was there."

"I helped out a bit while I was waiting. The head surgeon was appreciative."

The Jumps nodded in unison. "Make yourself useful," Joe said. "That's the way to get ahead. Hell, we'll be calling you lieutenant before this war's over."

Christopher shook his head. "Not if I have anything to say about it."

SOMETIME MID-AFTERNOON they got orders to move out. Anyone with a leg wound, such as Nathan Jump and Charlie Locker, were allowed to ride in the supply wagons. Everyone else had to march. Christopher was allowed to store his knapsack in a wagon. He'd rigged his cartridge box to ride on his belt, so he had nothing over his left shoulder. But, it didn't take long for his rifle to get heavy carrying it one-handed.

They were quite a sight as they marched down the road toward Maryland. Most of the men had spare shirts and undergarments, but not jackets or pants. Almost every man in the 8th had a ragged, blood-stained hole somewhere on his clothes. They limped and shambled along, heads down and shoulders drooping. More than one man was yelled at by a sergeant or officer for letting his rifle drag in the dirt. Fortunately, they only marched a few miles before stopping for the night. Even so, it was well after dark when they stopped, and soon the entire regiment, except for those on picket, was fast asleep.

It was like that for the next several days. They would march a few miles, stop and rest—sometimes for a whole day or longer. No one seemed in much of a hurry to catch Lee before he made it back over the Potomac River. But, with each passing day, the regiment seemed to grow stronger, the men no longer shuffled and winced as they marched. Instead, their strides grew strong and their backs straight. The only downside was the rain.

It started raining on the second day of the march. It was a summer rain that hit with fierce intensity. At first Christopher appreciated the downpour as it washed out much of the surface grime on his skin and clothing. But, then the road got muddy, and soon that mud was sticking to his feet. Each step seemed to add to the clump of mud that clung to his shoes and pants legs. Men were having to stop to retrieve shoes that had become mired in the muck, keeping up a steady stream of curse words the entire time.

By the end of the march Christopher's thighs trembled with exhaustion. It was too wet to build a fire. His knapsack had sat in the wagon's bottom in a puddle of water all day, soaking its entire contents, including his blanket and shelter half.

During that second day, they passed through Taneytown, Maryland, where the orderly told him Ezra had been sent. He wondered how his best friend was faring and asked Captain Reid if he could make a detour by the hospital to find out, but the captain denied his request. The old Christopher probably would have gone anyway, he thought. But the old Christopher had never known the pain and exhaustion he now felt. His shoulder throbbed, his muscles ached, he had a chill from his wet, torn clothing, and worse, since running out of opium, he had a pounding headache.

They didn't move out the next day. Instead, they waited for the rain to pass and spent the day drying out, resting, and cleaning up. They moved out a couple hours before dawn the following day, and, with the rising sun promising a respite from the rain, they entered the town of Frederick, Maryland.

As they marched down the main street, Christopher became self-conscious of his appearance. The sole of his right shoe was coming undone at the toe and flopped with a loud clap at every step, and his jacket and pants were threadbare and sun-bleached, torn in several places and stained with his and Ezra's blood.

In contrast, the New York militia occupying Frederick that lined the street to salute the passing veterans wore new uniforms of a deep, rich blue, with leathers of gleaming black patent, and bayonets that reflected the light of the rising sun with an intensity that hurt the eyes. The militia stood at attention with their rifles at shoulder arms the entire time the Second Corps marched through town, only moving to present arms as each regiment's colors passed by.

Someone started singing *The Battle Cry of Freedom,* and it spread throughout the corps. Soon, a thousand voices were echoing off the brick buildings and cobbled streets of Frederick. When they got to the fourth verse, the men shouted out the line:

And we'll hurl the rebel crew from the land we love the best!
Shouting the battle cry of freedom!

Christopher could have sworn some of the militia boys were crying—he almost was himself, his voice catching on the last chorus until it was just a whisper.

While we rally round the flag, boys, we rally once again,
Shouting the battle cry of freedom...

ON THE OTHER SIDE OF Frederick, they started hearing artillery fire in the distance. As they marched the sound grew louder, and they were finding it hard to breath or think of anything else. The distant booms, like thunder on a cloudless day, carried with them the promise of death and destruction.

Officers rode up and down the column, urging the men to pick up the pace. Those that could, did. Christopher felt it—there was an eagerness in everyone's step born on a hope that this might be it, the battle to end the war. The recent victory was uplifting, but it wasn't enough. They had to win the war. Then they could go home. Home to loved ones, clean clothes, plenty of food to eat, and no more fear of a sudden and violent death.

Someone tried to start up *The Battle Hymn of the Republic,* but most of the boys were too winded for it to spread. The singer and the few that joined him only lasted a couple of choruses. They marched for several miles in silent determination before the adrenaline wore off, and men started to drag. By late afternoon, the column was back to a bedraggled route step when finally someone called a halt. With a sudden burst of energy, men went to work gathering firewood, building fires, and boiling salt pork. As the sun began its descent in the west, Christopher settled down with Joe and Nathan Jump (all that remained of his mess) for a meal of salt pork with hardtack fried in the fat rendered from the pork, washed down with copious amounts of coffee that had a salty flavor from their having used the same pot to boil off most of the salt from the pork before frying. Then, using his hat and rolled up jacket as a pillow (his knapsack still being in a wagon somewhere), Christopher fell asleep.

Christopher was dreaming of Spaulding again, of starving and helplessness, of Daniel and rows of bloated bodies when the bugle call for assembly sounded through the camp. Someone poked him in the leg with a piece of firewood, and he jerked awake. Wide-eyed and out of breath, he looked around at the activity of an army preparing to march. Everyone appeared to be ignoring him, but he knew that they'd all seen his outburst. He felt his cheeks burn with embarrassment as he struggled to his feet, still favoring his left arm. Joe gave him a wordless nod, but the rest just continued donning traps and kicking out the fire.

So much for being free of the dreams, he thought.

They marched a few more hours, then stopped again, just as the sun set.

THE NEXT MORNING, THE sound of artillery fire was closer and more intense, sometimes sounding like a constant roll of thunder that seemed to go on for minutes. Christopher was sure he could smell a hint of gun smoke on the morning breeze.

After marching down the road in columns for a couple hours, the entire Second Corps spread out across a freshly plowed field in several battle lines. The 8th was in the second line. It was raining again, and the fresh-turned earth made a fine mud. Once mixed with the many puddles of standing water, it created a soupy mess that coated the thousands of men and horse-drawn cannon. Christopher could feel it oozing into his shoes, soaking his socks, and squishing between his toes. Once again, it felt as if he had an extra ten pounds on each foot, and the lines buckled as men stumbled and army mules protested the extra weight they had to pull.

They were almost to the edge of the field when the blast of several hundred rifles appeared on the tree line ahead, felling several men in the first line of battle. Christopher had been so focused on reaching more solid ground that the sudden onslaught took him by surprise. He stopped, ducking and cringing, and the man behind him in the second rank stumbled to keep from running into him.

Christopher made a quick apology and hurried to catch up to the line as best he could with the blocks of mud on his feet. He watched as the first battle line fired a volley into the trees, followed by a slow, awkward bayonet charge. He focused his attention on the trees, but there were no more volleys from the enemy. By the time the first line reached the tree line, they were already gone.

Christopher thought this would be like that first year of the war, with them chasing an enemy that was always just beyond reach. Then a cavalry brigade came riding up the road from the rear, yipping and cheering like a bunch of wild Indians. They were soon out of sight, and Christopher expected to hear gun fire any minute, but it was almost a half hour before there was the sound of small arms fire in the distance ahead. By then they had left the open field behind and were struggling to keep their lines straight as they worked their way through the woods.

They met the returning cavalry on the other side of the woods. Given the speed at which the enemy had retreated, Christopher assumed that they, too, were cavalry—Lee's rear guard, meant to slow them down long enough for the rest of the army to escape across the Potomac. Like hounds on the scent, the men perked up, kicked the mud off their feet, and pushed ahead. *This is it*, Christopher thought. *The end of this war lies just ahead.*

But it was not to be—at least not that day. Other than a series of running skirmishes between cavalry, there was no more contact with the enemy that day. Once again they went into camp with the setting sun, eating a quick meal, and collapsing into the deep sleep of utter exhaustion.

The next day was a repeat of the last, with the corps spreading out into battle lines. But, now Christopher was sure they were close. He could feel the river somewhere ahead by a slight drop in temperature. They would catch the Army of Northern Virginia in mid-crossing and annihilate them.

They were crossing another field, with another patch of woods at its edge. The 8th was once again in the second battle line. Christopher watched the first line enter the woods and disappear behind the foliage. He was squeezing and rubbing his rifle, and it was all he could do not to rush ahead. Soon, their line reached the trees and stopped. Christopher could see the first battle line had also stopped and was digging trenches. They were going into a defensive position!

"Captain Reid! Why aren't they attacking?"

"Quiet, Galloway."

"But—"

"I said quiet! It's none of your concern."

Christopher could see activity on the other side of the woods. The cavalry appeared to be engaged.

He heard the gunfire rattling like rain on a tin roof and saw glimpses of blue cloth amid the swirling white smoke. Why weren't they moving forward to engage?

After a few minutes the skirmish stopped, and all was quiet. Christopher could hear the sounds of digging, the murmurs of men voicing their frustration, flags snapping as they caught a sudden breeze. Then, the bugle call to advance.

He watched the front line climb over the entrenchments they had just been working on and exit the woods. Then his line moved forward and took their place. Captain Reid passed down the order for them to continue digging the entrenchments. As Christopher dug one-handed with his bayonet, he kept looking up trying to see what was going on. The enemy was just across the next field. Beyond that he could see glimpses of blue water through the trees, shimmering in the sun. They must be somewhere near the ford.

The first battle line exchanged volleys with the enemy line, supported by artillery brought up while they were waiting, but they did not press the attack. As he dug, Christopher watched the sun waning in the west. Soon, it would be too late, and the enemy would once again disappear into the night.

There was all the makings of a great battle, with the enemy trapped between them and the river. If they attacked in force, there would be nowhere for them to go.

Once the parapet before them was high enough, the men stopped digging. Christopher sat in their entrenchment and watched as the first battle line, supported by dismounted cavalry and artillery, exchanged fire with the enemy, dug in on the other side of the field, until the sun set.

As he watched their opportunity slip away, his breathing became more ragged, and he clinched his rifle so tight his right hand hurt. Once it was dark, he sank down in the trench with his back against the wall, rested his good elbow on his knee, and hung his head between his shoulders. Now there would be more attacks on Virginia, more counter-attacks into Maryland or Pennsylvania, more men would die, and it would go on and on until there was nothing left.

No wonder they were instituting a draft. They would need it to replace all the dead and maimed men they were creating.

Chapter Seventeen

T he next day, they marched to the ford where the discarded equipment, bodies, and wounded men left behind told the tale of a desperate effort to cross the Potomac under fire. They policed the area, rounding up prisoners and helping the wounded, and stayed there until the following evening, when they headed toward Harpers Ferry. On the way, they passed the Antietam battlefield, and Christopher was able to steal away that evening to go visit his brother's grave.

It was dark by the time he arrived at Roulette's farm. He stumbled around until he found the barn that had been used for a field hospital. From there he could work his way along the fence until he reached the orchard where the 8th's fallen had been laid to rest. He moved as carefully as he could through the dark orchard, tripping on roots and bumping his shins on the wooden planks made into headstones. He stopped to light a candle and began reading the names. When he found Daniel's, his breath caught in his throat, and his hands shook so badly he almost dropped the candle.

Christopher dropped to his knees next to the grave, still void of vegetation except for some weeds and a few clumps of grass. Shoving his fingers into the dirt, he scooped up a handful and squeezed it to his breast. *Danny. Oh, Danny, why did you have to leave me?* Tears coursed down his cheeks, but he didn't move a muscle or make a sound as he knelt there reliving that awful day.

He dropped back down into a sitting position and threw the dirt back on the grave. "Well, brother. You would not be pleased with the way the war is going. Even when we win, we lose. We keep having all these, 'last big battles,' where the big bugs get a bunch of us killed for no good reason. We can't give up now, I know that. We've come too far. Too much blood's been spilled.

We have to see this through. But, oh Lord, how I wish I could tell them all to go to the devil and just go home. Ma and Da miss you. Lizzy misses you. Little Becky and Rachel...well, in some ways they miss you most of all, though they can soldier on the way only small children can. The rest of us are a mess. Damn this war. Damn the South. Damn stupid generals and politicians. Damn it all to hell." He stopped and took a breath. "I wish you were here..."

Christopher's voice faded away, and he sat in silence until the dew soaked through his pants. As he scrambled to his feet, still favoring his left arm, a wind came up, and a low moan made its way across the orchard-turned-graveyard. Christopher thought maybe it was Daniel's way of telling him he understood and that he wished he could be there, too.

Christopher made his way down the farm lane, and he realized he was going the wrong direction when he came to the plain above the sunken road, now known by all as the Bloody Lane. In the meager starlight, he could make out the shape of the landscape, and his imagination filled it once again with lines of men, marching toward a rebel-filled lane, stepping over their comrades as they fell. The mournful cry of the wind continued, maybe even intensified.

Christopher could see in the distance the winking of lights from the windows of farmhouses. He couldn't imagine how anyone could live in this God-forsaken area, cursed by the thousands of violent deaths it had witnessed.

He made his way down to the main road, headed back toward Sharpsburg, and found his way back to the road he'd followed from where they had made camp. He arrived shortly before dawn and collapsed next to a fire pit, not having set up a tent before he left, and slept a dreamless, deep sleep until reveille two hours later.

THEY SPENT TWO DAYS camped near Harpers Ferry, resting, foraging, gambling, drinking, and doing whatever else a soldier thought he could get away with while not campaigning. Many men suffered from great quantities of pent-up aggression and could not stay still. They were constantly on the prowl, foraging for anything that wasn't nailed down, or playing rounders, or putting on boxing or wrestling matches. Those not actively playing were drinking and gambling on the outcome of the games and matches. Others, particularly those nursing injuries, were content to laze around the camp when not on picket duty or policing their company area. They grouped together near a simmering coffee pot, mending clothes, whittling, reading, or just idling the hours daydreaming of home. No matter their background, there were three things they all had in common: gambling, drinking, and gossiping. Christopher was still avoiding alcohol, and he had gambled away all his available cash and was unwilling to go into debt, but he was not immune to gossiping any more than any other soldier.

The two biggest rumors going around were, one, Lee was somewhere in the Shenandoah and that soon they would march out in pursuit, and two, that they would send veteran troops to New York to help quell the draft riots.

The morning of their second day by Harpers Ferry, Christopher was drinking a cup of coffee while Charlie Locker read aloud the news from a New York paper he'd traded for that morning.

"These riots in New York are terrible. Do these people think they are better than us? Too good to fight?" Charlie complained.

Christopher nodded and frowned in agreement, but was trying not to smile. He thought the way Charlie said the word "good" was funny. It sounded like "goot," as in "Foraging was profitable last night—the loot was goot." Christopher tried to suppress a giggle, but it burst out with a mouthful of coffee. Unfortunately, Charlie was reading the description of a lynching that took place during one of the riots, and the German's eyes flashed with anger.

"Christopher! You think this is funny?"

Christopher shook his head, but was coughing too hard from swallowing the coffee the wrong way to respond.

"I am no champion of the black man, that is for sure. But, what they did to this poor man was barbaric! How can we say we are better than the savage when there are men that will act like this? And you! You should be ashamed!"

A familiar voice came from behind Christopher. "Aw, come on, Charlie, you know Chris is one of the biggest nigger lovers in the army. He was probably just thinking of a funny story and ignoring you completely."

Christopher spun around. "Ezra!"

There stood Ezra Rouse, in a new uniform, complete with shiny black belt and cartridge box and a rifle so new it oozed packing grease around the breach and barrel. Christopher stood, and the two friends exchanged a hug, then quickly broke away, grimacing from their still-healing wounds.

"When did you get out of the hospital? How did you get here? You missed a wet, muddy march. Then we just let Lee's rear guard slip away back into Virginia." Christopher waved his right hand in frustration.

"Slow down, Chris," Charlie broke in. "Let Ezra get comfortable. Here. Come sit. Take off those traps and get comfortable. Coffee?"

Ezra lay his rifle down, keeping the breach side up out of the dirt. He removed all his equipment and unbuttoned his jacket, wincing repeatedly as he moved. Finally, he sunk down to the ground, sighing with relief, and pulled his tin cup out of his haversack.

"I just got out of the hospital the other day and caught a ride down here on a supply wagon. I tell you, it wasn't fun. Every bump hurt like Hades, but here I am. Spent the last hour wandering the camp looking for the 8th."

"It's good you're here," Charlie said, and Christopher snickered. Both men gave him a funny look before Ezra continued.

"The doc said I was one lucky cuss cause that bullet didn't even break a rib. It just smacked me in the chest and stayed there. Course, I still could have bled out on the field if you hadn't gotten me back to the hospital, Chris."

Christopher shook his head. "Wasn't me. I tried, but passed out trying to haul your fat ass back behind the line. Someone else came along and picked us both up and loaded us on a meat wagon."

Ezra cocked his head at Christopher. "You hit, too?"

Christopher nodded. "Left shoulder. Cut my cartridge box strap clean in two."

"Looks like you can move your arm okay."

"Just scraped a little off the top. Kinda like my ear." Christopher's fingers brushed the flat top of his left ear. "See any other Company D boys in the hospital?"

Ezra nodded, then looked down. "Gridley was there. He was in a bad way, but he held on for several days. One night, he'd just had enough and never woke back up."

Christopher felt a pang of sorrow. Gridley had just been promoted to sergeant, and it was a well-deserved and long-overdue promotion as far as Christopher was concerned. Gettysburg was his first battle as sergeant—and his last.

"Well, what's the news? You pick up any good gossip back in the land of big bugs and Sunday soldiers?"

Ezra nodded. "Word is Lee's in the Shenandoah. We'll probably try to catch him there."

Christopher dismissed that with a wave of his hand. "We heard the same thing. I mean something good."

"Well," Ezra said, leaning forward and looking both men in the eye before continuing. "We may not be going with them."

"What? Why not?"

"Well..." Ezra smirked. "They say they're gonna send western troops to New York to stop the riots—western troops from the Army of the Potomac, not from the West. Probably Ohio and Indiana regiments."

"Why western troops?"

Ezra shrugged. "I guess they figure we won't hesitate to bust New York skulls if we have to."

"They got a point there," Christopher said, and the three men laughed.

Ezra continued. "I tell you, iffen they do send us to New York, I'm gonna get me one of those New York City whores."

Christopher felt his cheeks flush, and he found something interesting in the fire to occupy his gaze.

"Careful, Ezra," Charlie warned. "You don't want to catch the venereal disease."

"I'll be all right. I'll wash up afterward."

Charlie looked at him skeptically. "If it was that easy, there wouldn't be so many cases vexing our hospital corps."

"They probably won't send us, anyway," Christopher said.

"Well, pard, if they do, we're gonna have a good time, that's for sure. That New York is one big city—even bigger than Cincinnati!"

Outwardly, Christopher laughed with Ezra. But, at the same time he worried about the temptations of a place as wicked as they said New York

City was, with its many brothels and drinking houses, and gangs of pug-uglies roaming the streets armed with knives and clubs.

THE NEXT DAY, THEY left for the Shenandoah. They marched twenty miles a day over the hilly countryside in grueling heat, barely stopping long enough for the men to refill their canteens. Soon soldiers were dropping from heat exhaustion at an alarming rate. But they pushed on, leaving it up to the chaplains and medical personnel to help the fallen soldiers.

At first, Ezra kept up, talking about what they would do in New York and joking how it would take more than a summer stroll along the countryside to slow him down. But, after a few miles, he stopped talking. Christopher could tell his pard was hurting. The vacant stare and the sheen of sweat that covered Ezra's face was from more than just the heat.

Sometime that afternoon Ezra collapsed. One minute he was walking along, head down, shoulders slumped, like so many of the boys that afternoon. Then he stopped. He didn't look up or say anything. He just stood in the middle of the road as soldiers streamed around him on both sides. Then, slowly at first, like a tree being cut down, he pitched forward. Christopher reached out to catch him, but there was little he could do to slow Ezra's fall.

"Ezra!"

The cold dread of the battlefield seized Christopher chest at the sight of his prostrate friend. He threw down his and Ezra's rifles and dropped to his knees.

"Ez. Ez. Are you all right?" He shook Ezra's shoulder and got a low groan in response. Christopher released some of his anxiety with a sharp exhalation. Then he rolled Ezra over, doing his best to support his friend's head as he did so.

Christopher shook Ezra's canteen. It was empty. He shook his own canteen and could tell from the weight and the sound that there was only a couple swigs left. He pulled the cork with his teeth and put the canteen to Ezra's lips. "Here ya go, pard. Drink it all up."

Ezra drank and seemed to recover somewhat. He looked around in confusion. "What am I doing down here?" he asked.

"Nappin," Christopher replied, smiling. "That's Ez, always shirking when there's work to be done."

Ezra gave a half smile. "I ain't no beat." His voice was raspy, and he still seemed listless.

Christopher knew it would take more than the few sips of water from his canteen to rouse his friend. He looked around for help. But they'd been straggling and were at the back of the column, surrounded by strangers. "Anybody spare a swig from your canteen?"

His query caused heads to turn away and a quickening of pace from those around him. "Come on, boys! Can't you help a fallen comrade?"

"Ain't no one got any more water, boy," someone said and hurried past.

Then Christopher spotted an officer on horseback. His hopes rose when he saw it was an army chaplain. "Sir! Sir! Over hear."

The chaplain gave no sign he'd heard Christopher, though he was well within shouting distance. "Sir!" Christopher waved his right hand over his head to get the man's attention.

Soon, the chaplain was almost alongside them but made no effort to slow down. Christopher reached out, grabbed a rein, and gave it a sharp tug.

The chaplain started as if woken from a nap. His expression quickly changed from startled to angry at the sight of Christopher holding onto the bridle of his horse. "What—See here young man, let go of that rein!"

"No, sir. I got a sick pard here, and we need help."

"Is your friend dying, son?"

"What! No! He just needs water."

"Then I can't help you. See to the medical staff."

"There ain't no medical staff around, and you're the only officer in sight. I figure you're riding, you're more likely to have water than these web feet."

"Young man, you realize you are talking to an officer of this army and your superior."

Christopher knew he was on thin ice, but he wasn't about to back down. He frowned until his eyes were slits, belaying the next words he spoke. "Sir. Sorry, sir. I have a sick friend who needs water. I assumed, you being on horseback and a Christian to boot, you would most likely have water and be willing to share it with a fallen soldier. Sir."

The chaplain stared at Christopher like a schoolmaster might an errant child. He opened his mouth to say something, then thought better. Whether he feared what Christopher might do, or he suddenly remembered his Christian duty, Christopher didn't know. But suddenly the indignation just disappeared. The man reached back to one of his bulging saddlebacks and pulled out a clay bottle.

He handed the bottle to Christopher. "Here. It's mixed with vinegar, so your friend should be as good as new in no time."

Christopher stared at the bottle. Was he really going to pass Ezra by when he had had that on his person the whole time? Then he quickly reached up and snatched it before the chaplain could change his mind.

"There are thousands of you boys. You fill your canteens with whiskey and eat and drink with no thought to the future. I can't help you all."

"I didn't ask you to help us all. Just him...sir."

The chaplain rode on. He looked back once and gave Christopher a hard stare as if memorizing his features. Christopher didn't care. He dropped to his knees and gave the life-saving fluid to his friend, who puckered his lips and sputtered at first but then greedily drank.

The army marched well into the night, and it was long after that before Christopher and Ezra found their way back to the 8th. Both were half asleep when they started out the next morning. But they both made sure their canteens, and the clay bottle Christopher had kept, were full of water.

There were several skirmishes as they continued chasing shadows around the Shenandoah valley—mostly by the cavalry. The closest the 8th got to the enemy was spending an afternoon in reserve, watching a minor battle take place in the valley before them. After a couple weeks of this, they marched back toward the Rappahannock River. It was there they received the orders the men were hoping for. The 8th would be a part of the contingent sent to New York City to quell the riots and ensure the draft went off without interruption.

Ezra gave Christopher his best "let's get in trouble" smile. "This is it, pard. We're gonna have a bodacious time. Look out New York City!"

Christopher returned the smile as best he could, but his heart was no longer in it. He would go to New York, do his duty, and come back none the worse for wear. No drinking, no fornicating, no nothing that would get him in trouble or damn his soul. Now he just had to figure out a way to tell that to Ezra.

Chapter Eighteen

Christopher sat at the table with Ezra and the Jump brothers, staring at the half-empty glass of whiskey sitting before him. It was rotgut, no better than what the sutlers' sold, but the first glass left him with that warm glow he'd been missing every night since he stopped drinking.

But now, all he could think of was how he'd failed. He'd resolved not to drink anymore, yet here he was, halfway through his second glass of whiskey. He'd resolved not to let Ezra lead him into trouble, yet now he sat in a saloon in the basement of a multi-story brick building that had seen better days, somewhere in the heart of New York City, surrounded by prostitutes, gamblers, and gangsters.

Christopher looked up from his drink, his eyes flitting around from person to person, wall to wall, as he berated himself for temporarily losing track of his surroundings in such an alien and dangerous environment. It was all as he'd imagined. Bare brick walls, blackened from tobacco smoke and the soot from the oil lamps (much of New York City was lit by gas, but not this place). The decor seemed to lean toward the nautical, with paintings of wooden ships, netting, and coiled rope and even a large wooden steering wheel mounted on one wall. Most of the people were also as he'd expected. There were the prostitutes, scantily dressed and heavily made up, their lingering stares a mix of lust and defiance, and the gamblers, dressed even prettier than the prostitutes with their three-piece suits, diamond pinned cravats, and beaver-skin top hats. As one of them passed their table, Christopher noticed he left a sweet fragrance in his wake. Hell, they even smelled prettier than the prostitutes.

The only thing that exceeded his expectations were the rowdies and gangsters. They were a colorful lot, their attire eccentric almost to the point of the ludicrous. They wore a wide assortment of outfits, almost like uniforms used to distinguish their gang affiliation. Some in red shirts with wide, white suspenders and knee-high boots looked almost like firemen. Some wore top hats or bowlers with rumpled suits and long old-fashioned coats. Some even adorned their clothing with swatches of rabbit pelts. Whatever their affiliation, they all gave the four soldiers a long, hard stare when they'd walked into the establishment. Thankfully, they'd let them be—for now.

Christopher looked around the table at Ezra and the Jump brothers. Ezra seemed oblivious to the pulsing danger that surrounded them, while the Jumps looked as nervous as Christopher felt. Ezra let out a loud laugh, cupped his big hand around the back of Nathan's neck, and playfully shook him. The sudden outburst drew the attention of one nasty-looking character with a jagged scar across one cheek. He was one of the ones with a rabbit pelt sewn into his clothing—they seemed the worst of the lot.

Christopher nodded at the man and raised his glass. The man gave Christopher a blank stare for a full thirty seconds before turning back to his companions and leaning into the table to say something.

Christopher leaned forward and hissed at Ezra. "You want to keep it down, pard? We don't want to be drawing any unnecessary attention to ourselves. Remember, a couple weeks ago most of the people in this room were rioting against boys in blue."

Ezra waved his hand and scoffed, "Pshaw. That's all in the past. We're all on the same side here." To emphasize his point, he stood and raised his glass to the flag hanging in the corner. "To the Red, White, and Blue!" He got a chorus of huzzahs and raised glasses in response. "The Union forever!" the response was much smaller and less enthusiastic. Ezra took a big swig of whisky and sat back down.

"See, patriotic Americans one and all."

Christopher looked back at the rabbit pelt guy, who seemed to still be casting glances in their direction as he talked to the other men at his table.

"Drink up, boys," Christopher said. "I think it time we were moving on."

"Moving on!" Ezra bellowed. "We just got here."

"I thought you wanted to see the city," Christopher shot back.

Nathan and Joe both took sips of their beers. "I'd like to look around some," Nathan said.

Joe nodded. "Me too."

"Then it's settled. Drink up, Ezra."

Ezra downed the remaining whiskey in his glass in one gulp, slammed the glass on the table, and belched. "Okay. Let's absqu—, absqwalate, abs—, let's go."

Christopher took a drink, the burning sensation and shudder down his spine provoked a wave of guilt. Joe and Nathan both took big gulps of beer, but they still had half-full mugs to finish. "We ain't all done yet, Ez. Give us a minute."

"Then I'm gonna have another while I wait." Ezra raised his hand to get the waitress's attention.

"No," Christopher said. "Wait until the next saloon."

Ezra stopped and stared at Christopher. Though neither spoke, Christopher sensed a shifting in their relationship. While Ezra had always shown a deference to the Galloway brothers in most things, when it came to his and Christopher's excursions, he'd always led and Christopher followed. But, no more. Christopher was setting limits now. From now on, Ezra would lead them down the path to trouble only so far. And Christopher was near that limit.

Ezra sat back with a sharp exhalation. "All right then." The two friends stared at each other for several seconds. Then Ezra belched. And laughed. "All right!"

They finished their drinks and left, only drawing half as much attention as they had when they'd entered the place.

Outside, Christopher once again marveled at the artificial canyons that made up the city streets. The buildings were all three or four stories high, some even higher, made of brick that came down to cobbled streets and walk-ways. Some alleyways were still dirt, as were the animal pens by the meat markets and livery stables; and the park where they had set up camp was filled with grass and trees. But, other than that, there didn't seem much natural about New York City. In contrast, even Main Street in Norwalk was still dirt.

And people! Pedestrians, carriages, and delivery wagons pulled by the biggest horses Christopher had ever seen clogged the streets. The sounds of arguing and laughing, playing and working, fighting and making love—the sound scape of people living their lives, blared out of every building they passed. People hung out windows, chatting to others on the sidewalk, or just watching while they enjoyed the cool evening breeze, however meager it may be. Merchants and newsboys hawked their wares, even at that late hour. To Christopher it was overwhelming and oppressive. He couldn't imagine how anyone would want to live like this.

It didn't take as long as Christopher had wanted for them to find another drinking establishment. He was hoping to have time to let his head clear, but Ezra seemed like a man on a mission to drink himself into oblivion.

The new place seemed a little more upscale than the last. It was twice the size, and instead of bare brick, the walls had paneling, adorned with red, white, and blue bunting, several eagles (some with the flag shield over its breast, arrows in one claw and vines in the other, and the "E Pluribus Unum" banner in its beak), and paintings of the nation's founding fathers; a band comprising piano, banjo, and violin, played in one corner; and in the back was an assortment of gambling tables. But the best feature to Christopher was that it was not in the basement, so it wasn't as dark and possessed more than one exit.

While the clientele still had its share of gamblers, toughs, and prostitutes, there were also what appeared to be honest workers and businessmen blowing off steam after a long day's labor, and more than a few soldiers in Union-blue. They still received several hard stares upon entering, but they also got a few nods, and were mostly ignored.

The four soldiers found a table not too close to the band, so they could talk. A barmaid wearing a shockingly low-cut blouse approached them. She had the disquieting habit of leaning forward while taking their orders, and Christopher did his best not to stare at the cleavage it revealed, but he didn't think Ezra had looked anywhere else. Joe, too, attempted to look everywhere else, and Nathan turned bright red and stared at his hands until she left.

"What'll you have, boys?" she asked.

"Whiskey," Ezra said to her breasts.

"You want the house, or the premium—we have Irish imported directly from the motherland."

Having a choice seemed to confuse Ezra, but it intrigued Christopher.

"How much," he asked.

"Two bits a glass"

Ezra sputtered and shook his head, and even the Jump brothers appeared shocked. But, the thought of a glass of whiskey, made in Ireland and imported by ship to the USA, was exciting to Christopher. Imagine telling his father he'd drunk real Irish whiskey. Besides, he'd promised himself this was his last drink. No more.

"I'll take the Irish," he said, much more authoritatively than he felt.

"Just bring me your regular joy juice," Ezra said. "As long as it doesn't eat a hole in my gut, I'll be fine."

The Jumps both stuck with beer.

"Sweet Jesus, did you see that?" Ezra exclaimed after the barmaid left.

"Humph. You act like you ain't ever seen a women's breast before," Joe said.

"Have you?" Ezra shot back.

There was a pause before Joe responded. "Well, not really. At least, not all bare and pushed together like that." Christopher didn't think it possible, but Nathan appeared to turn even redder.

Ezra leaned over so he could watch the barmaid's backside as she walked away. "We need to find us some fancy girls."

Christopher felt a shiver of terror and anticipation run down his spine. Before the night was through, he was sure Ezra would want to visit a brothel.

After a short time, the barmaid returned with their drinks. Christopher took a sip of the premium whiskey he'd just purchased and nodded with approval. It was smoother than he was used to. But, after a second drink he was almost certain it had been watered down.

Christopher was prepared to go into a rant on the vagaries of drinking establishments when a large man walked up and placed his hand on his shoulder.

"Welcome, Gents. What brings you four upstanding young men to the Golden Eagle?"

"The what?" Ezra asked.

The man waved his hand. "The Golden Eagle. This establishment. What brings you here? I take it you're in New York to quell the riots, and I'm guessing you boys have the night off?"

Ezra grinned. "Right on all accounts, my friend. It looks like all the fun was over before we even got here."

The man frowned and shook his head. "Nothing fun about it, bucko. It was nasty business it was, and many a fine fellow lost his life during those troubled days."

The four frowned and nodded in agreement.

"We're just glad it's passed," Joe said. "Last thing we want to do is take arms against American citizens."

"'ceptin' them in open rebellion against our government. Am I right?" Ezra bellowed.

Christopher stared at the man, not sure what to make of him. He seemed friendly enough and said all the right words, but there was something more. Something unsaid that lay just below the surface. And Christopher was sure it wasn't something good.

"What can we do for you?" Christopher asked.

"Why, nothing," the man said, appearing taken back by Christopher's tone. "The name's O'Malley, David O'Malley. I was just checking in on you fine boys in blue and makin' sure you were being taken care of proper."

Christopher nodded. "That we are. Thank you, Mr. O'Malley."

O'Malley waved his hand. "None of that, me boy. My friends call me Davey, and I'd like to think of you gents as my friends."

"Davey it is then," Ezra yelled. "My names Ezra Rouse, this here's Joe and Nate Jump, and my prickly pard over there is Chris Galloway."

"Galloway! Another son of the sod! Rouse, I take then you be a Hun, but Jump, that's a new one on me. Where you boys from?"

"Norwalk, Ohio."

"Ah, good, strong Midwestern stock. I hear that's what they were sending to deal with the rioters, and, well, here you are.

"But, you said something that caught me ear, Ezra. 'Pard.' What's a pard?"

The four soldiers looked at each other, at a loss for what to say. Finally, Ezra spoke. "Why, a pard's a friend or comrade, but something more. A pard is someone you can count on to stick with you when the bullets start flying."

Once again, Christopher stared at his friend as if seeing him for the first time. For someone so impulsive and lacking in book learning, Ezra could be insightful when he wanted to be.

"Well, I know what you mean, bucko. I got some pards of my own. In fact, maybe you boys would like to join us in a game of chance? All private-like in the back room."

Now warning bells were clanging in Christopher's head. The last thing he wanted to do was get all "private-like" with Davey O'Malley and his pards. But, he could see Ezra perk up at the mention of gambling, and Joe and Nate also seemed interested.

"We appreciate it, Davey," he blurted. "But, we were talking about finding some female companionship after this drink. Weren't we boys?"

The number of expressions that passed over Ezra's face in the following few seconds would have been hilarious under other circumstances. Christopher thought he'd rather face a rebel battle line that a naked fancy girl. But he was sure that, if they went somewhere private with Davey and his pards, they'd be lucky if they made it back to camp beaten and penniless.

"But, a quick card game beforehand wouldn't hurt nothin'," Ezra said.

"Ez, you don't know how to play a quick card game. We start gambling we'll be there all night. Then, it'll be time to report back, and we won't have gotten a chance to visit a New York City brothel."

"Yeah, I guess you're right," Ezra said with a slight pout. "I don't want to leave New York without saying I've had myself a real New York strumpet."

"No worries, boys," O'Malley said. "I can direct you to a fine establishment just a few blocks from here where I assure you the ladies are exceedingly friendly to our brave boys in blue."

To Christopher's relief, that seemed to seal the deal with Ezra. After giving the boys directions, O'Malley moved on, still on the hunt for someone he could lure into the back room.

Christopher leaned forward and hissed, "I don't trust that fellow. Something ain't right about his offer."

"He seemed fine to me," Ezra replied. "Seemed like a friendly enough fellow...for an Irishman," he added with a laugh.

"But, look around you," Christopher shot back. "There are dozens of card games going on in this room, not to mention farrow, chuck-a-luck, and there's even a roulette wheel. So why take us to some back room?"

Ezra shrugged. Christopher's reasoning was proving too much for him in his inebriated state. "Don't know. Don't care. We ain't doing it anyway."

"But, if he's up to no good, then he's probably directing us to someplace just as bad."

"You're acting like an old woman, Chris. Finish your drink and let's go. This place and your ditherin' is starting to bore me."

They downed their drinks, the Jumps much more slowly because they were drinking beer, and headed back out into the night. Though the sun had been down for several hours, it was still hot out, and the meager breeze was gone. Worse, the still air brought out the stink of unwashed bodies, garbage, and waste.

"I smelled sinks fresher than this place," Christopher mumbled under his breath.

"What you belly aching about now, grandma?" Ezra asked.

"I said this place stinks," Christopher snapped. "And you can cut it with the 'grandma' crap."

Ezra laughed and placed a hand on Christopher's shoulder and gave him a playful shake. Unfortunately, it was his bad shoulder, still not fully healed from Gettysburg, and the bolt of pain that shot down his arm made Christopher wince and pull away.

"Sorry, bub. Forgot about that shoulder of yours. I guess 'cuz I'm all healed, fit as a fiddle." Ezra slapped his chest, but too hard. Now it was his turn to wince. "Nearly so, anyways."

Then he took off, striding purposefully down the street. "Come on boys, I can hear the pus—"

"Ezra!"

"What?"

Christopher hesitated. He wasn't sure why he'd stopped Ezra. He'd heard his share of cussing and derogatory remarks while in the army and had contributed his share. But, it got old, and just once, he'd like them to treat others with some respect. Even if they were just women of the night. "Where you headed in such an all-fired hurry?"

"To the brothel," Ezra replied without breaking stride.

"The one O'Malley told us about?"

"You know of any others?"

"No, but I'm sure there are plenty around. Like I said, I don't tru—"

"Yeah, yeah. You don't trust the man—your fellow Irishman, no less. I swear, I don't know what's gotten into you, Chris."

Christopher didn't either. Maybe it was the strange, overwhelming environment, so unlike the small towns and open countryside he was used to. Or, maybe it was because his and Ezra's last drinking excursion away from camp had ended up so badly for him. Whatever it was, the longer they were out, the more nervous he was becoming.

"Hey, there's Davey O'Malley," Nathan said.

Christopher looked up. Sure enough, there came good old Davey O'Malley, striding up a side street, followed by five or six of his pards. Their speed and direction would have them arriving at the intersection at about the same time as the boys from the 8th. Christopher didn't think it was a coincidence. He looked the group over and noticed large bulges under most of their jackets. A few carried pipes or thick wooden sticks. Then, his eyes met O'Malley's, and there was no question any longer as to his intent. Even Ezra saw it.

"That scalawag!" Ezra huffed. "His whole act was one big humbug."

"I tried to tell ya."

Ezra shot Christopher a dirty look. "Well, we seen him soon enough, we just turn and go the other way." Ezra let out a big sigh. "There probably ain't even a brothel down that way."

"No."

Ezra's jaw dropped, and he stopped to look directly at Christopher. "No? What do you mean, no? You were the one wanting to retreat."

"That was before. Now it's out in the open and all, I say we give them a taste of what Ohio boys can do."

"You're daft! There's twice as many of them as there are us, and, in case you hadn't noticed, they're armed to boot."

"I seen. We'll move in fast, get inside their swing, and crack some skulls. They won't know what hit 'em. Besides, running's probably what they're expecting, and they'll be ready for that. Those brick-bats and sticks give them the advantage of reach. We need to negate that."

"No, let's get out of here," Ezra said.

Joe took Christopher's arm and said, "Listen to him, Chris. This isn't the field of battle, and those aren't rebs. This is one fight it's best to avoid." Pulling

Chris's arm, he turned to go the other direction and stopped. Christopher looked that way and saw four more b'hoys heading to cut them off.

"Not another 'I told you so' from you, Christopher Galloway," Ezra said. "We plow through these boys and keep going." The Jumps nodded in agreement. Christopher hesitated, but he couldn't argue with the logic of Ezra's plan.

"Okay," he said. Then he bellowed, "At the double-quick! MARCH!"

The four ruffians stopped for a second, put off by the martial commands. Then the Ohio boys were on them, their fists flying as they screamed a loud, wordless battle-cry.

It was over as soon as it had begun, three of the four stumbled back, their arms raised to block the flurry of punches. One b'hoy took a punch full on from Ezra that knocked him out cold. Christopher grabbed the unconscious man's stick, which was about the size of a rounders bat and made of hickory, and began striking the other three. He was smaller than his opponents, but given the speed and intensity of his attack, they never had a chance. Ezra had to pull him along as they made their get-a-way.

They ran several blocks, then ducked into another saloon. They were all out of breath, and Christopher still had the stick, which elicited several curious stares and a frown of disapproval from the bartender. Two men, both larger than Ezra, approached the four.

Ezra held up his hand and, as soon as he had gotten his breath, said, "No need for that boys, we mean no harm. We was just waylaid on the street and had to make a quick retreat." He pointed to Christopher's hand. "Give 'em the bat, Chris."

Christopher held out the hickory stick, and both men eyed the blood smeared end. "I think you gents need to be moving along," one of them said.

Christopher nodded and turned to go, but he kept the stick. "Come on, boys. Let's find somewhere we're welcome."

"You mean like Virginia?" Nathan quipped.

Still chuckling, the four stepped out onto the street.

"Well, pards," Ezra said. "I don't know about you, but that sobered me right up. Let's go find a drink and some fancy girls."

Joe shook his head. "You two are too rowdy. I think Nate and I will just call it a night."

Nathan gave his older brother a look of anger and disappointment. "Aw, come on, Joe. Do we haff ta?"

"Yeah, Joe?" Ezra said, smiling. "Do you haff ta? Let's have a little fun."

"Nope," Joe said. "Let's go, Nate."

His head hung low, Nathan followed his brother.

"Wait. Here, Joe," Christopher said and stepping up, handed Joe the stick. "Just in case."

Joe took the stick, but looked at Christopher. "What about you?"

"I'll be all right. I got this big gorilla to protect me." Christopher laughed and wagged his head toward Ezra.

The two watched the Jump brothers for a moment as they made their way back to camp. Christopher wished he could go with them, but he wasn't about to leave Ezra out here alone.

As he watched the two brothers walking side by side, Christopher missed Daniel more than he had in months. He felt as if his heart would break and quickly looked away before he cried. That was the last thing he wanted to do here on a strange city street with Ezra.

"Well, bub," Ezra said. "It's just you and me. Let's go find some women." Ezra put his hand on Christopher's shoulder and began walking, pulling the smaller man with him.

"Do you have any idea where you're going?" Christopher asked.

"Nope. But I suspect what we're looking for won't be hard to find."

And it wasn't. As they approached a row of brownstone houses, Christopher noticed women leaning out of windows, or lounging on the steps in nothing but their undergarments. Ezra stopped and stood, as if dumbfounded.

"Lordy me," Ezra said. "How do we choose?"

Christopher shrugged. "I have no idea. We don't want to pick the wrong place and get rolled or worse—the pox."

"Oh, don't worry about that," Ezra said. "Some boys from Company C told me if you wash right away afterward you won't catch the pox."

"You going to believe them over the Sanitation Commission?" Christopher reached in his pant pocket and fingered the rubber preventative they'd passed out to all the boys. Just having it on his person made him feel dirty and ashamed.

"Why not? Those old biddies at the SC just want to make sure we don't have no fun while we're off fighting for our country, facing all sorts of hardship and danger and the like. Here, let's try this one."

Ezra pulled Christopher through a door that two soldiers from another regiment had just come out of. After walking down a short hallway, Christopher found himself in a room lit by gas lamps, with a heavily gilded decor and wallpaper of red paisley. A pall of tobacco smoke hung in the air. Christopher took a big breath and coughed.

"You need to smoke more," Ezra said. "It'll toughen up your lungs."

"My lungs are fine the way they are," Christopher responded as soon as he was able.

A large woman dressed in a velvet skirt and a corset pulled so tight she spilled out of both ends approached the two. "You boys here for some fun?" she asked.

Ezra beamed and puffed out his chest. "Yes, ma'am! We're two hard fighting soldiers looking to blow off some steam."

She looked them up and down. "Ya look more like a couple horny teenagers looking to wet your willy for the first time."

Christopher felt his cheeks burning and, looking over at Ezra, saw his friend's face was as red as his felt. But Ezra also looked affronted.

"I'll have you know, I've , I've, you know, plenty of times."

"Uh, huh."

Christopher felt a soft hand grasp his left arm. Then, a breast, soft and unbound, pressed against him. It was like being struck by lightning, but the most wonderful thing in the world, all at once. His head felt like it was full of cotton, and his vision constricted to a small circle just before his eyes. He couldn't see the owner of the hand or the breast, but he could smell her—a sweet fragrance that mostly masked the scent of sweat—and he could feel her breath on his ear. "You're cute."

"That's Jezebel," the woman said. "Looks like she like you, runt."

"He's cute," Jezebel said.

"Sally!"

A skinny blond girl who could have been twenty, or thirty, it was hard to tell with all the makeup, ran up beside the woman in charge.

"You get the big oaf. The little runt's going with Jezi."

The blond smiled up at Ezra and came around to take his arm the way Jezebel held Christopher's. "Hi, handsome. What's your name."

Ezra's mouth moved for a few seconds before he got out, "E-E, Ez, Ezra."

Sally giggled. "Nice to meet you E-E, Ez, Ezra. You ready for a good time?"

Ezra's head bobbled up and down like it had become detached from his body.

"That'll be a dollar for the two of you."

"A dollar!" Christopher blurted.

"A dollar, runt. You want quality, you pay for it."

As Ezra and Christopher fished around in their pockets for two quarters, Christopher did a quick calculation. Fifty cents, here, twenty-five cents for the shot, fifty cents for meal they'd started the evening with, and the nickel shots he'd done, he would still have a couple dollars left of the five he started with.

The girls led Ezra and Christopher to a set of steep, narrow stairs. The second floor was a long hallway of doors, much like a hotel. As the girls led them to separate rooms, Ezra called out, "Enjoy yourself, pard! I'll see you in a bit!"

Jezebel closed the door and came around to stand in front of Christopher. She was heavier than he'd imagined, and the breasts that had immobilized him were large, almost pendulous as they hung down over the top of her corset, straining the fabric of her chemise. She had a smile that said she knew things he could never understand, and her eyes were colorless black orbs that glistened in the meager gaslight.

"What's your name, soldier?"

"Christopher." He surprised himself by getting his whole first name out in one breath without stammering.

"Chrissy," she said and giggled.

God, how he hated that name.

She worked the knot holding up her pantalets as she moved toward him. Christopher imagined a mountain lion stalking its prey moved much the same way.

When she was pressed up against him, it seemed all the air was sucked out of the room. Christopher took a deep breath to clear his head and regretted it. There was the smell of her perfume again, and her body odor was much stronger in the small room, but under all that was another scent, rich and cloying. Christopher's stomach flipped, and vomit came up to the back of his throat. He gagged.

The transformation in Jezebel was instantaneous. Her seductive smile turned to an angry frown. She stepped back and pointed to the door. "Oh, no you don't, billy boy. Not in here. Out! there's a piss-pot in the room at the end of the hall. You have to hurl, you can do it there."

Christopher tried to apologize and gagged again.

"OUT!"

Jezebel stamped her foot, and Christopher thought she would strike him. He opened the door and stumbled into the hall. But, instead of turning right and going to the end of the hall, he turned left toward the stairs, which he took two at a time, on the verge of tumbling head first the entire time.

Soon, Christopher was out the door and sucking in the cool night air until his vision blurred. When he had control of himself, he realized the nausea had passed, but his hands were shaking, and he felt as weak as a newborn. He thought about going back inside, but couldn't bring himself to face his shame. Besides, he'd been a knot and two buttons away from committing a mortal sin. He was sure it was Jesus himself who'd brought on the sudden sickness.

He walked down the steps and into the street, heading who knows where. He just needed to clear his head for a bit while he waited for Ezra. Turning, he tried to memorize the whorehouse's brownstone facade and the buildings beside it so he'd recognize them when he came back. Then he set out down the street in long steps that quickly carried him away from his weakness and sin.

AS HE WALKED, CHRISTOPHER thought of all the sin and depravation he'd taken part in since joining the army—the drinking and fighting and killing—and now he'd almost had carnal relations with a woman out of wedlock. The thought of where his soul would end up if he should die on the battlefield terrified him. All those men and boys living each day like there were no consequences to their actions—hell must be getting mighty crowded.

Fearful of being waylaid, Christopher also kept on the lookout, eyeing everyone he passed trying to divine their intent. The women all met his stares with knowing smiles, or contemptuous sneers, the men with hard looks, like a non-verbal warning. Until a man surprised Christopher by nodding politely.

Christopher stopped and looked around. He'd gone farther than he'd intended and felt a moment of fear before realizing he'd made no turns and could just go back the way he'd came. The neighborhood he now found himself in was a definite improvement over those they'd been to so far. The people were better dressed, and the street was cleaner and better lit—with a gas lamp on every corner—and didn't smell so much of human waste.

It wasn't a rich area, the brick buildings still had a worn look to them, and the people dressed like workers, not the big bugs who ran things. As he was taking in his surroundings, an enclosed carriage drawn by two shiny black horses pulled up and stopped beside him. It didn't look like it belonged in that neighborhood any more than he. Then one of the dark red curtains that covered the windows opened, revealing the face of a pretty young girl, framed by black curly hair.

"Excuse me, young man."

Young man? She was no older than him, maybe even younger.

"Are you a soldier?"

Figuring she was simple and should be amused, Christopher removed his hat and gave a slight bow. "Yes, miss. Corporal Christopher Galloway, of the 8th Ohio Volunteer Infantry, at your service."

"Delightful. Please join me, won't you?"

"What?"

The driver locked the brakes and stepped down to open the side door. The man was huge, with a broken nose, cauliflower ears, and hands like anvils. *This is not your average fart sniffer*, Christopher thought.

He opened the door and gave Christopher a hard stare. "No hanky-panky. Keep your hands to yourself, and I won't have to crush you."

The threat didn't bother Christopher as "hanky-panky" was the last thing on his mind after what he'd just been through. But, he was nervous about climbing into the dark interior of the carriage. "What does she want?" he asked the big man.

The only answer he got was a brief shrug.

Christopher squinted and peered into the compartment. All the curtains were drawn and, other than some dark wood and fine leather, and a patch of knee-shaped silk skirt, he couldn't see anything.

"Well, are you coming or not?"

Christopher made his own brief shrug and climbed aboard. The big man closed the door with a loud bang and a definitive click that sent a shiver down Christopher's back. The whole carriage dipped to one side as the driver climbed back into his seat.

Soon they were moving. From the steady clop of the horse's hooves on cobblestone and the gentle sway of the compartment, Christopher could tell they were not going fast. He could jump if he had to.

He looked across the cab at his hostess. She looked to be in her late teens or early twenties. Though her hairdo was that of a girl, her clothing was that of a grown woman. She wore a silk or satin skirt and jacket over a white blouse with the largest broach he'd ever seen at her neck. On her right hand was a ring that looked like it cost more than he'd make in a year. When she looked toward him, her eyes appeared glassy and out of focus, though he didn't smell alcohol on her breath.

"How many men have you killed?"

She said it so quietly he wasn't sure he heard correctly. "Pardon?" He leaned forward.

A hint of frustration passed over her face and then was gone. "I asked you how many men you've killed in the name of freedom."

"I don't rightly know."

"Surely you've been in battle?"

"Yes, many."

"But you don't know how many men you've killed?"

"No. Frankly, they're falling so fast it's impossible to tell whose bullet's killing who."

"Ah!" She fanned herself with her hand. "Your bravery gives me chills. I don't know how you do it."

"Neither do I," Christopher said and leaned back in his seat.

She'd opened her mouth to say something, but his last statement seemed to confuse her. She paused with her mouth half open, staring at him in a manner that, though in no way threatening or malicious, still made him uncomfortable.

After a moment, she continued. "You seemed hale enough. I'm glad the rebel traitors haven't harmed you."

"I've had my share of misfortune." Though he normally tried not to draw attention to his mangled ear, Christopher found himself pulling his hair back to show her. "I got the top of my ear shot off outside a town in West Virginia called Red House. Half blown up at Antietam (he decided at that moment not to mention Daniel; it was none of her business), and a little chunk shot out of my shoulder at Gettysburg—"

She gasped and covered her mouth with one gloved hand. "You were at Gettysburg? Oh my. I heard it was absolutely dreadful."

"They all are."

The fanning motion intensified. "Oh, oh my. Your bravery is commendable and, quite frankly, your manly fortitude is quite...intoxicating."

"Thank you?" It came out as a question because he wasn't sure there was anything to thank her for. He found her attitude and line of questioning irritating.

She stared at him again, then said, "I pray this war ends soon. It's just too much. If it wasn't for these damn headaches, I would help more—roll cartridges or bandages or something."

"You are ill? I'm sorry to hear that." In the back of Christopher's mind he noted how, after what he'd been through that night, the sound of a woman cursing didn't seem so shocking.

She sighed with a great heave of her bosom, the sorrows of the common soldier overshadowed by her own misfortune. "Yes. Ever since my riding accident, I've been getting these terrible headaches. The only thing that helps is this medication I get from the doctor."

She reached into her silk purse and pulled out a small bottle that Christopher recognized. "Is that opium?"

"Don't be so vulgar. It's laudanum." She pulled out the cork and took a big swig.

Christopher remembered the headaches he'd gotten after the opium the surgeon gave him at Gettysburg ran out. But they passed after a couple weeks. "You know. I bet if you stopped taking that laudanum, your headaches would go away after a while."

She sneered at him and took another swig. "Are you a doctor, too?" She took another drink.

"No—"

"I thought not. Why don't you stick to killing and leave the healing arts to those with proper training."

Christopher thought about arguing the point, but he didn't care enough to try.

"You never told me your name," Christopher said to change the subject.

"No, I didn't." Her eyes were decidedly more glassy and unfocused, and her lids were starting to droop.

Suddenly, the coach came to an abrupt halt, almost knocking Christopher off his seat. The coach swayed again as the driver descended, then he opened the door. "End of the line, bub. Get out," he said in a gravelly voice.

Christopher stepped out onto the street and looked around. "What? You're just leaving me here? I don't know where I am."

"We've only gone a couple blocks. Head back the way we came, you'll be back where we picked you up in no time."

"She needs help, you know."

"Bugger off."

The driver climbed back into his seat and, with a crack of his whip, took off at a faster pace than he'd been going before.

Christopher stood for a moment and watched them drive away. He'd always thought of the rich as lucky, above the troubles that afflicted the common man, but what he'd just witnessed was a tragedy in the making. If that girl didn't get help, she wouldn't make it to thirty.

As he started back toward the whorehouse, it occurred to him the whole night had been one big tragedy. Men roaming the streets in gangs preying on the weak, women selling themselves for a few coins, young girls addicted to opium, it was all tragic. The war was a tragedy that burned hot, consuming everything in its path, but it would eventually burn out. This would go on and on, as long as man walked the Earth.

AFTER A FEW BLOCKS, Christopher saw Ezra talking to a man wearing a cheap three-piece suit and a bowler hat. The man was shaking his head. "Ezra!"

His friend's head whipped around and swiveled back and forth for a moment before he finally laid eyes on Christopher. His raised his hands, palm upward and, even from a distance, Christopher could see the relief and frustration in his expression.

When the two friends reached each other, Ezra tore into Christopher. "Dammit, Chris! Where you been? I come out of Sally's room looking for you, and you're gone. Jezebel's already got another customer, so I couldn't ask her. I been up and down the street looking for you, pard."

"I'm sorry, Ez. I was just walking and met a girl—"

Ezra's jaw dropped, and his eyes got wide. "Well, you horny ol' goat. One wasn't enough for you?"

Christopher shook his head. "It wasn't like that. She was in a carriage and they picked me up and we just—"

Ezra started laughing. "Wait'll they here this back at camp. Chris Galloway comes out of a whorehouse, and the first thing he does is get picked up by another woman."

Christopher tried again to explain, but Ezra was laughing so hard, he let it drop.

When he finally stopped laughing, Ezra wiped his eyes and said, "That was really somethin' wasn't it?"

"Uh, yeah. It's been quite a night all around."

"You can say that again. What do you want to do next? Want another drink?"

Christopher shook his head. "I'm done in, pard. I'm ready to head back and get some sleep. Don't forget, we have picket duty tomorrow."

"Oh, that's right," Ezra said and laughed. "We wouldn't want to fall asleep on picket here in the heart of enemy territory."

"Enemy territory or not, they could still shoot you for it."

"Yeah, that ain't gonna happen. We got boys sleeping on picket, trading with the enemy, even deserting. You seen them shoot anyone yet?"

"Don't matter what they've done, it's what they could still do that you gotta watch out for. Come on, let's go back. You want more to drink, we can pick a bottle up on the way."

Ezra nodded. "Deal." He threw his arm around his friend, and they started walking in what they were pretty sure was the direction of the camp. After a few steps, Ezra started chuckling.

"What's so funny."

Ezra snorted as he tried to stop laughing. After one more good guffaw, he finally got out, "We're gonna have to change your nickname from Notch to Two-time." Then he started laughing again.

"Just try it, Ez, and I'll pop you one good."

At that, Ezra let out a bellowing laugh. He continued to laugh and chuckle off and on all the way back to camp.

THEY SPENT ANOTHER week in New York City, but, except to frequent one of the nearby merchants to purchase some fruit and sweets, and some new writing supplies, Christopher made no attempt to leave camp after that night. Before Daniel's death, he hardly ever wrote home, letting his brother act as a conduit between him and the family. Now, he wrote home at least once a week and made sure he always had paper and pencil on hand wherever they went.

There were no more riots. The contingent sent north to quell the rioting spent their days policing their camp, picketing its parameter, conducting dress parades for the locals, and answering questions, lots of questions, mainly from young boys.

"What do you eat?"

"What's the farthest you've ever marched in a day?"

"Do you sharpen your bayonet?"

"What do you do when it gets cold? ...when it rains? ...when it's hot? ...when it snows?"

"How do you get over rivers?"

"What's them stripes for?"

"Have you ever killed someone?

Except for the questions about killing, Christopher answered everything with as much patience as possible. Ezra avoided the public and their curious questions and stares as much as possible.

The men spent their off time playing cards or chuck-a-luck; sometimes they played rounders, had boxing and wrestling matches, or held foot races—all resulting in more gambling; they read and wrote letters, sat around the camp fire singing songs and talking about girls and home; a few tried to put on a play; and they drank. They drank whether they were playing or lounging. Just about everyone had a flask in his jacket pocket, and they kept the local whiskey merchants busy making sure they stayed full. Even the officers were drinking every chance they could. Sawyer himself was sent back to his tent to sleep it off by the commanding officer, Colonel Carroll, when he was observed swaying in his saddle and slurring his commands.

When it came time to leave, even the cruise back down south was a relaxing, enjoyable experience—for those not prone to sea-sickness, anyway. The weather was good, and the waves were relatively calm. Christopher spent as much time as he could on the deck, breathing in the salty sea air. He wished he had Daniel's copy of *Moby Dick* to read on the boat. Which surprised him, because he couldn't remember ever wishing he had something to read before.

After a couple days navigating the coastal by-ways, they reached their destination just south of Washington City. From there, they marched through Alexandria, Virginia, and went into camp. After the camp was set up, the regiment was made to listen to the Democrat and Republican representatives and why their guy should be the next governor of Ohio. This would be the first time voting for Christopher, and he knew, like the rest of the regiment, he would be voting the Republican ticket. Then Christopher was called to Colonel Sawyer's tent.

As Christopher turned down the street that led him into officer territory, his thoughts were a jumbled mess of possible things he could be in trouble for. But, for the life of him, he couldn't think of a single thing that would warrant a visit to the colonel's tent.

Master-Sergeant Wilson Parker, who had been promoted out of Company D to replace Master-Sergeant Eugene Henthorne, who had been killed at Fredericksburg, met Christopher outside Colonel Sawyer's tent.

"Galloway," Master-Sergeant Parker said with a nod.

"Wil—er, I mean, Master-Sergeant," Christopher responded. Then he leaned toward the sergeant and whispered. "Do you know what this is about?"

Master-Sergeant Parker nodded with a smile. "That I do."

Christopher looked at him expectantly until it became clear the sergeant had no intention of sharing that knowledge.

Master-Sergeant Parker cleared his throat and said in a raised voice, "Colonel Sawyer, sir. Corporal Galloway here to see you, sir."

Colonel Sawyer's voice came from within. "Very good, Master-Sergeant. Show him in."

Parker pulled back the tent flap and indicated Christopher should go ahead. Christopher stepped inside and Parker followed, letting the tent flap fall back into place behind him.

Though there was a lit oil lamp hanging from a hook on the center pole, it took a moment for Christopher's eyes to adjust. Colonel Sawyer was sitting at his desk with the shadow of a smile on his lips. Master-Sergeant Parker stepped around to join the colonel in facing Christopher.

"Thank you for coming, Corporal Galloway."

Christopher nodded like he'd actually had a choice in the matter.

"Please, have a seat," Sawyer said, indicating a three-legged stool next to his desk.

Christopher looked at the stool, looked at Colonel Sawyer, then looked at Master-Sergeant Parker, who gave him a small nod of encouragement. He sat.

"You too, Wilson," Sawyer said. The master-sergeant retrieved another stool and sat it off to the side, creating a third point in a triangle of chairs.

Sawyer leaned forward and put his elbows on his knees. "Camp Dennison seems like a lifetime ago, doesn't it?" he asked.

Christopher nodded.

"I remember when you and Daniel were brought before me for fighting." He chuckled softly. "You two were quite the sight. I can't imagine what possessed you two to take on that big German."

Christopher didn't try to explain. He didn't think he had enough breath to get the words out anyway.

"Then, afterwards, I was well aware of your shenanigans, young man. Don't think I wasn't."

This is it, Christopher thought. *I'm losing my stripes—or worse.*

"But, since Antietam, you've been a model soldier. Exemplary in fact."

Exemplary, that's good isn't it?

There was a long pause, in which Christopher went back and forth in his mind from the worst to the best possible outcomes of this meeting.

Finally, Sawyer continued. "I promised your father I'd keep you two safe. Did you know that?"

Christopher barely moved his head side to side. The two of them had been talking on the platform when he'd arrived the morning they left for camp, he just assumed it was about business, horse racing, or politics—the kind of things he'd thought men talked about.

Sawyer continued, now staring at the top of his desk. "After Daniel was killed I wrote him, apologizing for not being able to keep my promise. But, no one expected that it would be this bad." The colonel looked up, and his eyes bore into Christopher's. "No one."

He's sending me home. He can't do that. What'll the boys think? I'll be branded a coward.

"That's why I have mixed feelings about this. Privates think non-commissioned officers have it easy—almost as easy as commissioned officers. But, that's not true. There is a lot of responsibility in that position. Responsibility that leads you into dangerous situations.

"But, dammit! This war is decimating our regiment. I've lost so many good men. So many...I need responsible, experienced men in leadership positions. Company D lost two more sergeants at Gettysburg, and...and that's why I'm promoting you."

Sawyer shuffled through a stack on his desk and pulled out two three-stripe chevrons. He handed them to Christopher. "There are a few other promotions. They'll all be announced at tomorrow's dress parade. I just wanted to take a moment to speak to you. For your father, for Daniel. I pray that someday we make it home and, instead of officer and soldier, we are once again fellow citizens of Norwalk, Ohio, sharing a drink at reunions or passing each other on the street with a nod. Both free men of these United States of America."

Sawyer handed the chevrons to Christopher, who hesitantly took them. "Thank you, sir. I won't let you down."

Sawyer smiled sadly. "I know you won't, son."

Sawyer stood, and the two enlisted men shot to their feet.

"Rejoin your company, Sergeant," Sawyer said. "But, wait to sew on your new stripes until after tomorrow's ceremony."

Christopher came to attention with a snap of his heels. He raised his hand to his forehead and looked the colonel in the eye. "Thank you, sir."

Sawyer returned the salute with a wave of his hand. "Carry on, *Sergeant*."

Once he was outside and alone, Christopher looked at the stripes with disgust. *Damn me*, he thought. *Damn me for a fool.*

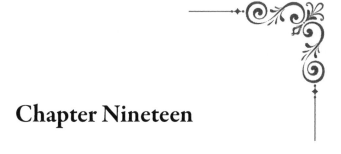

Chapter Nineteen

The difference between a corporal's duties and a sergeant's was mostly a matter of degree. Now, instead of just having a four-man square he was responsible for, Christopher had an entire squad—eight men whose performance and demeanor were his responsibility. If the company had been at full strength, it would have been many more.

He asked to have Ezra in his squad, but First Sergeant Ennis refused, saying their friendship would impede their relationship as superior and subordinate. Though he would have liked to have kept his friend closer, Christopher had to agree. Ezra's reaction to his new promotion was the same as it was to his last promotion—how could he use it to his advantage? Only, this time, Christopher sensed an undercurrent of resentment as well.

Christopher barely had time to adjust to his new position before they were again on the march, chasing the Confederate army across Virginia. Both on the march and in the line of battle, Christopher had to act as a file closer.

After marching several miles, the 8th created a single battle line with the rest of their brigade, but only as reserve for the cavalry, who were engaged with the rebels outside Culpepper Courthouse. Christopher's responsibility as file closer was limited to encouraging the men to keep up on the march and keep the line straight as they prepared for battle. He never had to close a gap in the line created by a casualty or stop a man from trying to go to the aid of a fallen comrade. The other possibility, that he would have to stop someone who broke and ran, never occurred to him, it had been so long since that had happened.

The Union cavalry won the engagement outside Culpepper Courthouse and chased the Confederate cavalry through the town. Afterward, the Second Corps marched through the town in strict formation, like a conquering army putting on a display of force. As they passed one house, Christopher looked over and saw a woman in the window, dressed in mourning attire, her fist clenched and face screwed up in hatred and pain. Her lips were constantly moving, and it looked as if she was cussing. As they marched on, Christopher thought of his own mother and how Daniel's death had broken her spirit. He was thankful that she hadn't gone mad with hatred and grief like that poor woman.

A few days after returning to camp, their division was called out to witness the execution of two deserters. While it was a well-known fact that the official punishment for desertion was death, but until now Christopher had never heard of that sentence being carried out. Usually, deserters were never heard from again. If they did return, the consequences were minor.

But, the draft, and the new policy of offering signing bonuses to new recruits, changed everything. Now, there were men signing up in one regiment, pocketing the bonus, and then deserting to go sign up somewhere else. And draftees, lacking the conviction of the volunteers, had little incentive to stay if they thought they could get away. So the army was cracking down. As far as Christopher knew, these would be the first executions in the Second Corps. But he feared they would not be the last.

The entire division marched out to a hill, at the base of which two graves had been dug. They lined up in a three-sided square around the graves, with the hill acting as the backdrop for the firing squad. A space was left open at the end opposite the hill for the executioner's procession. At the head of the square next to the graves were two lines of officers astride their horses—General French, the division commander, and the brigade commanders, sat in the first line, and the regimental commanders in the second.

As they stood waiting, the two thousand men attending kept up a constant chatter that seemed to echo off the hillside. The officers did little to quiet the men, apparently deciding it was better to let them expend some of their nervous energy than it was to maintain strict military discipline. It was late September, and the sun was shining after a cold, rainy night, warming the men in their wool uniforms, but there was a coolness in the breeze that said fall was just around the corner.

After several minutes, the sound of a brass band playing a death march, came in on the breeze and silenced the nervous chatter. For a few moments, it became so quiet it seemed every man was holding his breath. Then, Christopher heard the creaking of wagon wheels, and the stomp of marching feet.

A wagon entered the square carrying two caskets. Sitting on those caskets bound in chains sat two men. The provost guard, a chaplain, a doctor, and the band, still playing its dirge, followed them. The wagon stopped in the middle of the square, and the band ceased playing. A single cough punctuated the silence that followed.

The provost sergeant shouted commands. They brought the condemned men down, and the caskets were taken to the foot of each grave. The chaplain went to the men and prayed with them. Christopher stared at the condemned men, unable to look away. They were both crying and appeared to be half crazed with fear. One seemed to be muttering to himself and the other shaking his head as if he could deny the reality he now faced. Both ignored the chaplain.

Then two guards came over and led the men to the caskets. The one who had been shaking his head reached out, grabbed the chaplain's hands and dropped to his knees. His wail hit Christopher like a slap to the face; all the energy seemed to flow out of him. He felt nauseous and closed his eyes until it passed.

The guards dragged the wailing man to the left-hand casket and sat him atop it. Then they attached his chains to two stakes that they drove into the ground so he couldn't stand up.

The muttering man went willing enough to the other casket and let the guards attach him to the stakes. But his lips never stopped moving.

The chaplain approached, continuing to pray, and the sergeant placed a black sack over each man's head. Some of the men in the ranks muttered their displeasure, but otherwise everyone but the provost sergeant was silent. His voice rang out as he ordered the guard detail to retrieve loaded rifles from the wagon and line up, four to each man.

Once everyone was in place, the sergeant called out the familiar commands.

"READY!"

The guard detail brought their rifles to their shoulders. The condemned men stiffened, as did their audience.

"AIM!"

Christopher fought the urge to yell out, "Stop!" The nausea was getting worse, and now he was sweating despite the cool breeze. He couldn't imagine what those poor souls were going through. This was much worse than marching into battle. At least then you had a fighting chance.

"FIRE!"

Christopher flinched. But, instead of the thunderous roar of a well-timed volley, there was one rifle shot and seven snapped caps. The man on the left fell back, writhing in pain, blood soaking his shirt on his left side. The other man was unhurt, but he jumped up and down and pulled on his chains, screaming.

The crowd let out a collective moan, and there were several shouts, cursing the incompetence of the provost guard.

The sergeant screamed at the men to retrieve another set of muskets from the wagons. As the firing squads were retrieving new weapons, the screaming, struggling prisoner pulled out one of the stakes, ripped the sack off his head, and started tugging on the other stake with all his might as he screamed for mercy. The four guards assigned to him ran over. Two struggled to subdue the writhing prisoner while the other two drove the stake back into the wet ground. Once he was secure, they put the sack back over the prisoners head. The sudden muffling of the man's screams seemed to emphasize the cruelty of the events.

While that was going on, the chaplain and doctor helped the other prisoner sit back up, where he swayed, moaning, his left side now covered with blood. Several audience members jeered the provost guard until threats from their officers silenced them.

Again the guards lined up and the sergeant gave the commands, and again most of the rifles misfired. The already-wounded man fell back dead, the bullet this time having struck him in the middle of the chest. The other man was now a gibbering mess, his clothes soaked in sweat and piss.

A low moan escaped the lips of several hundred men.

Christopher looked toward the mounted officers, hoping someone would call a stop to this fiasco. But they just sat there atop their horses, their faces frozen in angry scowls. General French was so red faced, Christopher wondered if his heart would give out.

The provost guards had no more rifles and, not wanting to take the time to pull the unfired rounds out of the ones they'd brought, had to retrieve new rifles from a squad who had been preparing for picket duty.

A guard brought out a cartridge box from one of the wagons, and the four guards whose prisoner still lived loaded the new rifles.

The man next to Christopher leaned over and whispered, "How much you want to bet they set all this up last night and then left the whole shebang in the wagons last night in the rain?"

Christopher thought about it and nodded.

This time, instead of having the men line up and fire a volley, the provost sergeant had each man step forward, point his rifle at the condemned man, and pull the trigger. Every single rifle misfired. The prisoner jumped at the snap of each cap and by the end was violently shaking, no longer having the faculties to even try to escape.

Despite the officers' best efforts, the crowd was now booing its displeasure at the provost guard and demanding the prisoner be set free.

The provost sergeant cussed out his men. He looked at the officers for salvation but only received stony stares. He looked to the crowd and saw barely contained hatred and rage. After a brief moment of indecision, he pulled out his pistol, stepped up to the prisoner, put the end of the barrel against the poor man's forehead, and pulled the trigger. The gun fired, singeing the sack that covered the prisoner's head and blowing out the back of his skull. Gore spattered the top of the casket as the prisoner's head snapped back. The murmurs and jeers from the audience stopped. The body sat there for what seemed an eternity before falling back onto the gore-stained coffin.

It was over. Christopher could see the sergeant's pistol shaking as he reholstered it.

General French rode out into the middle of the square. He looked at his men and his mouth moved a few times. It seemed the general intended to make a speech after they carried the sentence out, but there were no words. He shook his head, tugged sharply on the reins, and rode away, the other commanding officers following along in procession by rank.

Chapter Twenty

After returning to camp, Christopher sought out Ezra. He needed someone to talk to, and since most of the work details for the day had been canceled because of the execution, they had some free time. As he looked through the crowd of men, hurrying to get to wherever they were going, he spotted his friend heading for the sinks.

"Ezra!"

Ezra made no sign he'd heard. Christopher hurried to get closer and tried again. "Ezra! Hold up."

Ezra raised a hand and gave him a wave, but did not slow down.

"You got the flux, pard?"

Ezra shook his head and kept going. Christopher let him go and turned back to their company street. If there was one thing he learned after two years in the army, it was to not hold up a man in a hurry to get to the sinks. Diarrhea was a near-constant in the life of a soldier, and Christopher suspected it had killed more men that all the battles they'd fought combined.

As Christopher was stoking up a fire for coffee, Joe and Nathan Jump joined him.

"My Lord, do you believe what they done to those men?" Nathan asked.

"I think you have to be extra stupid to qualify for the provost guard," Joe said. "Don't those boys know no better than to keep their powder dry?"

"Extra stupid, but extra honest," Christopher said, thinking of the 8th's turn as provost at Harpers Ferry after Antietam. They'd been relieved of the duty after only a couple weeks when a warehouse full of bread turned up half-empty one morning. "They kick us off provost duty because some bread goes missing, but if you torture a couple boys to death, that's okay." He looked at the Jump brothers. "And make no mistake about it, what we just seen was torture, plain and simple."

The Jumps nodded in unison.

The water was just about ready to boil, and Christopher was starting to worry when Ezra finally returned from the sinks. He sank to the ground with a groan, his face pale and coated with a waxy sheen of sweat.

"You doing all right there, Ez?" Christopher didn't offer him any coffee. Ezra shook his head.

"I know it makes you shit more, but you need to drink plenty of water—keep up your strength," Joe said. Everyone nodded but Ezra.

"No water. I'll be all right."

"The boys that drink something do better in the long run." Christopher was starting to worry about his friend, so didn't feel bad pushing a little.

"No, dammit. I said I'd be all right, so leave me alone."

Ezra didn't look all right. He looked like he was in pain. But Christopher let the matter drop. He figured he'd try to get Ezra alone later and try again. Maybe he'd be more receptive without the Jump's around.

But, as time passed and Ezra showed no desire to eat or drink anything, Joe took up the cause.

"You gotta drink something, Ezra. If you don't keep your strength up, that stuff will kill you."

"I'm all right. Don't press me, Joe."

"Ez—"

"No!" Ezra stood up and stomped off.

Joe looked at Christopher. "I was just trying to—"

"I know. Don't worry about it. I'll have a talk with him."

Later, Christopher returned to the dog tent he shared with Ezra. He was being pressured to bunk with the other non-commissioned officers and thought he'd have to give in when they went into winter camp, but as long as they were campaigning, he'd stay with Ezra.

But, Ezra wasn't there. Christopher hung around outside the tent and waited for him to show up. Eventually, he saw the big man approaching from the direction of the sinks. Even from a distance, Christopher could tell he was still not well. He looked like he'd swallowed a dose of castor oil and followed it up by sucking on a lemon.

Christopher didn't wait for Ezra to sit down. "You need to go see the surgeon. First thing tomorrow. I'll put you down on the sick roll."

Ezra didn't respond.

"I mean it, Ez. First thing tomorrow. The flux'll kill you. You know that."

After almost a full minute of silence, Ezra finally responded. "I ain't got the quick-step."

"What? What is it then? You been spending half the day at the sinks."

"I can't pee," Ezra whispered.

"You can't pee?"

"Shhh!" Ezra looked around. "Keep it down, would ya."

"Well, why can't you pee? I don't—Ohhh." Christopher's eyes got wide, and he could feel his cheeks redden as it finally sunk in. "I thought you were gonna wash up afterward."

"I did, dammit. I guess just not good enough."

"You shoulda worn one of those preventatives the Sanitation Commission gave us."

"Spilling your seed is a sin."

"So's lying with a prostitute."

"Yeah, well. There ain't no sense in compounding sins now, is there."

Christopher could not argue with that logic.

"What about you?" Ezra asked. "You had two women that night."

Christopher looked away. "I didn't."

"You told me you left the whorehouse and met a girl."

"I did. That doesn't mean we fornicated."

"Well, what about Jezebel?"

"I got sick."

"You got sick."

"Yeah, I got sick. And she kicked me out. Afraid I was gonna puke on her or something."

"Did you?"

"No! I told you, she kicked me out."

"So you didn't dip your stick at all?"

"Nope."

"Well, I'll be. Here you been lettin' me believe you were some boss stud."

Christopher felt his cheeks burning and couldn't look his pard in the eye. "That's beside the point. Now you really need to see the surgeon."

"I can't."

"You can, and you will."

"Maybe it'll go away."

"It won't go away. You seen the pamphlets same as me."

"Well, maybe what I got is something different."

"How would you know if you don't go to see the surgeon?"

Ezra was quiet for a moment, and Christopher thought he was getting through to him. Then, he shook his head.

"I can't."

"You can, and you will. Or I'll put you on report!"

Ezra's eyes shot open so wide, Christopher could see the whites all around his pupils.

"You wouldn't!"

"I would!"

"Well, I see how it is. You been a sergeant all of a tinker's minute and already you're lording it over me. That's how it's gonna be the rest of the war?"

"I don't know what else to do. I'm worried about you, Ez."

"Hmm, mmm. I gotta pee." Ezra stood up and stormed off toward the sinks.

The next morning, Christopher spoke with First Sergeant Ennis and got permission to take Ezra to see the surgeon since they didn't trust him to go by himself.

The two strode through camp in silence. Ezra hadn't spoken two words to Christopher since the night before. Christopher regretted it had come to this, but he had to get his friend help.

When they reached the Second Corps hospital tent, Ezra hung back with his arms crossed and a pout on his lips, so Christopher had to speak to the orderly on duty.

After Christopher explained the situation to the orderly, the man nodded. "You boys part of the contingent sent to New York?"

Christopher gaped at the orderly for a moment before responding. "How'd you know?"

"A lot of you boys have the same affliction." He looked at Ezra, pointing to a corner. "You can wait over there with the other VD patients. The surgeon will see you as soon as he can."

Christopher and Ezra looked to where the orderly was pointing. There were already close to twenty men waiting in the space he'd indicated. "They all got the pox?" Christopher asked.

"I gotta wait for all them to go first?" Ezra asked.

"No. Some are waiting for their second treatment."

"Second treatment! How many are there?"

"I'll let the surgeon explain. But you can expect to be seeing a lot of us over the next couple weeks."

Ezra groaned.

"Go on now. Be a man about it, and all this will soon be behind you." He turned to Christopher. "How about you, Sergeant? Any discharge or burning?"

"What? Me? No, no, no."

"Yeah, he was too scared," Ezra said.

"Well, given who's about to get silver nitrate shot up his penis and who isn't, I would say you got the little end of the horn on that deal, Private."

The light in the hospital tent wasn't that good, but Christopher thought for sure Ezra's face lost all its color. "What are they gonna do to me?"

"The surgeon will explain. It's not my place to say."

"That ain't stopped you so far," Ezra mumbled.

"You can return to your company, Sergeant. Private Rouse will be here awhile. We do two initial treatments, then he'll have to come back twice a day for at least a week, depending on how bad it is."

"A week! Oh, Lord, help me."

"You should have sought the Lord's help when you were facing temptation. You're in our hands now. So, get over there. Shoo." The orderly waved his hand at Ezra.

"I'll see you when you get back, pard."

"Not if I see you first!"

On his way back to camp, Christopher fumed at Ezra's attitude. It wasn't his fault Ezra was in this mess. It wasn't his idea to visit a whorehouse. Hell, it wasn't even his fault he didn't go through with it. He might have if he hadn't gotten sick. The Lord must have been looking out for him that night.

When Ezra returned to camp, he took advantage of his sick status to spend most of the day in the tent. That evening, after supper, when Ezra went to the sinks, Christopher could hear him howling all the way back at their camp. The friends spent two days in silence, except for Christopher making sure Ezra went for his treatments, before things finally began to thaw.

Chapter Twenty-One

S pring 1864. Christopher was finding it harder and harder to concentrate on his duties as the 8th's muster out date of July 13th approached. It didn't help that it was turning out to be a hot and dry spring. Though only April, the temperature most days was already reaching the eighties, and Christopher couldn't remember the last time it rained.

It had been a relaxing winter for the men. After a series of skirmishes late last fall, the army had settled down into winter quarters a couple weeks before Christmas. As usual, they decimated the surrounding woods for firewood and logs to make winter cabins.

Furloughs were distributed so many men could go home for a short time—some even got to spend Christmas with their families. Christopher did not get a furlough, he'd already had his the previous spring, but they offered Ezra one, which he declined. He said that there was nothing for him back home, and he'd stay with the only real family he'd ever had.

The winter cabins were made to hold six to eight men, and Christopher finally gave in to the pressure to bunk with the other sergeants instead of Ezra. After Christopher pulled rank to get Ezra to seek treatment for the pox, the bond between the two seemed to have loosened, and Christopher's bunking with the other sergeants drove them further apart. When they spent time together, Ezra took every opportunity available to make snide comments about Christopher's rank, and Christopher chaffed at Ezra's attitude.

Christopher liked his new bunkmates. They had all started out as privates and had known each other since Camp Dennison. First Sergeant Virgil Ennis was, at twenty-three, the youngest first sergeant the 8th ever had; Second Sergeant Charlie Locker had been one of Christopher's original messmates, and next to Ezra, his best remaining friend in the regiment; Third

Sergeant William Wells, at thirty the old man of the group, was the most level-headed of the bunch; Christopher was Fourth Sergeant, the junior of the bunch in both age and rank.

Despite their differences in age and experience, the four shared a common bond. They were not officers, but they were expected to be leaders. They were fighting men, carrying a rifle and standing in the line with the men, but they were also coordinators and helpers, keeping the ranks straight and the files closed, and helping when a man's gun jammed or ammo ran low. Christopher found that being a corporal was just a taste of what it was like to be a sergeant and that there was a lot more to leadership than just standing around telling others what to do.

Morale was boosted when they received the announcement that General Ulysses S. Grant, old "Unconditional Surrender" Grant, was coming east to take control of the army. Mead would keep his position as commander of the Army of the Potomac, Grant was replacing Henry Halleck, that prissy, old egghead Lincoln had made General-in-Chief after Winfield Scott. Halleck had been cautious and timid and never pressed his generals when they acted the same. Grant was a fighter, and he wouldn't stand for such nonsense. Now, when they struck, they'd strike hard, and keep striking until old Lee cried uncle.

It helped, too, that the men knew the South was about played out. The blockade on the east coast and the closing of the Mississippi in the west made trade impossible. The male population was decimated, and Lee could no longer replenish his losses. All they were doing now was delaying the inevitable.

The talk around the campfires, and in the cabins that winter, largely comprised boasting and verbal chest thumping. The men repaired their equipment and cleaned their rifles and dreamed of the day they'd get the chance to put them to use once again.

Until spring came. As the weather warmed, the men's fighting spirit cooled. And it cooled even more so when the men looked at the 1864 calendar with its big black circle around the date of July 13. On that day, win or lose, the 8th would cease to exist. By April, the regiment that had taken part in almost fifty battles and skirmishes in two-and-a-half years, who'd stood the

line before the Sunken Lane at Antietam for four hours, who'd marched out
onto the field at Gettysburg and single-handedly attacked a division, who'd
helped its brigade earn the title of "Gibraltar Brigade," lost its desire to fight.

It started as talk around the campfire, one topic among many in the standard bitch sessions of the common soldier. Then, it grew. The men began having rallies to drum up support. They distributed a petition requesting the 8th
be held back in a support role when the campaign started. Then, the leaders
of the group started proclaiming in public that they would not fight. Other regiments whose enlistment ended that summer took notice and started
their own petitions. And Ezra was right in the middle of it.

It came to a head on a hot April afternoon. The men had formed a crowd
and marched to the general headquarters of the Second Corps, intent on taking their grievance all the way to the corps commander, General Hancock
himself. Ezra was in the front row, along with a mix of men from several regiments. Christopher followed behind with a group of officers and sergeants.
He'd tried the night before to reason with Ezra and get him to quit the
protest movement, but his old pard was determined to see it through. And
after the execution last fall, Christopher feared what the army might do to
him.

"Ezra, you know as well as I do that this army ain't gonna let a bunch of
privates tell them what to do. Hell, even if they were thinking about holding
us back in reserve before, they ain't gonna do it now. Just to prove a point."

"It's the principle of the thing," Ezra replied. "You'd see that yourself if
you weren't so blinded by them stripes."

"My rank ain't got nothing to do with it."

"You wanna die for nothing? You wanna bleed out on some field in Virginia knowing you were this close to going home? It's cruel."

"Cruelty is the bread and butter of war, pard. The army is cruel to us so
we'll be cruel to the enemy. It's like when your da whups ya so you kick the
dog. It's how they do it."

"It ain't fair!"

"No it's not, but it's what we signed up for. We promised three years, and
they're gonna take every day of it."

"Did you sign up in July of '61?"

"You know I didn't—"

"That's right!" Ezra puffed up in victory. "We signed up in May, so that's when our three years should be up. Three years after we signed. Not three years after they got around to recording the regiment in their book or whatever it is they do."

"We've known all along that our discharge date was July 13th. If you disagreed with that, you should have said something before now."

"I didn't even know if we'd live this long."

"Just one more push, Ez. One more campaign, and we can go home in victory with our heads high, knowing we did our duty to the letter. And if the army cheated us out of a few days at the end, so what? It just means we're the better men."

"You can't hold your head up when you're dead."

It went on like that for an hour, back and forth. At one point, Christopher feared the two friends would come to blows. But, finally they agreed to let it go. Ezra would not change his mind, and nothing Christopher said made a difference.

Now Ezra marched with his new pards, the beats and jonahs, the shirkers and complainers, who brought bad luck with them wherever they went. Somehow, they convinced themselves they could argue with the corps commander, and he would listen. It would not end well. Christopher just hoped that he could somehow pull Ezra out before it got too bad.

The crowd never made it to the general's quarters. A line of provost guards, armed with bayonet-mounted rifles at port arms, blocked their path. As Christopher made his way around the crowd to see what was going on, he saw that the rifles were at half cock, with fresh caps on the nipples. No doubt the rifles were loaded and that, if things went too far, the provost guard would fire into the crowd.

A voice rang out. "We demand to see General Hancock!"

"Your demands aren't worth horse shit!" the captain of the provost guard shot back.

Then General Hancock appeared on horseback, followed by his division commanders. Christopher saw it was true what they'd said—the general's wounding at Gettysburg had taken a lot out of him. His left arm hung unmoving at his side, he'd put on weight, his skin was pale, and there were dark circles under his eyes. But those eyes blazed with anger.

"Captain of the guard!" the general bellowed.

"Yes, sir!"

"Take the men out front into custody. If they resist, or anyone tries to stop you, shoot them."

Several guards stepped forward and grabbed the five men. Ezra was one. The rest of the guard stepped back into a ready position, prepared to fire.

A murmur started in the crowd. Christopher couldn't tell if it was from doubt or defiance.

"The rest of you listen," the general said. "These men are to be taken to the stockade where they will receive fifty lashes. If you do not desist in your protests and defiance of general order, they, along with anyone else who continues this resistance, will be shot for cowardice in the face of the enemy!"

The murmuring stopped. No doubt many men remembered the botched execution of the two deserters the year before.

"Now, go back to your commands, and be thankful you're not in chains." The general turned his horse around and rode away, never looking back to see if the crowd did, in fact, disperse.

The provost guard dragged Ezra and the four other men away. The rest of the crowd only lasted a couple minutes before turning around and heading back to their respective regiments. Since most of the protesters were from the 8th, the men Christopher walked back with were quiet and subdued. Just as well, he thought. He was prepared to thrash any man who continued to press their complaints. Ezra would not be shot. Not if he had anything to do with it.

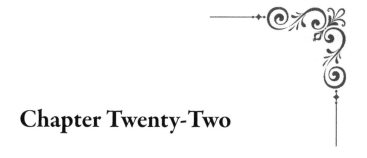

Chapter Twenty-Two

It was the middle of the night, and pitch dark. The 8th was passing through a densely wooded area on its march south, which blocked out what little moonlight there had been when they'd started. They'd set out around midnight, the men complaining about the lack of sleep and wishing for just one more cup of coffee as they fell in line behind the 14th Indiana.

But, after marching awhile in the cool night air, their spirits rose, and groups began belting out marching songs, sometimes more than one at a time. At one point, almost the whole brigade was singing *Battle Cry of Freedom,* unconsciously adjusting their steps to the time of the music, until the stamp of their feet created an accompanying rhythm to the song. Most of the men couldn't carry a tune, but the multitude of voices seemed to smooth out the imperfections. Christopher's voice soared with the hundreds of others, and his feet seemed to move of their own volition, with no strain or effort. By the end of the song he felt goosebumps on his arms and a joyful feeling that he was where he belonged. If they'd met an enemy battle line at that moment, he might have charged them by himself.

This was their first campaign since Christopher's promotion to sergeant, and he wanted to be vigilant about keeping an eye out for stragglers, helping those along who needed it and pushing those along who were slacking. But, in the darkness he was too intent on not tripping to pay much attention to what was going on around him. Maybe when the sun came up, he would do better.

This was also their first campaign under General Grant, and speculation was at an all-time high. Grant would win the war. Grant would get them all killed. Grant was a military genius. Grant was a drunkard. Everyone had an opinion, and no one that night was shy about sharing it. The excitement and heady spirit of the troops reminded Christopher of their marches that first year of the war. Before they knew what they were marching to.

What Christopher heard was that Grant would try to get between Lee's Army of Northern Virginia and Richmond, move toward the rebel capital, and forcing Lee to fight on ground of his choosing. It seemed like Lee was always trying to get between them and Washington, and they were always trying to get between him and Richmond. So far it had led to three years of stalemate and the loss of many a fine soul for nothing. He wished someone would come up with a better idea.

A steady breeze kept Christopher dry and cool. He appreciated the night march (though he would have appreciated a full night's sleep more). The weather was still hot and dry. It was only the first week of May, and the temperatures were already getting into the nineties.

Besides, this way they would be across the Rapidan River and well on their way to passing up Lee's army before the enemy even knew they were on the move. Maybe this time their plan would actually work.

The eastern horizon was taking on a soft, golden glow when they reached the river. There, the 8th marched to a ravine to wait while the rest of the division crossed. Christopher settled in for a long wait. At Gettysburg, a normal division of the Second Corps had been about 4,500 men. But, over the winter they had disbanded several corps and their regiments either sent west or folded into the remaining corps. Now, the division the 8th was a part of totaled almost 9,000 men, and they were in the third brigade, so they would cross last. Not that he didn't appreciate the rest, but a late start meant the sun would be high in the sky by the time they moved out—and blistering hot.

Before getting too comfortable, Christopher set out to make sure his men had full canteens. They had orders not to build fires, so there was no coffee, but he encouraged everyone to drink plenty of water and to eat what they could. There was no telling when they would get another chance.

As he was making his rounds, he kept an eye out for Ezra. They had hardly spoken since they had released Ezra from custody, and when they had, his old friend had been cold and distant. Christopher was reluctant to check Ezra's water and remind him to drink as it would just highlight further the growing distance between them. The thing that had always bonded the two men had been their disdain for authority and their "us versus them" attitude. As far as Ezra was concerned, Christopher was now a "them." But, despite their differences, Christopher owed it to Ezra to give him the same consideration as every other man in the company.

Christopher covered the entire Company D encampment without seeing Ezra. So he expanded his search, assuming the always-outgoing Ezra would be sharing a snort with someone in another company. But, after covering the whole of the 8th with no sign of his pard, Christopher started to worry. Had Ezra dropped out of the march sometime in the night? Had he deserted?

Please, Lord, don't let Ezra do anything so stupid, he silently prayed. He also prayed that, if Ezra had deserted, that they would not catch him.

Christopher was wandering the outskirts of the regiment when he spotted Ezra passing a canteen around with a couple men from the 14th Indiana. That was not surprising; the 14th had been a sister regiment of the 8th's since the beginning. But, the way the men were passing that canteen around and laughing told Christopher that it contained something other than water.

As Christopher got closer, he saw that the other two men were Si and Shorty, the two beats that had tried to rob their cabin the winter before. He couldn't imagine why Ezra would be falling in with these two.

Then, Ezra spotted him. He said something to the other two that Christopher couldn't make out, but the canteen disappeared.

When Christopher stopped before him, Ezra pretended to be surprised. "Well, if it ain't my old pal turned sergeant. How are you doing, Sergeant?"

"Fine, Ez. You boys ready for a long hot march?"

"Pshaw," Ezra said with a wave of his hand. "My guess is they'll be stopping us by noon. Just in time for a light lunch and an afternoon nap." He laughed, and the other two joined in.

"I don't think so. Not this time. We're going to push all the way through "the Wilderness" and get behind Lee. Grant ain't no shirker."

Ezra shrugged.

"Whose canteen was that you boys were passing around?" Christopher asked.

Ezra looked his old friend straight in the eye. "What canteen would that be, *Sergeant*?"

"The canteen you were passing around right before I got here."

Ezra shrugged again. "I have no idea what you're talking about."

Christopher looked around the ground, kicking aside anything that might cover the canteen. Finally, he saw it behind Shorty's feet. He kicked the man's feet out of the way and, ignoring the howls of fake pain and outrage, reached down and snatched up the canteen.

"This canteen. Whose is it?"

The three looked at each other, but no one responded.

Come on, boys. It's gonna be a hot one. You don't want to be marching in this heat with no water. Whose is it?"

The three again looked at each other, then the other two looked away. Ezra sighed. "It's mine."

"Okay. That wasn't so hard. Mind if I have a drink?"

Ezra shot to his feet as Christopher uncorked the canteen and brought it up to his nose. Christopher's head shot back at the sharp burn of alcohol in his nostrils.

"Ez! What were you planning on doing for water?"

"I don't need no water. We won't be marching that long."

"But we will. We're gonna flank Lee."

"Yeah. I heard that before."

Christopher held the canteen out away from him and turned it over so the contents spilled out. "I saw a stream over yonder. We're gonna go make sure you have a canteen full of water."

The expression on Ezra's face almost made Christopher take a step back. But he held his ground. "Let's go, *Private*."

The two started back with Christopher in the lead. The Indiana boys had not said a word while Christopher was confronting them, but has soon as his back was turned, they went at it like a couple old hens. Christopher just caught one of them saying, "Well, don't he think he's a huckleberry..." before they were out of earshot.

They reached the creek, and Christopher looked upstream to make sure no one was pissing in the water. He then handed Ezra back his canteen with the look that all parents and sergeants learn early on. The look that says, "You know what to do, so do it."

Ezra filled his canteen while Christopher watched. When Ezra stood back up, he thought about taking the canteen and giving it a shake to make sure it was full, but then decided he'd humiliated Ezra enough.

"Come on," he said. "Let's go back. You need to stay with the regiment. We don't know when we'll be called up."

"Aye, aye," Ezra responded with a limp-wristed salute that Christopher ignored. He also considered saying something about the naval phrase but didn't have the stomach to continue the confrontation any longer.

Several hours later it was the 8th's turn to cross the river. By that time, the sun was well above the horizon and promising another hot, dry day. As uncomfortable the incident with Ezra had been, Christopher was glad he'd done it. Now, his pard wouldn't be falling out of the march drunk and dehydrated.

The heat-baked road had already been pounded to dust from the thousands of feet and wheels that had passed over it. Soon, the men were a uniform tan from head to toe. They tied bandana's over their faces and squinted as much as they could and still be able to see where they were going. Sweat soaked through their jackets and dripped down their faces where it dried, leaving streaks lined with clumps of mud on their cheeks.

Christopher took a swig of water under his bandana and grimaced. The water already had a gritty taste, despite his best effort to keep the dirt out. He swished the water around in his mouth, trying to clear the buildup from his teeth and gums before swallowing.

The men had marched out the night before under full marching orders, meaning they had brought everything with them they would need to live in the field for several days. Every enlisted man wore a knapsack filled with a blanket, shelter tent half, a housewife and other repair tools, maybe some extra rounds of ammunition, a change of clothes, and various personal items. As the sun continued to rise, and the temperature with it, the men shed everything they didn't need for survival. Everything except rifles, ammunition, haversacks, and canteens were considered expendable. Blankets, knapsacks, shelter tents, and even a few great coats littered the road for miles.

After a few hours they passed the burned-out husk that had been the Chancellorsville mansion. Shortly after that, the 8th halted along with the rest of its brigade in the field where the battle had taken place the year before. Roll was called, rifles were stacked, and the men fell out, dirty and exhausted. Ezra had been right, it was only about noon and they were already done marching for the day. But, it didn't matter, Christopher didn't think he would have been able to go much farther, and the looks on the other men's faces said they felt the same.

The men scattered and collapsed wherever they could find shade. A few braved the thick vines and underbrush in the densely packed woods looking for firewood. Christopher and the other sergeants rounded up men for canteen details. Most of their canteens had gone dry several hours ago, and the men would need water if they were to recover from the long, grueling march.

As Christopher moved among the men, selecting several to assist with canteens, he wished he could lie down and join them and cursed the stripes he wore for that and many other reasons. Then he saw Company B marching into the woods for picket duty and smirked. One of the first things he'd learned in the army was, no matter how bad it seemed, things could always be worse.

After canteen detail, Christopher joined the other sergeants and several corporals for a meal. There was little shade in the area, except in the woods, but they were so thick it was hard to find a clear space big enough to build a fire. Given the heat and lack of rain, the whole area looked like a tinder-box to Christopher.

As soon as he'd eaten, Christopher looked for a place to lie down and sleep. He moved along the edge of the woods, but every shady area seemed to be taken already. Finally, he found an open area shaded by a large oak tree and clear of the underbrush and thorny vines that filled the woods. He wondered why no one else had claimed a spot under the tree as he quickly removed his traps and unbuttoned his jacket. He'd dropped his knapsack on the march along with almost everyone else, so he rolled up his jacket as a pillow and stretched out on the ground. The grass looked thick and that would offer some cushion.

He thought of home and family, of being done with the war, but he also thought he'd miss it—as bad as it was most of the time, there was a sense of belonging and excitement that would be nearly impossible to recreate in civilian life.

He rolled over on his side and a rock dug into his hip. At least it was round and smooth. He adjusted himself around the rock and tried to relax, but other rocks, smaller but sharper, kept poking him. That must be why no one else had claimed the spot. No matter, he was determined to get comfortable. He'd just brush away as many rocks as he could and those he couldn't, he'd dig out with his bayonet.

He sat up and dug around with his fingers. As he did, what he thought were rocks came loose, and he scrambled back. Poking up out of the ground where he'd been lying were human bones. He could see scraps of cloth around some of them, and what he'd thought was a smooth, round rock was actually the top of a skull.

He grabbed his gear and moved several feet away, but a close inspection of the ground there revealed the same gruesome results. The whole area must be a mass grave. That was why no one else was lying there.

Looking up, he saw several men watching him. As their eyes met his, they all turned and walked away, giggling among themselves like a bunch of schoolgirls.

Christopher scooped up his jacket and gear and headed for the tree. He might pick up a couple extra bugs that close to the wood, but at least no bodies would be buried there. As he drifted off, he wondered how many bodies filled the dirt next to him, and dreamt of them reaching up and trying to pull him down to join them.

THEY WERE BACK ON THE road early the next morning, the sense of excitement replaced by nervous anticipation. The day started with an artillery barrage, somewhere to the south and west. Then, as they continued to march, they heard the staccato bursts of rifle fire mingled in with the boom of artillery. So much for sneaking around Lee, Christopher thought.

They stopped around noon and rested with their rifles by their sides, ready to go wherever they may be needed at a moment's notice. They were encamped in a freshly plowed field next to a recently abandoned farmhouse, and the recently turned earth made for a soft bed. But, Christopher felt a little ashamed that all the work the poor farmer had put into preparing his field had been wiped out in a matter of minutes as the turned earth was tamped back down by the thousands of men now scattered across it.

While they awaited orders, some men passed the time going through the pre-battle rituals they'd developed over the last three years. Some prayed, some wrote home (giving the letters to comrades to mail in case they should fall), some cleaned their rifles and checked their rounds, some made nervous chatter and played practical jokes on their pards. What they didn't have to do this time was throw out their liquor, cards, dirty pictures, and any other evidence of their sins. If they should die and (bigger if) their possessions were collected and sent home, the last thing anyone wanted was that stuff mailed to their wives or mothers, but all that was already scattered across the Virginia countryside.

Their canteens were already empty again, and it didn't take long for them to run the farm's well dry refilling them. No one had a full canteen, and the temperature was already above ninety degrees.

Just like the woods where they'd spent the night, the woods surrounding the field were densely packed with spindly pine and cedar trees choked by an abundance of thorny vines and thick undergrowth. Looking at it, Christopher tried to imagine maneuvering through that tangled mess. It would be impossible to keep a straight fighting line. More likely, the command would become fractured and reduced to small groups of men fighting on their own. Also, your line of sight would be limited. You wouldn't be able to tell friend from foe until you were right on them.

Despite that, Christopher was excited and almost looking forward to the fight. He was excited because this time would be different. Grant was not like those other generals. But, hadn't they said the same thing about Burnside, and Hooker, and Mead? It had always been the same old dance: fight a big battle, lose thousands of men, and then slink off having accomplished nothing.

Sure, Grant said he would push through and keep pushing all the way to Richmond, but hadn't they all made big promises? And what if Grant did keep his promise? What would that be like? Would they fight and march, day after day, all summer long? Could they even do it? Would it be an Antietam, followed by a Fredericksburg, followed by a Gettysburg, all in quick succession? How many of them would be left after something like that?

As Christopher's excitement gave way to worry, he was interrupted by the bugle call to assemble. Grabbing his rifle, he rose slowly, groaning like an old man, and trotted toward the space in the line allocated for Company D. The worry gave way once more to excitement. It was now late afternoon, and all they'd done so far was wait and listen. Maybe now they would get a chance to fight before the day was done.

They resumed their march down the same road until it intersected with a plank road. The battle sounds were now almost on their right, and Christopher was wondering if they were going to turn down the plank road when the corps started breaking up in battle formation to the right of the road facing the battle. The 8th was on the far right, well away from the road and facing the wall of vegetation, when they received the command to move out.

The woods were just as bad as Christopher had imagined. The vines clung to everything—knocking his hat off, pulling his rifle almost out of his hands, wrapping around his feet and tripping him every few steps. The vines with thorns, though, were worse—they tore flesh and cloth alike. After only a few steps everyone's uniforms were in tatters, and blood dripped down their faces and hands. Christopher thought of Jesus and his crown of thorns with a new appreciation for the suffering his savior had gone through.

The bushes were so thick it took a great effort to push through them and the trees so close together he sometimes had to turn sideways to keep going. Just as he expected, the straight line fell apart almost immediately, and he could barely see the men next to him, let alone the rest of the regiment. No wonder this area was called the Wilderness.

The more Christopher struggled, the more he thought the Wilderness had an evil quality to it. It's misshapen trees and thorny vines that threatened to pull you down and not let you go made him think of the woods in old German folk tales—where the evil witch lived intent on snaring small children. Then they came upon the scene of a recent skirmish.

Christopher had seen many battlefields, and men killed violently by the score, but the sight before him took what little breath he had left away. The trees were shot to shreds, some actually felled by the volume of lead passing through them, and most of those still standing were little more than splinters going up to about seven feet off the ground. Glistening red blood dripped from the brownish green leaves and vines, the puddles on the ground congealed and almost black. The dead and dying lay scattered in stillness or in agony, some held upright by vines as if to deny them the rest they so richly deserved. But worse still, the intense fire of the opposing armies had caught the dry, brittle undergrowth on fire. Scattered around the carnage, dead leaves and vines smoldered, creating thick columns of dark gray smoke that rose up to mingle with the whitish gray canopy of gun smoke above their heads. The smell of burning foliage and gun smoke mixed with the smell of burning flesh where the fires had reached the dead. Christopher wretched and threw up what was left of the hardtack he'd eaten earlier.

He had no more time to contemplate the horror that these men had gone through. The enemy was on the run, and they had a chance to catch them. The bugle call to advance at the double quick sounded, and the men moved out, moving around the bodies and burning brush. Wounded men reached out for succor, but they were veterans and knew better than to slow their advance. There would be time for the wounded later.

As Christopher stepped forward the image of the man bleeding out next to him in the trench at Gettysburg flashed before his eyes. He pushed it aside and kept going.

The fighting and the rebels' retreat had cleared the way somewhat, making their pursuit easier. The sounds of fighting were growing with a steady crescendo, and an occasional cannon ball would come crashing through the trees, roaring like a freight train and obliterating everything in its path. *Any minute now*, Christopher thought. Then, they called a halt.

Once everyone had stopped, Christopher could hear better what was going on around him. Ahead, the battle continued, but not nearly as intensely. They were still near the plank road. Christopher could hear the booming of the planks as thousands of men, horses, wagons, and artillery passed over them.

They received the order to rest in line and wait. Christopher lay his rifle down, breech side up, and sat. He shook his canteen and the pitch of the splashing sound it made told him he was almost out of water. He took a swig and prayed there was a stream somewhere nearby.

As they waited, there was a flurry of gunfire from somewhere ahead on the plank road, followed by the sound of a wagon or caisson accompanied by many running men. Then it stopped as quickly as it had begun.

All around him, men speculated what was going on, and what part they might yet play in today's battle. But, the longer they waited, the quieter things became. Finally, Christopher decided they were done for the day. The fact that there was no call to retreat and that they did not strike camp told him that things would pick back up in the morning.

After digging a hasty entrenchment in which to pass the night, Christopher was ordered to take a detail back to where the plank road intersected with the road they'd come in on. There were supply wagons with ammunition, rations, and water barrels. After replenishing the regiment, everyone settled in for the night. Cook fires were built, water was boiled for coffee, and salt pork was fried for dinner. After a couple cups of coffee and a hunk of salt pork with hard tack, Christopher found himself unable to keep his eyes open. Fortunately, he didn't have guard duty, so he let the sleep take him as he lay in the freshly turned dirt of the rifle pit he'd dug for himself.

The dreams were particularly intense that night, full of mangled bodies and puddles of blood, but no dream-Daniel to soothe him. At some point, he became aware of his twitching and writhing, and slowly came awake. But, though he knew he was fully awake, he could still hear the screams. He opened his eyes and looked up over the dirt pile beside his pit. It was a dark night in the Wilderness, the moon and stars blocked by the dense foliage, but there were glowing spots scattered around them in the trees. Fires. The screams, though distant, took on an ominous quality.

He squinted to see who was in the pit next to him. Finally, he recognized Nathan Jump. "Nate, that you?"

"Yeah. Chris?"

"Yes, it's me. Is that the wounded screaming?"

"I think so. It's bad tonight. Even worse than usual."

Christopher remembered the smoldering bodies they'd passed that afternoon. "Why don't someone do something?"

"I think it's between the lines. I guess no one wants to get lost out there in the dark in this thick brush. Too easy to get killed or captured."

Christopher remembered his own time as a prisoner of war. Now there were horror stories going around that made his experience pale in comparison. There was one place down in Georgia called Andersonville, where escapees said thousands of men were crammed into a small stockade, with nothing to eat and living in their own filth.

Christopher bowed his head. He didn't think he'd have the courage to go out there either.

After that, he couldn't sleep. The amount of noise going on around him said only a few of them could. The screams and calls for help went on for a couple more hours, punctuated by occasional shrieks of pain and terror that would go on for a couple minutes before stopping abruptly.

Christopher managed to sleep fitfully for an hour or so before the sun started to rise. Then it was time to get up again and face the enemy once more.

THE DAWN WAS GREETED by cannon fire from both sides, followed by a crescendo of rifle fire as the armies continued their running battle. As the 8th moved forward, they passed through areas where first their soldiers, and then the enemy, had spent the night. It was apparent that the enemy was falling back, which made Christopher happy but anxious to get up to the front and get a few shots off before it was over.

After a couple hours, orders were passed down, and the 8th, along with the 14th Indiana and the 7th West Virginia, were peeled off from the rest of the brigade and turned left toward the plank road. Christopher wanted to know why, but he'd come to realize that as a sergeant, he didn't know much more about what was going on than he had as a private. You just move along wherever the orders take you and hope it's not straight into hell.

They were advancing by regiment, with the 14th Indiana in the lead, followed by the 8th, and the 7th West Virginia last. They paused at the plank road, letting the 14th cross first. The Indianians ran across the road, screaming huzzahs, the rhythmic booming of their feet on the wooden planks echoing through the trees. As they neared the tree line on the other side, they were brought to an abrupt halt by a volley of rifle fire from an unseen enemy. Several men fell. Those still standing returned fire into the underbrush.

Then the 8th was ordered forward. Knowing that they were either going to pull the 14th's fat out of the fire or join them in burning gave Christopher a thrill that he didn't understand. He should be afraid, but the fear was gone. Screaming as loud as he could, he had to control himself so as not to outpace the regimental colors. As soon as they were on the other side of the road, they moved into line on the 14th's left. As the men were taking their places down the line, they came under fire. The man next to Christopher fell, screaming in agony. That, he thought, should sober him somewhat, but it just seemed to fuel the flames. He wanted to gnash his teeth and rend his clothes, to fight like his ancestors with sword and club. He fired as soon as he was in line, not waiting for orders.

They fought until there was no more return fire, then they entered the woods in pursuit. Soon, they had the enemy in sight, and a running battle ensued. Men loaded their rifles on the move, stopping only to fire. As smoke filled the woods, they could no longer see the enemy and had to follow the sounds of their running and firing. After a few minutes, Christopher got the sense that the return fire was getting closer, and increasing in volume.

Then they were hit by a volley of rifle fire like a physical barrier, stopping the regiments cold, killing and wounding hundreds in an instant. The line of smoke before them extended as far as Christopher could see on either side. As the smoke cleared, the enemy appeared—black shapes in the swirling mist, standing shoulder-to-shoulder in a line that reached as far as he could see in either direction. Another massive volley of rifle fire once more hid them in smoke and another wall of lead tore into the men who, only a moment before, thought they were pursuing a defeated foe.

Screams of agony and panic filled the air. All his senses overwhelmed, Christopher became completely disoriented and didn't know which way to shoot or run. More gunfire erupted to the sides. The enemy line extended well beyond theirs, and they were being flanked! The bugle call to retreat sounded—needlessly, Christopher thought, most of the men were already on the run.

The euphoria he'd been feeling evaporated, and an unreasoning terror took hold of Christopher like he'd never experienced in any other battle. The lack of any visual indication as to where anything or anyone was, combined with the overwhelming noise of gunfire coming from multiple directions, left him completely disoriented. He was afraid to move for fear he would run right into the enemy line.

He caught a glimpse of their regimental colors and followed. The foliage seemed to increase its efforts to tear his clothes and flesh, to hold him back and keep him from safety. His hat was the first to go. Then his rifle was ripped out of his hands. He momentarily contemplated leaving it, but didn't want to face the rest of his regiment without it. He turned, grabbed it where it hung wrapped in vine, and pulled it free with a massive tug. Before turning back around, he saw what appeared to be thousands of gray-clad men pushing their way through the underbrush.

Christopher came out of the trees at the plank road, where the fractured command was trying to put itself back together again. On the other side of the road was a hastily erected entrenchment, occupied by another brigade. Christopher took heart at the sight of fresh troops and thought they would have a chance to regroup on the other side. But, as soon as the retreating Federals reached the entrenchment, the soldiers occupying it took off running. As he jumped down into a shallow rifle pit, Christopher looked back and saw what looked like an entire division of rebel soldiers coming out of the trees.

Officers were screaming orders. Christopher looked around. Not a single member of the 8th was to be seen. On his left was a man he recognized from the 7th West Virginia; to the right, he saw several members of the 14th Indiana, including Si and Shorty.

They fired another volley, which had all the effect of slapping a bear, then took off running again.

Though the woods were opening up from all the flying lead and men running through the underbrush, it was still thick enough to separate the retreating men. He could hear others crashing through the brush, but Christopher could only see a handful of other men around him as they made their way toward the rear. After a few minutes, Christopher and the others stepped out into an open area and found themselves facing several hundred rifles. Fortunately, they belonged to another brigade from the Second Corps, and, after an initial rush of panic that he would be shot by his own side, Christopher felt a flood of relief that left him weak and wobbly.

As he and the rest of the retreating men pushed their way through the front ranks, they were met with a few words of encouragement and a lot of ribbing.

"What's a matter? You boys lost?

"Did you see a rebel and get scared?"

"I haven't seen running like that since we sent the secesh packing at Bristol Station."

"You boys looking for your mommas?"

Christopher smiled and nodded, then said, "Laugh if you want, boys, but while you were back here lollygagging, we were up front fighting."

"How'd that work out for ya, hoss?"

"Just fine. So fine in fact, we invited a few to come join us. I 'spect they'll be along any minute now."

"We're ready for them!"

Christopher looked around and thought of the mass of men pursuing them. "I hope so."

Christopher moved to the rear to try to find the rest of his regiment, expecting any minute to hear the front lines begin firing. After several minutes, he became curious. Hadn't they pursued them across the road? Surely they wouldn't have passed up the opportunity to wipe out a couple regiments? As he wondered what may be going on, Charlie Locker walked up.

"Come on, Chris. We've got what's left of the regiment back together, and we've been ordered to the rear."

"That's welcome news. My cartridge box is about empty."

"As is mine. Hopefully, those ammo wagons are still down there."

The two sergeants walked toward their company. As they approached, Christopher saw Ezra joking with the Jump brothers. Smiling, he approached the three men hoping for a reconciliation. "Looks like you boys came out of that little fracas none the worse for wear."

The Jumps nodded. "That was a close one," Joe said.

"I couldn't see nuthin' running through those trees," Nathan said. "All I could think of was I hope I don't run right into a company of rebs. Last thing I want is to spend the rest of the war in Andersonville."

Christopher nodded. "They couldn't feed their prisoners three years ago. I can't imagine how bad it is now." He looked over at Ezra. "That's a pretty nasty cut you have on your cheek, Ez. You should—" Christopher caught himself before he finished the rest of that sentence. The flash of anger in Ezra's eyes told him that telling him what he should do would not help toward the two reconciling.

Fortunately, Nathan kept the conversation going. "Ez was telling us he saw an officer with the seat of his pants torn open. Showing the enemy his about face he was." The younger Jump brother laughed.

"Did you see that New York soldier at Antietam?" Joe asked. "Lost his whole pants and marched out on the field buck naked from the waist down."

"I didn't see it, but I heard about it," Christopher said.

"I don't know how you could miss it, they were there at the Bloody Lane."

Christopher shrugged. "Busy, I guess."

"Them New York boys are all cowards," Ezra said. "He probably did it hoping to get out of the fight."

"Now, Ez," Joe said. "That's no way to talk. We're all on the same side, ya know. Besides, after the reorganization, we have a lot of New York boys in the Second Corps."

"Great," Ezra responded to Joe, but he was looking at Christopher. "Taints the rest of us with their stink of cowardice. Pretty soon, we'll be just like the 11th."

"There's no call for that," Joe said, raising his voice.

Christopher stepped between them. "Whether they're cowards or not, it's nothing to get riled up about."

"Yeah, Joe," Ezra said. "Listen to the sergeant. Ain't nothing to get riled about. Is there, Sergeant?"

"Why do you keep calling Chris that?" Nathan asked Ezra. Joe put a hand on his brother's arm and shook his head. Nathan shook his head back.

"No. You two are pards. We got some hellacious fighting coming up, and you don't want to possibly meet your maker with anger in your hearts toward—"

"Sergeant!" Lieutenant Manahan approached the group. "Get these men lined up. We're pulling back."

"Yes, sir!" *That didn't help none*, Christopher thought.

"I didn't hear no bugle call to assemble," Joe pointed out.

"Maybe the bugler's dead," Ezra responded.

As they approached the assembly area, Christopher tried one more time. "You know, Ez, Nate's right. We shouldn't be going into this campaign all mad at each other."

Ezra's eyes flicked to him, then away, but in that brief flash Christopher thought he saw something. "Maybe so. But things are different now. That's a fact, and there's nothing you can do about it."

"A lot of sergeants and privates are friends. What about Parker? Or Charlie?"

Ezra shrugged. "They were corporals to start, so they were always over us. That's just the way it was. Hell, a year ago, you was a private same as me."

"But I'm still me. The stripes didn't change that."

"Mebbe. Don't you have some sergeant things you need to be doing?"

Unfortunately, Ezra was right; he did have to ensure his squad was lined up and ready to go.

THEY MARCHED TO THE rear, near where they'd camped the night before, and were reunited with the rest of their brigade. There, on the road they'd come in on (which Christopher learned was called Brock Road) was a line of supply wagons, loaded with rations, ammunition, and water barrels. The sound of intense fighting was still going on all around them, so they filled their canteens and cartridge boxes, stuffed a few hard crackers in their haversacks, and steeled themselves to go back in.

The brigade marched up Brock Road to where it intersected with the plank road (Christopher still didn't know the name of this one "Something Plank Road" he assumed). There, the vast majority of the Second Corps was assembled behind a line of parapets and rifle pits that hadn't been there that morning. Out front were several yards of tree trunks buried in the ground at an angle with their sharpened ends sticking out, creating an effective abatis.

As they waited to either be attacked or sent somewhere else, Christopher thought that there was less artillery in the fight for this battle. Batteries were firing with regularity all over the vast area where the battle was taking place, and he'd seen and heard more than one cannon ball crashing through the trees, but there weren't the tremendous booms of massive artillery barrages that were a staple of every major battle he'd been in since Antietam. Maybe the thick undergrowth made it too hard to move artillery and too hard to see where to aim.

Christopher looked around for Ezra. He would have liked someone to share his thoughts with, but Ezra was at the other end of Company D, ignoring him. Then an artillery battery, accompanied by a battalion of cavalry, came riding up Brock Road, and the 8th was ordered to accompany them as they probed the left flank.

They marched up Brock Road beyond the plank road for a half mile, where the battery lined up across the road and the cavalry went ahead to probe further. The 8th formed a battle line on either side of the road as support for the artillery. After a while, the cavalry returned and reported no enemy activity. The artillerymen hooked their cannon back up to the caissons, and the force returned to the main body of the Second Corps.

By now, it was late in the afternoon, and fighting had been going on at different places around a wide area since sunrise that morning. The 8th joined its brigade in line behind the men manning the parapets and waited. That large force that had attacked them was still out there somewhere, and no one thought they would leave without attacking.

Sure enough, as the shadows began to extend across the road, they heard the enemy's approach. The crashing of underbrush had become a common sound that day, and Christopher could tell by the extent of the commotion that they were being approached by a large force. After several minutes, the first line of enemy soldiers appeared out of the trees. As they were straightening their line, more men in gray appeared and began forming new lines behind the first. And then, more and more men appeared, until the first lines were forced forward, ready or not.

Suddenly, the sound of crackling underbrush was overwhelmed by a massive rebel yell. The yips and screeches were unnerving at first, but Christopher had long ago gotten used to it. He watched as the rebels ran, bayonets forward, toward the front line. Christopher said a silent prayer for the boys up there and hoped the line held.

The rebels hit the abates, and their forward momentum came to an abrupt halt as men got hung up on the prickly array of sharpened logs and branches. Say what you might about the area, Christopher thought, but at least there was plenty of material for barricades.

As the first line of rebels became mired in the abatis, the second line had to stop and wait. As they did, the Federal line opened up on them, mowing men down in droves. Anger and frustration gave way to fear as the survivors of the first volley saw their comrades falling like wheat before the scythe. Their efforts to break through and reach the breastworks intensified, but it seemed the harder they struggled, the more entangled they became. And now they had the wounded and the dead to go around as well. Another volley, and the attack began to disintegrate.

Christopher felt a thrill as the Federal forces began cheering. The men on the line began going over the breast works and, without orders, the 8th and the rest of their brigade followed. Christopher yipped and yelled his own version of the rebel yell as he climbed over the pile of logs and dirt, pushed his way through the makeshift abates, and shot down rebel soldiers almost point blank. Almost at once, the entangled enemy threw down their rifles and surrendered. Those not in the abatis turned and ran.

Afterward, as they marched down the road with their prisoners, Christopher felt an overwhelming sense of accomplishment and pride. He knew that the 8th had taken a lot of prisoners at Gettysburg, but he'd been wounded and out of the fight by that point. He looked at his dejected foe and the smiling faces of his comrades and felt hope. Hope that it would all soon be over, and they'd get to go home. Hope that he'd outlive this bloody war yet. Hope that he had a life ahead of him after all.

So this is what winning feels like, he thought.

Chapter Twenty-Three

D arkness and rain.
    Christopher couldn't see anything, or feel anything but wet—and an insistent poking forcing him awake. It had been a deep, dreamless sleep, the kind only days of marching and fighting could induce, so consciousness was slow in coming. Where was he? Why was it so dark? Who was so rudely poking him and exhorting him to get up?

Christopher sat up, rubbing his eyes. But still they were so crusted over all he could make out was shapes carrying lanterns as they moved through the sleeping troops, kicking and poking men awake. Then he heard the command to fall in being yelled all around him. Why didn't the musician just blow assembly? Did they think they would take the enemy by surprise or something? A bugle call would have been no louder than all this yelling.

Christopher rolled up his wool and gum blankets, tied the ends together, and draped it over one shoulder. He then limped (courtesy of an enemy Minié ball that had grazed his left foot and torn a gash in his shoe) over to where they'd stacked arms the morning before.

They'd spent the day digging trenches and building up defensive works and hadn't got to sleep until well after dark. Now this. *Did the big bugs think they were machines that could run for days on end with only a little oil?*

As he approached the assembly area Christopher looked for Ezra and imagined the running dialog of complaints they would have been going through if they'd been lining up together. As bad as things got, it never seemed as bad when you had someone with which to share your misery. But Ezra was at the other end of the company line.

It was almost an hour before the 8th moved out. They'd spent that time standing in line watching a steady progression of soldiers, little more than black silhouettes in the starless night risking chastisement by carrying on a steady stream of complaints as they marched. But the officers didn't seem to care.

It looked to Christopher as if the entire Second Corps was on the move. This promised to be big—not the piecemeal skirmishing they'd been doing the last few days since the battle in the Wilderness. Christopher recalled the fight to take the ridge called Laurel Hill—where he'd damn near got his foot shot off. After struggling through another densely packed woods—this time cedar with a lot of dead logs to go over and dead limbs to snag and rip their clothing—they came to the base of a hill with a well-entrenched enemy presence at the top. The slope of the hill consisted of loose, sandy soil which, coupled with its steepness, slowed them down. Men struggled for a foothold, sliding back some with each step forward, out of breath before they even started, and the enemy mowed them down in droves. Many a fine man had died trying to take that hill, including the 8th's color bearer, and then they just went around the damn thing.

But in the dark, Christopher had no idea in which direction they were marching. For all he knew they were slinking back to the Rapidan with their tails between their legs like they'd done so many times before. But he had the feeling that was not the case. The officers seemed determined—nervous, but determined.

At least Grant was keeping his promise to push on, no matter what. Christopher, like many other men in his company, wasn't too impressed with Grant after their first battle with him in charge. They'd out-numbered and out-equipped the enemy when they'd met in the Wilderness, but, from everything Christopher heard, the result had been, at best, a draw. If Lee had had the same number of men, rested, well-fed, and with an endless supply of ammunition, then most likely he would have beaten them soundly.

Maybe now the enemy was as tired and worn down as they were, and the Army of the Potomac would finally have a decisive victory. No more lame excuses. If Christopher heard the term "strategic win" to describe a battle where they lost more men and gained no ground, he'd puke.

The rain that had been coming down in blinding sheets off and on the last couple days was at the moment only a cool mist. A cool mist that penetrated every tear in his clothing and left him cold and shivering while they waited to march. *Wasn't that just the way?* Christopher thought. *Either it's blazing hot and there's no water to be had, or it's freezing cold and more water than we know what to do with.* He'd never insult God with such a label, but maybe Mother Nature was a bureaucrat.

For such a massive formation, they were quickly underway. That's when the real pain began. With each step, Christopher's foot ached more and more, until every time he put his weight on it a sharp pain shot half way up his leg. His shoe was coming apart as well, and it seemed every few steps a sharp rock found its way inside.

He was wondering how much farther he could go when he heard the call to halt. Stopping was such a relief Christopher's whole body went limp, and he almost collapsed. He leaned on his rifle, swaying, while they waited for orders to fall out.

Instead they formed two long battle lines, with the Second Corps' first two divisions in the first line, and the third (including the 8th on the left) and fourth divisions in the second line. There they were to rest on arms until dawn.

Christopher pulled off the soggy blanket that hung over his shoulder and collapsed where he stood. He didn't go to sleep right away as everyone around him seemed to do. Instead, he removed his left shoe, shook out the gravel, and tried to determine, by feel as much as by sight, if the wound was bleeding again. The rain made it difficult, but he figured that blood would feel thicker than water.

After determining that his foot wasn't bleeding—at least not too bad—he tried to tighten the leather string he'd used to sew up his shoe. There wasn't much he could do, though; the leather had stretched and was too wet to untie and tighten. He would just have to get by until the rain finally stopped and everything dried out, or he had the time to replace the string. Not that it would help much longer—the sole was coming away from the upper. It wouldn't be long before the shoe fell apart. Since the supply wagons were only bringing up rations and ammunition, he would then have to take shoes from a corpse.

Christopher used his gum blanket to wrap his rifle and lay down on the water-logged ground, using his soaked wool blanket as a pillow. He was just drifting off when a shrill bugle call pulled him back to his wet, miserable existence. He crawled up, moaning like an old man. His foot throbbed and his muscles ached in ways he'd never dreamt possible. At least the wet coolness seemed to sooth the many cuts and scratches that covered his body. Or so he imagined. Truth be told, he couldn't remember what it felt like to not hurt all over.

The sun was rising, but a heavy fog covered the ground, limiting Christopher's vision to just a few yards. He could make out the line before them, and he could see down the line he was in at least as far as the 8th went, but a swirling white mist hid everything else. The bugle call to advance sounded, and they stepped off.

Christopher limped heavily at first, fearful of dropping back. But, after a few steps it got easier, and, though the pain was still there and his shoe threatened to come apart at every step, he was able to stay in line.

The ground they covered appeared to be made up of a series of rolling ridges. They would march up to the top and then down into a swale. At the top of each ridge, Christopher tried to see what lay ahead, but the fog hid everything from view. At the bottom of the swales, all he could see was the line in front of him, struggling up the hill.

Then, he crested a ridgeline and saw the enemy entrenchments before them. It was just a shape in the mist, like some kind of medieval castle on a foggy shore. Then they went down into the next swale, again blocking his view. As his line came up, the sun was trying to pierce the fog, and he could see some detail of what lay before them. It was a parapet made of logs and earth, in places taller than a man. Before it was several yards of abatis—sharpened logs and branches placed close together and pointing outward to ensnare attackers. The whole thing was at the top of a ridge that seemed to dominate the rolling hills they had passed over.

The first line had just reached the end of the abatis and was working their way through the logs. The second line stopped at the top of a ridge and waited—giving Christopher a clear view of the attack.

As he watched, a line of men rose up over the top of the parapet and raised their rifles at the attackers. A volley of rifle fire shattered the morning calm. Squawking birds flew up from the trees, and men fell among the logs. The front line increased their effort to break through and reach the parapet, yelling and cheering as they struggled to push their way through the abatis.

Christopher looked for artillery positions in the defensive works, and, though he saw what he thought would be good spots for cannon, they appeared to be empty. Also, the volley could have been much worse; it sounded like many of the rifles misfired. He hoped his cartridges would be dry enough when the time came.

There were a few more pops of rifle fire, and then the first line was through and at the base of the parapet. As they struggled to climb over, men from the other side began clubbing the attackers with shovels and hatchets. The attackers responded by thrusting their bayonet-mounted rifles up into the defenders. There were several rifle shots, and then the attackers were on top of the wall. Many leapt down among the enemy on the other side, while others paused to fire their rifles down into the enemy before following their brethren into the fray. Again, it sounded to Christopher as if many of the rifles misfired, increasing his concern about the condition of his own rounds.

As Christopher listened to the sounds coming from the other side of the parapet—screams of anger and pain, accompanied by a melody of cracking wood and clanging metal—a visual image appeared in his mind of the pits of hell. His breathing and heart rate increased to the point that he was getting dizzy when it all went quiet.

After a long moment, the shrill blast of the bugle call to advance disturbed Christopher's growing fear that the two leading divisions had been broken and destroyed. Then, Union soldiers appeared on the top of the wall, accompanied by a few Confederates. The rebels' hanging heads and drooping shoulders told Christopher they were beaten men—the Union had won. The several thousand men awaiting the outcome of the battle broke into a cheer—pumping fists and throwing hats into the air. Soon a steady stream of rebel prisoners were making their way over the wall and being led away by armed guards.

A hand slapped Christopher on the back. He looked over to see Lieutenant Manahan's smiling face. "This is it, Galloway. With this breach we can split the rebel line in two and defeat them in detail," the grinning lieutenant said.

Christopher stared at the man and nodded but was thinking Manahan had never said more than two words to him in the three years they'd served together. Even as an enlisted man he'd been standoffish; now they were best friends?

A massive rifle volley sounded from the other side of the parapet. Men on the wall managing the removal of prisoners raised their rifles to fire in response, and, with a piercing rebel yell, their charges took advantage of the situation to turn and attack.

The bugle call to advance at the double quick sounded, and officers ran out front with swords raised. "Forward!" Lieutenant Manahan yelled.

They ran down into the last swale and then hit the abatis on the other side. The straight lines fell apart, but the men pushed through. On the other side of the abatis, Lieutenant Manahan scrabbled to the top of the wall, raised his sword, and turned back to look at his men. He opened his mouth as if he was about to say something, and the top of his head blew off. He collapsed over the side onto his men.

A couple men pulled the lieutenant out of the way while the rest climbed the wall. The logs, Christopher noted, were fresh cut and still had their bark, which made it easier to climb. He didn't pause at the top to see what he was getting into, the death of the lieutenant taught him that. He just jumped.

On the other side, Christopher found himself in a crowd of men packed so tight he could barely move his arms. A line of fresh Confederate reinforcements were pouring lead into their attackers even though their own men were mixed in with the enemy. Those on the outskirts of the crowd were returning fire, and as they fell others stepped forward to take their place. More men were still pouring over the wall, forcing the crowd forward. Then, as if by mutual agreement, the two sides charged each other, thrusting their bayonets before them. Once the two forces intermingled, they went from thrusting to clubbing, raising their rifles over their heads and bringing them down onto whatever was before them. Many men lost their rifles and resorted to punching and kicking. Some snatched up the hatchets and shovels that lay strewn about the area and began swinging.

Christopher held onto his rifle until the bayonet caught between the ribs of a rebel trying to split his skull with a hatchet, pulling it out of his hands as the man fell. He grabbed the rifle and tugged, eliciting a cry of pain from his enemy, but it wouldn't budge. So he ripped the hatchet out of the man's hand.

Before Christopher could straighten, the man grabbed the sleeve of his left arm with a bloody hand. Blood poured out of his mouth as he gurgled an angry epithet at Christopher and tried to pull him down with him. Christopher cleaved the man's skull with his own hatchet.

Christopher threw himself forward with the bloody hatchet over his head, screaming what he thought an Indian war cry might sound like. A rebel thrust his bayonet at him, and Christopher grabbed the rifle with his left hand, deflecting the thrust, and brought the hatchet down on the man's wrist, half severing his hand. He followed up by knocking out the man's teeth with the back-side of the hatchet before pushing on.

It seemed to go on like that for hours, but it was probably only minutes, before the press of Confederate reinforcements became too much, and the Federals retreated back over the wall, leaving in their wake piles of dead and dying men from both sides.

On the other side, the Union men hunkered down at the base of the wall. After fighting so hard, no one wanted to give any more ground than they had to. Nor did they want to get shot in the back trying to work their way through the abatis. So the two sides occupied the same area, separated by a single wall of logs and mud, about six feet high and three feet wide.

CHRISTOPHER SUNK DOWN in the mud with his back to the wall, sucking in big breaths of air. His head was swimming and his vision blurred. He couldn't get the images of the damage the hatchet had done out of his head. It was like something out of a nightmare, only he was the monster.

He dropped the hatchet and took stock of his condition. His clothes were now even more torn and ragged than before. They were also drenched in mud and blood—some of it his, some not. He had several cuts and bruises, but nothing life-threatening. Sometime in the fight he'd lost his left shoe, and the bandage had come undone.

He removed the bandage the rest of the way and looked at the wound. It was swollen and tender to the touch. If he thought about it, it also throbbed a dull pain even when he wasn't touching it. He should have had a surgeon look at it, but it was too late now.

Looking around, he saw several dozen corpses laying in and around the abatis. There were plenty of shoes available to him. He spotted a dead man whose feet looked about his size. Limping his way around the mass of men trying to stay close to the wall, he went to the corpse, knelt down, and untied the shoes. The leather shoestring was soaked through, so the knot was almost impossible to loosen. The entire time he picked at the knot, a spot between Christopher's shoulder blades tingled in anticipation of a rebel bullet. Finally, after much picking, he loosened the knot enough to grip it with his fingernails.

He soon had the shoe off, but putting it on his own foot had its own challenges. Trying to pull the wet shoe onto his swollen foot sent waves of pain shooting up his leg. When he finally got it on and tied, he leaned back on his elbows, out of breath and exhausted.

"Better get back here under some cover, Sergeant."

Christopher looked up at the man who'd spoken and saw several men lifting their rifles above their heads and firing over the wall. The Confederates were doing the same thing and bullets were smacking the logs of the abatis all around him. He grabbed the dead man's rifle—fortunately it was an Enfield and not a Springfield, so his rounds would fit—and crawled as quickly as he could until he was under the trajectory of the bullets passing overhead.

Christopher nodded to the man that had warned him and looked around. He recognized no one. They all had Second Corps badges, but there was no one from his brigade, let alone his regiment or company.

By now, most of the fog had burned off, though it was still cloudy and gray. He could see the wall curved around at the ends, forming a salient that stuck out from the rest of the Confederate line. *That must be why they'd chosen this spot to attack*, he thought. Facing the wall, the sounds of a fresh assault started on his right, so Christopher turned left, and he made his way down the line, calling out for the 8th Ohio.

After only a few minutes, he stopped to rest. He felt like an old man trying to make it up the stairs. There was a kid sitting next to him, probably no older than Christopher had been when he'd joined up. His uniform, though muddy and torn, didn't look as worn out as most. *Probably a replacement*, he thought. The kid was crying and staring out at the field beyond the abatis.

"What's your name, bub?" Christopher asked.

The kid started as if pulled back from thoughts far away. "Jimmy."

"Jimmy what, Private?"

It looked as if the boy blushed a little. *At least he can still feel embarrassment*, Christopher thought.

"Danner."

"You scared, Private Danner?"

The boy looked away and gave one quick nod.

"Me too."

Jimmy Danner looked back at him.

Christopher nodded.

"You're thinking of making a break for it, aren't you?"

Jimmy stuttered and shook his head. Now there was no mistaking the deep crimson that manifested itself under the dark tan of his cheeks.

"It's all right, Danner. I don't blame you. It's not what you expected, is it?"

Jimmy shook his head.

"You want to go home?"

Nod.

Christopher pointed out to the field. "That ain't the way."

Jimmy's eyes narrowed.

"You make a run for it, if the Johnnies don't shoot you in the back, your own people will. And if they don't now, they'll hunt you down after the battle, bring you back, and shoot you then. And even if you don't get caught, you'll be a wanted man for the rest of your life, never able to go home."

The tears were back, and Jimmy's lip quivered.

"Unfortunately, for you and me, and all these other boys in this pit, there's only one way home." Christopher paused. "Over that wall."

Jimmy shook his head, his eyes like saucers.

"Over that wall, through them rebs, and all the way to Richmond. For us, that's the only way home."

Christopher watched the emotions war inside Jimmy's head through the myriad of expressions the boy made. Eventually, resignation won out, and the boy sighed, his shoulders slumping. "I'll stay and do my duty," Jimmy said to the mud at his feet.

"I know you will, bub," Christopher said.

Christopher was wondering if they would try another assault when he thought he heard his name being called. He sat upright.

"Galloway!"

There it was again.

"Chris Galloway of the 8th Ohio! Where are you, pard?"

Ezra.

Christopher scrambled to his feet. "Over here!" He limped toward Ezra's voice.

Soon the two men were facing one another. If he stood upright, the top of Ezra's head was higher than the top of the wall, so he had to stoop over. He looked like an old man, a ragged, bloody old man. But he was smiling from ear to ear.

"I had one of those, what-ja-call-it, a piffiny, and thought if we was gonna die, I wanted it to be side-by-side with my old pard, the way it's always been."

Christopher was stuck on "piffiny," and he took a second to catch up to what Ezra was saying. *Epiphany.* Christopher burst out laughing and threw his arms around his friend. "Me too, pard," he said, his voice breaking.

Behind Ezra were the Jump brothers. Christopher was glad to see they were both still standing. "How you boys doing?"

"As well as can be expected," Joe Jump said and Nathan nodded.

"That was somethin' wasn't it?" Ezra said.

In his mind, Christopher saw the cleaved skulls, the severed limbs, and he nodded.

No one knew where the rest of the 8th was. *Probably scattered all up and down the wall*, Christopher thought.

"I guess we'll just follow whatever officer's around when the time comes," Christopher said.

"I sure would like to make a run for it," Ezra said without a trace of shame.

"Yeah, me and Jimmy Danner here just been talking about that," Christopher said, indicating the young man who'd come up behind him.

"Pleased to meet ya, Jimmy," Ezra said. "This here is Joe and Nathan Jump."

As they were all shaking hands and greeting one another, Ezra leaned over and whispered in Christopher's ear. "Did that pup follow you home?"

Christopher smiled and nodded. "I talked him out of jackrabbiting," he whispered back.

Ezra looked Jimmy up and down. "I hope he makes it."

The bottom dropped out of Christopher's stomach as he said, "Me too."

SLOWLY, A COMMAND STRUCTURE coalesced. Officers strode up and down the line, gathering up men and preparing for another assault. They brought mules laden with boxes of ammunition up all the way into the abatis—which by now had almost completely fallen apart—and ammunition was distributed. The sounds of fighting on the right flank had tapered off, so Christopher figured they were about due.

A captain came by and addressed Christopher. "Sergeant, these your men?"

"Yes, sir." Christopher decided to include Jimmy in his squad for now.

"You know where your regiment is?"

"No, sir."

"Well, no matter. Listen for the command. We're going over the top again."

"We'll be ready, sir."

"Good man...Boys," he said, including the rest of Christopher's squad. "We got fresh ammunition. Once we're on the other side of this cursed wall, form up with whoever you can and pour it into them. We will take this salient come hell or high water."

"Or both," Christopher mumbled, looking at the red stained puddles around them.

At the command, they climbed to the top of the parapet. There they unleashed a volley that again proved ineffective because of so many damp rounds. As they leapt down on the other side, the rebels fell back—but not far. They countered with a devastating point-blank volley that felled men by the score.

It was one of those experiences that filled Christopher with feelings of extreme elation, fear, and guilt all at the same time. A peculiarity of chance that reinforced his belief that the Lord was looking out for him. The men on either side of him fell to the ground screaming. A bullet buzzed by his head so close he felt the breeze like a gentle caress on his cheek, only to hit the man behind him.

As he loaded his rifle, Christopher looked out the corner of his eye and saw Ezra two files down, bloodied but still standing. On the other side of him were the Jump brothers, also still standing. Jimmy?

Christopher looked around for the boy. *Had he bolted after all?* Then he remembered, Jimmy had been standing beside him. Christopher looked down and the boy's sightless eyes stared back up at him, his jaw and a large chunk of his throat shot away.

Christopher brought his rifle up and tried to take aim, but his eyes were clouded over. He fired into the swirling gun smoke that obscured the rebel line. Why hadn't the Lord spared Jimmy? Or Danny? Or so many others? *Why me, Lord? What did I do to deserve this?*

The opposing forces stood toe-to-toe, pouring lead into one another until the rebels brought up several artillery pieces. Canister shot chased the Union men back over the wall. Dropping back into the puddles on the other side, Christopher remembered wondering why there had been no cannon on the parapets that morning. No matter. They were here now.

The two sides spent the next several hours shooting at each other over the top of the wall though the rain continued to make shooting unreliable. There were also holes cut in the logs for firing through without exposing yourself to enemy fire. The problem with those, though, was the proximity to the enemy on the other side. If someone stuck a rifle through a hole to shoot, someone on the other side would grab it and pull. If the shooter tried to hold on, he would get a hatchet or bayonet to the arm.

They continued to bring up ammunition throughout the day, but no one bothered to send up food or water. Christopher's canteen and haversack were empty by mid-afternoon, and by late afternoon he was getting weak and lethargic. He spent most of his time sitting with his head tilted back and mouth open, trying to catch some raindrops on his swollen tongue.

Toward dusk, reinforcements appeared just beyond the abatis. *That can only mean another assault*, Christopher thought. But, where were they going to put them all? They were already crammed up against the wall three or four men deep, and space on the other side was even tighter. They would just create a solid mass where the enemy couldn't help but hit a man with every shot.

But, again they went over the top. The rain had picked up, so they had to revert back to hand-to-hand fighting. But this time, Christopher was too weak and tired to put up much of a fight. His muscles ached from cramping, and his foot throbbed, sending bolts of pain up his leg with every step. The myriad of cuts he'd accumulated throughout the day had scabbed over, gluing his clothes to his flesh. When he climbed the wall, his clothes tore the scabs off, leaving him twitching in anticipation at every movement.

When they were on the other side and the rebels counter-attacked, Christopher jabbed his rifle before him until someone grabbed it and ripped it out of his hands. He reached for the hatchet still in his belt as a rebel stepped up and thrust his bayonet into Christopher's side. He looked down with a dull curiosity as the blade pierced his flesh.

Time seemed to stop. Christopher watched as his jacket pressed against his skin, then gave way to the bayonet's point. The blade entered him with the efficiency of a drill exercise, straight and true. Then, an agonizingly long time later, it pushed out his back.

Christopher looked at the man who'd killed him with curiosity. Why didn't it hurt more? Dying should be painful. But it was just a dull ache.

The man pulled the bayonet out. That hurt. His blood sprayed out with the blade, and Christopher felt a surge of adrenaline. Screaming in anger, he raised the hatchet over his head and lunged at his attacker. The rebel responded by reversing his rifle and clubbing Christopher in the face with the butt end.

Stars exploded out before his eyes—an expanding ring of light on a black background. Then nothing. For Christopher Galloway, the struggle was over.

Chapter Twenty-Four

Silas Horner was a draftee and beat of the first order. You couldn't insult him with the moniker though—he was proud of it. He spent more time in the stockade or on punishment details than he did on the battle line but, looking around at the piles of bodies, stacked like cordwood and covered in mud, he didn't consider that a bad thing. These boys fought all day yesterday and all night last night to take this little bump in the enemy line, only to have the rebs move back several hundred yards and make a new line. At the rate Grant was going through men, there'd be no one left by the time they got to Richmond—except old Silas.

"Horner! Get to work."

Damn that provost sergeant. He'd like to take that bayonet on the end of his rifle and shove it—

"What are you standing around for? These bodies aren't going to bury themselves."

"Yeah, Sergeant. It's just that the ground's still so wet the holes we dig fill with water."

The sergeant looked around. Silas continued to lean on his shovel, and, turning his face to the sun, he smiled. Let that pushy bastard figure it out; he would enjoy the sun. Seemed like forever since he'd seen it last.

Finally, the sergeant spoke. "Most of them are gathered around the rebel side of the wall. Just push it over. We'll bury the bastards with their own defensive works."

Silas cackled. "So, they dug their own graves. We just have to fill them in."

The sergeant nodded absent-mindedly. "Just make sure you get our boys out before you do that. I don't want you burying any good Union men with those dirty traitors."

"How we supposed to tell the difference. They're all so covered in mud the uniforms all look the same."

"Figure it out, Horner. Try to do something right for a change."

Silas clicked his heels together and brought his shovel to order arms. "Yes, sir, Sergeant. Will do, Sergeant."

"Shut up, Private.

"O'Reilly! Help Horner here go through the bodies. Pull out the Union boys, and then get some boys to help you tear this wall down on top of the rebs."

"Yeah, Sarge."

O'Reilly was a rat-faced weasel of a man, called Billy-go-lightly for his nimble fingers. Formerly a pick-pocket who worked the docks in New York City, he and Silas got along all right. The two men were staring at a large pile—maybe three feet high and almost as long as the salient was wide—wondering how little they could get away with and still keep the sergeant off their backs when Silas heard something that sounded like a cough and a moan. He felt the hairs on the back of his neck stand up as he looked closer at the pile.

"What is it, Silas? Seeing ghosts?" O'Reilly grinned, showing a row of rotten teeth and omitting a nauseating smell.

"Thought I heard something."

"Probably just the wind. They gone through and pulled out all the wounded already. This meat ain't gonna make no more noise ever." O'Reilly thought for a moment, then added, "Unless it's to fart out their gasses." He cackled again. It was a high-pitched, irritating laugh.

Silas ignored him and took a step forward, turning his head to the side so he could listen better. There it was again. He stared at the pile, moving his eyes from body to body looking for movement.

O'Reilly poked him. "Let's get on with it, pard. The sergeant's coming back, and he don't look too happy."

Then Silas saw a hand flutter in the pile.

"Sergeant! Over here! We got a live one."

The sergeant was intent on watching where he stepped as he made his way to the two men, but at that he looked up. "What's that you say?"

"I think this man's still alive." The man was near the top of the pile, and Silas pulled the corpse on top of him off and dragged it aside. The three men converged on the pile and stared at the man, who was now moaning again.

"Good Lord, how's that even possible?" Silas asked.

"Don't matter," O'Reilly said. "If he ain't dead now, he probably will be in short order."

"We're not worried about the 'short order,' O'Reilly," the sergeant said. "Only the here and now." He stepped forward and picked up the man's hand. "It's warm."

"Horner, go get a stretcher."

Silas hesitated. "You sure, Sergeant? He's just a reb, and, like Billy said, he'll probably be dead in no time, anyway."

The sergeant turned on him and poked Silas in the chest with his finger. "Union man or rebel don't matter. That's somebody's darlin' laying there, and we still got enough Christian sense in us to help no matter the side." He glanced over at O'Reilly. "Most of us anyway." Then he stepped up to the pile and pulled a corner of the wounded man's jacket back exposing a small section of blue cloth. "See here, he's a Union man. Now, get that stretcher!"

When Silas returned with the stretcher, the sergeant and O'Reilly had taken the man off the pile of corpses and laid him out in the mud. Looking at the man's blood-soaked side, Silas wasn't sure that was the best thing for him, but he kept his mouth shut.

The sergeant was corking his canteen.

"You think that's the best thing for him?" Silas asked, jutting his chin toward the canteen. "Looks like he may be gut-shot."

"If he was gut-shot, he'd probably be dead already," the sergeant replied. "Looks like he got it in the side. Anyway, you two put him on that stretcher and get him to an ambulance. If he is going to die, I'd rather it not be while he's under our care."

The man cried out as they lifted him up, and his moans grew in intensity as he bounced up and down with every step, until finally he passed out.

"He's dead," Billy gasped. "Let's drop him here."

"No, he's probably just passed out. Let's keep going. It's not far."

The deep mud that covered the battlefield made regular walking difficult, but carrying a load it was brutal. They sunk up to their ankles with every step and had to tug hard to free their feet again. Both men were stumbling and out of breath when they finally found an ambulance.

The ambulance driver checked to make sure the man was still breathing before they loaded him onto the back of the ambulance. As the wagon pulled away, O'Reilly made a hawking noise in the back of his throat and spit onto the ground. "He ain't gonna make it," he said.

"I don't know," Silas responded. "He's tough enough to make it this long, I give him 50-50 odds."

"Too bad we'll never know, otherwise we could have bet on it."

Chapter Twenty-Five

Darkness and pain.

Mercifully, Christopher slept most of the time, helped along by regular injections of morphine. When he was awake he could barely see or hear, and his whole body throbbed in agony.

People talked to him, but he couldn't understand what they were saying. He wondered why he couldn't just die and be done with it.

He was awake more now, but still so overwhelmed with pain it consumed all his senses. He lay staring at the ceiling for hours. People would put their faces in front of his to get his attention, and he could see their mouths moving. But there was no sound, and he was too tired and hurt too much to care.

Danny sat with him much of the time, rarely speaking and just behind his shoulder so Christopher couldn't see him, but he was there. Sometimes he would lean over and whisper in Christopher's ear, "It's all right. I'm here." Christopher would try to respond, but his brother would lay his hand on his shoulder. Cool, yet firm, it soothed him. "You're the bravest man I know, little brother. You can beat this."

Darkness and pain.

CHRISTOPHER WOKE WITH the sun in his eyes. He was in a tent, full of men lain out on cots and its sides pulled up to let in air and sunshine. He could hear birds singing, and a cool breeze carried most of the stench away. At first, his coherence surprised him, and he looked around to assure himself it was real.

There was an orderly at the foot of his bed, sweeping the floor. He looked up, and his eyes met Christopher's. "Well, would you look at that? Lazarus

268

awakes." He lay the broom down and knelt by Christopher's side. "You in much pain?"

Christopher nodded.

"Wanna shot? The surgeon will making his rounds soon. I could tell him you need a little something."

Something in the back of Christopher's mind said the pain was good. It meant he was alive. He shook his head.

"Suit yourself. Your last injection probably hasn't worn off yet. When it does, you'll change your mind."

Christopher tried to speak, but only managed a croaking sound.

Take it easy. You've been dead to the world for the last two weeks. You're probably parched.

The orderly hustled to a table at the end of the row of cots and came back with a tin cup half filled with water. He held up Christopher's head and brought the cup to his lips. Christopher took a couple sips and coughed. When he did, blazing pain consumed his side. He remembered the feel of the bayonet piercing his flesh—front and back. He remembered being surprised at the lack of pain. It was making up for lost time now.

He writhed, and that made his left foot flare up. Was that thing still bothering him? It hurt almost as much as his side. He tried to look down to see how bad the swelling was, but couldn't lift his head up high enough to see.

"Where? How... how bad?" he got out.

"You're in Fredericksburg. Brought you straight here from the battlefield. As to how bad you're hurt, that's not my place to say. Like I said, the surgeon will be along soon. He'll go over everything with you."

That made Christopher nervous. What was so bad that the orderly didn't want to say? He tried to lift his head again, but he was too weak. Despite the pain, he soon fell back asleep.

THE SURGEON WAS A HEAVY-set, middle-aged man. He looked at the cards hanging from the foot of Christopher's bed, nodding and ah-ha'ing. Then he looked at Christopher's foot and then his side. He gave the nurse accompanying him some instructions and read the placard hanging around Christopher's neck before finally looking him in the eye and addressing him.

"Well, I guess the first order of business is to find out who you are. You're our little miracle—picked out of a pile of dead. Other than the fact you're a sergeant, we know nothing about you."

Christopher stared at the man, his lips half parted. He knew who he was, but the words wouldn't come. *I'm...Galloway. Galloway...Spit it out, Chris!* His lips moved, but nothing came out. Fear caused him to tense up, which heightened the pain. He gasped, and the surgeon put a hand on his shoulder, his eyes full of concern.

"G...Gallo..."

The surgeon leaned forward, frowning. "What's that? Gallows?"

"G...Galloway."

Relief washed over Christopher like a wave. As the tension subsided, his muscles relaxed, and he let out a sigh of relief.

The surgeon smiled. "Galloway. Well, Sergeant Galloway, you'll have to tell us what regiment you belong to so we can get word back to your people."

Christopher nodded. The *y probably listed me as killed in action.* "The 8th Ohio."

The surgeon looked at the orderly. "Find out what you can on the 8th Ohio and get word to their commander."

"Second Corps," Christopher gasped.

The orderly smiled. "Thanks, bub. That helps."

"Well, Sergeant Galloway," the surgeon said. "I'm optimistic. You were in a bad way when you came in and all that time in the field I was sure an infection would have set in, but the bayonet wound seems to be discharging properly—as long as it continues to do that, it should flush out the bad humors that may otherwise take hold. As to the foot, we were able to take that before the infection worked its way up too far, so you still have most of your leg. You'll be able to get a decent prosthesis for that eventually, and you'll get around just fine. Your fighting days are over, though."

Christopher had stopped listening at the words "take" and "foot." He was confused. If they cut off his foot, why did it hurt so bad? With the help of the orderly, he sat up enough to look down at his body. Sure enough, there was the right foot pushing up the blanket, but on the left—nothing. The left leg just ended somewhere below the knee.

He looked at the surgeon and saw sudden understanding, then embarrassment, on the man's face. "You didn't know," he said.

Christopher shook his head.

"I'm sorry, son. I should have assumed that. You had been so delirious. Don't fret though. As far as amputations go, it's not that bad. Like I said, we were able to save most of the leg. Once you get used to it, you'll be able to do just about anything a whole man can do. And after this war, you'll be in good company. Every city and town in these United States will have its share of amputees."

Christopher couldn't process what he felt. Sad? Yes. He felt an overwhelming sense of loss. Scared? Yes. It was easy for the surgeon to say it wouldn't be that bad. He wouldn't be the one having to learn how to get around, to live with the stares, the restrictions, and the disfigurement.

He'd been thinking of going out west after the war. Maybe even joining the regulars and going out to fight Indians. That door was now closed. How many more closed doors would he face in the years to come?

Overwhelming despair washed over him. Then, a kernel of hope. "When can I go home?" he asked.

"Oh, it'll be quite a while yet. Like I said, you're not out of the woods yet. The wound in your side is still fighting an infection. You need to rest and concentrate on getting better. I'll move you up to a half-diet so you can start getting your strength back and start a regular dosage of whiskey so we can cut back on the morphine. We've loosely bound the wounds so they'll continue to drain, but I'm a firm believer in cleanliness and insist they be washed twice a day. We'll give you opium pills for that. The scrubbing of the wound can be exceedingly painful. Now that the delirium has broken, we'll be putting you on a hospital ship to Washington City, where you'll continue your convalescence in one of the new general hospitals there."

"I need to write home. Let them know I'm still alive." His voice was still raspy, but at least Christopher could think clearer. When he realized he might be listed as killed in action, his first concern was for his family.

"Of course. I'll make sure someone sends for the chaplain. He can help you compose a letter. He'll also get you some writing supplies. Assuming you can read and write, once you're strong enough to sit up you'll probably want to write your own letters.

"You may want to talk to the chaplain about your amputation as well. He's helped many a boy come to terms with the loss of limb. He'll talk with you, pray with you, listen—anything that may help."

"Thank you, sir," Christopher said to the ceiling.

"Get some rest, son."

THEY KEPT CHRISTOPHER drugged for most of the trip to Washington. The slightest movement would cause an agony in his side that seemed like a burning brand thrust into his body. In an infuriating twist of irony, the foot that was no longer there continued to hurt as well.

Once he was in his new location, though, he had to admit it was nice. It was a newly built facility, with multiple wings that stuck out from a central building in a star-shaped pattern, each wing big enough for up to one hundred patients. There were also several outbuildings for cooking, storage, maintenance, and staff housing. Vegetable gardens covered the open space between buildings, manned by the ambulatory patients (who also helped the staff with cleaning, cooking, and anything else the army could think of for them to do to earn their keep). The grounds even had a stable that housed milk cows so the patients had fresh milk every morning. It was a far cry from the converted hotel he'd spent almost two months recovering in after he was released from a Confederate prison back in '62.

Christopher lived every day in fear of the many infections they said he could still get—deadly illness with names like gangrene, pyemia, and staphylococcus something or other. But every day, when he woke up feeling a bit stronger, a bit healthier, the fear lessened just a bit more. When the doctors learned they had found him in a pile of corpses, they marveled that he was still alive at all.

"I don't think we'll ever fully understand the power of the human body," the head surgeon said to him during his Sunday afternoon visit to the ward. "You, son, are a testament to God's hand in our creation. Only a divine creator could have created something as wondrous as the human body."

Christopher appreciated God's creation, but he wished He'd made him a little sturdier. Maybe then he'd still have two feet.

He followed the war news, reading papers and interrogating new patients in the ward. He found the papers a little more up to date. The patients, having spent time in a field hospital before being transferred, tended to be a battle or two behind.

It was amazing how Grant was pushing Lee back. Battle after battle with little rest in between, Grant had the wily old fox holed up in Petersburg now. And with Sherman going south to cut the Confederate states in half, it was just a matter of time.

He wondered often how the 8th was faring and watched for a familiar face with every new patient. But, with the multitude of hospitals handling thousands of patients, it wasn't likely another member of the 8th would appear in this hospital, in this ward. Still, he watched and hoped. Truth be told, he was lonely, and bored.

He got a calendar and began marking off the days until July 13th, which he'd circled so many times he'd almost broken through the paper. It was almost July now. In two weeks, he would no longer be a soldier. He didn't know why he counted, though. He'd ceased to be a soldier the day they sawed off his left foot.

Another aspect of this hospital he had mixed feelings about was the female nurses. While he appreciated the women who came from all over the country to help, the tender care they provided, and the feminine touch they added to the ward, they made him feel self-conscious of his feeble condition, his amputation, and his all-around helplessness. But, to wake up to a smiling face, full of tender caring and affection, made it more than worthwhile.

His thoughts of female nurses and mustering out of the service were interrupted by a male nurse, who grinned mischievously as he said, "Galloway, you old dog, you got a visitor."

Christopher looked at him with slitted eyes. He didn't know anybody in Washington. Who would visit him? Then he thought it might be someone from the 8th, and his eyes went wide. "Well, who is it? Show him in."

"It's not a him, it's a her—and she's a looker." The nurse whistled.

For a moment, Christopher was stumped, then he thought it must be his sister. It would be just like Elizabeth to do something like hop on a train and come all the way to Washington to make sure he got home all right. But, if it was Lizzy, that nurse had better cease his whistling, or he would have to give him a good thu—

All thoughts fled from Christopher's head as Susan Johnston walked into the ward. Though she was still wearing half mourning clothes (a plain black dress and black shawl over a gray blouse), she seemed to light up the whole room with her golden hair and alabaster skin.

Susan saw him a moment after he saw her, and she broke into a shy smile. Then her eyes widened, and her cheeks seemed to lose all color. Christopher followed her gaze to the foot of his bed and his face burned with embarrassment. His first instinct was to shift around to hide the amputated limb, but to move that much would be too painful. Besides, there was no hiding something so obvious, and it would highlight his weakness. He was stuck where he was, in all his feeble glory. All he could do was put on a brave face.

But, what was she doing here?

Susan recovered quickly and hurried to the side of his bed, seemingly as lost for words as he was. She looked around for a place to sit, and the nurse grabbed a chair and brought it over for her. Smiling, she thanked the man, and he stumbled over a limp "you're welcome" before shuffling off.

She sat, and they stared at each other for what seemed an eternity. Several times, one or the other would start to say something and then stop, looking away in embarrassment.

"Miss Johnston," Christopher finally managed. "It's good to see you. But, why are you here?"

Her cheeks flushed, and she fiddled with her handbag. After a short pause, it all came out in a rush. "I heard from Elizabeth that you were hurt, and, well, it wasn't really that far. You see...well...I was here already. I've been working as a nurse for the last year. Doing my part. After you left Norwalk last, I did a lot of thinking and finally decided I could no longer sit idly by and let so many brave men and boys fight this horrid war and do nothing for them. I...I was so wrong in how I treated Daniel. I didn't understand. I thought it would be for the best. But, I didn't think it would be so hard on him, being so far from home and family. I let my father have his way because it was easier that way. Then, I was so ashamed when Daniel died. I couldn't tell your family that our relationship had ended. And they took me in and shared their grief with me and let me share mine with them, and...and I felt like such a fraud."

She was crying now, and Christopher wanted to reach out and take her hand, but he couldn't.

"When I heard you'd been wounded and were here, I couldn't lose another Galloway boy. I just couldn't. Not that—I mean, it's just, I had to do something. So I put in a request to be transferred here. So I could take care of you."

Christopher felt a lump in his throat, and his eyes were wet and itchy. He quickly rubbed them with his sleeve. "That was awfully generous of you, Miss Johnston—"

"Susan, please."

"Susan. But quite unnecessary. When I found that letter, I was angry with you, and I carried that anger with me every day—until we met on the street that day. But, then, after hearing your side and coming to understand the pressures you must have been under, I understood. That anger is gone."

"You forgive me?"

"I do. And I think Danny would, too, if he were here."

At that she burst into full throated sobs, earning Christopher several angry stares from the nearby bed. Then he did reach out and pat her hand. "There, there, Miss—Susan. It's all right. Everything is all right. You didn't have to come here."

She shook her head. "I wanted to. And I told you, I was here already. Some of these hospitals...well, some aren't as good as others, and I wanted to make sure. I didn't want you dying for lack of care. You and Danny, your whole family has sacrificed so much. Let me do this for you."

"But, your father."

"Bah!" She shook her head, causing her blond ringlets to bounce. "We parted on bad terms, and I fear we may never reconcile, but I don't care. I had to do this. I left with what little money I had saved up and have been living off my nurse's salary, eating the same food prepared for the men and sleeping in the women's quarters." She looked him in the eye. "But, it was worth it."

Susan proved to be a much better nurse than most, especially the men, who mostly were just walking wounded waiting to be sent back to their regiments. The women, too, were mostly volunteers who usually only stuck around for a couple months before getting sick themselves, or just over-whelmed, and going home. Susan had been nursing now for over a year, had already learned many of the procedures, and had proven sturdy enough to handle the worse assignments, even assisting with surgeries on occasion.

But now she was putting in her shift wherever they assigned her and then staying to look after Christopher. Christopher worried she was doing too much and would weaken herself until one of the many illnesses that plagued a hospital took hold. He tried to reason with her and get her to go home, but having found her strength and determination, she was proving impossible to sway.

"Susan, please—"

"Don't 'Susan, please' me, Christopher Galloway. They're not cleaning your wound nearly enough. Now pull up your shirt, and let's have a look."

She sat the basin of warm, soapy water down and pulled on his shirt. Christopher snatched the cloth and resisted briefly. The first time, she'd al-most had to pry his fingers open one by one, but over time he learned that compliance was his only option.

He relaxed and looked away has she pulled up his shirt, exposing the loosely bound cloth that covered his open wound. She pulled back the cloth, took a sniff, and nodded. She cleaned the wound with a warm, wet sponge as gently as she could. All the while on the lookout for streaks of red or black splotches of dead skin. Finally satisfied, she sat back and dropped the sponge in the basin.

"Let's give it some air for a while before wrapping it up, shall we?" She smiled at him sweetly.

"Oh, yes. Let's," he said.

"Sarcasm doesn't become you, Mr. Galloway."

"Neither does exposing my stomach to pretty, young women."

She batted her eyes and tried to pout over the smile she was trying to contain. "Do you think I'm pretty?"

"Well...Ah..." He saw even his exposed belly was turning red. *Dammit!*

He sighed, steeled himself, and looked her square in the eye. "I think you are the most beautiful woman I've ever seen."

Now it was her turn to blush, and this time her demureness was real. "You're embarrassing me," she whispered.

"I'm embarrassing you?" Christopher laughed. "You're not the one laying here with your—"

He stopped himself just in time. He looked at her fearing he'd gone too far.

She giggled in response. "Let's get this bandage back on so we can cover you up like a proper gentleman. Shall we?"

Dammit. She always gets the last laugh.

JULY 13th came and went. The 8th Ohio was no more. Christopher received a letter from his father describing the grand reception the City of Norwalk gave for the boys of Company D. Colonel Sawyer—now Mr. Sawyer—had told him of the mustering out ceremony they'd had for the regiment in Columbus. Christopher was sorry he missed it, but it was done, and that was that.

He enquired about Ezra's wellbeing. He'd not heard from his old pard since the Bloody Angle at Spotsylvania. (That's what they were calling it—the Bloody Angle. From the Bloody Lane to the Bloody Angle, it was one long, bloody war.) He'd written Ezra, in care of the 8th and then in care of his parents in Norwalk but had heard nothing. Ten days later he got a short note back from his father saying Ezra had not been at the reception, and he'd not seen him around Norwalk, but he would find out more and get back to him.

That had filled Christopher with dread, and he wrote letters to everyone he could think of, trying to find out what had become of his friend. Finally, he heard back from Colo—Mr. Sawyer. Ezra had been shot through both legs at Cold Harbor, shattering his femurs. He'd undergone a double amputation and was recuperating at a hospital in Georgetown, Virginia.

Christopher looked at his own leg and was embarrassed about feeling sorry for himself. Ezra was not a smart man, and would have used his body, not his mind, to make a living after the war. Christopher didn't know how he'd do that now or what would become of him.

But, whatever it was, he would be there for him. He would not abandon his best pard.

By this time Christopher was sitting up most of the time and getting around in a wheelchair. His amputation flap was healing well, but the bayonet wound continued to flare up with debilitating pain if he strained too much, so he still needed help to get in and out of the chair, and he was still too weak to go very far on his own, but Susan was there to help more often than not.

The non-stop pace of keeping up with her regular duties at the hospital as well as taking care of Christopher was wearing her down. Little by little, she was letting things go. Her golden ringlets drooped and frayed, her clothes were stained and dirty, and she had lost weight. She was also slowing down, and dark rings had formed around her eyes that never went away. Christopher was as worried about her as he was his own condition, and he begged her to slow down.

"I think you may get your wish, Christopher," she said one day. "I'll be getting some relief soon."

Christopher's stomach flipped as he imagined his days without her. Was she leaving? Or just cutting back? "Really?" He'd hoped to have sounded more nonchalant, but there was an eagerness to his voice that let slip his fears.

She gave him a wane smile. "Yes, really."

"Well...where...er, I mean, what are you going to do?"

She reached out and put her hand over his. "I can't tell you any more. It's a surprise."

"You're talking to a veteran, Miss Johnston. We don't like surprises."

She giggled. "You're back in the civilized world now, Mister Galloway. You will have to get used to them. Sometimes they can be quite enjoyable."

He nodded. "Indeed. Like the moment you appeared at the foot of my hospital bed. It was more than a surprise, it was a total shock. And I am exceedingly glad for it."

Susan looked at him with a slight grin for so long he squirmed.

"What?"

"I knew it."

"Knew what?"

"That 'aw shucks, ain't this, ain't that' talk of yours was all an act. You can be quite the refined gentleman when you want to be."

"Well, my ma done learned me right."

She laughed, and he liked the sound of it. "I guess the trick is getting you to want to be."

It was almost a week before Christopher found out what the surprise was. By then he'd forgotten all about it. He was busy working on becoming more self-sufficient and spent most of his idle time thinking about Susan.

If left on his own, he probably would still be bed bound and feeling sorry for himself. Instead, he was now making it all the way to the water closet on his own in the wheelchair and taking several steps at a time with the crutches.

The only thing he still couldn't do on his own was transition to and from the wheelchair, or stand up to brace himself on the crutches. But, he was determined to tackle that as quickly as possible. Not that he didn't like Susan's help with that chore—she had to put her arms around him and lean into it to get enough leverage to lift him, and he in turn put his arms around her for support. But, where things got awkward was at the water closet. For that he tried to wait for a male nurse, but sometimes the need to go didn't wait for when it was convenient.

The first time she helped him onto the seat with a hole in it, where he could evacuate his bowels into the running water below, was mortifying. The room was barely big enough for the two of them, and he insisted on keeping his drawers up until she stepped out. But afterward, he couldn't get his drawers back up by himself and she had to step in and help him. Though she had kept her gaze averted, and the closeness of their bodies was exhilarating, the incident left him so embarrassed he could barely look her in the eye for the rest of the day.

Later that evening, he had wondered how many men she got that close to during her normal rounds. Try as he might, he couldn't get the thought out of his head. It became a constant thought nagging at the back of his mind. Something he had to push back and ignore as much as he could. After all, she was just doing a job—a dirty, thankless job that few women of her stature would even consider.

It was during one of their awkward embraces, as Susan was helping Christopher out of bed, that his surprise came.

"I hope I'm not interrupting anything."

Christopher had his arms around Susan and his face half buried in her shoulder, but he would have recognized that voice anywhere. "Da!" Though Christopher was half up, they both quickly let go. Susan stepped back with a small squeak, and Christopher fell back onto the bed, causing a bolt of pain in his side that momentarily distracted him from his embarrassment.

"Mr. Galloway," Susan said. I didn't expect you until tomorrow.

"I caught an earlier train. I certainly didn't expect to find the two of you locked in an embrace—"

"It wasn't an embrace, Da. Susan was helping—"

"I was just helping him up into his chair."

Jack Galloway's eyes swept his son and stopped where his left foot would have been. His eyes went from shocked surprise to sorrow in an instant. Jack rushed to Christopher's bed and sat down next to him. He grabbed Christopher's hand with both of his and brought it to his lips. "Oh, my boy, my boy." His eyes were now full of tears. "I knew, but nothing can prepare you for the sight..."

Christopher looked from his father to Susan, who was crying as well. "This was your surprise?"

She nodded.

Jack sat back and reached for a handkerchief. "Forgive an old man his maudlin way. I find myself more sentimental with each passing year."

"Nothing to forgive, Da—"

"No, no, no. I shouldn't go on making such a fuss over your, your condition. It was just a shock is all."

"You think it was a shock for you? Imagine how I felt?" Christopher smiled, and his father chuckled briefly. Then he got serious again.

"I've come to take you home, Christopher."

Home. Christopher choked up at the thought. It was almost over. Completely over.

He looked at Susan. "Are they releasing me?"

She shook her head. "Not yet. But soon."

Jack cut in. "I wanted to be with my son. I'll be here as long as it takes."

"But, the business—"

"Bah! the business. I think I was better off a humble cobbler fixing shoes in me own shop than trying to be some big wig negotiating contracts with the government, dealing with labor problems and city planners. I'd just as soon leave that all to someone who likes that kind of stuff—and is good at it." He looked around conspiratorially and lowered his voice. "Someone like your sister."

"Lizzy? Running a company? But, she's only...what, eighteen?"

"She's wise beyond her years, that one, and tough as nails to boot. But, no. A woman running a large business like that wouldn't be proper. Especially not one so young. No. I've hired a man to look after things while I'm gone. But, he has orders to take everything to Lizzy. While I'm here I'm not to be bothered."

"I should leave you two to catch up," Susan cut in.

"But, but." Christopher didn't want her to leave. But, he had been pushing her to get some rest. This was her chance but—"I still need to...you know." He jerked his head toward the end of the hall.

Susan bent over and whispered to Jack. "Mr. Galloway, would you care to help your son to the water closet?"

Jack beamed. "I would like nothing better."

She stood back up. "There you have it. Mr. Galloway, the surgeon begins his rounds at 9:00 in the morning. If you could be here then, you can speak to him about Christopher's future care and when they can release him."

"Certainly. What about you, my dear? Will you be there for the discussion?"

Susan blushed. "I...well...I'll be on duty then, but I'll try to get away."

"Wonderful. See you then."

When she was gone, Jack looked at Christopher and said, "She's a wonderful girl, she is. She's kept us better informed of your progress than you have."

"She's..." Christopher looked toward the end of the hall where Susan had just disappeared around the corner. She was what? Christopher felt like he was on the edge of something he wasn't sure he was ready for. But when had that ever mattered?

Epilogue

Elizabeth Hastings nee Galloway stood on the train platform, waiting for her brother and his grandson to arrive. Looking away from the tracks, she took in the city street, with its paved surface and electric lines that powered the street cars. So different from the muddy road it had been over thirty years ago when newlyweds Christopher and Susan Galloway left to go out west. What would Christopher think now of the little town he had grown up in? As she watched, an automobile drove by, scaring horses with its obnoxious chuffing and stinking up the air around it. Thank God there were still few of them. What a horrid place the world would be if they ever starting mass producing the new-fangled abominations.

Elizabeth put a hand on her ample midsection and took a deep breath. Her girdle pinched and strained and she scowled slightly. Maybe the century would bring with it a change in women's fashions, and she could finally get rid of that particular torture device. Say what you will, the "Gay 90s," with its emphasis on exaggerated hourglass figures, was anything but gay for full-figured women.

It was at that moment her sisters appeared, their husbands and children in tow. A decade younger than Elizabeth, both Rachel and Rebecca managed to maintain slim figures and an air of healthy robustness that Elizabeth envied. Maybe it was too many long hours in a stuffy office and the strain of running a business that had sapped her strength and willpower. Maybe it was the fact that most of her business activities were, by necessity, done behind the scenes that was the real source of her affliction.

The three women nodded, and Elizabeth opened her mouth to say something when the whistle of an approaching train cut her off. All three women looked down the track with nervous excitement, their husbands and grown children tensed, and the grandchildren squealed with delight and began running circles around the adults. To Elizabeth and her sisters, that whistle marked the return of their only remaining brother, whom they hadn't seen since their father's funeral. To the others, it signaled the approach of Christopher Galloway, fabled Civil War hero who went out west and carved out a successful career in cattle (the distribution, not raising—his war wounds preventing the latter).

Rachel took Elizabeth's hand. "I can't believe he actually came," she said.

Elizabeth scowled. "He'd come for his precious 8th if not for us," she replied.

"Fiddlesticks." Rachel pouted. "I'm just glad he's here, whatever the reason."

"Then you approve of the monument they're putting on the land where Daniel died?"

Rachel straightened her back. "I am. They've sanctified that land, which is only fitting. So many boys gave their life there to preserve the union—and look what we've become. One nation, stretching from one end of the continent to the other. That would never have happened without their sacrifice.

"Though I do wish He'd spared Daniel," she finished in a whisper.

The incoming train overwhelmed everything else for a time. The whistle blew and the engine huffed, its metal clanking and groaning as it released its steam onto the platform. There was a bustle of activity, and soon the passengers started exiting the cars.

The excitement of the Galloway clan (for such was how they saw themselves, though none bore the name any longer) grew as, one by one, people descended the stairs and either scurried to the baggage claim or greeted those awaiting them. It wasn't until the cars were almost empty that the grizzled old man who once fought in some of the bloodiest battles in the nation's history appeared.

Elizabeth almost gasped. Had she changed that much? Christopher's hair was solid white, his eyebrows and mustache dominated his face (much like Mark Twain, Elizabeth thought). As he descended the steps he tightly gripped the railing with one hand and an oak cane with the other. Railroad employees helped him with every step.

Then a youngster in his early teens stepped out behind Christopher, and for Elizabeth it was almost too much. Her eyes filled with tears, and she choked off a sob. He was an amalgam of her two brothers, Daniel and Christopher, at that age. She looked to Rachel and Rebecca, but they seemed unaffected. They had been too young to remember their older brothers as boys. She looked back at Jack, Christopher's grandson, as he took his grandfather's arm and helped him toward the crowd that were, to him, strangers.

Then she looked back to Christopher, who walked with a distinctive limp, his face showing the strain of every step. But it wasn't the side with the missing foot that seemed to give him troubles, it was the other side, with its old bayonet wound. *That war will kill him yet*, she thought.

Christopher and Jack stopped before Elizabeth, and the old man smiled. There was the old smirk, with the mischievous twinkle in his eye. Then it was too much, and Elizabeth broke down in tears, throwing herself on her brother much the way she did that day in the kitchen so long ago. Jack held fast to his grandfather to steady the two as they embraced.

Then Rachel and Rebecca were there, adding their hugs and tears to the mix. Their husbands and teenage children stood back respectfully and gave the siblings their moment together. Not so Elizabeth's grandchildren. They surrounded the group hug, firing questions at Christopher and trying to pull on his coat tail to get his attention.

"Children!" Elizabeth snapped. "Wait your turn."

Christopher laughed and pulled a handful of licorice sticks out of his pocket. "Here you go, kids. Enjoy," he said. His voice was deeper than she remembered and had a gravelly quality that almost sounded mean. She imagined he could be a real terror when he wanted to be.

Introductions were made—all except Elizabeth's husband. "Where's the dude?" Christopher asked.

Elizabeth pursed her lips. Christopher had taken to referring to her husband as "the dude" shortly after their marriage, and she didn't like it. She was well aware it was not a flattering term out west. "Horace is at the office," she replied. "He couldn't get away, but he'll join us later."

"I assume he'll be along for the trip?" Christopher asked.

"Yes, of course." Elizabeth nodded. "In fact, he's made most of the arrangements."

"Bully," Christopher exclaimed, his eyes lighting. "I can't wait to see my old pards again...those still above the sod anyway."

THE COACH RUMBLED DOWN Main Street in Hagerstown. Christopher sat in the backseat and looked across at Elizabeth and her husband. Horace was a small pinch-faced man who, if not for his wrinkles and gray hair, would have appeared almost child-like next to his sister. The man reminded Christopher of the Jew from Cincinnati who was a POW with him in Winchester. What was his name? No matter. The man had been a clerk who had the misfortune of taking a wrong turn while delivering a message for a general or colonel or something. He was not accustomed to fighting and had fallen apart when things got ugly.

Next to Horace was their oldest grandson Philip, just a couple years younger than Jack, who'd won out against the other children for the chance to ride in the first carriage with the old war hero. Next to Christopher sat Jack, a constant comfort to the old man, and on the other side of him sat Petunia (God, who would name their child that?), Philip's mother.

As the Hagerstown Turnpike intersection approached, Christopher thought of his old pards from the 8th, most long dead or lost track of. He thought of Daniel and wondered what it would be like to once again stand on the spot where he'd died. He thought of Ezra, who never adjusted to the loss of his legs and blew his brains out in the spring of '65.

As the tears threatened to well up, he distracted himself by wondering if the Jump brothers would be there, or Charlie Locker. He surely hoped so, especially Charlie. He missed the only other member of his original mess to outlive the war and not for the first time felt a pang of regret for having lost track of the old German.

"Is this it, G-pa?"

Christopher looked at his grandson. He could look on that boy forever and never tire. He was a mix of Galloway, Johnston, and Mexican from that little gal his son had married—a face for America in the new century. He wondered once more if Jack's mother had not died in childbirth, would Daniel not have joined up at the outbreak of war with Spain? Maybe then he'd not have lost another Daniel to war, and his Susan would not have died of heartbreak, and they'd all be with him still.

The boy sat patiently waiting, used to his grandfather's long periods of silence. Finally, Christopher remembered he'd asked him something. "What's that, Jack?"

"Is this it? the road to Antietam?"

Christopher looked out the window. They'd turned south onto the turnpike and had left the town behind. Staring out at the fields of corn, punctuated by white houses surrounded by white picket fences, he was drawn back to that day, a lifetime ago, when he and his older brother had waded Antietam Creek and marched out onto a similar field and into a horror from which only one of them returned.

"Yes, son," he whispered. "I suppose it is."

Acknowledgements and Bibliography

The Galloway books probably never would have happened if it weren't for the 6th Ohio Volunteer Infantry Re-enactors, who rekindled my lifelong passion for the Civil War period and gave me an inkling of an idea what it must have been like for the Civil War soldier. More specifically, I'd like to thank Mike Davis and Steve Spohn of the 6th for taking the time to read my rough drafts and providing me with their knowledgeable insight.

A Military History of the 8th Regiment Ohio Voluntary Infantry, by Franklin Sawyer, acted as the framework of my story and provided me with a wealth of secondary characters. Every member of the 8th portrayed in the Galloway books, except for the Galloway brothers and Ezra, was an actual member of the 8th OVI. Where I could, I looked them up in census records to find out more about where they were from and what they did before the war. For the most part, I had to guess as possible familial relations, going by birthdates and shared residences in the census. But the fact that there were so many members sharing the same last names, it's obvious to me that going to war in the 1860's was a family affair.

The Valiant Hours: An Irishman in the Civil War: Eighth Ohio Volunteer Infantry, by Thomas Francis Galway, helped fill in the details left out of the official regimental history, such as the drinking shack near Romney, WV. Reading Sawyer's account and then Galway's was invaluable in my efforts to get as clear a picture of events as possible.

There are hundreds of books written on Civil War battles and I referenced several. For my purposes though, the most invaluable was Antietam: The Soldiers' Battle, by John Michael Priest. Priest's *Antietam* is a chronological retelling of the battle taken not from official documents and scholarly analysis, but from letters and memoirs of the men who were there on the front lines. More than once I wished Priest had written a book in the same format for every battle the 8th fought in. It would have made my life a lot easier. Also, it was after reading <u>Antietam: The Soldiers' Battle</u> that I first got the idea of writing a novel centered around the common soldier.

While most books on battles cover a larger strategic analysis of events, for the purpose of writing the Galloway series I used them to flesh out Sawyer's descriptions of where the 8th was and what they did during the fight. In addition to Priest's <u>Antietam</u>, some of the books I drew from are:

<u>"We are in for it!" The First Battle of Kernstown</u>, by Gary L. Ecelbarger

<u>The Fredericksburg Campaign</u>, by Francis Augustin O'Reilly

<u>They Met at Gettysburg</u>, by General Edward J. Stackpole

<u>Gettysburg</u>, by Stephen W. Sears

<u>Nowhere to Run: The Wilderness, May 4th & 5th, 1864</u>, by John Michael Priest

<u>Bloody Angle: Hancock's Assault On The Mule Shoe Salient, May 12th 1864</u>, By John Cannan

But the Galloway series is about more than just the battles, it's also about the day-to-day life of the common soldier and the human impact, both physically and emotionally, of the war. For that I referenced the following books:

<u>This Republic of Suffering: Death and the American Civil War</u>, by Drew Gilpin Faust

<u>The Life of Billy Yank: The Common Soldier of the Union</u>, by Bell Irvin Wiley

<u>Hardtack and Coffee</u>, by John D. Billings

<u>Life in Civil War America</u>, by Michael O. Varhola

<u>Embattled Courage: The Experience of Combat in the American Civil War</u>, by Gerald F. Linderman

<u>Civil War Hospital Sketches</u>, Louisa May Alcott

<u>Doctors in Blue: The Medical History of the Union Army in the Civil War</u>, by George Worthington Adams

And last but not least, <u>Corporal Si Klegg and his Pard Shorty</u>, by Wilbur F. Hinman which, while fiction, was a great source of inspiration for me in trying to understand both the Civil War soldier's life and common 19th century fiction. Hinman was Civil War veteran who served in the 65th OVI in the western theater.

But, after all that reading and research, the Galloway Series is still a work of fiction written for a 20th-21st century audience. It doesn't fully embrace the 19th century style of writing or language and is not always true to events. Timelines are distorted and things left out or exaggerated to accommodate the narrative. And sometimes I just got it wrong. Also I'm not afraid to admit that sometimes I was just lazy. As with the commands, which were taken (and sometimes mangled) from the 1862 edition of Hardee's <u>Rifle and Light Infantry Tactics,</u> by Lieutenant General William James Hardee, CSA. While Hardee's first addition was published in 1855 for the U.S. Army, when the revised 1862 edition was released he was a general in the Confederate Army. While I do not know what manual of arms the 8th used, I'm pretty sure it was not Hardee's 1862 edition. But Hardee's is the manual I am most familiar with so that's what I used.

Some may ask, since the Galloway Series is a work of fiction, why put all that effort into research? Because I love history and I love fiction, and when those two things come together it's a wonderful experience for me. But nothing ruins that experience more than a glaring error or anachronism that thrusts me out of the story and the time line. Also, I wrote them for all the people who are mildly interested in history, but not enough to read the non-fiction books which can sometimes be less than entertaining. I hope these books, <u>Road to Antietam</u> and <u>The Way Home</u>, will spark an interest in those readers' hearts to learn more about that time period, and history in general, and they will look back on these books fondly as the genesis of that interest.

Don't miss out!

Visit the website below and you can sign up to receive emails whenever Tom E. Hicklin publishes a new book. There's no charge and no obligation.

https://books2read.com/r/B-A-JWIH-UEYAB

BOOKS 2 READ

Connecting independent readers to independent writers.

About the Author

Tom Hicklin was born and raised in Colorado, and has had a strong interest in American history and the Civil War for as long as he can remember. After a brief flirtation with writing in college, he spent most of his adult life working in accounting or IT. He has since left the rat race and is now concentrating on his two great passions—history and writing. He currently lives in Cincinnati with his girlfriend and two dogs.

Read more at https://tomehicklin.com.

Made in the USA
Coppell, TX
07 November 2019